A Land Like You

THE AFRICA LIST

A Land Like You

TOBIE NATHAN

Translated by Joyce Zonana

LONDON NEW YORK CALCUTTA

www.bibliofrance.in

The work is published with the support of the
Publication Assistance Programmes of the Institut français

Seagull Books, 2020

Originally published as Tobie Nathan, *Ce pays qui te ressemble*
© Editions Stock, 2015

First published in English translation by Seagull Books, 2020
English translation © Joyce Zonana, 2020

ISBN 978 0 8574 2 788 5

British Library Cataloguing-in-Publication Data
A catalogue record for this book is available from the British Library.

Typeset by Seagull Books, Calcutta, India
Printed and bound by WordsWorth India, New Delhi, India

With you . . . With you . . . The world is so beautiful with you . . .
Whether you accept me, whether you reject me, whatever the city,
*   whatever the land, wherever you go, I will go with you.*
With you . . . With you . . . The world is so beautiful with you . . .
—*Wayak*, Farid al-Atrash

Come, my beloved,
Come join me.
Look at me, see the effect of your absence,
How I'm reduced to speaking with your ghost . . .
—*Ya habibi taala*, Asmahane; lyrics by Farid al-Atrash

My sister, my child,
Just think what delight,
To live and to love,
To love as we please,
To love and die as one,
In a land like you.
—*Invitation to a Voyage*, Charles Baudelaire

Turn, my beloved, and be thou like a roe or a young hart upon the
mountains of spices . . .
—*The Song of Songs*

1925

Haret al-Yahud

Egyptians are cannibals. Consider a fava bean—study it well. You'll see how much it looks like a foetus. Since antiquity, Egyptians have been fava-eaters, foetus-eaters. My mother's name was Esther. She must have eaten thousands of foetuses before finally becoming pregnant . . .

Esther rose before dawn, as she did every morning. She made coffee by candlelight, black coffee, very black, in a *kanaka*, the little brass coffee pot with the long handle. Then she prepared *ful*. With a fork, she mashed boiled favas while ladling on oil and adding little bits of hard-boiled egg. She brought her face close: the fragrance of a happy morning. It wasn't every day they could have favas and eggs for breakfast. Usually, it was a plain crust of bread and a cup of nearly translucent tea. But the night before, she'd stopped by to see her Aunt Maleka, who'd insisted. Of course, Esther had refused— they weren't beggars after all. Out of pride, yes, but not just that— out of politeness as well. You never accepted gifts without being forced. First the other person had to stuff something into your pocket, to pretend to be angry, to swear it was a question of life and honour: 'For the love of God, you have to take these favas—you have to!' 'But never! We don't need them!' 'I swear you won't leave here until—.' It was only then, as if unwillingly, and after several offers, several refusals, that you agreed to accept anything. Sophisticated etiquette that grants the greatest generosity to the receiver. Thanks to this haggling, Esther had returned home with a basketful of dried favas, dates, coffee and apricot paste, the sweet we used to call *qamar al-din*, 'moon of faith'.

She hadn't admitted any of this to Motty, her husband. He would have been angry, she was sure of it. He might have stormed out, slamming the door. He'd done it before. And she would have had to seek him through the alleys of the Mouski. She was wild with anxiety whenever he went out alone. So she'd silently put the supplies away and waited for him to fall asleep before soaking the favas; later, she'd cooked them by the dawn's first gleams.

She arranged everything on a tray and sat down beside the bed, waiting for the meal's fragrance to filter into her husband's dream. She sat still, her eyes unfocused, thinking back to last night's sorrow. For the first time ever, Motty had been silent all evening. A tear had even rolled down his cheek. She knew what was troubling him—nothing good. A couple, she knew, owed its existence solely to joy. And she had to admit that, during their seven years of marriage, they'd certainly had their share.

At twenty-one, Esther was a woman. Her breasts and buttocks bouncing under her light cotton gown; her brown hair with reddish highlights cascading like an Amazon's over her shoulders; her open face; her fresh, blooming lips; her way of walking, as if her feet floated a few inches above the ground. Oh, she could drive men wild! But she didn't mean to, for, when it came to men, Esther thought only of her own. In all of Haret al-Yahud—the Jewish Quarter known as the 'Alley of the Jews' or simply the *hara*—no one was happily married. People married because they breathed, because they walked, because they ate favas and onions, because it was time. These two had married like all the rest, but they'd been granted love as a bonus, truly a gift from God.

At the time, she'd been fourteen, and he twice that. They were cousins, yes, but because of their age difference they'd never played together, never even spoken. He was handsome. He seemed grand in his immaculate *galabia*, but he'd been blind since early childhood—at the age of three, an untreated infection, so common among us. His eyes were clear, overly clear; two faded pearls, fixed. She was young, a gazelle—but ever since her fall at the age of five from a second-floor balcony, people thought her mad. She'd lost consciousness. Everyone took her for dead. The whole alley huddled around her, and while her family mourned before the small lifeless body, a dog—

most likely female, though no one thought to check—came and licked her. Several minutes went by like this, the humans struck dumb by the warmhearted animal. Little by little, the child's fingers began to twitch, first her right hand, then her left. Her right foot jerked. She opened an eye and uttered this peculiar sentence: 'He is powerful!' Of whom had she spoken? At first people thought it must be the dog; they looked for it, but it had fled, chased off by children throwing stones.

'It's a miracle!' exclaimed Nafoussa, Esther's mother. ' "He is powerful." That's what she said, isn't it? She was speaking of God, who came and revived her when she was dead. Don't we say in our daily prayer: "Blessed are you, oh Lord our God, who revives the dead"?'

The old women agreed. God had restored the little one, already on the road to Paradise. But Aunt Maleka, her mother's sister, the envious one, with eyes clear as jade, immediately suggested another meaning.

' "He is powerful." Yes, that's what she said, all right. I think, though, she was talking about a demon'—and of course she used the Arabic term for demon, *afrit*— 'who entered her during her absence. When you lose awareness, you no longer have a guard watching over your soul's threshold. Did you see how that dog came and sniffed her, licked her? He recognized a familiar, make no mistake about it, no more, no less.'

'No more, no less,' Esther's mother repeated, mocking. 'No more, no less—oh my, oh my!'

From that day forward, and for almost a year, it was as if Esther had withdrawn from the world. Sitting on her bed, she no longer heard anything, no longer learnt anything. She spent hours rocking back and forth, every now and then uttering words in an incomprehensible language. Most likely her soul had fled during her fall. They questioned Mourad, the rabbi who, after a stint with the Alliance Israelite Universelle, had dedicated himself to rooting out the ancient superstitions of the filthy ghetto Jews.

'She had a shock,' the rabbi decreed. 'That's all. A traumatism.'

The word impressed them: 'traumatism'. A medical term that seemed to explain everything and which they repeated whenever Esther's behaviour frightened them. 'Shush. She has a traumatism.' They pronounced it 'traumatisism'.

'Leave her alone,' Mourad scolded during another visit. 'In a few weeks, she'll be back to herself, just like before. A traumatism is a sort of wound, a wound to the soul. It takes time to heal.'

The rabbi was right. Esther eventually emerged from her stupor. But he was also wrong. It was not time that healed her, but the death of her mother which affected her like a new traumatism. Sett Nafoussa, the empty-headed, had been carried off by typhoid fever in just a few days. (Poor thing! May God enfold her in His womb!) That's when the little imp emerged from her stupor to take charge of the household, to care for her two little brothers, to prepare their meals. And here she was, as energetic as ever, whirling from house to house, rushing through the alleys. The family taunted the rabbi: 'A traumatisism took her away, a traumatisism brought her back. As we say in Arabic, "Fear cures fear!"' And he went off, shrugging, muttering into his beard: 'Wasn't it God who created science? Why don't they want to believe in it?'

Although Esther had indeed returned to the human world, she'd come back from her adventure among the demons with some strange ways. People called her 'topsy-turvy'; they claimed that the afrit, the devil made from the Nile's mud who'd possessed her since her fall, had turned her inside out like a sock that needed darning. Her conduct was the inverse of a young girl's. She swore like a water-seller, reeling off strings of curses, insulting grown-ups in the street, even the men of her own family. She was gentle only with animals—and not all of them—mostly just a scrawny black alley cat with a ragged coat and an evil eye, which she alone could approach. Aunt Maleka, who'd become her guardian after her mother's death, kept repeating: 'How will we get her married? An ignorant little slattern, half-crazy. She'll have to marry her cat!'

A new crisis arose when she got her first period. She lost consciousness, and this time no dog showed up to drag her back from the world of the dead. She remained absent from humans for one whole day and one whole night. As soon as she came to, she crawled to her bed and lay there for a month, able neither to speak nor to eat or drink, nor even to do her business. For a second time, they thought her lost. Mourad, the rabbi, was called to her bedside. 'Say some prayers to drive away the devils!' pleaded Maleka, Adina and Tofa'ha, Esther's three aunts. He refused. What a strange rabbi, not to believe in miraculous prayers. They, of course—well, it wasn't so much that they believed in them but they knew that such prayers contributed to the order of the universe. This man seemed bent on destroying it. They insisted, invoking the memory of the old rabbi taken by dysentery, the one with the blessed hand, the hand he used for healing but which he never failed to slide down young girls' arses.

'That bastard Entebi, may God enfold him in mercy, would have made an amulet.'

'Yes! And he would have pinned it to her gown.'

'Just below her breast, over her heart. He was a real rabbi!'

Mourad didn't want to get into a philosophic discussion at the girl's bedside, but really, there were after all some basic truths, indisputable, as evident, as true, as God's existence. Didn't they know, these superstitious peasant women, that religion, more than anything, was the struggle against idolatry? And that's what they were asking of him: idolatry! But the opposite thought also struck him: if, after all, a simple trick could relieve suffering, why refuse to help? And then, he wasn't averse to testing what emanated from him. Would he be able to transmit *baraka*? Did he have a scrap of divine power, like the celebrated Entebi, his predecessor? It wasn't impossible. His father claimed their family was directly descended from a great Kabbalist. 'And so?' the women urged. And so, grudgingly, but in a spirit of experimentation, he ended up placing his prayer book on Esther's forehead and murmuring a psalm. It was one of the longest. Minutes went by. Eyes closed, Mourad chanted in an undertone, and

7

chanted some more. He'd withdrawn into himself. It was something to see! The three sisters hanging on his lips, trying to guess his words, and he, solemn as a sultan in his black kaftan. Then he hiccupped, and then again. He yawned—not a small, stifled yawn, but a large, huge yawn, his mouth wide open, accompanied by a rattle. Suddenly, everyone jumped. Esther had sat upright. The aunts cried out, 'It's over! Look—she's cured!

If she'd sat up like this, it was that he'd left. They meant the demon, of course, the afrit. Hadn't Mourad chased him away through the power of his prayer? Everyone knows that baraka emanates from sacred words, sometimes even in spite of the rabbi who utters them. And they gazed at him, questioning, hoping for confirmation of this little local miracle. Mourad rubbed his eyes as if emerging from sleep. Seeing how the women were watching him, he realized he was about to become a saint. He foresaw how often he'd be summoned to the bedside of one or another of them. He grew frightened.

'What's the use of all this?' he began.

And they, their eyes wide, as if before an apparition: 'You think it means nothing to rescue a poor innocent girl from the jaws of death? But what kind of a rabbi are you?

'Do you want to know what I saw?' Mourad tried to explain. 'Do you really want to know? Well, I'll tell you: she suffers from a lack—'

'A lack?' the aunts cried in unison. 'Meaning what? A lack of what? Hmm. But she lacks nothing.'

'In her belly,' the rabbi continued, 'there's something like a beast, a ravenous beast. When I place my hand like this, look—' He slipped his hand under Esther's shift. They all drew closer. 'I feel it moving beneath her skin, there, in her lower belly.' And he pressed his hand down hard. Esther cried out. 'You see! This beast—listen, I'm not saying it really exists, am I?—this beast is hungry.'

'And so?' the others asked in unison, 'And so?'

'The beast,' the rabbi went on, '—it's not a real beast, you understand?—this beast feeds on the substance halfway between blood and milk, half and half.'

'What's he babbling about?' Aunt Maleka grumbled. 'I'm telling you, the prayer has made him mad! What a bloody lunatic!'

'Listen, listen to me carefully.'

And, for once, he obtained silence.

'This substance made of blood and milk is the one men carry within themselves. Do you understand? The drop of life—that's what the beast feeds on.'

'Oh, I understand!' exclaimed Uncle Elie, until now silent in his armchair. 'I understand. The drop of life—what we have in our eggs!'

'In our eggs. No, but this one,' Aunt Maleka grumbled, 'he certainly doesn't have it in his brain.'

'And so?' the other two aunts asked again.

'And so,' the rabbi finally decreed, 'and so, she must be married! In this way, the beast will receive its daily portion and leave the poor child in peace.'

A beautiful theory, in fact, that limned the order of the universe. The beast, this creature that does not exist, lives within the woman— who certainly does exist—at the heart of her womb, awaiting its nourishment, the husband's sperm. The beast was thus the condition for marriage between men and women; or, perhaps the marriage of humans should be understood as nothing more than the visible aspect of the beast's meal. But to get Esther married—was he joking or what? Who would marry her? Who would want a halfwit?

When her cousin on her father's side, Mordecai Zohar, known as Motty, learnt of the rabbi's recommendation, he declared his intention to Uncle Elie. He'd deliberated long and hard. He hoped to ask for Esther's hand. Seriously? Absolutely!

'How do you know she's attractive?' asked the old man. 'You've never seen her. When—may God protect us—you lost your sight, she wasn't even born. You don't know her face.'

Motty, his gaze absent, took hold of his uncle's hands. He squeezed them, kissed them, begged him, 'Tell me, Uncle, she *is* pretty, isn't she? I can feel it. I know it. When she walks in front of me, it's as if someone were uncorking a vial of myrrh. And when she serves me a drink and I brush her arm, warmth fills my chest.'

Overcome with emotion, the old man didn't know what to say. Esther was indeed a hard worker, honest and devoted to her family—the very qualities that would make her a good wife—but . . . but he didn't dare voice his opinion. You should never let loose malicious words. No. Never. They always ended up proving true. Should he tell Motty she had something missing, as if reason had abandoned her soul since her fall? Or, not that. Something extra. Yes. That was it. There was even some*one* extra. That's what Uncle Elie was thinking: if Motty married Esther, there would be two in her bed, her husband and the demon inside her. But how to make him understand?

'Do you know the story of Tobias?' Uncle Elie asked.

'Tobias? You mean, as in the Book of Tobit?'

'Exactly. Tobias, the son of the blind man, Tobias and his cousin Sarah, who was possessed by a demon.'

Motty knew the prayers by heart, from the first line to the last. His blindness had sharpened his other senses, especially his memory. He knew how to recite not only the three daily prayers but also those for feast days, those for the dead at the cemetery, the seven marriage blessings and large portions of the psalms. He knew them so well that at the Haim-Capucci Synagogue, named for a seventeenth-century Kabbalist who'd lived in Cairo, people often turned to him, the blind man, to verify the precise wording of a verse, a pronunciation, the order of blessings. But although the prayers contain whole sections of the Torah, the Book of Tobit does not figure at all, not even with an allusion—the Bible has always distrusted demons. Of course, Motty knew the story, but he'd never heard the exact text; he would have remembered it. He remembered everything.

'Tobias also ended up marrying his cousin, didn't he?' he asked his uncle.

'Yes,' replied Elie, 'and it was to everyone's satisfaction, for she was destined to him. But do you know that when Tobias approached Sarah, the demon that possessed her had already killed seven fiancés who'd presented themselves to her, one after another? Seven! Do you hear me? The beautiful Sarah, so sweet, so desirable, his sister, his love, was also the door of hell.'

'Oh, well, that won't happen to me. The demon won't bother with a blind man.'

A wave of emotion once more flooded Elie. 'What makes you think that, my son?'

'Don't people say that a demon uses the power of the person he possesses? If he uses my eyes, then he certainly won't see me.'

Elie thought for a moment in silence. Motty seemed genuinely attracted to Esther. And his opinion wavered. He told himself that, all things considered, this marriage wasn't such a bad idea: a half-mad woman with a blind man; perhaps the two together would make up one sound person. But they would have to watch that Motty not be destroyed by the demon, the djinn as educated people called him, or the afrit as he was called in the alley. Whatever his name, if he existed, may God destroy him! . . . That's what Elie thought.

Elie, the oldest man in the family, had some pull. He knew how to convince Esther's aunt. Once the loose-tongued Maleka had been won over, the rest of the family easily fell into line. They had to admit that, in one stroke, this marriage resolved two problems: Motty's blindness and Esther's madness.

But a week before the ceremony, Uncle Elie was seized with misgivings. He spoke to his nephew, counselling him not to go near his wife for the first three days after the wedding.

'What do you mean, Uncle? That I not go near her, not sleep in the same bed? Is that what you mean?'

'Yes. Neither the first, nor the second, nor the third night. You will wed her on Wednesday'—the 'fourth day' as it is known— 'and wait till Saturday night, well after sunset, to join her.'

'And I shouldn't even stay in the same room?'

'You can stay in the same room, but always make sure another person is between the two of you.'

'And speaking to her? Can I speak to her, Uncle?'

'What are you getting at, with all your questions? What will you say to her? All you have to do is pray to God that your destined bride come to you with her soul whole.'

Motty was struck by his uncle's words. He did not understand them; they whirled through his brain. He repeated them to whoever wanted to hear, as if to extract their full meaning: 'My bride will come to me, her soul whole.'

Some people made fun of him. 'You think you're marrying one woman, but it's an entire tribe that invades you. Lucky if they're children of Adam.' 'Children of Adam'—that's what human beings are called in Hebrew and Arabic, to distinguish them from those others, children of the creatures people are afraid to name—demons. Some others pitied him. 'Poor Motty who can't see the ruts in the road and stumbles at every step.' In the Alley of the Jews, people often spoke in images. Day by day, Motty grew more anxious. He returned to his uncle with new questions. He had so many. People were saying that Esther was 'accompanied'; some even called her 'possessed', that she didn't own her body, not even her voice. That's how they explained her abrupt mood swings, her angers, her absences, her losses of consciousness. Another will was expressing itself through her, another personality—angry, vindictive, sometimes violent. But how to make sense of that? Esther had too strong a character to let someone else decide for her, speak for her. He didn't know what to think. Motty was like that, both simple and deep. His blindness hobbled his imagination—he was too afraid of illusions. And so what he heard acquired the force of law. He didn't know that humans speak mostly to lie, and often to wound.

Uncle Elie took him by the shoulders and hugged him. 'I'll take care of it,' he promised. 'I'll go tomorrow to the perfume souk to buy some incense. You'll burn it for three days and three nights in the room where your bride will wait. She must not move from there, do you understand? Even if she protests, okay? She must bathe in the scents that will envelop her like the *hijab* that envelops Arab women.'

'Incense? Are you talking about incense?'

'Yes, the incense will cover her like a veil for three days and three nights. On the fourth night, at the end of Shabbat, her aunt will take her once more to the ritual bath. She'll purify herself and then she'll await you on her bed. It's only then that you may go near her.'

Here is what the women were singing on the night of Motty and Esther Zohar's wedding, a sort of poem they'd composed for the occasion:

'He has married the orphan, she has married the prophet. He has married the orphan, who meets her father on her nightly path without seeing him. She has married the prophet, who cannot see today, for he already lives tomorrow. To him, Esther has been given, the way a dog is given to a blind man. To her, Motty has been given, set on her lips like God's name to draw her from evil. She was speaking of him—she had his name on her lips. He was holding her hand—she was the light of his eyes. He has married the orphan, she has married the prophet.'

And the song made sense: Esther's name rang in Motty's heart, and Motty's face shone in Esther's eyes. That night, people sang in the streets, they danced and drank. And that night, the Jews, their hearts caught up in celebration, forgot to lock the ghetto's gate. But that night, there was no quarrel with the Arabs.

Following Elie's advice, Motty did not go near Esther, even though she was his wife. On the third day of the incense ritual, he returned to confide in his uncle. For two nights he'd been unable to sleep. On the first night, Esther, arrayed in her beautiful bridal clothes, had collapsed onto the bed and immediately fallen asleep. As for him, he'd remained at the entrance, near the brazier. As soon as the fragrance faded, he'd tossed in new bits of incense.

And he'd heard her talking in her sleep. 'There were groans, uncle, and shrieks and tears—'

'Groans, shrieks, and tears? And words too?'

'I could make out only one, which she repeated dozens of times: "No!"'

'Are you saying that while she slept she repeated No? Just No?'

'Yes.'

'And she was shrieking and groaning?'

'She was crying too, yelling "No" and fighting in her sleep.'

'You didn't go near her? Are you completely sure?'

'No, Uncle. I stayed on the other side of the door, as you told me. I tried to speak to her gently, but I heard only rage.'

Motty was hoping for an explanation; Elie didn't offer one. He only recommended that Motty go to the synagogue and 'clear the way', meaning give alms to every beggar he met. And Elie promised to spend the next night, the third, with Motty.

That night, after the meal, they set up the *tawla*—the backgammon board—brewed a full pot of tea and sat down in the street outside Aunt Maleka's house where Esther was sleeping. Elie couldn't understand how the blind Motty managed to beat him at backgammon. Of course, he had to announce the outcome of each toss of the dice in a loud voice. And he said it in Kurdish, as we all do: *Docha*, 'double six'; *dorgui*, 'double four'; *shesh-besh*, 'six-five'; *habyak*, 'double one'. Each time, Motty got the best combinations. But what was most astonishing was how perfectly he envisioned the board and the placement of the pawns, not hesitating for a moment before moving them. That night, he won game after game. What's more, he succeeded in bearing off all his pawns before Elie could take any. Which earned him double points, '*marz*'.

'*Marz*!' he exclaimed, laughing.

His uncle protested. 'Come on, I let you win! But tell me, how do you keep the whole game in your head, knowing where the pawns are without seeing them?'

14

'I see the numbers,' Motty answered. 'The numbers are people.'

'People' is a strange word in Arabic—it means 'humans' but also 'spirits, non-humans'. In Arabic, people are sometimes not-people.

'But what are you saying?'

It must have been midnight. Elie was holding the two ivory dice between his thumb and forefinger, about to toss them when a deep groan emerged from the room where Esther was sleeping. The two players paused. The groan began again. A solemn sound, fearful, the groan of a trapped wild animal fighting to be free. And then a roar of anger, followed by an almost human cry, sharp, tearing.

'He is caught!' Elie exclaimed. 'Move away. He will come out now.'

'What? What are you saying?' Motty hesitated even as he sought shelter in an angle of the wall.

They heard a creaking, the breaking of a wood plank, the bursting of a chest or table (or maybe a chair); then the distinct sounds of running and panting. Lightning crossed the sky, here and there, revealing pairs of gleaming eyes. The thunderclap that followed terrified Elie who covered his face with his hands. An awful howling wind swooped down the alley. Motty recited a prayer. Flung from his chair by the force of the gust, Elie rolled on the ground, repeating in Arabic: 'In the Name of God, in the Name of God, the Most Compassionate, the Most Merciful,' not realizing that was how Muslims opened their prayers. The wind blew for several minutes more, and then, just as suddenly, calm returned. In the alley, shutters opened. A man asked if anyone needed help. Then Esther appeared on the threshold, her face all sleepy. She was holding her head in both hands. She looked around, but her eyes seemed to see nothing, neither her old uncle nor her young husband. Like a sleepwalker, she went back in and lay down. Feeling his way, Motty approached Elie who was still lying on the ground. He struggled to lift him up; the old man had received a blow to his thigh and could no longer place his left foot on the earth.

That is what happened on that infamous night of 21 September 1918, in an alley of the Jewish ghetto of Cairo. The following day, Motty joined his young wife, and Uncle Elie remained lame. People said the old man had absorbed the blow the demon intended for the husband. Later, many recalled strange happenings that night: a storm without rain; violence without a perpetrator; cries and groans without animals. And in the annals of the Jewish community of Cairo, the Chief Rabbi recorded, in the Rashi script usually reserved for esoteric commentaries, that it had been done in accordance with the recommendations of the Book of Tobit, to bring the bride to her husband. That's how Esther, daughter of Shmuel Zohar and Salha Cohen, was delivered from the being who'd oppressed her for years, becoming the wife of Mordecai Zohar, her first cousin, whom she'd married the preceding 18 September.

It was also on this 21 September 1918 that, in Palestine, General Edmund Allenby won the Battle of Megiddo that decided the outcome of the First World War in the Levant, chasing the Turks from the region. During the days that followed, Elie soberly recalled that the night determined destinies, for, as the Talmud teaches, every event is a child of night. Egypt became more and more British, and Motty set up house with Esther on the mezzanine of the grocer's shop Elie owned on Nasir Lane, near the Haim-Capucci Synagogue, named for a kabbalist who'd cured the sick with sacred words and amulets.

Motty immediately took stock of his responsibilities. Now that he was the head of a household, he had to earn a living. As he'd explained to his uncle that remarkable night of the demon's racket, numbers were people he saw moving before his eyes. He ascribed to them colours, smells, ways of moving, mating, breeding. In Arabic script, zero was an almost invisible point, the tip of a spear, a sexual organ. Zero, called *sefr* in Arabic—from which French drew the word for numeral, *chiffre*, and Hebrew the word *sefer*, meaning 'book'—was red and had the same smell as blood. Zero was the demiurge, the origin of all numbers, the one through whom all the numerals were able to constitute the structure of the universe.

Without zero, the others would remain separate, only numerals, never numbers. One was the wife of Zero, his complement, enjoying no existence without him and becoming a totality as soon as he appeared. One was unique because Zero preceded it; One was transformed into infinity when Zero followed it. That's why the first letter of the alphabet, the one associated with unity, the *aleph*, goes from one to a thousand when you remove a single letter. In Arabic, a thousand is *alph*, while *aleph,* the first letter of the alphabet, is one. One was yellow, like gold, with a scent as strong as resin. Zero was the father and One the mother; together, they had eight children. The slyest, Five, was a snake, and he was green. He represented the source, for the hand with its five fingers was the origin of everything; when you're done counting your fingers, all you can do is start over. Five always protected, in the form of the hand used against the evil eye.

Numerals, which had kept Motty company since his childhood, peopled his long hours of solitary thought. He was excited by their combinations; he rejoiced at their unions and tried to mediate conflicts, to avoid ruptures. It was more than a passion; it was in fact a kind of obsession. Everything pertaining to numerals was a province of his kingdom; in secret, he ruled over a populace of numbers. That's how he could remember infinite lists after having heard them just once, and could mentally complete the most complicated calculations faster than any machine. For many years, he'd used his gifts to entertain the family; now that he was married, it was time to draw a profit from them. He became the accountant for Jewish craftsmen in the gold, silver and brass souks. Within a few weeks, he'd memorized the books for each of the hundred shops that made women's gold rings and bracelets, silver ornaments for Torah scrolls and brass amulets to ward off the evil eye. People said Motty's brain was a pyramid— on its walls, the smiths' accounts were engraved for eternity, as if on cartouches. Every morning, Esther led him through the market stalls, and he went from one to another, discussing buying and selling, profits and losses. He concluded by giving a number. Of course, the shopkeepers continued to record their transactions in their account books, but they no longer looked at them, so reliable was Motty's memory. They didn't pay him much, and, besides, he never asked for money. At the end of the week, on Friday during mealtime, after having brought Motty to the synagogue, Esther threaded her way through the Khan al-Khalil until she reached the jewellers' alley. She entered each stall, sat for a moment and awaited the meagre reward for his efforts. And so life went on like this: the gold engraved by the smiths' hands left to adorn a wealthy bride; a few piastres, enfolded in her handkerchief, came to Esther; and the record of the transactions was inscribed in Motty's memory.

From the very first night they spent in the same bed, Esther loved Motty, the mysterious one. In the darkness, equally blind, they explored each other with their fingers, lost in the scents of their bodies. From the first night, Motty loved Esther, the wild one. They spoke little, whispering each other's names. He exhaled onto her neck; she inhaled from his mouth, each depositing a fragment of breath on the frontiers of the other. She called him 'my eyes', she who was his eyes. He called her 'my soul', he who was her name. At daybreak, she kissed his hands, thanking God for having made her a woman. At night, she lay down first. Reciting a verse from the Song of Songs, he approached the bed and took her face in his hands; he always ended by declaiming her name, 'Esther, Queen Esther . . . Esther, the divine Ishtar . . . Esther, the Astarte of my nights.' In the morning, they rejoiced at the thought of a day won from darkness. When the sun set, their bodies thrilled at the thought of lying next to each other.

While Motty worked on the jewellers' accounts, Esther, her chores completed, sat on their doorstep. Why did the women come to talk to her? No doubt they sensed the strange calm emanating from her since her marriage; no doubt they sensed the power of the earth that underlies all. They brought cones of grilled watermelon or sunflower seeds, sat down beside her and told her, she who'd barely left childhood, their women's problems while splitting the seeds with their teeth and spitting out the shells, like parakeets. Esther smiled to herself, for the questions were always the same: 'How to restore desire when it was eroded by revulsion at pregnancies, everyday anxieties, morning cares?' She always answered methodically. 'First touch it,' she'd say, 'touch it!' In Arabic, the word means 'touch', 'sensation' as well as 'emotion'—the language knows that the person who touches is also touched, that you cannot touch without love. 'You have to take his bird in your hand,' she'd say. 'All men are children. They all had a mother who washed them, didn't they?' And the women would giggle, their noses in their zinc pots which they called *zingo*.

One morning, one of the neighbours looked at Esther defiantly and retorted, 'You think I don't know how to transform the chicken's neck into a rod, the way our father Moses once did with the serpents in front of Pharaoh?' Everyone laughed. Esther went one better, 'But do you know how to put the red spice in the sauce that moistens the rice on Shabbat eve?' 'The red spice?' 'What spice are you talking about?' 'The red spice, obviously!' 'You mean saffron? Or turmeric?' 'Or maybe red pepper?' another added. One woman, suddenly understanding: 'No! She means the spice that flows from women when the moon is full, right?' Another, the eldest, voiced her disgust, 'Ugh! Stop talking about such filth.' And they burst out laughing again. It was then that Esther shared her recipe.

'On the last of the five days, you have to take the final drops, when the blood is darkest, and expose them to the first light of morning.'

'On a plate?'

'How can you talk about such things?'

'Yes of course, on a plate. You need to collect as much as the mark left at the bottom of a cup after you've drunk your coffee.'

They drew closer to Esther, asking her to go on in low voices.

'And then?'

'You let it dry until you can reduce the blood to a powder, as fine as turmeric. One day is enough. Then you store the powder in a dark place. It must not see the light. And then—there you are!'

'What do you mean, "there you are"? What do you mean?'

Esther let herself be begged. It wasn't enough to tell them that they knew what came next, that all they had to do was to include the powder—called, she said, 'moon powder'—in the sauce. The others demanded a detailed description. What sauce? With what ingredients? Did you first have to fry onions?

She agreed to reveal a few more specifics: You had to spice up the sauce, so your husband would suspect nothing. Along with onions, tomatoes, naturally, and some red pepper, some saffron.

'And then?' they asked again.

'Then when you add the moon powder, you have to recite a sentence.'

'A sentence? What sentence, my dear?'

Esther was silent. The women drew closer. Finally, she breathed in a low voice, 'The sentence from the Torah: "You are a blood-groom to me."'

She repeated it in Hebrew. Respectful, deathly silence. A woman who quoted the Torah—she must be either a man or a witch.

The women tried Esther's recipe, of course. On Friday, they prepared the dish without anyone's help, hiding from daughters and mothers-in-law. Then, they went to the *hammam* where they spent more time than usual. Slowly, they epilated themselves with caramel, rubbed their skin with a rough loofah, made their hair sleek with henna, then perfumed themselves in the most intimate recesses of their bodies with myrrh, frankincense and oud. When they heard the Muslim afternoon call to prayer, they put on their blue gowns and burnt incense throughout their homes. It is said that on that night, the serpents proudly lifted their heads beneath their husbands' galabias. The experiment, frequently repeated, earned Esther a solid reputation as a sorceress. Soon, many were the women who came to chatter on the steps of her house at the hour when the lizards stirred. They presented her with the most troubling problems. Cousin Tayeba, who'd brought five girls into the world, one after another, feared her next pregnancy. If another daughter came, her husband would most certainly repudiate her.

'But no!' one of the women exclaimed. 'He wouldn't dare. He's too afraid of his uncle.'

His uncle was also his father-in-law.

'Of course he would,' another replied. 'Haven't you seen how he ogles the little Narguess? She's told me several times how he's tried to corner her in the hallway that leads to the kitchen. The hallway, can you believe it? Right under his wife's nose. Of course he's already thinking about remarrying.'

And, turning to Esther, her youngest aunt, Tofa'ha, 'the apple', asked if she could make a son come into Tayeba's womb. What a question! The others seemed shocked. How could she? If she'd asked for such a miracle from a man of God, like those you sometimes met on Yom Kippur, who spent the whole day and night praying and lamenting. Perhaps to one of those men, God could grant such a favour. But to women, who knew of religion only the stink breathed by the old stones, and whose actions, if Rabbi Mourad was to be believed, were nothing but idolatry and offerings to Baal. 'It's *haram*!' said the first, meaning 'sinful, forbidden'. 'Haram, totally haram,' added another.

'But,' Tofa'ha concluded, 'it's because it's haram that it might work, no?'

They no longer knew whether to laugh or be afraid. The women drew closer to Esther. She pulled back her hair and breathed deeply. What emerged from her was a sensation of physical power. To impose a sex on an infant, she explained, you had to summon the strength of animals—and the dead.

The dead? You didn't utter such words. You didn't say, 'the dead,' even less, 'death'; it wasn't done. And when you spoke the name of someone who'd died, you always added some protection. For example, you said, 'My Grandfather Soli, may God protect his soul,' or even, 'Our-father-Soli-may-God-protect-us,' as if, after death, his name had been modified, recomposed, augmented, transformed into a formula. It took a demon like Esther to let loose such wild sentences—containing death and the dead—without anxiety, without fearing the wrath of God. To ask for help from the dead? To use the power of animals? And, what's more, how the devil did she know this, she who'd never studied a thing? It's that the earth thinks; the neighbourhood, the hara, the Alley of the Jews, thinks; the ancestors think and there are sensitive souls that take in all these thoughts. That's what was going through Tofa'ha's mind.

'I'm not sure I can succeed,' Esther replied. 'You'll have to help.'

The women grew frightened. She was asking them to be her accomplices in sorcery. They sought other solutions.

'People say you should change the placement of the bed.'

'Yes! The head of the bed should face the first star.'

Tayeba shrugged. 'Really? Dozens of times, my dear, dozens of times, I've heard that tale about the head of the bed. At my house, the bed faces the star, my husband looks at the star, and me, I'm still searching for a son.'

'They say you should make love on your side.'

'Yes! On the right sight if you want a son, on the left for a daughter.'

'To make love on your side—what nonsense! When you move in bed'—that's how they described the act of love— 'you roll on all sides. And you always end by getting up, don't you? So, everything gets all mixed, right? The hot, the cold, the blood, the milk, everything. It's nothing but nonsense.'

'I heard you need the foreskin of a boy just after circumcision.'

'Yes, I heard that too. A boy from your family. You dip it in hot water and make a broth. You add nothing, neither salt nor spices. And you drink that broth right before welcoming your husband.'

The women affirmed this proposal with a nod of their heads. Such a recipe, they didn't know why, must be effective. But it imposed certain conditions—above all, acquiring the primary substance.

'So how do you get that foreskin?' Tayeba asked. 'Should I steal it, maybe? Have you seen how the grandmothers surround a baby after circumcision? You might as well try to steal the sacred carpet destined for the Prophet's tomb on his feast-day. Maybe that way of having a child is effective, I'm not saying it isn't, daughter of I don't know what—but it's impossible to accomplish, more difficult than acquiring the penis of a wolf or a hyena. No, the child's mother would have to give me the foreskin as a gift. And I don't know anyone who would.'

'She'd be too afraid her son would never marry.'

'Or that he'd become a "follower of Lot"'—meaning a homosexual.

The women turned again to Esther. 'You, Sett Belila.'

That's what they called her when they wanted a favour from her. Sett Belila, 'Lady Wheat Porridge', because, they said, her wheat porridge was the best.

'Sett Belila, you must have a solution.'

'Yes,' Esther answered, 'but I'm not sure how it will turn out. I've never done it before.'

'And so? Even if you've never done it. Does that mean you never will?'

'You're right, by my eyes! What does it hurt to try?'

On a Thursday, a little before noon, at the hour when they knew the men were in the synagogue for the Torah reading, they left for the cemetery. Esther was in the lead, walking with a sure step, followed by her Aunt Tofa'ha and Tayeba, the suppliant. They'd also enlisted Mahmoud, the ragman, who followed them, walking some steps behind. It's not acceptable for women to walk alone through the city. On their heads, they carried large pots of water to wash the tombs. Esther seemed to know the neighbourhood.

'It's definitely not the first time she's been here,' the other two whispered to each other. 'You see how she never once hesitated.'

'People say she comes here at night.'

23

'Do you think so? As for me, I'd never come here alone in the middle of the night.'

Children were everywhere, dark-skinned and dirty, running around barefoot on the burning sand. Women emerged from the tombs that were their homes. They spread their washing on the graves, holding it down with heavy stones. This place was inhabited by as many living as dead. Oddly, no one spoke. Despite all the activity, an unusual silence reigned.

'Here,' Esther said.

'Where?'

'Right where you're standing. It's an unmarked grave.'

'Is it at least a Jewish one?'

'Of course,' Esther replied, 'it's the grave of your grandfather's maternal uncle, Tall Saad. He was skinny and stiff as a reed. People say he died standing up, leaning against a wall, and that he stayed there until night. Everyone thought he was dreaming, lost in his hashish haze. And when they finally realized he was dead and wanted to carry him, they saw he'd been transformed into a wooden statue, truly stiff as a bone. So here's someone who died without living. His life was useless, he didn't leave a child.'

The two women looked around. They felt dozens of eyes following their slightest move. Even if the grave were not Tall Saad's, this was surely a Jewish section. They could make out Hebrew writing on some of the scattered tombstones.

'All right ladies, to work!'

They began to scrub the stone covered with earth and sand. And Esther began to sing in a Judaeo-Arabic sabir: 'You who sustain the lame, who open the doors of the prisons, who give life and death, who can revive . . .'

An hour went by like this. Little by little, the stone regained some of its chalky colour. They poured the water from their pots and stood, motionless under the sun, watching the stains evaporate. Tayeba was thinking: there are many more people below the earth than on it. Tofa'ha was turning over in her mind this phrase from the Bible, 'From dust you came, and to dust you shall return.' Most assuredly, God must know Egypt, this land where it was hard to distinguish men from dust. Esther was staring fixedly at the hole beneath the stone. 'Look,' she said, 'There! You can see his tongue.'

The two others drew closer. She pulled them back. 'No. Wait. You'll frighten him.'

Indeed, you could see a tongue. It was long and agile, perhaps the tongue of a snake, flicking forward as if to taste the terrain before venturing out.

'I'm afraid,' Tayeba said.

But Tofa'ha couldn't help joking. 'What are you afraid of? A child also comes out of a hole, doesn't it?'

'And he too comes from the dead,' Esther added solemnly. 'That's why we give him a grandfather's name.'

They saw a head appear, a heavy, helmeted head, as big as a fist.

'It's a warrior!' Esther cried as she grabbed the pot.

Drawn by the water, the chameleon emerged slowly, one step after another. He was exactly the colour of the stone, even up to the stains and blotches. His eyes, mounted on turrets like cannons on an assault tank, explored the four directions.

'Your son will be a warrior, that's for sure.'

You need to know that 'warrior' is the Arabic word for chameleon, and the one emerging from the tomb fit the word well, with his helmet so much larger than his head. When he reached the centre of the slab, Esther stepped forward and covered him with her pot. Tofa'ha helped her wrap her prey in a rag, and there they were, all three, heading back to the Mouski. Along the way, they were thrilled to have conquered their fears of the dead and of snakes. They sang a sort of ballad, a love song, and the chameleon leapt in the pot, like a foetus in its mother's womb. That night, Esther gave the tip of the tail to Tayeba and advised her to swallow it raw. The two women were not surprised by the prescription; they only wondered how

Esther had managed to kill the chameleon. Had she slit its throat, the way it's done with a lamb, or had she cut off its head, like a dove?

'In one month you'll be pregnant,' she told Tayeba, 'and it will be a boy. Don't forget, you must name him Saad, like your grandfather's uncle.'

Afterward, the two women often questioned Esther, asking her what she'd done with the rest of the chameleon. But Esther always answered the same way. 'A chameleon is like a woman. It hunts with its tongue. You'd be better off holding yours!'

Esther was the youngest of those gathered on the steps of the alley known as 'Thursday's' in Haret al-Yahud. The others loved her a little but criticized her a lot when she wasn't there; deep down, they also feared her. Indeed, something strange happened during the year of Tayeba's pregnancy, something that magnified their fear. One Friday, Esther was returning from her visit to the jewellers' souk, holding her skirt tightly. She was running, her hair in the wind, like a greyhound. When she reached her neighbourhood, she bumped into Adina, the second of her aunts.

'Where are you running like that? Did you meet a devil in full daylight?'

Esther was naive enough to tell her aunt that old Amine Lichaa had given her a pound—that's right, one hundred piastres!—for Motty's work. That was the change she was holding tightly in a fold of her gown.

'A whole pound? You don't say. That man who's so miserly? But what came over him?'

Esther shrugged and then burst out laughing.

'And to think he's a Karaite,' jeered the aunt, 'who claims to be Jewish and takes off his shoes to make prostrations like a Muslim. What a disgrace! Perhaps you granted him some other favour?'

Adina, who had a filthy mind, suspected that her niece had let the old miser pinch her arse or even caress her breasts. Esther didn't understand the allusion. She was ignorant of sex, knowing only love—ignorant of desire, knowing only God's call in the hollows of her body.

'Give me the money,' her aunt demanded. 'I'll keep it for you. What can you do with such a large sum?'

But why should she give it to her? All along her route, Esther had been imagining the silky cotton fabric she'd buy in the market to make a new galabia for Motty. Maybe there'd be enough left for a *tarbouche*, a fez; his old cap was moth-eaten. She shrugged again and disappeared into the mezzanine.

On Shabbat eve and the next day, she sang to herself, joyous. She even went to synagogue and remained quiet in the women's section. She was not uneasy, made no signals to the men, did not gossip with her neighbour, neither yawned nor burst out laughing. But the following day, Sunday (which they called 'the first day'), when she returned from the jewellers' souk after bringing her husband there, the money had disappeared. She cried out—and fell. It was the first time since her marriage that her demons showed themselves, and it was much stronger than the last time, when she got her first period. Shrieking, she rolled on the ground, hitting herself; then she rose, rolling her eyes; then she fell back down, crying out again. It was a deep cry, a wild animal's cry. Old Massouda, Uncle Elie's wife, came out of the house shouting, 'Come to me!' She repeated, 'To me! To me!' The other women ran to her. But what could they do, other than helplessly witness Esther's fit?

'Let misery befall me. Let me die!' Massouda howled. 'I didn't do anything. I didn't even speak to her. I was in the kitchen. She came into the room. I heard a scream. And when I got here, she was rolling on the ground as if fighting a demon.'

'The poor child,' Adina mourned. 'I'm sure that Karaite jeweller is to blame, that Lichaa, son of a dog.'

'Dog, son of a dog!' someone else added, spitting on the floor.

The women considering sending for Rabbi Mourad, but the fit lasted only a few minutes. Esther rose, mechanically arranged her gown, untangled her hair with her fingers. Her Aunt Maleka offered her a glass of water. She swallowed it in one gulp. Then she glued herself to the house's wall and turned her back on the gathering. What was she up to?

'Esther!' called old Massouda, 'Esther!'

She didn't react; she seemed to be praying. Everyone was aware, though, that she knew no prayers and that at synagogue she didn't even pretend by moving her lips the way the other women did. Suddenly, she struck the wall with the flat of her hand and said, 'It is written on this wall! What was hidden today at night will appear tomorrow with the sun!'

She turned to them, her eyes bulging and bloodshot. One by one, she stared at the women, letting her glance linger on each. The atmosphere was so charged the children ceased their play. The matrons, standing in a semicircle, looked at her open-mouthed. Then, turning away, she went into the mezzanine to make lunch. Little by little, life resumed.

It was Aunt Maleka who broke the silence: 'She was always like this, poor thing.' And she explained what she meant: 'Spirited.'

'Spirited?' Adina was surprised. 'Inhabited, you mean.'

'Yes, inhabited!' Tofa'ha went further, 'Worn by a djinn who uses her like clothing.'

'Don't say that!' Massouda pleaded. 'May God protect us. May it be in accordance with His law!'

News of these events immediately spread through the little community. Everyone knew that Esther had fallen after discovering the disappearance of the money the jeweller Lichaa had given her. Someone had stolen the hundred piastres hidden under her mattress. That explained her seizure. But it was impossible; there couldn't be a thief in the hara. The Jews lived so on top of one another that everyone knew what was in their neighbour's pockets better than what was in their own. No! It could only be a trick of the spirits, the afrits. Everyone knew they were mischievous. Sometimes they moved things. You looked for them, and, when you finally accepted they were lost, they turned up elsewhere, in an unexpected place. Someone mentioned the disappearance of a shoe; someone else, a coffee pot. 'The money will reappear, somewhere or other—don't be upset!' Still, a pound, a hundred piastres—no one had ever heard of such a thing; no one had ever heard that spirits cared about silver coins—modern silver, legal tender.

The next morning, Aunt Adina couldn't get out of bed. From her head to her toes, she was covered in spots. They summoned her mother, old Helwa, whom everyone called Ommi, which means 'my mother'. She was Esther's grandmother. She must have been at least eighty-eight years old and adept at healing. When she saw the spots, she cried, 'Terrible! It must be measles, which she caught when she was very little. She nearly died from it.'

There were some twenty spots just on Adina's face. Massouda was the first to notice their shape: 'Look! What a disaster! Look!'

'What?' Maleka asked.

'Don't you see?'

'Speak already! What should we look at?'

'The spots, there.'

'So? The spots?'

'Look! They're piastres.'

The women drew closer, looked carefully. It was true, the spots resembled coins, perfectly circular, with some sort of bas-relief design. But the ones on her face were too small. When they examined her legs, they discovered a spot the size of a coin, and this time they could even make out the king's profile in relief. They asked her to turn over. At the base of her back, a spot of similar size had at its centre the number One. A piastre. The hundred piastres Aunt Adina had stolen from Esther—had they reappeared in the form of spots on her body? The women counted them. There were indeed a hundred—exactly one hundred. One woman shrieked, then a second. Massouda fainted.

The aunts were the first to understand that it was impossible to harm Esther, that she was protected (they said, 'enveloped'). Moreover, any harm redounded upon the aggressor, like a mirror, attacking and denouncing at the same time. Adina thought she would recover when she returned the money, which she hastened to do. But the rash lasted for more than three weeks, almost a month. During that time, the story made the rounds of the neighbourhood. People told it to their children, to their employees, even to Arabs. Many tried to slip into Adina's room to see the coins inscribed on her body. It was said you could grow rich just by touching them. But the family guarded her. It would have been understandable if Esther drew power and influence from this. But the opposite was true. Some stayed away, avoiding being alone with her; others were cautious, careful not to say the least thing that might offend her. In either case, relationships were strained, and, little by little, Esther resumed the pariah's role that had been hers during her childhood.

'What's wrong?' her husband Motty asked one evening. 'I can tell you're unhappy. It seems as if joy has left your heart. Daytime or nighttime worries?'

He caressed her with his hands, brought them to her face. Esther could not repress a tear.

'Are you crying, my daughter?'

You could hide a lot from blind Motty but not your emotions.

'It's nothing, "uncle".'

Esther rarely used this Hebrew word, which meant both 'uncle' and 'darling'; only when her whole being leant towards him.

'Your joy gives me strength,' Motty replied; 'your sorrow erases the world's existence.'

'Tayeba is pregnant,' Esther said simply, 'she who people said was fated to grow old surrounded by stones, abandoned by her husband and by God. It will be a boy, she will call him Saad, because, as she said, his arrival in her belly filled her with joy.' (*Saad* means 'joy' in Arabic.)

Motty didn't answer. He kept Esther's hands in his. Did he know she was the one who had drawn little Saad from the ancestors' domain?—that she had known how to tame him, to convince him to leave the confined atmosphere of the tombs to come and join the family in Haret al-Yahud, the Alley of the Jews in old Cairo? Perhaps not, but he knew what women said about them as a couple. Until then, he'd never paid it any mind. Often, he repeated the sentence from the Talmud Uncle Elie had taught him: 'God poured ten measures of words into the world. Women took nine, and men just one.' So, you had to let them talk, to listen to them from afar, like birdsong. But some words pierced the heart like needles. You shouldn't avoid these but confront them, to nullify their effect, and perhaps even to answer them. The women claimed Esther was a witch—that was why she had no children. Her real husband, they sometimes added, was not Motty with the dead eyes but a demon with four eyes, two in front and two in back, an afrit. It was true they'd been married for seven years and his wife's belly had never grown round.

At first, they'd attributed it to Esther's youth, barely fourteen years old when they were wed. A child can't have a child. But when she was seventeen and her breasts had grown round like two ripe pomegranates, the child did not come. When she was nineteen, and her body had grown firm and her scent developed the strength of jasmine, Motty began to think that he himself was the child that would never come to Esther. And time continued to flow like the Nile's water under the bridge at Al-Gezira. Now she was twenty-one, and some women were saying terrible things. They said she devoured children in her womb. They said that was what gave her the strange power to reverse fate.

'Tomorrow,' Motty said, 'I'll go see Mourad, the rabbi, and ask him for a cure.'

'A cure?' Esther exclaimed. 'I'm not ill, you're not ill.'

'I'll ask him to intercede with God so we can have a child.'

Accompanied by his Uncle Elie, Motty went to the synagogue to meet the rabbi. They did not have the courage to speak, but

Mourad knew something was weighing on their hearts. They began to wander through the alleys, chatting. Children followed them, asking questions. So they ventured out of the ghetto, through the gates of the Mouski and entered the city. They walked for a long time, the two who used their eyes to see framing the one who gazed with his heart. When they reached the river, they sat on the ground, on the bank. They still hadn't broached the subject. Annoyed, the rabbi described to Motty what he was seeing: 'Do you hear how the breeze is making the leaves quiver? It's carrying the feluccas sailing with the speed of birds.'

'Yes,' Motty replied. 'I know. I can see the wind, I can see the scents and the weather. All that, I can see.'

Elie gestured to the rabbi to not take his nephew's words seriously. In Haret al-Yahud, people responded to sorrow by multiplying jokes. And so, to distract the rabbi, Elie said, 'He sees at night the way cats do, and women pull his tail.'

'How do you expect God to one day send us the Messiah if you talk like bargemen?' Mourad replied, looking severe.

After several hours, after having exhausted all the jokes they knew, unreeled all the crudeness hidden in their tongue— that Arabic mingled with Hebrew expressions and words from many other languages—Elie finally revealed the reason for their visit. It was seven years since his nephew married the beautiful Esther with the belly of fire, but no child had come nor even acted as if it would. Yet, as the rabbi knew well, the couple respected Shabbat and all the family purity laws. Motty was always the first at services. Although they were poor, they never failed to give a coin. As we say, God makes sure there are people poorer than you, so that everyone can offer charity, an obligation. So if the child was not coming, no doubt God had some plan. They knew, of course, that our father Abraham did not have his first child until his wife Sarah was a hundred years old. Motty was barely thirty-five. They weren't complaining. They were simply wondering. They weren't wise enough to interpret the puzzle they'd been posed. That's why they'd come to question Rav

Mourad. He would know what they must do to guide the child of these two into their home.

Mourad reflected for a long while.

'We realize,' Elie added, 'that you know prayers that can drive away demons. Perhaps you also know others to guide souls on their path towards us.'

'Wait,' the rabbi said, 'wait! We must consider the problem from all angles. First of all, does Motty know the usage of his wife?'

'The usage of his wife?' Elie was stunned. 'Which means? Is a wife like those automobiles you sometimes see on the street along the Nile, by the islands, over there? Most certainly, if that's the case, neither Motty nor I—his uncle, after all—know the usage of one.'

'The usage of his wife,' the rabbi continued, 'the usage of his wife—I mean—listen, Motty, since we're among men, I'll speak to you as a man. You see, it's not just a matter of penetrating your wife with your bird.'

'But what are you saying, Rav Mourad?' Elie sputtered, 'You're not speaking like a sage. Perhaps you're abusing *zbib*, anisette, or something? We come to ask you for a prayer, and you speak to us of a bird?'

'Listen! Listen to me, you animal. God gives you three ways of understanding—by spirit, by feeling and by reason. I'm suggesting you use your reason. And so, if you want to know why a machine isn't working, you first ask yourself if you know how to make it work.'

'Which means?'

'So now I'm speaking to you Motty, my prince, my pasha—please, answer me. I was saying it's not just a matter of putting your bird into your wife's secret, you should also move, do you know that?'

This was too much! This rabbi always wanted to appeal to reason; he should maybe first have determined if he had the usage of it himself. Of course Motty knew that he should move. He was blind but not an idiot. He even knew that when he moved, Esther also moved, and he was always surprised to discover how much they were in unison, how the movement of one wed the movement of the other. He shrugged and walked away alone, hastening his steps. Elie followed him, limping. And Mourad stayed where he was on the bank, his arms dangling by his sides.

That evening, everyone knew the question he'd posed Motty. Discussion flourished. 'They say it's with her afrit husband that Esther has children,' said Doudou, Adina's husband, 'and this blind fool has no idea of a thing.' Elie shot back, 'Motty is a *hakham*, a true sage. He's a blind seer. He sees the wrong side of things better than you see the right.' But Doudou insisted: 'Motty should give a *get* to his wife, he should leave her. To not have a child is proof of adultery.' A *get*? How they went on. After all, we're not pharaohs to repudiate a wife we love because she hasn't given us descendants. Mourad couldn't quiet the men who filled the alley with their loud voices. Back home, hiding, Motty sat on the floor, his face to the wall. Esther did what she could, not daring to interrupt what she took to be a meditation.

But soon, no longer able to restrain herself, she knelt before him, kissed his hands. 'Motty, O my eyes, O my soul.'

He didn't answer.

'Why pay it any mind? Men talk. And so? Do we always know why dogs bark? Most of the time they don't even know themselves.'

He ended up uttering words that remained engraved in Esther's heart: 'My sister, my sweetness, what have we done to deserve such misfortune, that of bringing forth nothingness? Who are we then, who have received life and do not know how to give it in turn?'

Esther was gripped by his plaintive voice, the words barely murmured, words she had never heard from him, as if all the pain he'd endured all his life—the humiliations of a blind man; the stones thrown by Arab children when he walked alone in the city; the mockery of the malicious and the fearful—had come to express itself in one sorrow, brute, complete. Her heart constricted, but she did not weep. Instead, she stiffened, determined. They would not take her Motty away from her. He was her life, her soul, her name. She vowed she would find a way to have a child since that was what he wanted, what the family expected. For that, she would do anything— even go naked into the synagogue, just as Hanna, mother of the prophet Samuel, had done when she despaired about her infertility.

The chance to do something (her aunts would later say 'anything'), presented itself the following Saturday. She'd accompanied Motty to the synagogue, but she hadn't gone in—she was standing against the wall. Through the open windows, she could hear the tenor voice of her husband as he began each verse of the psalm. When Motty sang, everyone for miles around knew, for kites came by the dozens to rest on the building's dome. Some said the kites weren't birds but souls, those of generations of Egyptian Jews buried in Bassatine, coming to claim their return to Jerusalem. And so, when people raised their eyes to heaven and saw the kites descending and hovering harmoniously above the Mouski, they said, 'Today Mordechai Zohar has risen to sing.'

Esther was standing in the shadows, her head lowered, lost in dark thoughts. A poor Arab woman passed, dressed despite the heat in several layers of filthy fabric, her head wrapped in a large scarf. As she drew near, she extended her hand. She was accompanied by a young man about twenty years old, barefoot, wearing a torn galabia, his head covered in a sort of odd, motley-coloured skullcap—her son, most likely. He seemed dim-witted, and a thread of saliva drooled from his mouth.

'The poor child,' said Esther, 'Doesn't he speak?'

'Not with the children of Adam,' the woman replied. 'But his mind is sharp, and beware, his hand is quick. Don't come complaining he's robbed you. He's hungry.'

'I have nothing. You know that on Shabbat, we Jews never carry any money on us. But I'll give him the bread with favas I made for my husband.'

Esther offered it to the boy. Gingerly, he took hold of the packet wrapped in old newspaper, sniffed it, caressed his face with it.

'You may,' his mother said, 'Take it!'

The young man's eyes shone with joy, two large clear eyes, lined with black, like the eyes of a gazelle. He ate the bread. The woman clasped Esther's hands.

'May God bless your hands, my sister! The bread is plant flesh, and the favas you've given my son will be as many children that God will grant you.'

'Alas!' Esther sighed. 'Here it is seven years that I've known my husband and my womb has remained empty until today.'

'Oh, my poor child,' replied the woman. 'Do you know what I'm called?'

'Tell me your name, that your day be lit up.'

'Sett Oualida, "Lady Momma", that's what they call me, because all I have to do is look at a water buffalo and before I've turned my back, there she is, pregnant. I know the plants, the stones, and the words that bring children forth. I also know the actions that make them leave. That's why I'm called Lady Momma, I who preside over children's arrival when you wish for them and their departure when they've come to hinder life. People fear me and peddle ugly rumours about me. You shouldn't pay them any mind. They accuse me of being a witch. Don't believe them. I untie wombs. I also know how to untie the strings of husband's wallets. Look—'

The woman lifted the hem of her gown, displaying her thighs before Esther's entranced gaze.

'Of all the children that have passed through this womb, only this one remains.'

She let her gown fall and tugged the young man's ear; he grimaced.

'When I go near Bab al-Zuwayla, the neighbourhood where I was born, the mothers say to their children, "Here's the Baboula, she'll steal you away and devour you." At the sight of me, children run and hide. You see how unjust they are, I who am the queen of children, who gives them their souls'—the Arabic word also means 'desire'—'and who makes them leave.'

Esther looked more carefully at the woman. She was tall as a man, with the dark skin of people from the South. A certain sweetness shone on her face. Esther had faith in her words. She told herself, 'God has answered my prayers. He doesn't want a soul as pure as Motty's to be destroyed by sorrow.'

'Can you do something for me?' she asked.

The matter was soon settled. Esther would come and find her over there, in her world. Sett Oualida lived outside, sleeping under porches, and spent her days wandering through the old city.

'You'll find me in front of a mattress-maker's shop. The workers sometimes give me bread. Sometimes I help them clean the cotton.'

Esther would have to bring her gown and *mandil*, her headscarf. The woman promised that not a year would go by before a son would come to rest against her breasts. At these words, the young man placed his face against his mother's breasts. The woman looked around. The alley was empty. All the Jews were praying inside the synagogue, and Arabs avoided passing this way on Shabbat. In one movement, she bared her breast. It was heavy and firm, the aureole nearly black, the nipple prominent. The young man delicately positioned his lips. Then, closing his eyes, he began to suck. In the synagogue, they were beginning to read the Song of Songs. It was the passage, 'Your two breasts are like two fawns, twins of a gazelle, which feed among the lilies.'

'Hurry up, fool!' his mother scolded, accompanying her advice with a little tap on his head.

Esther was silent, contemplating the scene which she didn't try to understand. After all, when a donkey nurses, it stands and is strong like this young man.

After a few minutes, the woman pushed her son away and covered her breast.

'God gives to everyone,' she said. 'Happy are those who accept His gifts. I can offer him Paradise five times a day, he who doesn't know how to pray.'

She limped away lightly, leaning on the young man's arm, trailing behind her a strong scent of musk.

'May your day be blessed!' Esther called after her.

Without looking back, the woman replied, 'May our Father keep you, O my sister!'

The children were already beginning to leave the synagogue.

Bab al-Zuwayala

The next day, at the laundry hour, unable to stand it any longer, Esther told her three aunts about her encounter.

Maleka, sharp-tongued, cried, 'I know her, that witch! Her name's Khadouja—don't go near her! She'll swallow all your children, you poor thing!'

'Witches aren't so stupid that they'll eat absence,' thought Esther, and shrugged.

Adina, malicious, spat out some of those poisoned words that were her specialty. 'Go see her, then. The child that comes to you will be just like hers. I hear she feeds him her milk by day, and he feeds her his sperm at night.' And she snickered as she hid her face in her hands.

That left only Tofa'ha, the youngest, to sigh thoughtfully. 'Children are born from the triumph over the forces of evil. If the medicine of the Jews has not been able to liberate the child destined to you, perhaps the medicine of the Arabs will manage to open your belly.'

Esther smiled then, struck by these words. She felt reassured. She'd often thought: 'We live beside the Arabs the way a man might live beside his innards. Our tales fill their Qur'an, their tongue fills our mouth. Why aren't they us? Why aren't we them?'

'Will you come with me, my aunt?' she asked Tofa'ha.

'Would I allow my daughter, the daughter of my oldest sister, to face a wild beast alone in Bab al-Zuwayla, without lifting a finger? Bab al-Zuwayla . . . '

And all four of them burst out laughing, so pleasing was the sound of the words 'Bab al-Zuwayla'.

Two weeks went by before Tofa'ha came to fetch her niece one morning, reminding her to bring along a gown and a headscarf as Sett Oualida had instructed.

They found her seated on the ground, not far from the Zuwayla clan's gate, her back against the wall of one of the minarets. Her son was sleeping, his head on his mother's lap. Over and over, she was softly singing a song that began with these lines: 'Has my love betrayed me, making me long for him each day and dream of him each night?' When she noticed Esther, she shook her son. He rose quickly, shielding his face with his arm—he knew how quick his mother's hand could be. She invited the two Jewish women to have a seat on the dirty cloth, as if it were a set of armchairs in a middle-class parlour.

'May your day shine brightly!'

'May your day be as white as jasmine!' replied Tofa'ha. 'I've brought semolina cake with honey for your son.'

'My son, that ass, what does he know except his mouth's pleasure?'

Esther noticed the gleam in the young man's eyes. She recalled her Aunt Adina's words and wondered if it was just the anticipation of cake or thoughts of other, more forbidden, pleasures.

'Your son, may God keep him, we don't know his first name.'

'Does he know it himself?' exclaimed the mother. 'To me, he's Naji. Who knows what those he speaks to when he's sleeping call him.'

They chatted like this for a while, in the shadow of two minarets guarding the entrance to the Muslim holy city—speaking of families that didn't exist, of a past they invented, a future that would never come. Philosophy of the present moment, which knows that words are void of meaning. Words to pass the time, words to breathe, words to play your part in the city's cacophony. When the conversation seemed to peter out, Tofa'ha drew Esther's mandil from a fold in her gown and handed it to Khadouja. 'Here's what you asked for.'

'Did she sleep with this scarf on her head?'

'Yes.'

'And the gown?'

'We have that too,' Tofa'ha replied, pointing to the parcel Esther held under her arm.

The woman took the scarf and sprinkled it with a reddish powder from a rusty metal box. Then she struck a match and set it alight. The fabric crackled and emitted multicoloured sparks. 'Look!' she said, 'The colours.'

The flames kept changing colours, from blue to red, sometimes yellow, sometimes green. Real fireworks. Then Khadouja threw the scarf onto the ground and it began to move, still crackling, like an animal, like some kind of spider, creeping towards Esther.

'Oh, Momma!' cried Esther, jumping back.

The fire burnt down and the strange thing subsided. Nothing remained but a small pile of cinders. Esther drew closer. When she reached out her hand, the fire suddenly flared up again. She quickly retreated. The thing, giving off a disgusting smell, ended up burning down to the last thread.

'Did you see?' asked Khadouja.

The other two gazed at her, wide-eyed.

'You saw, didn't you? They are seven. And they have a leader. I know this one'—she sneered— 'by his smell. He's called "Nofal the Red". That's why we'll need a sheet of copper.'

When they returned to Haret al-Yahud, both aunt and niece were visibly uneasy. To the questions of the other two aunts they replied evasively, not daring to recount their adventure. Truth is, they'd been frightened by Khadouja's strange proposals. They were ashamed, too, to expose their gullibility in broad daylight. They'd left the gown with her. What would she do with it? Everyone knows how easy it is to cast a spell on clothing imbued with someone's scent. Would the cure they'd gone in search of prove worse than the disease? If the men learnt where they'd been and what they'd done, they would inflict severe punishment on the beggar woman and her imbecile son. They decided to keep their secret.

The following night, Motty smelt a strange odour in the kitchen. 'Go and see if a rat hasn't died in the trash.' The trash was empty; everything was perfectly clean. Still, Esther scrubbed the floor with buckets of water. Then burnt incense. But the odour persisted. It was worse the next day. On the night that followed, a fire suddenly blazed in Tofa'ha's bathroom, a bizarre fire, as if the air itself were aflame; you couldn't tell what was burning. The next day, when the women climbed up to hang laundry, stones fell onto the terrace from out of nowhere, as if from the sky. Each day, each night, something new happened, now at Esther's, now at Tofa'ha's. The most ordinary objects disappeared, especially kitchen utensils. The little clay water jugs where water was left to cool were mysteriously emptied of their contents. One morning, when Tofa'ha went to put on her slippers, she had a strange feeling. Then she realized they'd grown so big you could put two feet into each one. Day after day, strange things continued to happen: water rose up from drains; doors and windows opened backwards; glasses broke by themselves. At the end of a week, unable to stand it any longer, the two women finally spoke to each other. Until then, they hadn't exchanged a word about Khadouja's recommendations.

'We'd better return,' Esther stammered.

'She said, "the first night of the new moon." '

'That's tomorrow!'

*

They went at dusk. They heard the singing from afar—

'O the beauty, the languor of night. I have seen his breast by the light of the moon. And his face reflected in the Nile's water. O Nofal, O Nofal, O Nofal. Red, your colour is your power, it is the guide of our lives.'

The voice seemed to be coming from nowhere—a man's voice, strong, deep, with perfect pitch, an interval of pure music. The solitary note lasted, *a cappella*, for minutes at a time. 'O . . . O Nofal, O Nofal, O Nofaaaa . . . ' Suddenly the voice was silent, leaving an anxious void in space. Then it was the tanbur, the traditional six-stringed lyre, that skilfully took up the melody. Then the rhythm, beaten by dozens of hands, and then, soon, the counterpoint—the tarabukas, the drums—first the heavy ones, the big bendir frame drum, then the village tabla. Then the second rhythm, the taks and doms of the tablas, then the clicking of the cymbals, and there they were, on their way—a caravan jolting along, the throbbing rhythm of camels, the bouncing of riders in their saddles. Once the rhythm was established, the voice returned, somewhat hoarse, plaintive, the voice of a worker, a peasant who, at close of day, takes pleasure in honouring his land and singing its mystery: 'O Nofal, O Nofal, O Nofal . . . O Nofal, O Nofal, O Nofal . . . I saw the moon light up his breast. Such beauty exists only in dreams.'

In luring peasants into its mirages, the city of Cairo gives birth to thousands of nostalgic poets whose tears emerge in moonlight like clouds of mosquitoes, escorts of invisible camels. In this way, through their songs to the spirits, the Nile peasants endure the city where poverty has brought them; in this way, the city draws strength from the centuries-old silt.

The woman, Khadouja, the witch, the one they called Sett Oualida, 'Lady Momma', had brought them into a courtyard, a sort of patio. Some thirty women were bustling about. A dozen or so musicians stood against the wall, tuning their instruments. In the four corners, torches burnt.

That evening, Khadouja, dressed entirely in black, looked almost elegant. The beggar woman had transformed into a priestess, outlined her eyes with kohl. Here, she was the assistant of the *kudiya*, the mistress of ceremonies, an old woman with muscled arms, stronger than a man's. When they passed through the door of the courtyard, the kudiya pointed to Esther and asked in a man's voice, 'Is this the one who sees, who touches, and who holds back?'

'Your word is sweetness, O you who rule,' Khadouja replied.

The kudiya measured Esther, using a cubit-long stick and announcing numbers: five, then seven, twelve, and finally ten. She unfolded the gown Tofa'ha had entrusted to Khadouja the week before. It had been visibly prepared, perfumed. 'Put on this gown,' she ordered Esther, 'We'll read the signs.'

Oh, to read the signs! . . . To seek in impalpable substances—the air that burns, the drums that beat, the dance that whirls—the traces left by the invisible ones . . . That's what it is, to read the signs!

Then the kudiya raised her hand in the direction of the musicians and the voice of the man, an ageless peasant in a striped galabia, rose again, imposing silence: 'Aaaaa. O Nofal, O Nofal, O Nofal . . . O Nofal, O Nofal, O Nofal . . . Those who descend are happy in the depths, those who rise blossom in the sky. How beautiful she is, her eyes black like a fawn's. I have seen the moon light up her breast. Each mistress of ceremonies has her own vision. Aaaaah. O Nofal, O Nofal, O Nofal . . . '

That's how the dance, the trance, the ceremony of presences began. That's how the rite of the lords, sometimes called the *zars*, began. A woman flung herself into the centre of the room. Her feet flew, led by the drums. She became wind, odour, essence. Khadouja slipped behind her, her feet keeping time. When she saw her panting, sensing she was ready, she draped her head with a black cloth. The woman began to spin to the rhythm of the instruments. One taraboka player came forward with an endless solo. The others accompanied him with their cries: 'Play, my son, play on.' The women ululated. The dancer whirled faster. A verse then came to the singer—it was not what they called 'moments', well-known songs repeated week after week, but an improvisation: 'Look, Abdallah, see the beauty that arises from woman and radiates throughout the world . . . Play, play on!'

The musicians responded as a chorus: 'Give me beauty, give it to me. I play for you until night's end. Give me beauty, that I might cast its veil upon the earth. Each mistress of ceremonies possesses her own vision . . . Aaaah . . . '

And the woman fell, face down, on the ground, twitching. The other dancing women approached her, tenderly stroking her head and back. Then they helped her rise and brought her outside the circle. Then they led her into another courtyard where she could catch her breath, caressed by their hands.

Night of presences, night of madness. A second woman came forward. This one was quite young. Her thin, sweat-soaked gown revealed her shape more clearly than if she were naked. The voice of the first singer took up the refrain: 'I saw his breast by the light of the moon . . . ' She danced; the musicians played verses, the drums competed in virtuosity. She too ended up falling. Her voice was heavy, the voice of vegetable hawkers in the market as she rolled on the ground, crying: 'O Nofal, O Nofal, O Nofal . . . ' And the musicians replied: 'Aaaah . . . You married in the dark of night and deepened the blackness of your eyes.' She rolled from side to side, groaned, unreeled incomprehensible phrases. The old women came to take her from the centre and carried her, nearly unconscious, into the back courtyard.

That evening, more than ten women fell, one after another, for Nofal, suffused by the musicians' words, offering their voices to the spirits. The music had carried them into the night's heart; their human souls gathered into one composite being of heightened sensibility. They were no longer many; they were no longer themselves; together, merged, they'd become Nofal. It was he whom they sensed vibrating, leaping, feeling, playing. Nofal was their gathering, and, as he took possession of each, he dwelt in their dance, their song. Nofal was presence! And when each sound, each breath, each word had become a rite, Esther began suddenly to tremble. Her arms trembled, her belly trembled, her mouth trembled and a strange smile lit up her face. Her aunt gripped her by the shoulders to hold her back. But she shook her off and took her place at the centre of the group.

The musicians left the wall and approached the novice: 'Each mistress of ceremonies has her own vision. O Nofal, O Nofal, O Nofal . . . Aaaaah . . . The beautiful one has left the dream. She has placed her foot on the earth. Come to me, O beautiful one, come to me. You who resemble the spirits of the night, you with the grace of a gazelle. O Nofal, O Nofal, O Nofal . . . '

Esther had never danced, but that night the music possessed her feet, her hips, her belly. 'No!' cried Aunt Tofa'ha who, at every turn, tried to catch hold of her, to draw her out of the enchanted circle. Impossible. Esther went towards the musicians' wall, to the lyre-player, caught the cigarette dangling from the corner of his lips, carried it to her mouth, and inhaled one long puff. The men groaned. One of them cried, 'O the valiant one! O the lord . . . ' This time, they used an old word. When they used the word 'lord', it meant 'master of the night', 'master of the hidden'. The zars were descending to visit the living.

The women ululated. 'O Nofal, O Nofal, O Nofal . . . ' The dizzying taraboka solos succeeded one after another, calmed each time by the steady voice of the first singer who was endlessly invoking Nofal, calling on his presence, he to whom they offered women's beauty. Esther was still puffing on the cigarette. Then she was seized by a forward and backward movement—she threw her hair back against her neck, then flung it forward until her eyes were hidden, backward and forward, backward and forward. The taraboka player came up and followed her rhythm, accompanying her for a few minutes before quickening the pace. Esther took a step forward, threw herself forward; stepped backward, threw herself back. Her hair followed the movement of the torches' flames.

'Look how she's casting her eyes, the betrothed, look how her eyes are casting flames, the betrothed. I sing, I sing, I sing, until the lovers' dawn. I sing, I sing, I sing, for the pleasure in their eyes.'

The ensemble of musicians took up the chorus: 'Sing, sing, O sing, the love of the betrotheds. O Nofal, O Nofal, O Nofal . . . It's the first time they're seeing each other with their eyes. O the beauty, O the beauty, O the beauty . . . '

Esther made her way to the corner of the room, took hold of a torch and brandished it before her as she danced. She spun, a top now, having become flame—so much so that you couldn't tell the difference between the firelight and the shining glint of her hair.

As she brought the flame close enough to her face to touch it, Tofa'ha grabbed Khadouja's arm: 'You won't let her burn herself, you good-for-nothing!'

Khadouja slipped behind Esther and gently withdrew the fire from her hands. Then she stretched a red scarf above her head, letting it float like a banner, and Esther's movements grew more suggestive. Her pelvis began to gyrate; she panted and let out little cries.

'I sing, I sing, I sing until the lovers' dawn. I sing, I sing, for the pleasure in their eyes.'

Her hips' moved faster and faster, pulsing, following the drums. Her body began to quiver as if she'd been shocked by an electric current. Then, sighing, she sank to the ground. Khadouja covered her with the red cloth.

The men let out heartrending cries, as if weeping: 'Ay, ya, yay; Ay, ya, yay; Ay, ya, yay. We have thrown time away. We have lost eternity. O Nofal, O Nofal, O Nofal . . . O the beauty, the beauty, the beauty . . . '

The musicians stopped short. The silence fluttered for a moment before falling over the gathering like a cloth. At the centre lay Esther, stretched on the ground, struggling to breathe. Despite the burning heat, she seemed to be trembling with cold or fever. The women came towards her, one by one, and draped her body with veils—red ones, yellow ones. Khadouja approached the brazier where the incense was smoking and smudged Esther's body with its fumes.

The kudiya, the mistress, sitting in an old wooden chair like a throne, gestured to Tofa'ha to sit beside her. Then she spoke into her ear: 'All this, you see, stems from an ancient wrong. The sultan of the djinns, in love with a pharaoh's daughter, wanted to marry her. He asked her father for her hand. But the pharaoh refused. So, the djinn took possession of his daughter's body, and refused to leave unless they organized an evening for him, like the one you've just witnessed. The more gifts the pharaoh offered, the more the sultan of the djinns honoured her, but he always delayed the day of the young woman's deliverance.'

Tofa'ha listened, her eyes wide open, not knowing what to make of it but unable to refute it.

'Give me some money!'

'How much?' Tofa'ha asked.

'Whatever you have. It makes no difference.'

Tofa'ha held out the few coins she'd hidden in a fold of her gown. It wasn't much, barely enough to buy a few rounds of bread. The kudiya rose, turned the money seven times around Esther's head and went to offer it to the musicians. The women ululated.

That was the first night.

Through the following weeks, Tofa'ha often accompanied Esther to Bab al-Zuwayla for more dance rituals. Each time, Esther fell sooner, more quickly; each time, her dance was more beautiful. They never spoke of it. They never discussed the dancers' wanton movements, the songs' wild eroticism, the musicians' lustful looks, nor the fiery atmosphere that penetrated them to the core. They shared a secret of which they were ashamed, and yet from which they drew pride. Of course they knew they were transgressing the boundaries of both community and propriety—yet they were convinced they were acting for good.

One evening, they found no musicians in the courtyard. They heard only the repeated sound of a hammer, striking rhythmically. A red-haired man in a long white galabia, a turban on his head, was standing in a corner in front of a fire that a young assistant was fanning with a bellows. He was sweating as he worked on a copper sheet. Esther and Tofa'ha stepped back, frightened.

'Don't be afraid,' the kudiya said. 'Tonight I will set you free.'

And that night, they sealed a copper bracelet around her ankle, similar, no doubt, to those placed in antiquity on the feet of slaves. The kudiya did not explain how a slave's anklet could liberate the zars' captives. She offered no advice. She simply pronounced some Muslim blessings, accompanied by unknown words, most likely from villages in the South. Amid the Arabic, Esther recognized 'In the name of God,' 'the Merciful who grants us mercy,' and another sentence, 'The betrothed has entered the house of the lord,' words that resonated within and were forever inscribed in her memory.

When she returned to the Alley of the Jews, Esther hid her anklet, her *kholkhal*. She developed the habit of wearing long gowns that covered her feet. But such an object could not remain hidden for long. There was the hammam, where the women spent so much time, often entirely naked, examining one another, massaging, combing, epilating.

'My oh my,' breathed Adina, the first to notice. 'Arab jewellery. Excuse me, my dear, but I find it vulgar. If your husband saw it—'

Esther shrugged scornfully. Motty had immediately sensed the kholkhal. He'd touched it with his fingers but made no comment nor asked any questions. Most likely he'd understood its necessity, for he'd whispered in her ear, 'When our son is born, I'll give you seven gold bracelets.' And that night was like the first. He caressed her at length, whispering words that spoke to her belly. 'My beauty, my eyes, light of my days, sweetness of my nights.' And when she let herself slip into his hands, verses from Bab al-Zuwayla danced through Esther's soul. 'Sing, sing, sing, until the lovers' dawn . . . ' No, she thought, no! She could never tell him.

Aunt Maleka put on a serious look to reproach her. She knew about such anklets; it wasn't just a piece of jewellery—she was well aware of it. She wanted to say something, but not in front of the others; it was too serious. Did she know what Jews called what she'd done in that pile of garbage Bab al- Zuwayla? Amid that filth, those daughters of nothing. No! She didn't know, because she was ignorant. And, she added pompously, 'As our sages say, it's through ignorance that evil enters a family.' Oh well, she'd teach her, this illiterate. What she'd done had a name. 'It's called "serving strange gods". It's haram, a sin. You don't understand. It's serious, very serious. I'll have to present the matter to Rav Mourad. Perhaps he knows how you can be cleansed after such disgrace.'

Esther lowered her eyes—because you need to respect your aunt, your mother's sister—but didn't feel guilty. As for Mourad, she had nothing against him. Quite the opposite, she was grateful to him, he who'd been able to stand up for her during her adolescent crises, keeping her family from rejecting her and treating her as if she were mad. But, after all, Rav Mourad was not a woman. When God wants to send a soul to the earth, he addresses not rabbis but women's wombs. So, there was no point in his saying 'you should do this, you shouldn't do that.' To lead a horse, you first have to mount it. This sentence that came to her—she didn't know from where—seemed to make sense. So that's how she answered her aunt.

'To lead a horse, you first have to mount it.'

Who knows what Aunt Maleka thought; she probably perceived some sexual allusion in the sentence for she responded by slapping Esther.

'Daughter of a whore!' she shouted. 'These things don't exist in our family.'

The dispute grew poisonous. Other women joined in, all in support of the aunt, except for old Helwa.

'You have a voice, that's true,' said the grandmother, 'and your tongues move in your mouths. But does any reason guide them? Look at me! Has anyone ever accused me of serving strange gods?'

The others grew silent, taken aback. Helwa lifted her gown and shook her left foot. A kholkhal surrounded her ankle, but not made of raw copper like Esther's. It was also copper, but worked with gold designs, burnished by time.

'Look! I too have taken part in ceremonies of presence.'

'You, O my grandmother!' exclaimed Esther. You have also danced to the drums?'

'I went there for a long time, for years.'

'But why?'

'For no reason!' the old woman lied. 'You feel better after you've danced, that's all. But I never went back since Tofa'ha's birth. You see, it was a long time ago.'

And Helwa traced a dance step to show that her body still remembered.

'Sing, sing, sing . . . ' she chanted.

Esther smiled as she recognized the melody that had been running through her head for weeks.

Despite this theatrical display, Maleka didn't let up. She dragged her niece to the rabbi. The old woman went with them.

'It's certain!' Mourad said. 'It's certain. The dance to the drums, the fires, and colours, oh yes! It's definitely "serving strange gods". It's the worst of all. Because, in Hebrew, we call this impious act *avoda zara*. And do you know what the ceremony Esther participated in is called?'

'The zar!' the three women answered in unison.

'The zar! May God protect us. The zar, exactly! Zar, zara. You see, when our sages defined strange gods, they used the word *zara* because they were thinking of the zar. Because for them, of all the strange gods, the zar was the strangest.'

The three women, impressed by rabbi's lucid reasoning, nodded with an air of understanding. But after a while, they felt as if they'd been tricked. Helwa was the first to react.

'And tell me, my son,' she asked, eying him, 'if we serve a strange god, well—what's supposed to happen to us?'

'Um,' Mourad hesitated, 'if you believe what's written in the Torah, the person who commits such a monstrosity will be withdrawn from the bosom of her people.'

'Oh, my child! Withdrawn from the bosom of her people! What does that mean, withdrawn?'

'It means she will go away and not return. Even die, perhaps.'

'Ah yes,' sneered the old woman before getting angry. 'May your mother withdraw you from the bosom of your people, you son of a dog!'

'O Mother!' Maleka complained. 'We can't talk like that to the rabbi.'

'And may his mother go to join him in Gehenna where they'll both burn for a thousand years. We can't? Why can't we? Does he have an extra leg? Do rose petals come out of his arse? Did you see them? I'm telling you, this one has a knife up his arse.'

Mourad was young and didn't yet know the fervour with which the hara's inhabitants could speak. But he understood the urgent need for some diplomacy.

'Wait!' he exclaimed. 'Wait!'

'He has a knife up his arse, I'm telling you,' the old woman insisted. 'That's why he can neither stand up nor sit down.'

'But let me speak!'

'Yes, let him speak, O Grandmother!' Esther put in.

'There are some exceptions, of course,' the rabbi began, twisting himself into knots.

'Exceptions, what do you mean?'

'I mean, exceptions. When it comes to healing yourself, for example.'

'Aha!' sang out the grandmother.

'Yes. When someone is sick and has concluded that known cures do no good, that person may resort to strange gods. But only to be healed, right? Do you understand?'

'And not to go and act like'—Maleka couldn't find the word—'the zar's whore.'

'Shut up, you monkey!' her mother said, shocked.

'Didn't you say, "to be healed"?' Esther asked.

She reminded him then that she had consulted him several times for an amulet or even a prayer to lift the sorrow afflicting her belly. And he had replied—did he recall?—that God alone could grant a child, certainly not human knowledge. Her husband himself, the poor man, despite his blindness, had abased himself in front of him, had kissed his feet—it's a manner of speaking, of course—and this stone-hearted man, 'as if he'd been born on the island of Gezira or the island of Rhoda, my oh my,' had never lifted a finger. No! What did he say? Do you know what he said to poor Motty? He told him to move! Move, he said, as if scratching could cure an itch.

Old Helwa suddenly became more conciliatory.

'And so,' she suggested, 'if you were saying that to be healed of an illness whose only treatment is Arab women's treatment . . . If you were saying that's why my little one went to Bab al-Zuwayla, hmm? . . . You would agree to present the matter like that to silence the words swirling through the hara?'

The rabbi scratched his beard for a long time.

'I'll say it's women's business, and that women know how to handle women's business That's what I'll say.'

The grandmother was not satisfied with the rabbi's response, too ambiguous, leaving room for doubt about the nature of the treatment. Her daughter also wasn't satisfied: she had not obtained a clear condemnation of her niece's conduct. As for Esther, she was thinking: 'What difference does it make, what people say, if a son is born to Motty?'

In the end, Helwa pulled the other two along with her. 'Come. We're going home. This one must be a mongrel. Tell me, what do mules know about drinking ginger syrup?'

They burst out laughing and turned their backs to him, reconciled in an instant at Mourad's expense.

The rabbi's words did something, and time did the rest. Soon no one paid any more attention to the kholkhal encircling Esther's ankle. Three months later, her belly grew round.

'Five on you!' the women said, invoking the five fingers of the hand of Fatima used to ward off the evil eye. 'I don't want any harm to come to you, my dear, you're blooming.'

'It's the breath of spring!' Esther replied.

It was the month of March, and in this year of 1925, the neighbourhood was abuzz with a thousand rumours. Marshal Allenby, victor at Megiddo, had just renounced his role as British High Commissioner, meaning to set an example. He hoped, through this symbolic act, to demonstrate his faith in the nation's independence. For the first time since the pharaohs of Antiquity, Egypt was about to become Egyptian.

At the same instant—was it by chance?—a giant was emerging from the sands. 'It seems we're about to unearth the father of terror.' That's what Arabs, Copts and Jews in Egypt called the Great Sphinx of Giza, who, until now, had displayed only his giant head, swimming in the dunes. Everyone added their own commentary or jokes—you couldn't tell one from the other. 'Under the earth, extending this head, is an enormous statue, a hundred metres high. It could be the body of the Golem, turned to stone when Moses withdrew the name of God he had first slipped under his tongue.' Stories by the dozen featured Goha, the simple-minded victor over the powerful, the divine Goha: 'The Sphinx, watching Egypt for five thousand years, knows everything better than the angel of death. Do you know why Goha sits in front of him day and night? No? He's waiting for him to tell him where his donkey went.'

The year the Sphinx emerged from the sand was also the year the communists tried to get a foothold in the Alley of the Jews. For several weeks, Joseph Rosenthal, founder of the party, set himself up on the edge of the Mouski, in the cafe next to the Nile Hotel. He accosted the men of the hara with a German accent you could cut with a knife: 'Proletarians, unite!' He handed out tracts written in Arabic which he himself couldn't read. And he used the French word for 'proletarian'.

'What does it mean, *brolétaires*, what does it mean?' asked Uncle Doudou.

'You know,' Elie replied, 'Rosenthal is a *shlecht*.'

'A shlecht. What does that mean?'

'A shlecht is a Russian or a German who doesn't like semolina cake with honey.'

'Can anyone not like *basboussa*?'

'Huh? What are you talking about?'

'It's true! Elie explained. 'Aunt Oro offered him a piece. He tasted it and then spat it onto the ground saying, "*Shlecht! Shlecht!*" Ever since, we call people like him "shlecht".'

Since Doudou didn't understand, he added, 'Yes! They have transparent eyes, they wear suits in which they hold themselves erect like puppets and they don't know how to pronounce the *aïn*.'

'Oh, you mean a *wouz-wouz*? And *brolétaires*, well, what is this *brolétaires*?'

'*Prolétaire*, hmm. It's to tell us we're poor—'

'We're poor? This plug-nose, this busy-body, may God curse his mother and his mother's mother,' Doudou cut in, then added, 'For ten generations!'

'Don't say anything bad, the poor man! Do you know what happened to him?'

'What happened to him, where?'

'Last year, they threw him in prison with communists from Alexandria. Don't nod, you don't know what communists are.'

'What? I don't know what communists are? I know! They are *wouz-wouz*, winter Jews, who want to become Christian.'

'Idiot! You're an idiot! It's a po–li–tic–al movement. Do you know politics?'

'Bolitik or boliturk, all that, it's like a sandstorm. The grains always end up falling back to earth.'

'Oh well, sandstorm or sand grain, they expelled him to Romania. And do you know what? The Romanians put him in a boat and returned him to Alexandria. Now, something that goes back and forth is called a yoyo. Yoyo Rosenthal!'

And the two of them burst out laughing. But that year it wasn't only communists who took an interest in the simple Jews of the neighbourhood. A man whose family had left the Alley of the Jews several generations earlier had become a minister of Fouad I, the new king of Egypt. Ennobled, he bore the title of *bey*, but used his French name, with a particle, like aristocrats. Moses de Cattaoui Pasha, banker and court Jew, dedicated a large part of his fortune to the social aid of the hara's poor.

That morning, the Hispano Double Phaeton, preceded by two pages in gold-brocaded livery clearing a path for it, had stopped at the entrance to the Mouski. Before ceremoniously opening the door of the automobile, the chauffeur had waited for the bey's retinue, arriving on foot and out of breath. The pasha, dressed in an immaculate galabia, his shoulders draped with a velvet cape and his head wrapped in a white turban, marched into the hara, majestic as a pope. He'd decided to select a dozen of the brightest boys, to offer them a scholarship to his school in Sakakini, where they taught in French, according to rules formulated by the Alliance Israelite Universelle. He hadn't reached the footbridge crossing the first street before a dense crowd surrounded him, seeking to touch the hem of his cape. Behind him, two secretaries, also in livery, distributed small coins one by one. It must not have been eight in the morning when he reached Uncle Elie's grocery. And it was exactly then that Esther and Motty left the house, she holding him by the arm, he feeling with his foot to avoid the stones and potholes. He bumped into the bey—felt the clothing of the rich man, stroked the velvet of the cape, lingered over the silk of the galabia. His hand reached the perfectly trimmed white beard, and for a moment he felt the face. A leaden silence fell onto the crowd. How would the bey react? With anger? Scorn?

'This man,' Motty said, 'is deeply worried about his daughter. He doesn't know why, for he is upright and fears the Lord. Don't we say, "The man loved by God, God also makes him loved by men"? He should know that this is a trial, he must not think of himself as a victim of injustice. A little patience. Just two more years and the tree he has nurtured in his garden will bear the most beautiful fruit.'

Motty withdrew his hands from the man's face and sighed. The others held their breath. The bey smiled, and, understanding that a blind man was before him, turned towards Esther.

'Is this your husband?' he asked.

'He is my brother, my master and my husband,' Esther replied.

'Bring him to me tomorrow morning, to the Cattaoui home, in Zamalek. I want to ask him some more questions.'

The next day Esther and Motty returned from the posh neighbourhood around noon. When the automobile arrived by way of Khoronfesh, threading its way with loud honks through the narrowest alleys, children emerged from the Goutte de Lait, 'The Drop of Milk', an institution where they could obtain a little bread for free, and began to shout, 'Motty Zohar is in the car, and the car moves forward!' Of course it wasn't the Hispano, only the small one, a six-cylinder Oakland, blue and gleaming. But in Haret al-Yahud they'd never seen such a thing—a Jew from the alley sitting like a pasha in the rear of an automobile! Esther got out first, helped by the liveried chauffeur. She'd put on her red gown, the one from the zar rituals. For once, she'd arranged her hair in a chignon and made up her eyes. She'd even borrowed shoes from Aunt Tofa'ha, which she rushed to remove as soon as her feet touched the ground of Haret al-Yahud. The two of them advanced arm in arm, with an Olympian gait, accompanied by dozens of children celebrating them.

'Look!' said Aunt Maleka. 'How she holds her nose in the air.'

'My dear, I've always thought so,' replied Aunt Oro. 'The djinns have jumbled her brain. She thinks she's Queen Nazli.'

'Oh! The *queen*, queen of the flies, more likely! What a daughter of a dog!'

'One day, someone will have to take her down a peg or two,' Adina added.

And the three sisters, Maleka, Adina and Tofa'ha, along with their cousin Oro, watched the couple pass, speechless. If at that moment they'd known that Moses de Cattaoui Pasha, the bey, impressed by the precision of Motty's divination, had bestowed upon the couple a gift of ten pounds—a thousand piastres, ten thousand millièmes—one of them might have had a heart attack, or thrown herself into the Nile, or maybe into a fire. Adina was content simply to spit on the ground.

A week later, Esther woke up in the middle of the night, feeling a slimy fluid between her thighs. She lit a candle and screamed—she was bleeding. The child she'd had so much trouble conceiving, that child was about to leave before even seeing his father. She began to cry. Motty woke up with a start.

'What's wrong, O light in my darkness?' he asked, his voice sleepy.

'I'm afraid, O my soul. Blood, the Torah says, contains the soul. If it escapes, the breath of life will return to God.'

Motty deliberated for a long time before each word he then uttered: 'We say, "God has given, God has taken away." Isn't that what we say? But no one says we can't try to make Him change his mind.'

'I understand!' Esther replied. 'Do you think I can go there in the middle of the night?'

'Stay.' Motty ordered. 'Don't move, don't make the slightest movement. At the first light of day, you'll go.'

When she heard Mahmoud the ragman stirring, she asked him to take her there. For five piastres, he agreed to carry her in his cart. And off they went, he pulling the handles of his cart, she repeating over and over the only phrase she had retained from the prayers, 'Hear O Israel, God is our god, God is Oneness.'

At the entrance to Bab al-Zuwayla, a ray of sunshine was lighting up the top of the minaret. She found Khadouja the witch lying on her rags, her idiot son asleep with his head on his mother's belly.

Esther shook her awake: 'Get up! Sometimes the children of Adam die at daybreak.'

'May I be cursed!' the other replied. 'What's happening?'

'You must take me right away to the kudiya.'

And so Khadouja led Mahmoud and his cart through the alleys of Bab al-Zuwayla. Esther studied the sky. The sun was shining as it had the day before; it was shining as it always shines in Egypt, powerful and so close by. The city was waking up, full of sound and strength. The world was indifferent to her suffering. Neither earth nor heaven makes a sign when trouble assails us, Esther thought. Whoever does not go out in search of signs will die in the street, alone, like a dog.

The kudiya laid her on a sofa and prepared some tea.

'Jealousy, O you the beloved, the betrothed. It's jealousy!' And she added, 'I'll take care of it.'

'Jealousy?'

'Yes! Jealousy has come in by the main door, because you don't know how to hide your joy. Did someone look at you? An old woman—think! She was wearing a pendant. Didn't you notice that her jewel stank? It stank of rot. Do you remember? Well, I'll tell you: her pendant was stuffed with a dead man's blood, killed accidently or assassinated or even a suicide. She must have got the blood from a cemetery, maybe the morgue. She soaked a handkerchief or an old rag in it, and enclosed it in her pendant. She leant over you. You inhaled death. That's the source of your misfortune!'

'And so?'

'We'll turn fate back against the whore, the daughter of nothing. She'll learn what it means to be a daughter of Nofal! First we'll clean you. You'll give me all your clothes, and we'll burn them. You'll give me your hair, and we'll bury it. You'll give me your nails, and we'll place them at the feet of a saint. And when you go home, you'll ask your husband for a new gown. We'll smudge it with myrrh, and I'll make a belt for you, a talisman. And your baby will be so happy within you that even after the ninth month he won't want to come out towards the light.'

'But here? Now?' Esther asked, worried, 'What will you do?'

'Let you sleep, O betrothed one!'

The treatment lasted a long time, almost a month, during which Esther never set foot in Haret al-Yahud. Each day, Gougou, a neighbourhood urchin, was sent by Motty to get her news. Each day, he returned, laden with requests. Three chickens were needed, ten metres of spun cotton, one pound to buy a sheep, dozens of candles. And of course Motty paid—so much that by the end of a month the sum they'd received from the bey had melted like snow in sunlight. Elie told him, 'Your gift, your ability to read the future, God didn't sell it to you, did He? He gave it to you. Do you think, now that it's in your possession, you can sell it?' And he added, nodding, 'God is a good businessman. He always takes back more than he gives. That's why you must spend everything and more in order to guarantee the existence of your child.' Esther was being cared for by the kudiya, but she was learning as well—the arts of placing coloured powders on a tray; of drawing cards and reading fate; of noting the series of numbers on throws of the dice and associating them with tales of the djinns related by the sheikha.

One day, a woman brought in a horned viper wriggling in a sack.

'Here's your talisman!' said the kudiya, brandishing the sack. 'Soon you'll be able to return to your husband.' She grabbed the viper by the tail and drew it out. Screaming, the women fled, but the old woman held it firmly, laughing. Then, with a practiced hand, she grasped its jaw between two fingers and made it bite into a thick piece of leather. Then she cleanly broke off the two venomous fangs.

'These are for that old woman who cast a spell on you!' she said.

It wasn't hard to guess that she was planning to use them to make one of those terrible objects that act from a distance. She carefully placed the fangs in an old iron box. Then she smashed the viper's skull against a rock. She grilled pieces of its flesh on skewers, and this was the first meat Esther was allowed to eat since her treatment began. When Esther grimaced at the idea, the kudiya said, 'Go on! Eat! It's certainly not permitted flesh but it's a remedy. What's more,' she added, winking, 'it's delicious!'

Out of the snake's skin, the kudiya made a belt with which she encircled Esther's waist. 'You see?' she said, fastening it, 'I've anticipated several sizes. You can make it wider as your belly expands. The snake will guard your child better than he would his own hole if he were alive. This, too, you must keep. Do you know what we call the snake? The master of the hole!—*Abu l'khorn*. We know how to sing his praises here, we also know how to honour and serve him.'

Esther left Bab al-Zuwayla one Friday morning, at the hour of the Muslims' second call to prayer. She was dressed in an immaculate, long white gown. Her hair, which had been shorn, was growing back as a light golden fluff. Her neck long and slim, her head high, she had the bearing of a princess. She moved confidently, her two hands resting on her small round belly. A gleam in her eyes drew the gaze of women who saw in it the look of the priestesses of a forgotten time—an atavistic memory perhaps. The men turned their heads away, disturbed, most likely, by the immodesty of a happy pregnancy. She crossed a section of the city on foot, without anyone permitting themselves a whistle, a comment, an insult. She entered Haret al-Yahud by Al-Moez Street, the least poor section. In Darb Mahmoud, she penetrated the narrow 'passage of the Jewish baths' and arrived in front of Rav Moshe, the synagogue said to have sheltered the relics of Moses Maimonides before he'd been taken away to be buried over there, beside his ancestors, on the banks of Lake Tiberius. Something impelled her to enter, as if she had to return to the source. Was it because she'd gone too far in her exploration of strange gods, the zars?

Scattered in twos throughout the main room, children were reciting their Talmud. Rav Pardo was fiercely debating a point of doctrine with the faithful. It was cool. The place breathed calm. Without asking permission, she descended to the crypt, placed her hands on the empty tomb from which the presence of the blessed philosopher still radiated more than seven hundred years after his death, closed her eyes, and promised in a whisper: 'Rav Moshe, if God allows me to present a son to Mordechai Zohar, my beloved, my husband, I will give him the name of Maimon, and his life will be devoted to study and his soul to good.'

Then she began to yawn, once, twice. Her eyes were closing, and a strange torpor seemed to be falling over her. She placed her hands on her belly and felt a warmth rising into her chest, her throat. She sat on a stone, turned onto her right side and fell asleep. And an image coursed through her like lightning, causing her to slip onto the hexagonal tiles of the synagogue's courtyard. She was startled but soon sank back into her dream. Then a huge silhouette rose before her—Rav Moshe himself: Maimonides, as she had seen him in pictures, both stern and kind, in a bright kaftan, his head in a turban, his beard trimmed, his black eyes piercing.

'Oh! Are you here?' she marvelled.

He showed her his hands, and his fingers seemed to be shooting out bolts of lightning.

'The fire,' he said, 'I carry it here, at the tips of my fingers.

And he rearranged his fingers, two by two, separating the pair made by the index finger and the central finger from the pair made by the ring finger and the pinky; the two thumbs came together naturally. His fingers continued to crackle. Then he stuck out his tongue, long and forked like the viper's.

'And the snake,' the apparition added, 'I carry it in my mouth.'

With his two hands joined in that strange position, he spread open his garment, exposed his stomach and indicated his navel. She turned her head away, telling herself she should not uncover a father's nakedness. But he insisted: 'And the dance, look! The dance—I carry it in my stomach.'

When she consented to raise her eyes, the garment was back in place and Maimonides was holding in his hands a blooming lotus flower at the end of a still-moist, long stem.

'You will extract the juice of this plant and mix it with oil. It's for your belly.'

And suddenly the apparition became fixed, an engraving again.

'Wait! Don't go! I wanted to ask you a question.'

Maimonides remained immobile, as if the breath of life mysteriously manifest through the power of Esther's dream had evaporated. But she insisted: 'Tell me, O my rabbi, you who, when you were alive, were the doctor of kings and princes, why do you care about us, worms crawling through the wretchedness of Haret al-Yahud?'

The image of Maimonides began to stir, then disappeared. In her dream, Esther saw the bare stone of the tomb and the empty crypt. She woke up and what appeared before her was identical—the same crypt, the same tomb. She wanted to ask another question, she wanted to ask if Maimonides was a dream or if he'd come to life before her eyes. But she heard footsteps on the stairs. So she arranged her gown. It was Rav Pardo, accompanying an aged woman in tears. Perhaps, Esther thought, she was coming to ask Rav Moshe to intercede, to heal someone who was sick.

'But I know you,' he said, 'you're Shmuel Zohar's daughter, may God bless his memory. How your eyes are shining! Do you want to tell me what Rav Moshe told you?'

'O my father,' Esther breathed, 'May God protect me from misfortune!'

And she ran up the stairs without looking back.

Motty was stretched out on the bed, absorbed in one of his meditations, but he recognized Esther's step the moment she entered the alley. He rose, felt around for his cane and went towards the door which was, as always, wide open. 'O my soul!' he called, 'Is it you whose footsteps I hear or only the beating of my heart calling you?'

'Shush, Motty, shush. Do you also want to climb the minaret to announce my return?' And she whispered: 'Yes, it's me, O my eyes. But I am only myself because I see you.'

Motty found Esther again and could not stop caressing her with his hands. Esther found Motty again and spent the day contemplating him in silence.

'What are you doing?' he asked.

'I'm filling my eyes with your presence,' she replied, 'like Rivka on her way to the spring, her jar on her shoulder.'

Esther asked Khadouja to bring her some fresh lotus blooms. Following the instructions received in the dream, they obtained a yellowish substance from the exudation of the flowers which they then mixed with olive oil. Esther massaged her stomach with this unguent whenever she felt any pain. And, day by day, her belly grew; it was round; it was beautiful; and she carried it proudly before her. But when the aunts asked her, 'Does he move at night? He kicks, doesn't he?' she didn't answer, because the child made no signs, as if he'd decided to pass by unperceived.

Motty was worried. 'Why does our child not move like other children?' But Esther reassured him. 'I know him. He wants to be forgotten, out of fear that people might harm him again.'

The pregnancy continued like this until the seventh month. Esther sometimes said, 'When I touch this round hard belly, I have the feeling I'm carrying an egg—the egg of a gigantic bird like the one Sinbad the Sailor met.' By the eighth month, the child finally began to kick his feet, to beat his fists. Day and night he wriggled in her belly. Nothing calmed him other than Motty's hands and his voice singing whole passages from the Song of Songs: 'There thy mother brought thee forth; there she brought thee forth that bare thee. Set me as a seal upon thine heart, as a seal upon thine arm: for love is strong as death.'

The child was born in Haret al-Yahud on 15 Cheshvan 5686; recorded in the civil state of Cairo on the same day, the 7th of Rabi al-Tani in the year 1344; it was the first day, a Sunday, 25 October 1925. He arrived early in the morning after a day and a night of labour, on the mezzanine of Uncle Elie's grocery store.

Fate would have it that, on the same day, the archaeologist Howard Carter finally opened Tutankhamen's tomb. The funerary chamber had been discovered three years earlier, in 1922; the wall of this room, pierced in February 1923, revealed four nested sarcophagi. The cover of the first sarcophagus, made of quartzite, was lifted in 1924, but they had to wait until October 1925, the final settlement of the conflict between British archaeologists and the Egyptian administration, for the golden face of the young king to be unveiled before the whole world's gaze.

Mouffetard Street

That's what I was born—in the land of the pharaohs, to a blind father and a mother possessed by demons. What could I do, caught between these two who loved each other with an infinite passion?

I'm made of demonic music, viper meat and lotus essence. For protection, I received fragments from the Song of Songs, and a name risen from a tomb. My birth earned my mother a new gown and seven gold bracelets. I was their first; I would remain their last. No one knew from where I came; no one could say to where I would go . . .

I began this tale at the beginning, with my mother's pregnancy. But I wonder—was that truly the beginning? If you're speaking of a child to be born, perhaps. But a child is only one manifestation of a being. The being most likely appeared earlier, before my parents knew each other, or perhaps even before their birth, who knows?

Egyptian brothers, I'm thinking of the pyramids. They say that we, the Jews, built them for you. As they say in Egyptian folktales, 'this was, or this wasn't . . . ' They aren't idols but rays of sunlight, turned to stone. Don't destroy them. I doubt that new ones could be built.

Egypt is called the mother of the worlds, *oum al-dounia*. It's also mine! I mean, Egypt is my mother, the womb of all my thoughts. I'm from there. We, the Jews of Egypt, are from there, since all time. We were there with the pharaohs. In a distant past, Egypt was invaded by Persians, and we were there; by Babylonians, by Greeks, by Romans, by Arabs, and we were still there. We Jews are like the young water buffalos, kneaded from the Nile's mud, the same dark colour, natives.

We were multiple, we were tribes. It's true that some of us also came from elsewhere, arriving during the third, eleventh, fifteenth or nineteenth centuries. We were Sephardic—Spaniards expelled by the Inquisition; Ashkenazi—Russians and Germans fleeing European pogroms; Mizrahi—Persians, Uzbeks, or Tajiks attracted by Ottoman promises. It's true we were strangers by nature, like the Roma, always others among others. But Egypt is our substance, the substance from which we're made; the Nile is the artery that irrigates our bodies. Today, we are no longer there. Egyptian brothers, dwellers in a land of relics, what you're left with are pyramids and a few empty synagogues. Take care of them! How can you live without us?

My name is Zohar, both my first and last names—I'm called Zohar Zohar. If you think about it, the world is made up only of letters—all the letters—isn't that right? I've studied, assembled and reassembled the letters of my name, seeking there the key to my fate. I was born at the end of October 1925. It's wasn't exactly yesterday—the day before yesterday, if you like. I grew up in Haret al-Yahud, the 'Alley of the Jews', the ghetto of old Cairo, a flower in manure, growing wild in the muck under Egypt's sun. I spent my childhood on the street.

The delivery was difficult, very difficult. I was the first; I opened up her belly from the inside. They immediately realized I was a problem—I was arriving feet first, the umbilical cord around my neck. Khadouja, wise Sett Oualida, 'Lady Momma', whom they'd gone to fetch from Bab al-Zuwayla to help my mother, said, 'It's serious! This one's coming against his mother.'

'What are you saying, you peasant?' protested Aunt Maleka. 'How can a newborn be against his mother?'

'He's coming against his mother,' repeated Sett Oualida. 'He's coming to make her suffer, to do her harm. He might even kill her.'

'May the fate that seeps from your lips fall elsewhere!' my aunt cursed, 'Go to the devil, daughter of the streets! Look how fat he is. You'll see, he'll be as strong as a lion.'

My mother, poor thing, was suffering so much her cries could be heard as far as the Karaite neighbourhood, in the al-Nahasin souk, the coppersmiths' market, and in Khoronfesh. Sett Oualida coated her belly with Rav Moshe's lotus oil and it calmed her a little. Then the contractions began again, and her terrible screams tore at my father Motty's soul. Ten men who knew how to pray were summoned and asked to sing psalms, to deflect the severity of God who wanted to call back the child and his mother with him. My mother screamed. The men prayed. And my father wept. Finally, after twenty-four hours of labour, my father Motty, who was standing outside in the dust of the street, came in. He placed his hands on my mother's belly and decided to chant the passage from the Song of Songs: 'There thy mother brought thee forth: there she brought thee forth that bare thee. Set me as a seal upon thine heart, as a seal upon thine arm: for love is as strong as death.'

The men repeated after him, changing only one word: 'Love is stronger than death.' And, according to what I've been told, at that very moment I turned over and emerged all at once, head first. Aunt Maleka didn't wait for me to be washed—she tied a red string around my neck, with a blue-eye pendant. And spitting on the ground three times, she said, 'Leave this place, son of night! This child belongs to us.'

Sett Oualida, priestess of the zars, burst out laughing. 'Do you really think a glass eye makes a difference to the lords? Go, bring a sheep and offer them its blood before night follows day.'

Everyone stopped talking, men as well as women, all gathered for a change in the mezzanine of Uncle Elie's shop. Now a single question hovered over them: Who should be thanked for protecting mother and child? The god of the Jews, mollified by the prayers of the ten men assembled around my blind father Motty? Or the lords, owners of the earth, Sett Oualida's afrits, who'd granted me permission to leave their world? They agreed to offer thanks to both. At dawn, a lamb was sacrificed in accordance with the lords' rite; all night long, the men read psalms and prayed in the Rav Moshe synagogue.

Despite everything, my problems weren't over. I had to be fed now, and my mother did not have a drop of milk. Her breasts were as dry as a balsam branch.

'Wait!' said my grandmother Helwa, 'tomorrow, her breasts will swell like a wineskin. Let her rest.'

But the following day, she still had none, nor the next. They tried soaking a cloth in cow's milk and giving it to me to suck, but I spit it up. Twenty-four hours after my birth, I hadn't yet swallowed a thing. If I was to survive, they would have to find a wet-nurse, a woman breast-feeding her child. And fast!

Ma'ruf Street

On the second day, as soon as the sun was up, Aunt Tofa'ha left with Khadouja the witch, whom they called Sett Oualida, and Naji, her simple-minded son (poor thing!), for a long trek to Ma'ruf Street. It would take them a good three hours to reach those infamous alleys hidden at the heart of the posh neighbourhoods, those dark dives where no woman ventured alone. A north wind had been blowing since the night before. They walked briskly to keep warm in the morning chill. They arrived through Ismailia Square, where they couldn't get their fill of the beautiful buildings, the luxurious cafes and the men in European suits, their heads adorned with tarbouches, the red felt fez. 'Look at that one, swinging his arms like a big-shot. You'd think his mother was holding him by his rompers and teaching him to walk.'

When they reached Champollion Street, the scene changed. First they recognized the smells, that blend of spices and dung, and frying fumes mixed with sewer stench. It smelt of Egypt again, the true Egypt, the one they knew, with its strong scent smothered in sand. Then the sounds—the cries of vegetable vendors, the creaks of cart-wheels, the horseshoes' clatter on round cobblestones, the camels' passage beneath the donkeys' scornful gaze. Some buildings had crumbled; within, amid the ruins, crude walls of mud bricks had been raised, with sheet metal or salvaged wood on top to make a roof. They knew they weren't far now. They hailed a poor woman accompanied by two children.

'Do you know Hassan al-Shebab's inn?' Khadouja asked.

'The inn? Why are you calling it an inn?'

'Isn't it an inn?'

'I dare you to sleep there, my daughter.'

'All I need is to meet a woman. Her name is Oum Jinane. Do you know her?'

She didn't. She only knew that men gathered at Hassan's place. Of course, they spent the better part of the night there, but she didn't think it was to sleep.

'The only women you meet in places like that are dancers and whores. The woman you're looking for, your Oum Jinane—is she a dancer?'

'Whether she dances, sings or climbs palm trees and picks dates, all I want is to talk to her,' Khadouja replied, 'and it's urgent!'

The woman pointed out a passage between two buildings. All they had to do was to follow it. It would snake around, grow narrower, double back—until a little square with a fountain. There, they would see a door on the right, like the entrance to a house. They would go through it, and, on the other side, they would find Ma'ruf Street, which they would take to the left. They'd walk a little further. 'Hassan's' was the name of the hashish den.

You could barely make out a house—a ruin, rather, open to the four winds, yet with a door, closed. Khadouja pushed it open. No one. They entered a long hall pierced by windows that opened onto shadows. They had to climb over pottery shards, shapeless basins, a carriage wheel, scraps of wood. Free-roaming chickens scattered as they passed. They reached a large room with a floor of beaten earth. Here, the blinds were closed. A babble of murmurs reached them, a buzz. They paused for a moment, letting their eyes adjust to the half-light. Khadouja recognized the acrid, intoxicating smell. Little by little, figures emerged—men sitting silently in groups of three or four, each sucking on the bamboo of his *goza*, the traditional water pipe with a coconut-shell bowl. Two young boys scurried about in a silent ballet, bringing smokers their doses of honeyed tobacco, adjusting the stems, stingily depositing blue specks of hashish with their fingertips. The women moved forward with a few timid steps. Out of nowhere, a woman arose to bar their way. Heavily made up, her skin shining, enveloped in a great transparent veil that highlighted her generous figure, she was swaying her hips. Under the veil, she wore billowing trousers with a golden butterfly over her privates. Her breasts were sheathed in two tortoiseshell cones from which hung garlands of pearls, so well placed that with each move she made the trinkets jiggled, tinkling endlessly. You could tell that when she danced, she knew how to make them spin to create spellbinding wheels of desire. And above all her voice, that high-pitched voice made to hail men, to make their hair stand on end, to bring their birds to attention.

'Oooooh! Where have you come from, you nightbirds? No one comes here to find their father or brother. These men have only one family, the family of blue smoke.'

She must have thought the two women were seeking a strayed husband.

'We haven't come to cause trouble, my sister, we left home with peace in our hearts,' Khadouja replied, extending her hands towards the woman and then bringing them back to her lips in a gesture of submission.

'May peace be with you!' the other said.

'And may our Father preserve you in life,' Tofa'ha added.

The woman took a metal goblet and filled it with water from a large earthen amphora resting on an iron tripod. Khadouja wet her lips.

'May God bless your hands!'

She extended the cup to Tofa'ha, who drank in turn.

'Even a camel is soothed when you offer it water.'

She offered the goblet to poor, backward Naji. Unable to tear his eyes away from the pearl garlands hanging from her nipples, it took him a while to understand. The women began to speak. The dancer was the Cairo wife of Maalem Hassan al-Shebab. She specified 'Cairo wife', because he had another in Kafr al-Amar, their village near Damanhour in Lower Egypt, in the Delta. During the day, she was in charge of serving, and supervising the waiters: 'You know, it's so easy to hide a bit of kif under your fingernail.' In the evening, she danced to rock men's dreams.

'And at night?' asked Khadouja with a wink.

The other clapped her hands and rolled her hips. 'O my sister! Our master's like a big monkey. When the Maalem wakes, his wives bow and turn their backs to him. When the Maalem tires, his wives massage him with perfumed oil. But when the Maalem sleeps, well, then, his wives can earn a bit of money.'

When Khadouja snickered, she added: 'Never neglect nights of pleasure! As they say, they will never return.'

They were well met, these two, thought Tofa'ha, her eyes lowered as she pretended not to understand their racy allusions. The conversation turned to the people in the house. At least five waiters prepared the charcoal and tobacco refills for the gozas. They earned a great deal of money, largely in tips and in a side trade she tried to combat. The men, the consumers, were for the most part regulars. Some procured their kif across the way, at Sheik Ahmed's. Here at Hassan's it was more expensive but of better quality. Many were *khawagates*, gentlemen from the posh neighbourhoods—Ismailia, the Risotto or Mehmet Ali clubs, Suleiman Pasha Square, even Gezira. Some were responsible men, heads of households, bank employees, but some were artists, journalists, students. As for the real ones, the ones she called *hashashins*—the ones so suffused that their lungs had turned blue—they lived here, sleeping at night on straw mats, performing odd jobs by day to pay for their rations.

She touched one with her foot. 'They're rags, lying on the ground like floor cloths. You can wipe your feet on their faces, they won't open an eye.'

There were also musicians, but they never came before night.

'And the women?' Tofa'ha asked.

When night fell, the streetwalkers posted themselves at the door or windows. They had to seize the fleeting moment after the second or third pipe, when the men were gripped by lust. Earlier, they were too busy procuring their pipes. The critical moment past, they were lost in dreams and no longer good for anything except dragging themselves from chair to rug. When lust seized them, the women led them outside into the alleys around the Sheik Ma'ruf mosque. These women were of course known to the Maalem and his wife, and especially to the little maids who filled the kitchen. Sometimes they came during the day to gossip or help with chores. 'It's too early. Right now, they're still asleep.' There was also a singer, but she hadn't worked since the final months of her pregnancy. She'd just given birth to a daughter.

'Oum Jinane?' asked Khadouja.

'Do you know her?'

Oum Jinane was twenty-six years old. Related to the Maalem, she was also born in Kafr al-Amar. A singer, she first sang there secretly, watching her father the imam who officiated at circumcisions, marriages and burials. From the age of seven, in front of the three water buffalo calves she grazed, she practised reciting her father's religious songs, songs she knew by heart. She was delicate, brown like a ripe date, and ran around everywhere like a boy. Everyone was stunned by the beauty of her yellow eyes.

One day, after she surprised the little cow-herder with psalms sung in her angelic voice, the landowner's wife spoke to her: 'If you sing for animals, you'll end up like them. See how sad and dirty they are. Come with me instead, and I'll have you singing in rich people's homes. You'll become rich and beautiful like them.' The woman obtained her parents' permission to enroll her in the kottab, the Qur'anic school where she learnt to recite the Qur'an, the only girl among the village scamps. And when she chanted the Fatiha, echoing her father's lines, when her voice rose, crystalline, leading the other children's voices, men paused in their fields, women dropped their washing, to listen. People said that even the goats came to crouch outside her door.

She grew up like this among the boys, a nightingale mired in mud, her head instructed in religion, her legs as skittish as a fawn's. At fourteen, her hips grew round. Her breasts, two pears freely swelling under her dress, drew looks. Finally, she was forbidden entry to the kottab. It was then that the landowner's wife, for a few piastres that her father pocketed, took her as a servant in her Damanhour home. Admittedly, the woman kept her word, for at night, after work, she invited musicians, and Jinane sang for the wealthy, the house's guests. She sang verses from the Qur'an, the only tunes she knew then, but her voice was so limpid that they never tired of hearing her. Then her mistress said, 'You can't sing only about religion—it's love that brings money, not prayers! Tomorrow, Gergess Hakim, the poet of Port Said, will dine with us. I'll ask him to write you a song.'

All night that thought whirled through Jinane's head—she couldn't sleep. And when she finally did, she heard a man's voice in her dream, deep and solemn, repeating, 'Sing! Sing! Sing!' It was the same voice she heard the next night when she served dinner, the voice of Gergess Hakim who whispered in her ear, 'You are open like a morning flower.' He was tall and fat, dressed in Western clothes, a white linen suit, his head uncovered, his eyes hidden behind sunglasses even at night. He spoke loudly, drank whiskey, smoked cigarettes of aromatic blond tobacco, told endless off-colour jokes.

When the meal was over, she cleared the table and hid in the kitchen, her breath short. From there, she could hear the three musicians tuning their instruments. As always, the simsimiya, the little lyre that picked out triplets, touched her heart. The moment she heard the first notes, she rose. She was trembling with excitement. Her body vibrated, her soul quivered. The musicians played their long introduction. Then she heard her mistress calling, 'Jinane! Come enchant the night.' She appeared before them, daughter of the Delta, planted on her two outspread legs, with her copper skin, her face round like a moon and her golden eyes. A gathering of notables dreaming they were European watched as a young Egyptian ancestress emerged from the back kitchen.

Jinane's voice wed the lyre's—like the lines of the right hand meeting those of the left. People say there's an angel whose heart-strings are the lyre's cords; alone among all God's creatures, that angel's voice crosses the heavens, causing humans to fall in love.

She caught the highest note and held it—for a minute, maybe more; then, closing her eyes, she ventured into the text as into a forest: 'There is no god but God.' No one was unfamiliar with the words, but, shaped by her voice which had become matter, they penetrated the listeners until they were possessed. 'There is no god but God. There is no god but God.' And their lips began to mouth it, their feet to tap time to it and their hearts to beat with the exact rhythm of the bendir. The profession of faith repeated five times daily by believers was transmuted by the grace of a wild young girl who opened a hitherto unknown path in their souls. Wedding the music, Jinane's body trembled, and the throbbing words became flesh. These words, heard thousands of time since childhood, arose that night from the depths of their dreams and came to life. God was majesty, the Prophet stood before them, and everything became possible, true; each moment breathed beauty.

She didn't sing for long, not more than half an hour, before she had exhausted her meagre repertory. The musicians instantly froze, their fingers still on the strings, their hands against the drum's skin. There was a profound silence. Aware that they had just witnessed a magical event, the guests didn't dare applaud. The poet, Gergess Hakim, a little tipsy, declaimed a verse that came to him on the spot: 'O beauty, O beautiful one, O you who give the world its colour . . . O you, you should be called "The World". That's when they applauded and applauded some more. Jinane, red with shame and pleasure, placed a hand over her heart, bowed awkwardly in acknowledgment, then ran to join the servants in the kitchen.

'She should go to sing in Cairo,' said one woman authoritatively.

'And the next time you come here to dine, will you be the one to enchant our evening?' retorted the owner's wife.

The discussion of Jinane's future went on for a while. Then they returned to their usual topics—the price of cotton that never stops climbing; the canals that needed to be dug again, choked each year with the flood's silt; the lands for sale; the question of agrarian reform that came up with each new administration.

The poet had disappeared, seeking the way to the kitchen. There he found Jinane alone, collapsed over the table, her head in her hands. She was weeping.

'My daughter, bring me a glass of water,' he asked.

She raised her head, frightened. 'At your service,' she replied, rising. And added, 'O my prince . . . '

He sat on the bench with difficulty, struggling to bend his legs. She stood before him, a bird with broken wings.

'Why are you crying, O beautiful one?'

'I am far from my family, my prince, and once I've performed the song that fills my soul, I am alone in my night.'

'Come! Draw near.'

He sat on his lap this young girl who had not reached her sixteenth year. All her limbs were trembling. He caressed her thighs, her breasts. Jinane's ears rang, and the world's din grew distant. He asked where she slept. When he learnt she had to go into the courtyard, into the servants' shack, he understood why she lingered like this, alone in the kitchen. Mournful solitude is better than degrading company.

'Come, join me in my room,' he urged.

She didn't reply.

He rose heavily, his step uncertain. 'Your voice is purer than the lyre's, your song the music of angels.'

She watched him totter away. She didn't know what to think. At that moment still a child of the village, friend of placid cows, but already, faintly, a young woman, secretly ripened.

The next day, Hakim wrote a song for her that began: 'Come, O beloved. Come, come to me.' For these were the words he'd uttered when, at the owls' hunting hour, Jinane, barefoot and on tiptoe, had entered his first-floor room. 'Come, O beloved. Come, come to me.' That's how the poet welcomed her.

Love touched the heart of Gergess Hakim, the Copt—love for the little Muslim girl, the daughter of Kafr al-Amar's imam. He loved her, and, overcome by the love he felt which made him think of music and words, he began to read the poets—the ancient ones, Abu Nuwas, Ibn al-Rumi, and above all the modern, Ahmed Chawki. He wandered around, book in hand, reciting whole passages from *Majnun Layla*, 'Layla's Madman', And, to imitate it, he played freely with Jinane's ambiguous name which could mean 'Paradise' or 'madness'. Mad for her, at least in his songs, he called himself Majnun Jinane; he called her 'his sweetness, his madness, his paradise'. For a whole year, Hakim wrote songs for Jinane. She locked them in a chest hidden in an attic corner, knowing it contained a treasure. They met in the afternoon, in the music room where he had her rehearse. They sometimes met again at night in the room he occupied more and more often, on the first floor of the Damanhour villa. He bought her gifts, dresses, perfumes, but never too much . . . He wanted her docile—at once earthly and divine, the unlikely emergence of the angel at the heart of the lyre in the voice of a filthy cowgirl. The landowner's wife was not unaware of their relationship, but kept her eyes shut as long as Jinane continued to work for her by day and sing for her guests at night.

For a whole year, Jinane sang for the rich landowners of Damanhour. Each time, more and more of them came. Her reputation grew, extending to other villages in the Delta. Her mistress agreed to 'lend' her for as much as two or three pounds per evening. They came to fetch her by car; she left to give recitals in the houses at Tanta, Mahalla, Mansoura. Hakim never accompanied her; he never saw men sticking banknotes on her forehead, slipping them into her corsage. All this money joined the song lyrics in Jinane's secret chest.

Soon her mistress realized her effect on men. She did not inspire them with lust like a dancer or a courtesan, nor with love like a bride, but with a sort of mystical passion, the irresistible urge to plunge into mystery. They begged her to allow them to guide the young girl along life's paths. 'Entrust her to me, I'll give her everything! She'll be more than my daughter, I'll treat her better than my mother. What more can I say? And, to compensate for your loss, I'll give you a hundred pounds. Two hundred.' They sought her as daughter and mistress, idol and spouse. Until then, Jinane went along with them, knowing neither how to desire nor how to refuse. Not that she was passive, but curious, rather, to learn God's will. Would He make her know glory? Wealth? Happiness? She never went so far as to think He was perhaps planning deception and bitterness for her.

One day, her mistress confronted Hakim: 'I know you won't marry her. She's not from your world, she doesn't share your faith. People are starting to talk, you know them. Words are a slow-acting poison. Soon, scandal will spill onto you and splatter over me. They'll say I let immorality flourish in my house. Perhaps they'll even accuse me of having planned it, who knows? Every day, your father augments the fortune he will bequeath you. You rich writers don't have to worry about anyone's opinions. For us business folk, it's never good to have a bad reputation. So, tell me, what are you planning to do?'

Hakim was having trouble waking up after a night of drinking. Judging from the heat of the terrace's tiles, he thought it must be around noon. The mistress' questions struck him like a bolt of lightning. Jinane was his inner freedom, the space he'd created for himself, where he moved as an artist. What did this greedy old woman want from him? Money, of course. That was it, yes! He gave her some, paying generously for her silence and the lodging he enjoyed almost nightly. He thought she would ask for more. After all, he had the means. But her manner disturbed him. The attack was underhanded; from a moral point of view, it was impossible to respond. Was he going to argue? To explain that, without the songs he'd given her,

Jinane would still be croaking in front of swamp frogs? No. He considered it beneath his dignity. To tell the truth, he was beginning to tire of this silent, ignorant peasant. So without a second thought, he settled his affairs and promptly disappeared.

In less than a month, they learnt that Jinane was pregnant. At first they tried to settle the issue there and then, in Damanhour. But the men, who just a little while ago were parading as Pygmalions, balked at the prospect of finding themselves the husband of a primitive girl, father to a most likely degenerate bastard.

And so it was, back to the village, to Kafr al-Amar, of a Jinane who'd left as a princess with a golden voice but was returning as a perverse prostitute. Her oldest brother slapped her when she arrived; her father the imam beat her in public; her mother never stopped crying; and one of her aunts made her swallow a concoction of wormwood, saffron and parsley. She grew feverish and developed dysentery. She vomited, she cried, but no one consoled her. When she lost her child one night, only a toothless old woman was there to help. For a long time, she couldn't walk. She huddled alone in a hut, humiliated and ashamed. But Egypt is the land of forgetting. She was not forgiven, not at all, but little by little the story of her misconduct and pregnancy vanished from memory.

Sometime later, she rejoined her water-buffalo calves in the marshes of the Delta. She rarely spoke to her fellow humans. Children playing in the fields reported they sometimes heard her singing at the prayer hour—hymns of piercing love that mingled with the sounds of nature. It was said that ducks and geese set the rhythm, a spontaneous percussion; cranes formed an echoing chorus; and ravens cawed in cadence, like hands clapping.

In all seasons, she went barefoot, her hair undone, her body draped in a large piece of fabric that enveloped her like the loincloths of women from the South. A legend grew around her. People said that Jinane sang with the animals, like King Solomon who'd spoken with them. They could become an army at her command. People feared her a little, ascribed malevolent powers to her. When a snake slithered into a house, everyone wondered if its mistress had offended Jinane; when a wild cat devoured a chicken, they made a chicken dish and offered it to Jinane so she would be appeased—as if they thought she could transmute into a feline at night. They pitied her too; they said she was condemned to the solitude of creatures deprived of soul. When they uttered her name, they always said, 'Jinane, with the empty spirit, poor thing.' Sometimes they added, 'See what happens to those who dare to defy God.' A few years later, everyone in the village had forgotten Jinane's wonderful talent for music and song— everyone except her cousin Hassan who'd bought a hashish den in Cairo.

'You see,' the woman explained, 'all the money the eternal youth Maalem Hassan al-Shebab earns—and trust me, he earns a lot!—all that money, he brings it back to the village to buy land. There, he had the most beautiful, solid house built, where he set up his other wife and all her children. See how he makes us live here, in poverty! Our master is crafty. Wanting to attract customers, he decided to bring music into his den. He needed an orchestra—I was the dancer. Men smoked, spellbound by the litanies of the lute, their blurred eyes on my naked belly. The kif-lover likes to prop up his blue dreams. In a few months, we'd captured all the customers on Ma'ruf Street. Sheik Ahmed's hashish lounge was empty, even Abu Ali's, the big place on Champollion Street. But that wasn't enough. He wanted to attract customers from Gezira and Rhoda—and he needed a singer. One day, he returned from the village with little Jinane. At first I thought she was one of those streetwalkers brought back from his trips to the villages of the South, the ones he set up in nearby slums. But when I heard her sing . . . '

Eight years had gone by since her melancholy departure from Damanhour. Jinane was now twenty-five, with the face of a child and a body burnished by hot winds. Hassan settled her in the little room at the top of the stairs. Although the way there was perilous, scattered with pottery shards and treacherous scraps of metal, the room itself was welcoming, with a cotton mattress on the bed and curtains on the window. She looked a long time for a place to hide her treasure, Hakim's songs and the banknotes that had evaded her family's searches. She found a cavity beneath a tile on the little terrace in front of her window.

She agreed to sing on the earthen mound Hassan had made, which he pompously called 'the stage', but she did not want to appear as a woman. It wasn't good to have talent when you were female. Her small size and muscular legs would allow her to pass as a young boy. They bound her breasts with cotton bands. They cropped her hair. They found her an outfit as a *saye*, one of those liveried pages who precede the carriages of the rich and powerful—billowing trousers, an ample tunic and a red vest with gold embroidery. On her head, she wore a flat little tarbouche, like that of Ismail the Magnificent, and in her hand she held a long staff which she beat on the floor to signal the musicians' departure.

That's how she appeared for the first time on the den's stage. Hassan introduced her as Ibn Ali, 'son of Ali', which was only half false since her father the imam was indeed named Ali. When, after the long introduction by the simsimiya, she caught the note and modulated it with her voice, there was silence. The women suspended their chattering; the smokers dropped their pipes; the waiters stood still, their mouths agape. She began with Hakim's first song. 'Come, O my beloved. Come, come to me. Your absence is agony. To see you is agony. To touch you is agony. Even to kiss you is agony. Come closer. Come closer still.'

Thanks to his new singer, Hassan's dive was never empty. Every evening, Jinane gave two recitals; the first around ten, the second at midnight. Some, who'd come only to hear her sing, stayed afterwards to chat and order a goza.

She avoided meeting customers. Other than the time devoted to music—afternoon rehearsals and evening performances—she refused to leave her room, remaining in bed, daydreaming. The image of her lost child secretly haunted her—a girl, she was certain. Sometimes

she cried about her, dreaming she might have been a fabulous artist—
a singer, a diva—like those Hakim had told her about. But most of
the time she spoke to the dead child as if to an angel, asking her to
protect her from the cruelty of the living.

She thought she could protect herself through her isolation, but
no one can avoid fate. Once it has taken a bite from your leg, it will
find you again you no matter where you hide. Again it was a rich
man, but this time he wasn't an artist.

Ever since he'd entered politics, Abdel Wahab Mazloum Pasha
had lived in a plush flat on Abdine Street, near the Royal Palace, leaving his wife and three children in his villa in Alexandria. He'd made
the headlines in November 1924 when he joined the Wafd, the
nationalist party opposing the British. Its leader, Saad Zaghloul,
under pressure from the British governor, had been forced to resign
from his position as prime minister. Until then, Abdel Wahab had for
a long time opposed the leader idolized by the masses, but, appalled
by Britain's bad faith, decided to join the struggle for Egypt's independence. Tall and thin, refined and elegant, he was always dressed
in a three-piece suit, his stiff collar secured by a white silk ascot, his
tarbouche slightly tilyed to the left. This obsessive concern with
appearance perhaps compensated for his graceless face. With his pit-
ted skin, sagging cheeks, thick eyebrows and small, piercing black
eyes, he could have played an assassin in the silent films shown at
the Gaumont Palace or the Metropole. His reputation matched his
appearance—people said he was hard on subordinates, severe with
friends and fierce against political rivals.

Some time ago, he'd begun to visit Hassan's den, where the waiters dreaded having to serve him. He arrived a little before midnight,
sat down, always alone, near a door, and ordered a pipe and a
whiskey. That night, he was startled by a voice that seemed to descend
from heaven—was it the influence of the blue smoke that made him
see, with his eyes closed, images of Paradise? An impregnable fortress
atop a craggy mountain, a shaded garden with immense flowerbeds.
He sniffed his fingers, subtly scented with jasmine and orchid. And

then, at the audience's request, Jinane began her heart-wrenching song for a second time: 'To see you is agony. To touch you is agony. To kiss you is also agony. To be within your body is the greatest agony. For I realize, O my beloved, that I am not you, not entirely, up to the movements of your belly . . . ' Abdel Wahab, his eyes closed, saw a dark woman with copper skin, naked, advancing towards him. The vision seemed so real that he abruptly opened his eyes.

Jinane had come down from the stage, as she sometimes did to honour her enthusiastic audience. She was standing in front of him in her oriental page's outfit. As she sang, she traced Abdel Wahab's outline with her staff. He blinked, not knowing for an instant if this was still a dream. He abruptly grabbed the staff—the staff was real, and, even more, the delicate little hand he was holding, this boy with the stirring voice of an angel.

The audience reacted wildly, crying 'Leave him! Leave him!' His eyes in those of Jinane as if hypnotized, he was transfixed, unable to react. In his mind, he saw himself rising, taking the boy in his arms, kissing him on the lips. 'Leave him alone! Leave him alone!' the men in the room kept shouting. And Jinane kept singing as she gently swayed her hips to the drums' rhythm: 'O my beloved, I am not you, totally you, up to the movements of your belly, the beating of your heart.' Abdel Wahab shook his head to chase away the dream. He rose, withdrew his wallet from his back pocket, took out a pound and extended it to the young boy. Jinane delicately grasped the note between two fingers and showed it to the audience as she sang the last verse: 'Love is an agony nothing can soothe.' Then she turned her back and regained the stage, beating the ground with her staff.

That night, the pasha fell in love with the young boy who was not one. Jinane, for her part, began to nurse strange thoughts. This man, she thought, would restore life to her lost little girl. She approached Hassan's wife, the dancer with the generous body: 'O mother, do you know the plants that permit you to have a child?'

'And I,' said the woman as she told the story to Khadouja, 'I, who had not understood what Jinane was planning, replied: "Before thinking about plants, my daughter, you'd be better off finding a husband!" What a fool I was—he was already there, established in her heart, dwelling in each nightly dream!'

The Maalem, her husband, knew better. For a goodly sum, he sold the pasha a night of song for himself alone—for fifty pounds, he promised to bring him Ibn Ali, the young page who would stay till morning. 'You'll see, O pasha, you won't be disappointed. All your senses will be gratified, and more.'

'But the boy won't know how to sing like that without the musicians,' protested Abdel Wahab.

The Maalem indulged in the luxury of naivety: 'So, you want musicians too, O my prince? I thought the boy would have been enough. For twenty more, you'll have three musicians. If you agree to another ten, I'll also bring you the dancer.'

'No!' replied the other, who didn't appreciate the joke. 'Your wife can stay in your sty and dance for the rats. I'll keep the musicians only until midnight. And for all of it, thirty pounds. If you object, count on it, tomorrow you'll have a police raid. Who can say when you'll get out of prison, you idiot!'

And so the Maalem bowed and kissed the pasha's hand. 'O pasha, O my prince, whatever sum your highness chooses to bestow on me will always be greater than what I merit.'

Cairo night, eternal night. The moon was full. A gala meal— Abdel Wahab had ordered the most luxurious dishes. A festive atmosphere: he'd burnt incense throughout his flat, placed candles in all the rooms, built a platform for the musicians. He'd brought along two friends, two soldiers with solid reputations as rakes, and paid for two girls, among the most beautiful. His singer needed an audience, after all!

Sinuous paths of fate—Jinane had also prepared herself. Following the women's advice, she'd chosen the day, a Thursday. In the afternoon, she'd gone to the hammam, where she'd sweated and been epilated, massaged, perfumed, made up. Every evening for the preceding week, she'd drunk an infusion prepared by an old woman, to which she'd added spoonfuls of honey so she could stomach its bitterness. Before donning her page's outfit, she'd studied herself in the mirror for a long time. Her breasts and hips had blossomed, her skin, shining with oil, smelt of jasmine and rose. Her face was taut with expectation. She forced herself to smile, trying again and again. Finally, she waved her hand over the mirror and murmured, 'With God's help.'

The musicians first played alone while Abdel Wahab and his guests drank whiskey. They were waiting for the singer, who was delayed. With alcohol's help, the conversation grew racier.

'I hear you're drawn to the young singer,' said the general. 'You shouldn't be ashamed. Do you know this poem by Abu Nuwas?

> *They ask him:* '*What are you drinking?*'
> *He replies:* '*In my glass!*'
> *They ask him:* '*What do you like?*'
> *He replies,* '*In the arse!*'
> '*And what have you forsaken, then?*'
> *The answer's plain:* '*Grace!*'

'Abu Nuwas is a great poet, I agree—one of our greatest! But I don't share his critique of religion. I have to admit, the grace of prayer always does me good, especially at night.'

Abdel Wahab clapped his hands. A server appeared. 'Bring us three *shishas*,' he ordered.

The three men sat in front of their pipes. The bubbles swirled in the opal bowls. Scents of caramel and hashish filled the room. The military men, meaning to honour their host, defended homosexuality.

'To return to our discussion: I would say that boys are superior to girls. Boys understand our pleasures better than girls can,' said the colonel, his hand on one of the girls' thighs.

They drank; they smoked; they called for new helpings of scented tobacco; they smoked some more; they laughed, louder and louder. The musicians played. The women disappeared, then returned, clad only in billowy trousers and bras. Making their long transparent veils whirl, they began to dance. They drew close to the men, brushing their knees with their hips, kneeling before them, enticing and submissive, grazing them with their lips, inviting them through their gestures to the passions of their bodies.

It was late when the musicians played the introduction to 'The Agony of Love', Jinane's signature song. Conversation ceased. They heard, first from the distance, a crystalline echo, then, louder, one note, a single, long note of suffering. Then, she appeared in a corner of the room, lit up by the moon, the little golden page, leaning on her staff. And her voice filled the room, like an eruption from the centre of the earth. 'Come, O my agony, come!' And the musicians and the revellers chanted in one breath, in harmony—a sigh, a cry, 'Aaah . . .' She repeated the verse, 'Come, O my agony, come'. And the others took it up, 'Aaah . . . ' Five times, ten times . . . She could have repeated it another hundred times; a hundred times her audience would have responded with a sigh, like an unending orgasm. While the lyre was picking out solo arpeggios, she came towards Abdel Wahab, and, when she was quite near, felt his face with her hand: 'Come, O beloved. Come, come to me!' He closed his eyes and sighed, 'Aaah . . . ' She repeated the second verse as she moved away from him. 'Aaah . . . ' When she'd rejoined the musicians, she sang, 'Your absence is agony.' Bound by the unendurable power of beauty, the audience, no longer able to withstand it, applauded. She repeated the verse, and again, the public sighed, each time, stronger, more present, penetrated by the poet's words. Jinane bent lightly forward, thanking them with a nod of her head, and repeated, 'To see you is agony. To touch you is agony . . . ' And the recital of lovers' agonies lasted a long time, a very long time, punctuated by the audience's sighs.

Abdel Wahab had closed his eyes, swaying slowly, assailed by visions of Paradise. Nude young women danced before him—not two but seventy. Their skin was white, and they were virginal, untouched by men or djinns. They flew through the air on green velvet cushions or rugs with intricate designs. Abdel Wahab sighed; his eyes closed, he sighed. And when Jinane again uttered, 'To see you is agony. To touch you is agony. To kiss you is even greater agony,' he suddenly opened his eyes, rose from his armchair, seized the page and kissed him on the lips. His mouth tasted of flowering orange trees.

It was black night in the room. Outside, the musicians had put away their instruments, and the two military men, each with his courtesan, had disappeared. The last rhythm still alive was the big pendulum's ticking, to which the servants attuned their steps as they silently put away the remains of the evening's pleasures. Abdel Wahab, standing, his head clouded with alcohol and carefree smoke, caressed the face of the little page captured in mid-song. 'Tonight, you'll sing for me, a song that comes from your belly.' He removed the embroidered vest and tossed it aside. Jinane was holding her breath. He removed the ample, fine cotton tunic. Jinane quickly brought her hands up to hide her breasts. Surprised, Abdel Wahab unrolled the long cotton band that enclosed her beneath her clothes. He stroked her breasts, but his mind was troubled. The boy had beautiful breasts, large and pointed. A hermaphrodite? Images of Paradise returned. Hadn't he learnt in theology class that there were demons, djinneyas, among the virgins? Some devils had a male sex organ on their right thigh and a female vulva on their left. When they were bored, they threw the right leg over the left to give themselves pleasure. The Shaytan? Seized by a sudden anxiety, he began to tremble. The drugs' influence was returning in waves. The Shaytan? The clock's ticking grew louder, merging with the beating of his pulse. He closed his eyes and squeezed his lids tightly to drive away terrors. 'Courage!' he told himself.

He removed the boy's trousers, caressing his thighs. Jinane, also standing, so tiny compared with him, gave a sigh of pleasure. They stretched out on the bed. The drugs returned. 'What are you?' he stammered. And the little page answered, 'Jinane.' And the images rose before Abdel Wahab's eyes: above the bed hung fruit bursting with juice, grapes. Thanks to hemp's magic, he had night vision, like a cat. And her eyes, Jinane's blond eyes. She spoke soothing words: 'Jinane, I'm Jinane, not a man, and no djinn has conquered me. My heart is a pearl hidden in a shell no one has opened.' Had she even uttered those words? Or had she merely guided his sexual organ, rendered timid by the blue smoke, as far as her corolla? Hashish strengthens love's bonds. Slowing the man's pleasure, it increases the woman's. They made love for a long time, silently, with no words other than their names, exchanged in murmurs. At dawn, the first light coloured the room's walls. Abdel Wahab's pleasure, until now dampened by drugs, dazzled him. Jinane felt it through the spasms of his belly.

'Why?' he asked her. 'Why did you travesty yourself as a boy?'

'God's gift is not for women. A woman who sings stirs up lust and ends up destroyed and defamed.'

'You're a woman then?'

She smiled. 'A *fellaha*, a peasant, a simple woman from the Delta.'

'The Nile comes to us from far, very far. Its torrents have rushed down Ethiopia's mountains, its turbulence has snaked through the Sudan. After unfurling across half the earth, when it reaches the cow's belly, exhausted at last, it separates into seven branches to create a giant green chandelier that feeds the world. You're not a fellaha, you are Egyptian woman. You are earth. You are Egypt.'

With these words, Abdel Wahab fell into such a deep sleep that the servants who came to wake him the next day at ten o'clock thought he was dead. After this night, he never again set foot in the hashish den of Maalem Hassan al-Shebab, called 'the eternal youth' by his family.

As soon as the man, sated with love and intoxicated by kif, fell asleep, Jinane withdrew without a sound, returning to the den of fleeting pleasures. During the days that followed, he sent her money and bouquets of flowers but did not try to see her again. As for her, liberated from her long sorrow, she wrote her first song: 'Jinane, I'm Jinane—not one man, not one djinn has ever conquered me.' She sang it at the end of each performance, after disappearing backstage as a page and returning as a Bedouin woman.

She waited five months until her belly was round as a small donkey's before letting him know she was pregnant—from him! He did not immediately reply. In his solitude, he only thought, 'From me, yes, and from all the others . . . ' It's the excuse of every man who lets his seed flow. But Jinane knew it was his, no one's but his. She hadn't been with any man since Gergess, and none after her night with Abdel Wahab.

After a few weeks, he finally made a decision: he invited her to his house. He sent his car and driver. She entered the flat on Abdine Street, which seemed less grand, less luxurious than she recalled. Dressed in a three-piece suit of fine grey cotton, his tie knotted over his stiff collar, his face red, he received her from behind his desk; he was playing with his fountain pen. It was hot. On the ceiling, a huge, aluminum-bladed fan spun slowly and powerfully, making a slapping sound that rang like words, voices.

Jinane looked up at it. 'May your day breathe jasmine, O pasha!' That's how she greeted him, and then added: 'You can make wind, but the breath of life comes from within.'

'May your day be golden like a river of honey under the sun,' he answered. 'The breath of life, my child, is introduced by the Creator in the drop of blood.'

Then he launched into a long political narrative. The British were hypocrites, sly deceivers, offering independence with one hand and establishing courts with the other, managing public finance and deploying soldiers at strategic crossroads, especially along the Canal. And if King Fouad let it happen, it's because he too was a foreigner, a Turk, an Albanian. For the country to be born at last, Egypt needed a patriot, a true Egyptian, like 'our leader Saad Zaghloul'. He reminded her that Zaghloul, head of the Wafd, his party, was a fellah, a peasant from the Delta just like her, issued from the earth as tall as a palm tree. He'd pulled himself up by his own merit to the level of the highest leaders, including those of foreign countries. Stunned, she listened to this speech whose meaning she didn't understand and about which she didn't know what to think. What was he trying to tell her? That the coming child was the incarnation of his recent realignment with the Independence Party? Perhaps this child should have been called 'Wafd'. Radiating politeness, the infinite sweetness of this land's people, she replied, 'Egypt is the mother of the world, is that not true, my prince? And I—all I will be is the mother of your child.'

'Do not think I am shirking, my daughter,' Abdel Wahab said solemnly. 'I will watch over your child, but from a distance. Rest assured he will lack nothing. He is coming at the moment when the forces held back for centuries, the forces of our country, Egypt, are finally about to be liberated. The Nile, restrained in a narrow corridor throughout its desert passage, is also liberated, in the place known as Batn al-Baqara, "the cow's belly". As you know, the cow swells in order to give birth.'

Jinane thought it was Abdel Wahab's head that was troubled and in need of liberation. She knew that overuse of hashish gave rise to strange words that persist in some men long after their last session, sometimes never leaving. She had seen such men in Hassan's den, prostrate for days at a time, their eyes haggard, not eating, barely drinking; men who, when they were questioned, pretended to be kings, princes or pashas. They gave orders to mice and battled enemies only they could see. But this was a real pasha and his words flowed like a torrent, his bright eyes fluttering, his hands restless.

'It's a girl!' Jinane announced, gently stroking her belly.

Abruptly, he rose from his seat and crossed the distance between them in two steps. Towering over her, he shouted, 'How do you know that? How? Who told you it's a girl? What witch did you question, with what magician did you lie? Why do you say it's a girl? Maybe it's a boy. Well, for my part, I think it's a demon, an afrit, a djinn—one of those creatures witches like you bring into the world!'

He was so brutal, so close to her, that she was frightened. No one was going to take her child away from her by violence again. Covering her head with her hand, she rushed towards the door. He grabbed her by her clothes and yanked her back.

'No! Stay!' Then, growing softer, a cruel smile on his lips, 'Stay, my daughter, stay!'

Reluctantly, she sat down again in the chair, hunched over to protect her belly. After a few minutes, out of breath, red with anger, he asked, 'What do you want? Tell me the truth: is it money? Is that what you want?'

What was it they all had about money? She had no need for money. She had hundreds of pounds in her safe, slowly amassed over the years. She hadn't spent a single one. No! All she wanted was her daughter; she wanted the return of the daughter ravished too soon by men's cruelty. She wanted to be sure he would let her return. And then, he was right, she was ready to acknowledge it—yes, she'd consulted a sorceress, a woman who read marks in sand. She, at least, had recognized that her daughter had returned: she was here, huddled in her belly, this daughter she was now protecting with her arms. She lifted her head. 'My daughter! I want my daughter.'

'But then why have you come to trouble me? What do you want from me?'

'That you name her!'

Name her? What did that mean? Most assuredly, he would never understand women. You didn't give a name until the seventh day, and this girl—yes, she was a girl—wasn't even born. Why choose her name now? And why did she have to give him this task? He wasn't even sure such an act was lawful, in accord with religious precepts.

'Her name, you know, is written by the hand of God somewhere in the sky.' And to explain to her that God wrote human destiny in a kind of book, he drew some letters on an invisible tablet with his finger in the air.

'What word did you just write, O my prince?'

'I don't know—Masr, Egypt—I think that's the word I was drawing in space.'

'So is that her name?' Jinane asked.

'It's not a name for a girl. Masr is a country—it's neither a man nor a woman, our country. But you could call her Masreya, "the Egyptian woman".'

She rose then, smiling. 'O my prince! Masreya will be her name. And when she will be of age to understand, I'll teach her that she was born from the cow's belly, distant daughter of the Nile's torrents.'

And Jinane left Abdel Wahab Mazloum Pasha's home. A few months later, he was elected member of Parliament.

*

Aunt Tofa'ha had a smile on her lips when she told the dancer, Hassan's Cairo wife: 'She's the one, Oum Jinane, she's the one we want to meet! Her reputation has reached us in the Mouski. Is it true what we've heard? Since she gave birth to her daughter, her breasts give so much milk that you can fill three big jars every day?'

'Words of light flow from your lips, my sister! Yes, it's true! Her daughter is barely two days old and already her face is round as a watermelon. In the morning, Oum Jinane's blouse is soaked, the sheets on which she's slept are soaked and the mattress is also wet. You'd think her bed had been watered in the middle of the night. And you can taste it, it's milk, pure milk.'

The woman led them through the back room of the den, along dark corridors, up to the first floor, to Jinane's room. A ray of sunlight filtering through a gap in the curtains traced a line of fire on the wall, as if it were split. They were both on the bed. The little one was greedily sucking to the rhythm of a refrain her mother was softly singing, 'I'm the Egyptian, natural child of torrents and desert, born from the belly of the cow, my name is Masreya ... O Masreya ...'

Moved by the sight, the three women bowed to the ground. Naji, the simple-minded one, was emitting little cries of excitement and was given a tap behind his ear. Then Tofa'ha greeted Jinane. Ancient images came to mind. She thanked God for having brought her here and thanked Him again. She knelt and kissed the mother's hands. To avoid the evil eye, Khadouja showered the infant with deprecating words, 'Look how ugly she is. With that rumpled face, you'd think she was an old witch.' And she tapped one hand on the other and then the other way around, 'Ay ya yay. How ugly she is, this Egyptian girl!' she repeated. And Jinane, filled with joy, thanked the women and thanked God at the same time—though it wasn't clear it was the same god.

Khadouja then spoke up, explained to Oum Jinane that over there, in the Mouski, in the Alley of the Jews, a boy had been born to a couple from the jewel family, the Gohars. Over there, they called them 'Zohar'. His face was so beautiful that when women looked at him, tears came to their eyes. Sometimes beauty has more power than strength does. When they drew near him, a fragrance arose, like incense. What she wanted to ask her was: Should they let this child die because its mother, poor thing, didn't have a drop of milk? Of course, they'd tried to feed him cow's milk, and sheep's milk, but he'd refused all nourishment. They'd sought wet-nurses from the neighbourhood, from the Jews in Haret al-Yahud, but he had turned away, spitting. Ever since he was born, he'd absorbed nothing— nothing at all. And so, here's what they thought: he was probably waiting for the milk of happy Jinane. And Khadouja cited a verse from the Qur'an that described Moses—for whom, as everyone knows, the pharaoh's daughter anxiously sought a wet-nurse— and said, 'Nurse him! Don't be afraid. Don't be sad.' And added, 'Trust me, he'll come back to you!'

Tofa'ha wondered what that last sentence meant: 'He'll come back to you.' Did it mean he would be Jinane's child and one day join her? Or perhaps he would marry an Arab, a Muslim? She shook her head in denial.

Masreya had fallen asleep at her mother's breast, her mouth half open. Khadouja continued her assault, unremitting. She mused out loud: 'Once, you gave life. But you couldn't do otherwise. In your belly, the child, drawn by the light and sounds of the world, wanted to emerge. All you did was to go along with its will, all you did was to help it with all your strength. This time, it's through your decision, your choice, that you'll give life to an infant who, without you, will go back among the dead. Will you refuse to give life by an act of your own will?'

At these words, Jinane accepted. She thought God would be grateful, and that, in exchange for her milk, He would grant a long, beautiful life to Masreya, her daughter, the little Egyptian girl cradled in her arms. Yes, she replied to Khadouja, she would go with her daughter to spend a few weeks in the Alley of the Jews, among the jewel family, so that their child would consent to join the living.

Tofa'ha clapped her hands exclaiming, 'Glory be to God!'—a God whom she called 'Allah' in Arabic, as did all the ghetto Jews. And Khadouja placed her hands on Jinane's head and brought them back to her lips, repeating, 'In the name of God, in the name of God.' And the women laughed and cried at the same time, and the idiot Naji clapped his hands.

After packing some things (it had to be done quickly), the women set off in a cart drawn by a big sorrel horse with a golden mane. Naji sat beside the coachman. Jinane insisted on a detour to the mosque of Sayeda al-Zaynab. What was the point of doing a good deed if God and his angels were not informed? It took so long that, by the time the carriage arrived in front of Uncle Elie's grocery, the sun was starting to go down in the sky.

'All day long, he hasn't stopped crying for a minute,' old Massouda, Uncle Elie's wife, complained. 'What do you expect? He's hungry. And his mother's withdrawn from the world. It's sad to see a mother weeping because she can't feed her starving child.'

They led Jinane of the beautiful breasts to a large wicker sofa. In one arm, she held Masreya, child of the Nile, who'd fallen asleep;

Esther's aunts placed the boy, who still didn't have a name, in her other. He seized the breast, and sucked for a whole hour, without stopping. Motty, his father, standing, leaning on his cane, also couldn't stop chanting in Hebrew a verse from the Song of Songs: 'Thy navel is like a round goblet, which wanteth not liquor; thy belly is like an heap of wheat set about with lilies.'

The news of the miracle spread like wildfire. A group formed in front of the grocery door, and Aunt Maleka went out to serve dates, exclaiming, 'It's a miracle, a great miracle.' Never had any neighbourhood in Cairo been so excited by a baby's nursing.

Until bedtime, the child nursed three more times at the breast of abundance. He took hold of one nipple, little Masreya another, and the two children's hands sometimes touched. You would have thought they were two lovers entering Paradise as they held each other's hands. The night was far advanced when they laid him, sated, in his mother Esther's arms.

Jinane was settled in the family's biggest house, the one that belonged to Aunt Maleka and her husband Yakoub, whom everyone called Poupy. She felt safe in the ghetto. She knew that no one would come looking for her in this realm of the excluded. She told herself that here her daughter ran no danger: unknown to her family, the excitable peasants of the Delta; protected from the evil eye of the women on Ma'ruf Street, and from the predictable fury of Abdine Street and its master, Abdel Wahab. The Jewish women of the hara, their hearts swelling with gratitude, treated her like a princess. Every day, they served her dishes whose secrets they alone knew: first wheat porridge with milk, the one set aside for those who've just given birth; then zucchini stuffed with meat, which they called 'Italian'; a veal ragout she'd never tasted that they called 'sefrito'; rice and lentils with dill; and, of course, multiple helpings of *ful*, dried favas, the delicious food of the Egyptian people. Between meals, they plied her with little cakes—hazelnut mille-feuilles dripping with honey; morsels of pastry stuffed with puréed dates; white-sugar cookies, round like the full moon, cleft like women's arses.

They never left her alone, not for an instant, responsive to each of her desires, talking with her about her parents, her childhood. And they pitied her. 'O God! How could you give birth alone, far from your mother, far from your aunts, far from the land of your birth?' said one as she raised her hands skyward. 'Poor thing,' another said. 'Nothing can replace her family, but we can help her forget.' And Masreya, the little Egyptian girl, was passed from hand to hand by the aunts, who washed and massaged and cradled her as if she were their own child, with the same privileges as Esther's son.

Tofa'ha, the youngest aunt, who'd developed a real affection for Jinane, asked Rav Mourad to make an amulet for the newborns, to repel Lilith, the female angel of death. She knew he was obstinate, their rabbi, but honest at heart, and above all learned. Yet when he tried to get out of it by saying, 'Listen, we can't make her a Jewish amulet—she's Muslim!' the dismayed women cried, 'And why not?' in one voice. 'So—do the demons, the sorcerers and the germs check someone's faith before attacking them?'

Maleka, the wisest, but certainly not the least offensive, declared, sententiously, 'To pray, each group is different, but to protect ourselves from death, we're all the same!'

And Tofa'ha appealed to him, 'So, do you want the death of Jinane's child, even though she's saved the life of ours?'

Of course Mourad ended up relenting, but silently cursed this Zohar family that feared neither God nor rabbis.

In the night's silence, despite his ill-will, he set to work. In his most beautiful handwriting, he copied, on a large, more or less rectangular parchment, the prayer he found in a book of practical Kabbalah he'd inherited from his grandfather: 'He will not allow your leg to stray, the God of our fathers. As it is written, He neither sleeps nor dreams, the Guardian of Israel.' Then in the centre of the sheet he drew a black hand with outspread fingers; to the right a fish and to the left an eye, a little like the eye of Horus in the engravings in books about ancient Egypt. And he let his imagination go. 'O, you evil eyes! Eye that looks to the right, eye that looks to the left! O you evil eyes! Baleful eye, piercing eye, eye that absorbs life, eye that brings death! O you evil eyes! Eye of the divorced woman, eye of the deceived husband; eye of the blind, eye of the lame.' There followed a long litany of toxic eyes, envious eyes—ending with the last, the most powerful: the eye that remembers the eye. Mourad addressed all these eyes and warned them: 'O, you evil eyes, the eye of God sees you and transfixes you. He prevents you from acting against these two infants, whom he protects with His powerful hand. You will be able to do nothing, neither during the day nor during the night, neither during wakefulness nor during sleep, neither in dreams nor in madness. You will be able to do nothing against them, neither here nor elsewhere, neither in Lower Egypt nor in Upper Egypt, neither in this world nor the next.' He called on the hundreds of angels he knew by name; he called on legions of demons whose names he distributed all around the parchment. At the very top, he inscribed the name of the most powerful, Solomon, lord of spirits and animals. At the very bottom, he inscribed the seventeen names of Lilith the destroyer, Shatrina, Abito, Kali and all the others. And in a corner, encircled by beautiful arabesques, he recounted the history of the prophet Elijah who recognized Lilith and transfixed her with his words. He consecrated two nights and a day to the creation of his amulet. Then, he brought it to Maleka's house.

When he welcomed him, Poupy, the husband, was startled by his shining eyes.

'What's happened to you, O my rav? Your eyes are wider than the doors of heaven. Have you encountered an angel, perhaps?'

Mourad went straight to Jinane's room. Sitting like a sultana on her wicker sofa, she was nursing the two children. Tofa'ha, who was massaging her feet, rose instantly.

'I hope you're not coming to tell us you couldn't make the amulet,' she said to him, looking distressed.

'Woman of little faith,' Mourad replied. 'Here it is!'

He unrolled the parchment. And she examined it, dumbfounded. Tofa'ha did not know how to read Hebrew—and even if she had, it would not have been of much use, since Mourad had drafted the amulet in Aramaic. But it was beautiful, this amulet, a sort of complex tableau, with the look of a labyrinth, its three designs encircled by dancing words and lost letters.

'Maleka!' she called, 'Maleka! Come quick to see the shield Mourad has crafted.'

'But there is one condition,' Mourad announced.

'What? A condition? What kind of condition?' Tofa'ha challenged, hands on hips.

'One condition, that's all! The amulet protects the two children, from the day of their birth until eternity . . . '

'And so?'

It was Mourad's little vengeance. Because it had to protect the two infants, it was necessary, for the amulet to work, that both of them remain together under its aegis. And Mourad added, 'This skin is an armour, an impermeable garment, but it can act only on the two children united.'

He placed the amulet at Jinane's feet and delivered his prescription: 'For seven days, the amulet must rest under the belly of Esther, the boy's mother. For the next seven, it must rest beneath Jinane, the girl's mother. After that, it must be hung on the wall, above the two children.'

'But you know very well, Rabbi, that Jinane is here temporarily,' Poupy complained. 'She'll leave in a few days with the little girl. How can we hang the amulet above the two children if one stays here with his mother, in his family, and the other goes elsewhere, into hers?'

Mourad, a little smile at the corner of his lips, raised his arms towards heaven in a gesture of impotence.

O Mourad, you have inherited from your ancestors, the time-honoured Kabbalists, this cunning, the demons' weapon, with which demons are combated. O Mourad, what thought crossed your mind? Do you know that your writing sealed these two children's fate? Why wasn't writing reserved for the gods? Why was this weapon of cunning and plots placed in human hands?

Around the table, gathered on Shabbat eve, the family discussed the problem late into the night and concluded that they didn't know how to resolve it. If God had decided to protect the two children like this, it's because He had his reasons. Elie decreed that Jinane would stay in Haret al-Yahud, in Maleka's house, for forty days.

'Why forty?' asked Tofa'ha who'd have kept her even longer.

'Because of the forty years in the desert?' Poupy ventured.

'But no!' Adina offered. 'It's for purification. Don't we fill the basin of the mikvah, the women's ritual bath, with forty measures of water?'

The men groaned. Why was she meddling, this one? How did she know how many measures of water were in the mikvah?

Motty went on all the same with his Talmudic commentary, 'Forty is the numerical equivalent of the word "water" in Hebrew,' he said into the silence.

'And so?' asked Maleka, who hadn't understood.

'Forty,' Motty continued, 'forty measures of *forty*, which is to say, water that makes water that is totally water, do you see? Thus, pure water, purified by its count.'

Everyone knew he was intelligent but this time it seemed his intelligence had muddled his brain.

'Nooooo!' exclaimed Adina, 'Do you really think we can follow you?'

And so it was Esther, silent until now, who came to her beloved husband's aid: 'But look! Forty days is the time required for the purification of the newborn. It's as true for Jews as it is for Muslims.'

She was right. A heavy silence followed, broken by Poupy. 'Agreed! But that shouldn't keep us from talking about it, all the same!'

The next day, they placed the parchment beneath the sheet on Esther's bed, and it spent seven nights under her belly. On the eighth day, the women examined the boy. He hadn't yet received a name. Motty, his father, was against it. 'What's the point of naming him if he must leave us?' They discussed it, nevertheless. If the child were to live, Motty wanted to give him his father's name, Abraham, first because it was tradition, and then because the name is fitting for a first born. Wasn't Abraham the first to acknowledge God? His mother, Esther, felt bound by her promise at the crypt. To her, he was Maimon. That's what she called him when she rocked him. Sometimes she called him by the philosopher's epithet, 'the Great Eagle'—she would use that lovely little Arabic word, *Nasr*, which means 'eagle', or *Nasr al-Gam'a*, 'the eagle of the mosque', or yet again *Nasri*, 'my eagle'. She even found a nickname, *Nasryouni*, 'my little eagle'. Poupy, Maleka's husband, wanted to name him Mourad, strategically, so the rabbi would feel constrained to do everything in his power to protect him. As for Uncle Elie, he wanted to call him Elie, because the whole world knew that the Prophet Elijah saved infants from death. Didn't he preside over every circumcision?

And indeed, the circumcision—that was the topic every evening. He should have been circumcised and named on the eighth day. He was reaching his twelfth day, and it hadn't been decided. For the child was sickly. They feared for his life. How many had died after circumcision, even those who were strong and healthy? As for him, strangely, although he let himself be fed, he didn't gain any weight. You could tell the difference by looking at Masreya, the same age, his twin so to speak, full-cheeked and chubby. He had a well-shaped head, gracious features, huge eyes wide open on the world, but a scrawny body with a big ballooning stomach. Adina called him 'the little dying one', and Doudou, her husband, seemed afraid to take him in his arms. 'Look what he's like, no bigger than a mouthful of bread.' Although Elie thought the circumcision might make him stronger, Motty, on the contrary, argued that they shouldn't submit him to it until he'd gained more strength. And: 'The Arabs don't circumcise their boys before the age of five.' The debate went on, endlessly: 'What the Arabs do isn't necessarily good—it's not necessarily bad, either.' Each day, they postponed the circumcision to the next.

After withdrawing the amulet from under Esther's mattress at the end of the allotted time, Uncle Elie examined it. He thought he noticed that the alephs had been lightly erased. He concluded it should be the first letter of the child's first name, hence, Elie. Motty pointed out that it was also the first letter of the name Abraham. They agreed. Esther protested, arguing that aleph was the most frequent letter in a Hebrew text and proved nothing. She knew he was Maimon, she felt it in her heart, her little Nasr. A mother's heart cannot be mistaken. Poupy, whose comments always swung between criticism and derision, offered a new hypothesis. 'They'll always have to remain united under the amulet,' he began.

'And then?' interrupted Maleka.

'And then—till when?' answered Poupy. It rhymed. 'Since the girl's name is Masreya, "the Egyptian woman", why not call him Yehudi, "the Jewish man"? Huh?'

'No,' Elie said, 'By that logic, we should call him Masri, "the Egyptian man". Masri and Masreya. What do you think?'

They decided once more to put it off, the name as well as the circumcision.

And they placed the amulet under Jinane's mattress. On the first day, they didn't notice any change. But on the second, a small young man appeared, out of breath, at Maleka's house, asking for Jinane. He'd gone to a lot of trouble to find her. He'd been sent by Hassan al-Shebab's wife, with an urgent message for Jinane. A music-hall producer, Marwan al-Halim, wanted her for his next production. He'd been impressed by her singing at the hashish den, and he was planning to mount a sort of musical comedy around her cross-dressing character. She needed to understand that it was a very promising offer. She would know glory, she would be the new Munira al-Mahdiyya, they would record her songs on the new machines and everyone around her would grow rich.

The boy punctuated his words with little leaps of joy. Jinane burst out laughing. It was the first time anyone saw her laugh like that.

'Why are you laughing at me?' the boy asked, turning red.

'It's no use for you to leap like that, my boy! You look like those little monkeys in vests you see in the markets.' (And she burst out laughing again.) 'The monkey in the vest, the red vest over his red arse.'

Everyone hooted, and the boy ended up laughing as well.

'Should I return an answer to the Maalem?' he asked.

She rummaged through the folds of her dress, unearthed a riyal, quite a nice coin, and handed it to him. 'You can go tell Maalem that I will answer him at the end of forty days!'

Two days later, more emissaries arrived. The amulet was especially active, it seemed. There were three of them, dressed in long striped galabias and caps, each with a thick moustache that obscured his face. They smelt of sweat and dust. They'd completed a long journey, first from the village of Kafr al-Amar to Damanhour on a donkey's back; then on a train for the first time in their lives, in those wooden third-class carriages that make a hellish noise. They had been so frightened that they hadn't opened their mouths in six hours. The two sheep they were pulling at the end of a rope seemed less anxious than the three strappers. They reached Cairo station, Bab al-Hadid or 'the Iron Gate'. Then they wandered for a long time through the city, dragging their two animals among carriages, automobiles and walkers. They were jostled in Ismailia Square; with difficulty they'd made their way among bankers and officials in European dress. There, a policeman had threatened to take them upstairs to the police station if they didn't get their filthy animals off the street. Not able to stand it any longer, the eldest had reacted,

'Because you don't know, my prince, that the meat you eat has a head, feet, and shits?' The policeman, dressed in white like an admiral, had shrugged and blown his whistle with all his strength. They'd finally reached Mouski Street, which they'd gone along for a whole hour before finding the entrance to the neighbourhood. But here they were, safe and sound, wishing to speak to beautiful Jinane, their child.

'May your day be like orgeat syrup,' Tofa'ha welcomed them, 'liquid and sweet.'

'May your day be for good, and may God keep you, beautiful woman!' answered the oldest of the three.

'You look tired, my uncle. Come, enter the house and drink a glass of water or a cup of tea.'

They explained to Tofa'ha that they were peasants from the village of Kafr al-Amar, a village where the wheat grows so high that when you're in the fields you can't see the minaret; where the chickens lay eggs as fat as eggplants. They'd been sent by Jinane's father, Sheikh Ali, the imam, who'd heard that his daughter had brought a child into the world. This child was their child. Not knowing if it was a girl or a boy, they'd brought with them a ewe and a ram, one for the naming, the other for the feast. They acted as if they were about to leave. When, from her room, Jinane heard her uncles' words, she couldn't hold back her tears. For more than ten years she'd thought she was an orphan, and now, in one day, little Masreya had brought her the village's warmth and her father's protection.

'Is that Jinane I hear crying?' asked the old man. 'Tell her that her father asks only to convey God's blessing.'

The three messengers remained in Haret al-Yahud for three days. The ewe was slaughtered for Masreya, but the ram enjoyed a reprieve.

They were still wondering about Zohar's circumcision. They appealed to the oldest male in the family, Uncle Elie.

'So?' asked the two anxious parents.

'We'll circumcise him next year, at the same time as the second son that may be born to you, *Insha'Allah*, God willing.'

And the two breathed a sigh of relief, so sure had they been that the little sickly one would not survive the cut of the covenant; the aunts, too, and even Elie, who'd just made the decision, and who added, 'The Torah tells us, "I have set before you life and death. Therefore, choose life!" '

That's how it happened that the child was not circumcised. A few days later, the ram was slaughtered and a great feast was held for Zohar's naming. Because, to make an end to it, they'd abandoned all the other names. They'd given him the first name Zohar, simply Zohar. Thus he was called Zohar Zohar, translated by some as 'jewel of jewels'.

Figtree Street

Summer should have started long ago, yet it rains every day in Paris, a cold, grey rain that blurs the landmarks.

A childhood between life and death—ever since my birth, and for a long time after, for years. As a nursling, I never stopped crying. I barely ate. I looked like those undernourished waifs whose pictures you sometimes see in magazines, with legs and arms like matchsticks and a big ballooning belly. It seems I didn't walk until I was two, didn't utter my first word until I was four. I never smiled, refusing to look at whoever was talking to me. Growing up in two tiny rooms on the mezzanine, the back room of a grocery, I couldn't find my place between my parents who loved each other passionately: my mother Esther, who became more of a sorceress by the day, devoted to hysterical fits, and to whom people came from the other end of the country to have their fortunes told; and Motty, my blind father, a kind of autistic man—today, we might say he had Asperger's. He knew by heart not only the prayers he'd memorized but also the account books. It was his job: official accountant for the Jewish merchants in the metalsmiths' souk. When he wasn't reciting lists of numbers in his beautiful voice, he was chanting the Song of Songs.

There's something about marriage that makes it impossible, institutionalizing the notion of love as a natural need. Love is not a need, nor is it even the result of desire—when it arises, love is always a rupture in the world's order. That's why true spouses, those who love each other despite marriage, touch each other only rarely and then always in accordance with some ritual.

As soon as I understood human language—it seems this happened relatively late—I realized that my mother repeated (the word 'repeated' is to be taken literally, for it was every day): 'Never marry a dark-skinned girl from the Delta, she could be your milk-sister. It's haram, forbidden!' Here, I should explain. Muslims, Copts, Orthodox, Karaites, Jews—we're all Egyptian. One law governs our marriages: the absolute prohibition against a milk-sister. You could almost marry your blood sister—your first cousin, for example—but in no case your milk-sister. Of course, I had no recollection of nursing. When I grew up, I learnt that I'd been saved by an Arab woman, a singer who'd spent forty days in my great-aunt Maleka's home. It was she who nursed me. I knew she had a daughter, my milk-sister, nothing more. But these were family stories. That's how they told them, the way you look at old photographs, laughing and joking. And then they moved on to other things. How to know what really matters to the Jews of Egypt, who've adopted *nokta*, joking, as their fundamental philosophy?

Time passed. Little by little, the economic situation improved. Some family members left the Alley of the Jews, going to live in Abasseya, an almost bourgeois neighbourhood, with clean buildings, big doors, lifts and marble staircases covered in rugs. One of my mother's brothers, Joseph—we called him Soussou—lived there. One morning, he came to fetch us from the hara in his automobile, a Model T Ford, the cars we saw in the silent films of Buster Keaton and Charlie Chaplin. His Ford was black—in those days, they were all black. He'd decided to take us to Alexandria, to visit the sea.

We all got in, my mother, my father, Aunt Maleka and her husband Poupy. Of course there were also Nanou, Soussou's wife, and their two children, Flore and Albert. I don't know how that old jalopy managed to hold us all. We left Cairo at seven o'clock. Every twenty kilometres, we had to stop to add water to the radiator. My father burst out laughing each time. He kept saying to my uncle, 'Soussou, you'd be better off taking a camel. It would drink less than your car!' And everyone laughed. It was a convertible—or rather, it didn't have a top, not any longer, only an enormous windshield that needed endless wiping with a wet cloth.

The sun had beaten down on us all day. It must have been around five in the afternoon. We'd just passed a little village,

Al-Baradi, when, at a turn, a sheep suddenly appeared, a small solitary sheep that had decided to cross the road. I was sitting in front, on my mother's lap. I screamed. My uncle couldn't brake. We heard a dull sound under the car's wheels. My mother screamed hysterically and Aunt Nanou fainted. The animal was dying on the side of the road. Soussou got out to examine the poor creature as it took its last breath. That's when we noticed a peasant, dressed in a long brown galabia, running towards us and brandishing an enormous knife. 'Come!' my mother shouted to her brother. 'Get in the car! Let's get out of here fast.' Instead, my uncle went towards the peasant. In Egypt, no one ever avoids a conversation. Panicked, we watched from afar. We saw the man gesturing, swinging his machete. Other peasants spilt out from a path and joined him. Then we saw them approaching the car. We were frightened. I heard the first one say to Uncle Soussou, 'What are you planning to do, *ya-ostaz,* "O my fine sir"?'

My uncle didn't hesitate an instant. 'May God bless you! I'll buy it from you, of course, my friend, I'll buy your sheep from you. Two pounds . . . '

Two pounds, that was some money! Maybe four or five times the creature's worth. Thrilled by the windfall, the peasant slit the sheep's throat right there and handed it to my uncle. My uncle stood there, with his arms dangling. What was he going to do with a whole sheep on our excursion? He suggested to the peasant that we eat it together, here, now, all together. The man was thrilled. He shook my uncle's hand for a long time. Then he went back to confer for a few moments with the others, then returned to Soussou, whom he kissed.

We parked the old Ford by the side of the road and off we went to the village. They welcomed us, clapping. The women ululated, as if at a festival. First they served us tea. Then they killed two other sheep and the families all gathered around us. We settled in. The women talked about clothes, the men animal husbandry. We chatted, we joked, we drank milk still warm from the water buffalo's udders. When night fell, the musicians arrived: the tarabokas, the simsimiya, the rattlers, the bendirs. They sang; we didn't know their music, but it was beautiful. At one point, the imam appeared; accompanied at first by only a small lyre, he chanted a religious song. It must have been inspired by a sura, for the others raised their open palms up to heaven, punctuating each stanza with 'amens'. I listened carefully to the words. I understood Arabic, of course, but the language of the Qur'an, poetic, of perfect purity—I couldn't understand one word out of two. My father, in contrast, seemed to know the song which he intoned with the imam. The villagers were pleased to hear my father's beautiful voice, trained through the psalms sung daily in his synagogue in Haret al-Yahud, the Haim-Capucci Synagogue.

Then the imam brought forward a young girl, and I was mesmerized. No one ever thinks about the passion children can feel for beauty. A wild girl, barefoot, with curly hair cascading to her waist. God, how beautiful she was! She had a pretty little brown face, with delicate features and big clear eyes, the colour of fresh almonds. He introduced her to the gathering, who already knew her, but he wanted to make it seem like a show. She was his granddaughter. Silence. Not shy, she held herself erect, proud, her head high.

First the simsimiya, in a long rain of semitones, that whispered the sadness of a motionless world. Then her voice rose from elsewhere, as if all the strings of the instrument began to play at the same instant, the perfect harmony of sound and wind. At the first word of her song—it was, I recall, *Ya-rohi*, 'O my soul'—at the first word, I fell in love with her.

She sang, then came to join us. We were sitting on the ground, tearing the rest of the flesh from the cutlets with our teeth. A man brought a goatskin pouch. He took a swig and handed it to my uncle. Soussou hesitated a moment, then drank. Then he took another swig before passing the goatskin to Poupy.

'What is it?' Poupy asked him.

'I have no idea. But it's good!'

He offered it to me; I drank. It was fermented camel milk—I learnt that years later. I took some more. The alcohol fumes began to fill men's spirits, and they rose to dance with their canes to the drums' rhythm. As for me, this first bumper of alcohol gave me the courage to speak to the girl. 'You're beautiful!' I told her.

That's what struck me, what drew me from my inner world—her beauty. Beauty, that strange quality that makes you think the world obeys an invisible order. I asked her, 'What's your name?'

'Masreya. And you?'

'Zohar!'

'Gohar?'

'If you wish.'

'Me, I'll call you Gohar.'

She took my hand and led me to a stable. We settled down in the straw. In the distance, we could hear the music, to which she was humming. I was looking at her, but I saw nothing. I looked at her more closely. When our eyes adjusted to the darkness, hypnotized by her lips, I heard her ask, 'Do you come from Cairo?' And without waiting for my reply, she continued: 'I'd like to live in Cairo.'

'Why?'

'I want to become a singer.'

'You sing well. Your voice—your voice is a bird's voice.'

'And a dancer too. Look at my legs.'

In the darkness, I couldn't make them out, but I'd admired them when she was singing. Her legs were fine and long, her gait that of a gazelle. She took my hand and placed it on her chest, inviting me to caress it. Her breasts were a promise, two tiny intense mounds that quivered like a bird caught in the hollow of your hand. My heart beat wildly. For the first time, I sensed the mystery of otherness. How to explain? I felt her pleasure in my own body. I was trembling. The more her breathing quickened, the more I felt myself there, beside her. I closed my eyes. She drew nearer, placing her lips on mine. It was warm, sweet, it was what had to be. It was—yes, that's it—it was what had to be. I kissed her. I don't know how I knew what to do. I was innocent. She was less so. In the country, people grow up closer to their feelings. We were glued to each other, not speaking, discovering desire and discovering each other. Her grandfather called her. We remained another moment, without moving, holding back our waves of anxiety, curiosity and, also, pleasure. He called again.

'I have to go.'

I was distraught. In the stable, the water buffalo mooed. I jumped. Masreya laughed. I wanted to stay there beside her. I wanted to stay there my whole life, beast among beasts, plant rooting itself in her as in the land. In one leap she rose and vanished into the night.

Let's see—that was in 1936. It was my first kiss. I mean, my first kiss of love. I remember, Farouk had just been enthroned. He was sixteen. I was eleven.

1942

Abul-Hassan Street

1932. Zohar wrenched himself from the Alley of the Jews with the same violence that had thrust him from his mother's belly. From the age of five, he ran everywhere, barefoot, dusty, eyes wild. When the residents of the hara found him on Mouski Street, they brought him back. His mother Esther welcomed him with a shrug. She never seemed concerned, simply curious. What was calling him away? Or rather, who? What being, what force? Sometimes she said, 'Let him run. Let's see where his feet take him.' Old Aunt Maleka scolded, 'Aren't you ashamed? He's your son. Do you have another?' Adina, vicious, added, 'Can she even make another?' The family had already waited five years for a new pregnancy. Tofa'ha lectured her, 'You kept him in your belly for nine months. Doesn't it break your heart when he disappears like this for days at a time?' Esther answered with words not one woman in the hara could accept: 'We don't know where he came from, only God knows where he'll go.' Her aunts knew she was mad, but that was no excuse. What was she thinking, abandoning her son like this to the street? Was she trying to get rid of him? Maybe she wanted to be alone with her husband? And they whispered among themselves that it wasn't good for parents to be too attached to each other. When adults think too much about love, children go to the devil. And when it's even more (you know what I mean) well, then—it's too much! It's normal for parents to argue about their children. A mother must take her son's side against his father, get angry with her husband on his behalf. As the Arab proverb has it: 'A son brings injury to his father.'

Motty's finances had improved. It was two years now that he'd no longer worked as the accountant for the souk's jewellers. With money lent by Elie, he'd started an alcohol business and was selling hundreds of bottles of *zbib*, that clear, fiery anisette. He sold it to the neighbourhood Jews, to Christians both Orthodox and Copt, and to the British who sometimes ventured this far into the bowels of old Cairo. As for Muslims, they commissioned a Christian to buy it for them. When people criticized him, accusing him of fostering immorality, Motty would reply with a laugh, 'For us Jews, drinking alcohol is a commandment from God. Don't we drink four whole glasses of wine on Passover eve? Isn't it a religious duty?'

In the morning, Esther helped him run the shop. But as soon as the sun began to go down, around four in the afternoon, she entertained women on Uncle Elie's mezzanine. She answered their questions, often about marital problems; she dispensed advice; sometimes she pulled out her cards, and the women knew then that she would tell their fortunes. She had fewer fits, or, rather, she knew how to recognize them by their first signs. Some mornings, she felt as if she were not herself—always after a dream, always the same one. She would see the wall of her room begin to pucker around a crack. Then it would open like the two lips of a scar, and a grimacing face would appear, a man's. Dressed in a long burnoose, the hood hiding his head, he would emerge from the wall. She recognized his voice as it intoned, 'A son should be beside his father.' Sometimes he was more specific, more insistent, even menacing. 'What have you done with my son?' he would scold. She understood the summons. She quickly made her way to Bab al-Zuwayla, to join the Arab women gathered around the kudiya. Most of the time, she stayed there just one night, sometimes for several days, but when she returned to Haret al-Yahud, wearing her red gown sprinkled with gold charms, her eyes shone like stars.

During her absence, the aunts took care of little Zohar, feeding him, dressing him, trying to tame him. When he was with them, he seemed quiet, right up until the moment when they looked away. Then he scampered off like a hare, disappearing for hours. When he returned, Maleka would ask where he'd been. He'd lower his head without answering. Once, he stammered out a phrase she barely heard: 'I'm looking for my friends.' Maleka slapped him. 'Your friends? At your age, you don't have friends, only relatives! Idiot!' He didn't shed a single tear—he never cried—but he dove between Maleka's legs and vanished for a day and a night. They thought he was lost. What could a six-year-old child who barely knew how to speak do for all that time in the poor districts of Cairo? He might have been run over by a cart, trampled by a horse—maybe he was dying, alone in the mud of the street, poor thing!

Motty, his father, who refused to intervene when it came to his son's upbringing, was taken to task. The aunts upbraided him for what they took to be his indifference. They pleaded with him to do something, to shout, to call him. Harassed by an enraged family, Motty wept and quietly lamented: 'O my Father! Where are you? Where are you my Father, you who had me survive until today? What to do, my God, what to do?' His head in his hands, he sat on the ground at the door of his shop. 'Sing!' Elie suggested. 'When Zohar was in his mother's belly, your voice calmed him. Sing, maybe he'll hear you.' And Motty found, as always, the verse from the Song of Songs that fit the situation. His lips closed, he hummed the tune, then he lifted up his voice, deep and clear in the night: 'Whither is thy beloved gone, O thou fairest among women? Whither is thy beloved turned aside? That we may seek him with thee?' Drawn by the singing, the women who'd left the house returned. They stood in front of the door, hearing those words in such pure Hebrew, those verses composed they say by King Solomon to glorify the people's love for their god.

Motty repeated the same verse, coming up with new harmonies each time. Then another verse came back to him from the Song, and this time, his voice was even stronger, like the ram's horn whose call we hear at the end of the Yom Kippur fast, 'Until the day break, and the shadows flee away, turn, my beloved.' He was silent. In the stillness, you could hear a small sound of approaching steps. And all at once, Zohar emerged from the night to fling himself into the folds of his father's long robe.

This story made the rounds of the hara, but it didn't lessen the aunts' anxiety. If on that night Zohar had returned at the sound of the Song, that would not stop him from leaving again, as soon as he had the chance. And no one knew where he wandered. The men reproached Motty for his indifference. 'You, a wise man, who know the texts by heart, how can you let your son roam like this?' Poupy argued. 'Do you want me to tell you? Your son is as light as a feather in the wind. One day he's here, the next somewhere else. Does a feather know where it will fall when it's swayed by the breeze? It's because he's not circumcised, because he hasn't entered into the covenant.' Not entered into the covenant? Did they want him in the cemetery at Bassatine? In the covenant, yes, but covered with earth—is that what they wanted? Doudou would then add, 'Do you know a single uncircumcised boy in all the hara? Come on! It's time! Circumcise him and his mind will open. He'll have access to reason.'

Oh really? Out of all the organs given to us by God, is it into this tiny bit of flesh that He's crammed the restraint of reason? True, the other boys never strayed from the hara, but they spent their days trying to snitch a hunk of bread or beg a few millièmes from a passer-by. And when he tried to gather them to transmit some Talmud, our age-old wisdom, they scattered like rats in the alleys' maze. What good had circumcision done them? The loss of their foreskins hadn't aroused their brains.

As always, Uncle Elie took Motty's part. 'Calm down, everyone! Zohar's circumcision can wait. He's not getting married tomorrow.'

The argument seemed convincing. The two others finally went along with the old man. It was urgent that they wait. In Egypt, no one likes anything that stops the river's eternal flow. In the days of the pharaohs, didn't they measure time with the water in the clepsydras? And Elie added, 'No one can tell if reason has developed in this child—for he speaks to no one.'

Everyone agreed. Zohar was like a stranger—a stranger whose language they didn't know, since they couldn't exchange a word with him; a stranger whose name, echoing like a mystery, was all they knew.

Elie let them talk, then his eyes lit up: 'As for me, I've seen him walking on his hands.'

Astonishment of the others. Amazement of the blind father who knew nothing of his son's physical prowess.

Elie continued: 'I even saw him doing somersaults like the monkeys in vests the Bedouins display in the souks.'

Poupy burst out laughing. 'The monkeys in vests who do backward somersaults!'

Just the mention of these animals, these humans in miniature held at the end of a chain, provoked his hilarity. Then Doudou recalled how one day he'd tried to take Zohar in his arms and the child had escaped, slipping from his grasp like a fish. 'And so I touched his stomach. It was hard as wood.'

'Strong and supple, like a monkey,' Poupy added, turning towards Uncle Elie. 'And so? He can walk on his hands—so?'

It was then that the old man revealed in hushed tones the plan he'd ripened in secret. The next night, he put it into action.

Once the Alley of the Jews was asleep, Elie and the two men left with little Zohar for a long walk. When they reached Abul-Hassan Street, in front an old three-storey building with *mashrabiyas* on its facade, they looked around. A feeble gas lamp was lighting the area so poorly that even a few yards away you couldn't make out any shapes. The street was deserted. Elie crouched, took the child in his arms and whispered for a long time into his ear. When he rose, Poupy could see a big smile brightening Zohar's face. 'Go!' Elie ordered. And the child clambered up the wall, tucking his bare little feet into crevices in the stone. Doudou couldn't restrain his delight as he watched him climb like a spider. 'Oh, that!' he exclaimed, 'Oh, that—what a devil.' Then he added, 'He's sensational!'

It was his word, and it would stick. 'He's sensational!'

When he reached the third floor, the child went in through an open window. The minutes flowed by. Poupy, who feared his wife more than he feared God, was the first to break the silence. 'If Maleka were to find out. If, tomorrow, the little one decided to tell her, what then?' None of the others took him up on it. He persisted, 'Well, I think if Maleka found out, she'd kill me.'

'Shut up, you milksop,' Doudou whispered, 'you're going to wake the whole street. Who thinks about their wives at a time like this?'

Poupy forced himself to banish his anxiety for a few minutes, but the child delayed his return, and this time, in a barely audible voice, he said, 'But what did you ask him to do, Uncle Elie?' Facing the others' silence, Poupy began to tremble like a fledgling fallen from a nest.

'Look!' Doudou suddenly exclaimed.

On the third floor, a sheet of paper was fluttering.

'Come down!' whispered Poupy to the child, making big hand gestures. 'Come back now! My God, what's he doing?'

Up there, Zohar, delighted, was brandishing the document.

'What is it? Are you ever going to tell us what he's brought?'

Once back at the grocery, Elie explained: 'What can I tell you? I bought four fifty-litre drums of oil. Abul Gheit, my supplier, so rich he has four wives and so miserly he keeps only two donkeys, made me sign a promissory note with terrible terms. I haven't even sold the contents of the first drum. When I realized I would be unable to pay him this month, do you know what he said? For every month that goes by without repayment, my debt will increase by fifty per cent.'

'He's a usurer!' exclaimed Poupy. 'And to think he's Muslim.'

'Usury is forbidden in Islam,' Doudou added. 'May God curse his faith!'

'And the faith of his mother!' Poupy added. 'And the faith of his mother's father!'

Elie carefully smoothed the sheet of paper he'd placed on the table. He moved his finger over the text as he went through it word by word. 'And so, here's the promissory note!' He waved the paper before their unbelieving eyes.

Then they smiled and laughed. 'It's definitely worth a glass of zbib.'

Motty, who hadn't slept while awaiting their return, uncorked a bottle. They drank straight from it—first Elie, then the two others, then Elie again.

'But tell me, Uncle Elie . . . '

'Yes . . . '

'How did this child who doesn't know how to read, who barely knows how to talk, how did he find your promissory note amid all Abul Gheit's papers?'

Uncle Elie winked, with a knowing look. 'I told him "A paper written in Arabic with a French signature." '

'That's all you said?'

'Yes!'

'He's as clever as a monkey!' Poupy said rapturously. 'He's sensational—sensational!'

Three months later, Poupy and Doudou wanted to be there when Abul Gheit visited Elie to demand the extravagant sums he considered his due. Elie agreed to pay for the merchandise, which he'd eventually sold, but nothing more. The wholesaler insisted on that sum plus the usury Elie had committed himself to in writing. Elie asked if he possessed any evidence, a piece of paper, an object he'd left as collateral. Had he signed a promissory note, say, or something like it?'

'What?' thundered the wholesaler. 'You want to challenge our contract? What kind of a liar are you? Yes! Yes, you signed something.'

'No, I didn't!' Elie protested with a smile.

Abul Gheit, who'd searched most of the night for the cursed paper, was growing flustered. His voice rose. That's when little Zohar showed up, no taller than the footstool onto which he leapt in one bound. Once more he was brandishing a sheet of paper.

'There it is!' shouted the wholesaler. 'It's a miracle! God always helps the faithful.'

'Give it to me!' Uncle Elie ordered.

The child jumped off the footstool, ran to the table and leapt onto it, still holding the paper in one hand. Poupy, who happened to be behind him, roughly tore it away. It couldn't be! He'd seen— with his own eyes, and they'd barely started the bottle at that moment—he'd seen Elie burn the promissory note, that remarkable evening when they'd returned from Abul-Hassan Street. It couldn't be the same paper—it was impossible. Where had it come from?

He studied it carefully. There was indeed an Arabic text that ended with a French signature: 'Elie Sroussi.' But Poupy didn't know how to read Arabic. 'It certainly looks like your signature, Uncle Elie.'

Doudou ripped the paper from his hands and read the Arabic text out loud: 'I thank lord Abul Gheit, wholesaler of grocery products, for having consented to a delay of up to one year for payment on four fifty-litre drums of olive oil, for a total of two hundred litres. Above all, and with all my heart, I thank him for having agreed to this delay without charging interest, out of kindness and for the love of God. Signed in Cairo, this 17 April 1932.' Doudou nodded his head in satisfaction and repeated: 'Out of kindness and for the love of God.'

'May our Father keep him, lord Abul Gheit!' said Poupy.

'Abul Gheit is a good man!' Elie reminded them. 'All these years, all I've done is congratulate myself on working with him. Let's go to my nephew's, blind Motty's, for a bottle of zbib. We'll celebrate this!'

'But, after all . . . '

'What's wrong, Abul Gheit? You refuse to rejoice with us?'

'Of course not! But, after all . . . '

'Well, what?'

'I'm Muslim! You're well aware of it, you rogue.'

'We know you're Muslim, we also know that's why you didn't want to charge any interest for the loan you offered our Uncle Elie.'

'I mean—I don't drink alcohol.'

'Well, for you, it will only be a cup of tea.'

And they burst out laughing. Abul Gheit nevertheless accepted a generous measure of zbib in his teacup and asked for more. The case concluded with the bottle's last drop. Once the wholesaler had left, the three men pondered the origin of this new promissory note, born as if by enchantment in Zohar's hands. They agreed that he certainly had not drafted this new version. It wasn't him. It couldn't be Poupy, who didn't know how to write Arabic. Doudou reminded them that he could never have penned such a document, he who was interested only in mechanical things. But who then? Who had drawn up this paper and how had Zohar got hold of it?

They spoke for a long time, two hours, and finally concluded that although Zohar had not written it himself—it was impossible!—it was through Zohar that it had arrived. That much was clear. There was no point questioning him about it; it was obvious he wouldn't yield any answer.

'Like a monkey, the little devil!' Doudou chuckled.

'Come!' grumbled Elie, 'This is serious. Maybe he used magic?'

'His mother's a witch,' Doudou reminded them. 'I'm not joking this time—a real witch!'

'In any event, he's sensational!' concluded Poupy.

And there they let it remain, at least for that day. Zohar's abilities would soon present other problems.

*

In the Bible, the name Gedaliah is associated with a crime that, in ancient days, had grave consequences. But the passage of time meant nothing to the Jews of the hara, contemporaries of the prophet Moses who'd forgotten them there when he left for the Promised Land, and of the other Moses, the philosopher Maimonides who arrived three thousand years after the first to remind them of the law. Gedaliah, you recall, had been appointed governor of Judea in 586 BC by Nebuchadnezzar II himself, to revive the province that was dying after the execution and exile of its elites. He was a just and courageous statesman, celebrated for having obtained the release of the prophet Jeremiah. But he had not been leading the country for more than seven months before Ishmael ben Netanya's tribe, stirred up against him by the King of Ammon, led him into a trap and assassinated him. It was a terrible loss for Judaea and the Jews. Ever since then, to commemorate this lamented leader, we observe a fast on the third of Tishri, exactly one week before the Yom Kippur fast.

But in Haret al-Yahud, Gedaliah was the name of a cafe where the consumers consumed nothing. Is that why it bore the name of a fast? Not at all—rather, it was because the owner was called Gedaliah and he ruled over a community of paupers. It was a cafe where men gathered every morning to play backgammon or dominos and trade tales of amazing nighttime adventures or daytime sorrows. It was also a kind of employment office, where the wealthy sometimes came, the khawagates, men who'd grown successful in the new Egypt of King Fouad, with its flourishing economy that drew immigrants from all over the Mediterranean. They would hire two or three strappers to help with a move; they'd ask for a minyan, the quorum of ten men for a funeral prayer; or they'd invite the poor to a thanksgiving feast, a *seudah*. On this morning, Soussou, Esther's brother, perhaps the only member of the family who'd seriously sought work, came back very excited from Cafe Gedaliah.

'Seudah! Seudah! Come quickly! Hurry! It's in a villa, oh my oh my—the di Reggio Villa.'

'No! You don't say.' Poupy marvelled. 'The di Reggios? Son of a bitch! In Zamalek? Son of a whore, you're not fooling, are you? May your faith be cursed if this is one of your tasteless pranks.'

'Hurry! Get ready! Take off your pyjamas, and, please, put some shoes on your feet.'

Poupy never took off his pajamas unless it was worth the trouble—to go to the synagogue, say, once a week on Sabbath eve, or during the Jewish holidays. Then he would don his only galabia, freshly pressed and perfumed with eau de cologne, putting his black jacket on over it, along with a gold chain to make people think he had a watch. He would slick his moustache with brilliantine, claiming it made him look like Garibaldi, and even place an old eyeglass lens, a kind of monocle scratched by time and falls, on his right eye. On his head he would stick a tarbouche, the only one in the hara that was purple, almost violet. Then, from under his bed, he would pull out his old pair of black shoes which he polished at least twice a day with spit and endless acts of love. He would admire himself in the mirror, call Maleka, his wife, and ask, 'And so? Hmm. Tell me. And so?' When she was in a good mood, she'd answer, 'Exactly like the sheikh of the alley!' But when she was in a bad mood, she'd fling out, 'It's not because you put henna on your donkey's arse that it becomes a pretty bride's face.' On that day, she was in a foul mood. He left with no further ado.

Thus outfitted, furnished with a stick masquerading as a cane, his head high, his proud gaze cast into the distance, Poupy passed in front of Darb al-Nasir, where the Haim-Capucci synagogue is found. He noticed little Zohar listening to the hazzan's chant. Zohar could spend hours there, his ear glued to the wall.

'What are you doing here, my son?'

The urchin raised confused eyes towards his great uncle. It would not have occurred to him to say that he was waiting for his father to sing a few verses from the Song of Songs, for he did not know it himself. Yet that was the music he was waiting for, like a sparrow accustomed to the crumbs tossed after a meal.

'Come with me! We'll eat cakes.'

And off they went, the two of them, looking for Soussou, Elie and the others, already on their way to the wealthy neighbourhood, beautiful Zamalek, flowering, perfumed, the garden of earthly delights. Poupy asked passersby for directions: 'Do you know the tram that goes to Zamalek?' Each one answered, 'This way, straight ahead—you can't go wrong.' And each one pointed in a different direction. Finally, it was the child, little Zohar, who, seeing a tram pass, pulled Poupy by the hand and urged him to jump on the footboard. Hanging onto the iron railings, creeping along at a snail's pace, amid the hubbub of the wheels and the shivering of the pavement, he asked him, 'But how do you know the tram, son of a dog?'

For once, the child replied, but Poupy did not hear him because of the racket. He asked again and Zohar repeated: 'Zamalek is the terminus!'

Poupy couldn't believe his ears. To himself, he repeated again, 'He's sensational!'

Salah al-Din Street, the di Reggio villa—a veritable three-storey Italianate palace, its ornate windows trimmed with blinding green shutters, huge doors with gold fittings and tall marble columns at the entrance. Two black guards, Nubians in white uniforms, were barring the way.

'We're guests,' Poupy proudly announced. 'Guests of lord di Reggio, may God acknowledge his good deeds and each day grant him twice the wealth of the day before.'

'The poor,' the guard immediately interrupted him, 'use the service stairs.' And pointed to a little path that circled the house.

'You are mistaken, my friend! You, a man of great wisdom nonetheless, come down from the cataracts of Nubia to brighten the sad streets of the capital with your dazzling smile'—an allusion to the two gold teeth the guard was making sparkle in the sun. 'We cannot take the service stairs—we are part of the family. Lord di Reggio will be angry, he'll think we are refusing to honour his house, he'll turn against you for refusing us entry, he'll send you back to your village, O my poor Abdu. Your master, you see, is his uncle'— pointing to the little one—'and he's my cousin!'—pointing to himself.

The guards remained impassive, like those at Buckingham Palace. They crossed their lances in front of the two louse-infested Jews, each lance surmounted by a blue and white pennant bearing the di Reggio coat of arms.

'Little one, go alert your uncle,' Poupy ordered.

And Zohar shot off like an arrow between the legs of the two Cerberuses.

'You little ass,' sputtered the guard, 'if you don't understand the language of the children of Adam, you'll understand the language of the stick.'

And, casting off the impassivity of a British guard, he chased the child up the stairs. Taking advantage of the ruckus, Poupy slipped behind the column and entered the palace. Impressed, he searched for words: 'What kind of a whore of a house!' he whistled. 'Even King Solomon's, I'm telling you, with its massive gold doors, was not as beautiful as this, may God forgive me!' And he fingered the velvet of the curtains, touched the brocade of the armchairs, inhaled, his nose in the air, the scents of vetiver. And he murmured, 'Gift of fate to people blessed by God. O Jacob (called Poupy) Shaltiel, the first, last and only son of Menachem Shaltiel, may God welcome your soul in his womb, you'd better pray much more than you do now, if you want to receive such rewards one day. You must be far off the mark, you mangy dog.' The grand staircase led him to the reception room, where he found himself beside the rich. No one paid him any mind; mesmerized, they were gazing at the lord of the house, Baron Ephraim di Reggio, descendant of bankers and advisers to the princes of Venice, now a banker and adviser to the King of Egypt, His Majesty Fouad I. He was entering to the sound of violins, holding the arm of a woman about thirty years old, slender, radiantly beautiful, attired in a lavish white silk gown. He led her to a raised armchair in the first row, bowed and kissed her hand, then helped her to a seat beside a rabbi in a black kaftan decorated with a minister's red silk sash.

'My dear friends,' he began, addressing the rich—the poor were behind him, hidden by heavy curtains. 'My very dear friends, thank you for having come here, to this simple house, to honour my father's memory, Baron Abraham di Reggio, who died exactly a year ago, on 15 Iyar 569, according to our calendar, which is to say, 2 May 1931, according to the Christian calendar. Thank you to Her Majesty, our Queen Nazli, the well beloved, for presiding over this benevolent meal. All of you know the devotion of my deceased father—may God protect his soul!—to the Jewish Community of Egypt. That is how I account for your presence, so many and so kind. Together we will say the Kaddish, our prayer for the dead, in memory of my father, and for each of our dead who died this year. We will then recite thanksgiving prayers. Then we will sing several psalms under the guidance of the Grand Rabbi of Egypt, Rav Haim Nahum Effendi, who has graced us with the signal honour of his presence. After this, you will consent to break bread in this house, you with whom I rub shoulders daily.' A moment of hesitation. He turned towards the drawn curtain: 'And you as well, our disinherited brothers of the hara, of Khoronfesh and the Mouski.'

A murmur could be heard behind the curtains, then, in unison, a loud 'Amen,' and immediately after, 'Amen, amen and amen!' Baron di Reggio was standing erect in his yachting outfit—perfectly creased white trousers, white shoes, a royal blue blazer. Some of his silver hair was peeking out from under his white cap. He had a proud bearing, stiff, his chin thrust forward, his eyebrows furrowed.

'I turn the podium over to our father, our master, our guide, the Grand Rabbi Nahum Effendi, master of justice, master of knowledge, as distinguished a historian as a theologian. The Grand Rabbi of Egypt—'

By dint of little sidelong steps, Poupy had managed to make his way to the enormous buffet laid out in the adjacent hall. As he passed, he gobbled two little meat pastries, stuffing three others into his galabia's huge pocket. In his haste to swallow them, he was seized by terrible hiccups just as the rabbi began his speech,

'Your Majesty, Queen of beauty and intelligence, may God shine upon your reign.'

Rabbi Nahum, his mitre on his head, a curious little beard on his chin, squinted myopic eyes behind thick lenses. From the other side of the curtains, you could hear a thundering 'Amen,' along with the burbling of Poupy's hiccups.

'Sir Baron, prince of business and prince of the heart, may God increase your wealth so that you might always, like today, come to the aid of our brothers in need.'

And from the room hidden by curtains a muffled sound arose. The poor were grateful. 'He is strong and he is blessed!' they shouted. Another hiccup, a double hiccup, and the rabbi went on.

'A tireless king has rendered our land prosperous and its people happy. Chance has it that, in this land, some are born rich and some are born poor. Know that the rich grow richer when they give to the poor.'

In the silence that followed this sentence, Poupy had an even louder hiccup, like a cymbal clash. The guards he'd eluded at the entrance were itching to jump him. A mere look from the baron stopped them.

'I would like to use this opportunity,' the rabbi continued, 'to remind you that the money you give in the temple on Yom Kippur is insufficient. You cannot donate just once like that and discharge in one gesture your responsibility towards your brothers. Are you heartless, like Joseph's brothers, who abandoned him in a dry well in the middle of the desert? Yes, my dear coreligionists, the money we collect is not enough to finance the schools, help feed the children, care for our aged relatives in need, maintain our temples and pay the salary of our rabbis. If you refuse to give . . . '

Poupy had finally made his way to a pitcher of water. He drank it all down happily, belched loudly, and couldn't keep from exclaiming, 'To the lion's health!'

'If you refuse to give,' the rabbi continued, furrowing his brows even more, 'if you refuse to give, you who have the means, God will take away everything you've accumulated. One day you'll find yourselves on a quay in the port at Alexandria, leaving for who knows where, nobodies once more, cast out to wander, your pockets empty and your eyes filled with tears . . . '

A voice could be heard from behind the curtains, the powerful voice of Doudou who was growing impatient: 'Hurry up a little, O lord! We're hungry.'

And a great burst of laughter.

'Come on! Move along!' someone else insisted.

'As it is written: "When thou hast eaten and art full, then shalt thou bless the Lord thy God." '

From the poor they didn't want to display, but whose presence was indispensable to the peace of the deceased, had risen a rumbling, like a wave threatening to break on a rock. Again they chanted, 'As it is written: "When thou hast eaten and art full, then shalt thou bless the Lord thy God." ' It was a verse from the prayer of thanksgiving the pious Jew recites after every meal. They were trying to say they'd be happy to thank God, but only after having eaten, not before. The rabbi, understanding the message, interrupted himself, thanked the host, his family, the Queen, her family, the community dignitaries and their families, the masses; and then, at last, he began to read the prayer for the dead.

'Oh no,' Poupy grumbled, 'there's more to go.' And, circling the buffet tables, he snatched up meatballs and spinach pastries as he went. Between two huge plates of *ful*, those mashed favas, primal substance from which Egyptians are made whatever their faith, his eyes suddenly lit on a shining object. 'What's that? Really—what is it?' he repeated into his beard with a smile. He drew closer. A silver spoon, most likely forgotten by a waiter. All the *sofragis* had of course been ordered not to leave any silver on the tables. The house knew the habits of the poor from the hara. One look to the right, another to the left. A little innocent gesture while turning his back to the table, and it was done. Then, pockets bulging with assorted foods and one silver spoon, Poupy began to edge away. Little discreet steps towards the columns that framed the stairs. Once there, he stood still, troubled. Zohar! Where had the rascal gone to? He hoisted himself onto the column's pedestal to look around. Nothing! Not a trace of the little devil. And Poupy thought again of Maleka, his wife, how she'd howl if he returned alone to the hara.

An idea suddenly came to him. What if the child had climbed up to the second floor? That would be just like him, the little monkey, always searching for heights. So he slipped into the staircase and reached the next floor, at the entrance to a long corridor. The first door was locked; the second opened onto some sort of storeroom filled with randomly stacked furniture; when he opened the third door, he was thunderstruck, his mouth agape. There was Zohar, comfortably seated in a deep, velvet armchair. He was wearing a white silk shirt, much too big for him, with sleeves that covered his hands. Next to him, an older child, maybe nine or ten, a rich boy, in British shorts and suspenders, high woollen knee socks, and a matching white silk shirt, tailored to fit. Each was smoking a gold-tipped cigarette. On the floor, the empty Craven A tin served as an ashtray. 'If Maleka could see this!' thought Poupy, who didn't dare imagine what would happen next.

'Zohar!' he scolded.

The child raised his eyes and for once answered. 'Yes, Uncle?'

Poupy leapt at him, grabbed him by the arm and tried to pull him away. The child arched back, his hands clutching the door frame, his two feet planted like a stubborn mule. He neither screamed nor wept but resisted with all his might. From the lower floor rose the songs and chants intoned by the poor and led by the Grand Rabbi of Egypt himself. The preliminaries were ending, soon the buffet would be opened—it was now or never for them to escape. In the crush, no one would pay them any mind.

Poupy tried persuasion. 'Let's go, O my son, O pasha, O my soul, what do you want, then? Tell me and let's get it over with, you brainless worm.'

Free to move again, the child readjusted the big shirt that went down to his knees, pulled on over his filthy little galabia, and gently approached the other child, step by step, like a little worried animal. When he was just a few inches away, he simply said, 'Joe!' Then he turned towards his uncle and repeated, 'Joe!'

'May the devil take you,' Poupy said, 'your new friend's name is Joe. Excellent. Delighted to meet you! Yes, yes. Delighted, I tell you, you jackass. His name is Joe. I'm honoured to learn his name and my heart drips butter. Now, come along, we're going back home.'

Wordlessly, little Joe led them through the maze of corridors to the service stairs; they ended up back in the garden without passing through the reception halls. Out of breath, Poupy looked at Zohar and smiled: 'And now, we're going to run to the tram, okay?'

The child had already taken off at top speed. When they reached the riverbank, panting, they sat on the grass. Zohar couldn't stop touching the silk shirt his friend Joe had given him. 'You're proud of your new shirt, is that it, you fool?' Poupy asked.

When Zohar didn't reply, he pulled out the silver spoon from his pocket. 'Look what I found on a table. It's beautiful.'

The boy grabbed it, examined it, sniffed it, touched it with the tip of his tongue, hefted it, made a face, and returned it to his uncle. Then he thrust his hand into the opening of his galabia and drew out a necklace sparkling with a thousand lights.

'What?' Poupy marvelled. 'What's that? Let me see!'

It was a magnificent piece of jewellery, with finely worked gold links, each enclosing a precious gem. The clasp was especially beautiful: on one side, the sort of boat that is the letter *noune* in Arabic; on the other, the hook that fit into it with a clever mechanism.

'No—don't tell me! But who are you then, child of the streets? Don't tell me, no. You frighten me. Yes, you do. And yet, you know, your Uncle Poupy is not a fearful man. You frighten me, you son of a dog. Don't tell me these are diamonds.' He rubbed one of the stones against his nail. 'No! Where did you find it? Huh?'

The child remained silent, a big smile on his face, delighted by his great-uncle's amazement.

'You'll answer me, this time, my little one. I mean—this is serious, you know—I could end up at the police station or—I don't know, in prison, maybe—O my eyes! Tell me who you took it from. O my master!' He implored the heavens. 'We'll return it to her. But to do that, we need to know who—or, rather, no! We'll bring it back, perhaps, give it to the two guards, and claim we found it in the garden and then, there we are.' He hesitated a moment, cast a glance skyward. 'No! We won't do that. Will we go and throw to a hundred thousand devils a gift sent by God himself? Or rather, no. I never heard of God sending a diamond necklace to his faithful. Oh my oh my! But why? Why? What sin have I committed to end up married to a witch's aunt? A witch whose son is a demon, an afrit.'

At that word, the child began to laugh.

'So that makes you laugh? Out of all the legions of devils, what kind of a devil are you? You laugh? So you smoke—and you laugh. Yes! That's it! That's the little Zohar! He smokes cigarettes and laughs at his Uncle Poupy.'

And he began to laugh in turn. The child exploded with laughter and the man as well, both of them now stretched out on the grass, as if seized by frenzy.

That evening, gathered with the others in the grocery, Poupy let himself be persuaded by Uncle Elie—but not without having first resisted—that they needed to return the necklace. The arguments were simple: they would certainly accuse the poor from the hara of having stolen it. They weren't going to suspect the Grand Rabbi or the baron's family, or one of those khawagates, those fine gentlemen. The police would storm the neighbourhood, search the houses. And then, the women would talk—they always did. The men would be taken to the police station, and, because they weren't foreigners, receive their share of beatings.

They weren't foreigners . . .

'What are you talking about?' Poupy asked.

The others looked at him as if he were dim. What? He didn't know? Uncle Elie patiently explained the very old law that allowed foreigners to benefit from special courts. In Egypt, when you were a foreigner, you weren't detained in the Egyptian police station, ruled by those brutes, peasants in uniform, who stank of onions and sweat and who shouted for no reason, but at the consulate of the country from which you came. And he presented the three men with a question: 'Tell me, you Poupy, for example, what's your nationality?'

'Egyptian!' Poupy replied without hesitation. 'I was born in Cairo, like everyone. And Cairo is in Egypt, right? Cairo belongs to Egypt like the fingers to a hand.'

'No!'

'What do you mean, no? So Cairo isn't in Egypt, is that it?'

'That's not it, you fool! I say no to explain that it's not because you were born in Egypt that you're Egyptian. Do you have an identity card, an Egyptian passport? Do you have any papers at all?'

'Yes!'

'You possess an identity paper, you, Jacob Shaltiel, son of Menachem Shaltiel, may God enfold him in his womb? Well, then—'

'Yes! The ketubah, the marriage contract the rabbi gave my mother the blessed day I left her thighs to join those of Maleka Zohar, your niece.'

'But that's nothing, that—it's nothing! Your wife's thighs are not a nation-state. Neither her thighs nor her arse you fool! You're like everyone else, an outcast from the hara. You have no papers, nothing! Is your name printed on a card, with a photograph and an embossed seal? Do you know what your nation-state is called?'

'No.'

'Listen carefully: it's not called anything. It's the opposite of a nation-state. A non-nation-state. I'm going to tell you what you are Poupy. You're stateless. *Apatride.* State-less. That's how you say it!'

In this Egypt awakening to modernity, so much so that people wrote in the papers that Alexandria was a great European port, most of the inhabitants of Haret al-Yahud were stateless—like Poupy, the naif with an open heart; like Doudou, the smart man with bulging muscles; like Elie, the silent one with tender eyes; like Motty the blind one, *a fortiori*. 'Stateless', political word, magical word which they repeated to each other, to say, simply, that they were nothing. And Poupy, who was discovering it, answered with a simple interjection: 'Toz!'

Which was more a sound than a word, the sound children make when they're pretending to fart with their mouths, a sort of interjection that means, 'These world events are nothing but wind.' And he repeated, 'Toz, toz and toz.'

'Toz or not,' Elie continued, 'Since you're neither a foreigner nor an Egyptian, no one will defend you. You're like an animal, Poupy. Have you ever seen anyone defend a donkey when its owner was beating it to make it move? You can go up and down all of Egypt and you'll never see anything like that. And so, toz on you!'

But another argument, presented by blind Motty, ended up convincing them. 'We simply have to wait a few days. They'll search for the necklace. Maybe they'll offer something, a reward, I don't know, to whoever finds it. That's when we'll return it, claiming we found it in the street or on a pile of junk. That way, at least we'll earn the reward money. It probably won't be much, but it'll be something all the same.'

Doudou, who already had a score to settle with the police, drew their attention to a problem. Motty's idea was good, yes, he agreed. But who would run the risk of returning the necklace? For, as the Arab proverb has it: 'Whoever tells me about an injury committed behind my back injures me.'

'Which means—?'

'Which means—the messenger is often punished for the bad news he brings.'

Doudou was sure that whoever risked returning the necklace would first be imprisoned, beaten, perhaps even locked up for months, maybe years. And the trouble with Cairo prisons was that while it was easy to find someone to put you in, it was much harder to find someone to let you out. And those wise heads of Haret al-Yahud had not even thought of that.

Then an idea crossed Poupy's mind, one of those solid, good ideas that solve a dilemma. 'I know!' he exclaimed. 'I know what we'll do. We'll send Zohar, the little one, to return the necklace. They won't imprison him. He'll put on a poor innocent look—he knows very well how to do it—he'll return the necklace and that will be the end of it!'

'This has gone on too long,' added Elie, 'it's enough! It's over. It's enough! It's over!'

'It's over?' asked Doudou. 'The reward too—it's over! Do you think they'll give the least bit of money to a child of seven?'

A week later, the men of the family were all gathered around Soussou and many others from the hara at the Cafe Gedaliah. They were so excited that Gedaliah brought them glasses of water, as in the grand cafes of Suleiman Pasha Square. It was an important occasion: one of them was being spoken about in the newspaper. Soussou was reading it out loud: 'Child Returns Necklace Lost by Queen Nazli at Zamalek Reception.' That was the front-page headline. A photo of the Queen leaning over graciously, stroking the head of a little boy in a galabia, just like the thousands of vagrant children you ran into everywhere on Cairo's streets.

'Listen! Listen to this,' Soussou continued, 'Oh, for the love of God! Unbelievable! "Her Majesty Queen Nazli, the mother, as we know, of four children, was moved to tears." '

And he repeated, 'Oh my, oh my, how beautiful! "Moved to tears," do you hear?' He continued: ' "Moved to tears before this poor child, inhabitant of a neighbourhood in the old city." '

Naturally, no one mentioned that Zohar was Jewish. The necklace, the Queen explained to journalists, had probably slipped from her neck when she was entering the car to return to the palace. "The child, whose name was Gohar ibn Gohar, was received in the Abdine Palace for an entire day." '

'Zohar, son of the blind man,' corrected someone, 'not Gohar ibn Gohar but Zohar ben Zohar.' And he added: 'At the royal palace, for the love of God. Blessed be His name!'

'It's certainly proof there's a God!' someone replied.

'And that He doesn't forget the forgotten,' concluded a third. 'Blessed be His name!'

'Whereas the forgotten forget Him—how long has it been since you've come to Sabbath service, you misbegotten bastard?'

'And do you know what?' Soussou went on. 'At the palace, he met the heir, Prince Farouk. God sees to everything! In the newspaper, they wrote that they played together. Farouk is nonetheless much older than he. He's eleven, I think.'

'Twelve!' corrected the other, drily.

What? He didn't know the prince's age? Everyone knows he was born in 1920.

'Okay! Okay! Twelve. But listen to the rest: "The necklace the Queen had lost and which she found again thanks to little Gohar ibn Gohar's honesty was specially made for her by a Parisian jeweller named Cartier. It is a true work of art worth several thousand pounds, part of Egypt's royal treasury." Several thousand pounds— enough to feed the whole hara for months.'

'And they don't specify how many—how many thousand. Several thousand—that's how many thousand?'

As his reward, Zohar received several royal gifts: a new galabia which didn't stay white for more than a day; a red skullcap he wore proudly; and a pair of leather slippers, much too big, which waited for two years under his bed. When he was brought back to the hara in an official black car, two pennants floating from the front fenders, his father, thanked at length, was granted a sack of rice, a drum of oil and a handshake from the chamberlain.

Calm returned to the Alley of the Jews, but the men would never forget that everything had been started by the child who'd pilfered nothing less than the Queen's necklace. 'Do you realize? Queen Nazli's necklace. He's sensational!' repeated Poupy. 'How did he manage it?' This question kept recurring, without an answer. Soussou, the most reasonable, claimed that the Queen had really lost it; Zohar, who trailed everywhere, simply picked it up. Much too banal a solution for the others. Doudou, more daring, thought the child had entered one of the rooms, perhaps where the Queen had left her things, and pocketed the necklace. 'He's a little thief, nothing more! Sufficiently quick and agile to take advantage of the moment, I suspect.' Poupy, who believed Zohar had uncommon abilities, thought he'd slipped behind Queen Nazli during the Grand Rabbi's speech, unhooked the clasp, then fled. 'Impossible!' argued Uncle Elie. 'Someone would have seen him, caught him, punished him. No! That's not how it happened. He must tell us.' And the old man redoubled his kindness to the child, trying to extract his secrets, always without success.

Because Zohar had demonstrated certain qualities, or at least some ability, they decided to send him to school. But it was impossible to keep him in his seat for more than a few minutes. Every attempt to settle him in failed. The family tried the schools available to the poor: first Rav Mourad's private lessons; then the Jewish Community's school; next, tired of fighting, the school of the Brothers of Saint Jean-Baptiste de la Salle; and finally, in desperation, the Qur'anic School. He never lasted a day. Which is why, the next year, when he began to work, no one objected. He assumed a trade known only to Cairo's inhabitants—*sabbarsagueya*, which might be translated as 'untiring collector of cigarette butts'. He scoured the pavements, foraging in gutters, a battered aluminium cup dangling from a string on his wrist. But although all the others sold their harvest by weight to a boss who made other children extract the old tobacco and roll new cigarettes in a shed, Zohar did all the work himself. He managed the whole cycle, from gathering the raw material to packaging the final product. Then he sold his cigarettes on the street at prices that defied all competition.

Industrious, focused on his task, he worked ceaselessly.

He worked so well that by the age of ten he was contributing much more than his share to the relative ease of his little family. He'd found an activity that suited his nature, outdoors from dawn until late at night, flirting with the secret desires of those he served, maintaining regular relationships with the shadows of the night, those smokers addicted to their drug. Out of nowhere, he arose beside the smoker in need—a man anxious before a rendezvous, a sated diner, an appeased lover—offering his cigarettes one by one, in little sachets of four, in packets of ten or twenty. He was called 'Zohar the Smoke', suggesting at once the substance he served and his ability to evaporate, like vapour. When people asked his mother, 'And what about your son Zohar?' she answered, 'We don't understand him. He's a good boy, but he floats above us, like smoke.' And when they asked his father, he answered with these strange words: 'Zohar is my father, maybe my grandfather, or older still. How can you expect me to know the motives of someone so old?'

Until now, Zohar had been true to form—since his birth, since his conception even. A stranger to his family, alone of his kind, indifferent to domestic matters—almost handicapped—and yet competent in certain realms. He went here and there, always alone.

He was abruptly transformed after the trip in Soussou's Ford and that night in the village of Al-Baradi near Damanhour. Since then, he spent long stretches of time lost in thought, motionless on his bed before falling asleep, and you could hear him talking in his sleep. You couldn't always understand what he was saying, but the word 'Masreya' returned often, and also, 'Come, come live in Cairo.'

His mother, having understood his words, was so frightened that she fainted.

'What's wrong, O my eyes?' asked Motty, her husband. 'What worldly commonplace has come to pierce your soul's sheath?'

'I heard our son talking in his sleep.'

'Why would that trouble you, O my sister? When angels appear in dreams, the dreamer sometimes answers them. And that often happens to children. Don't we say that, asleep, children have not yet forgotten the language of angels?'

'It's not that, Motty! Listen to me! He was naming Masreya, his milk-sister. He was calling her, begging her to join him.'

'I don't understand your reaction.'

'Listen to me, Motty! I took great care not to reveal his milk-sister's name to him.'

'Someone else might have spoken to him about her, why not? Probably one of the aunts.'

'No, Motty!' There was passion in his voice. 'A mother's heart can never be mistaken. He's in love.'

'At his age? It's impossible. You're making things up, O my beloved. And how could someone be in love with a memory that dates back to the first days of his life?'

Esther was not mistaken. Zohar, only eleven years old, was obsessed with the young Masreya whom he'd met only once. The furtive moments lived during that extraordinary night had become the background of his mental landscape, the earth on which his existence unfurled. Masreya's name echoed in his ears at each instant of the day. He smelt her body's fragrance, tasted her lips' flavour. He ran his hands down his own torso, imagining it to be hers; his legs, also hers. By day, during his walks through the alleys of the old city, he secretly called her; at night, he did the same during his dreams. He began to save, millième by millième, with the thought of one day buying a third-class train ticket to her village in the Delta.

Zamalek, Salah-al-Din Street

Three years later, Zohar and Masreya found each other again, under circumstances no one could have foreseen.

One day, news came that Joe di Reggio, son of the man people called 'the cotton baron', was requesting Zohar's presence. Joe's parents found the demand preposterous. What could their son, their only son and heir, have in common with those commoners who lived in the foul alleys, swarming like rats? Still, they gave in, but only under one condition: it would be an educational opportunity— as much for the millionaire boy with disastrous outcomes in his studies as for the louse-ridden child from the hara. Zohar's visits took place under the watchful eye of Mademoiselle Solange, a French-woman certified to teach philosophy. Zohar didn't go often, only when Joe asked for him, but his visits to the di Reggio palace gave him self-confidence. That's where he finally learnt the art of speech and how to handle languages. 'We thought he was *maboule*'—it's the same word in Arabic as in French, meaning 'simple-minded'— Poupy declared ecstatically when he saw Zohar's progress. 'For us, he didn't know how to talk,' Elie explained. 'The truth is, he hadn't found anyone to talk to.'

It must be said that Joe di Reggio, Zohar's millionaire friend, was, in a way, under house arrest. Of course he owned everything a child could dream of—even a little motorcar which ran on petrol like a real one, a half-scale reproduction of a Bugatti 35—but he couldn't go past the perimeter of the Zamalek property, neither in his car nor on his pony nor on foot. He went out only when accompanied by his parents, his governess, or—in an emergency—by the two Nubian guards. His parents feared bad influences. Mademoiselle Solange ini-tiated him into general culture, and two private teachers, also French, instructed him in sciences. But Joe learnt nothing. Stretched on the sofa in his silk garments, he spent his time daydreaming as he watched kites fly in the sky. He was a good-looking child, with long limbs, an open face, an angelic smile, wild hair and burning eyes. It seems that Mademoiselle Solange, who at twenty-eight had known only young girls' boarding schools, was a little in love with him—she doled out affection at every turn.

Despite all this, the only time Joe paid any attention to his masters' lessons was during his friend Zohar's visits. Although much younger, Zohar easily memorized scientific explanations, mathematical theorems and French poetry. Joe was most deficient in religion. Twice a week, Rabbi Bensimon came to prepare the boy for his bar mitzvah, the religious coming-of-age ceremony expected of every Jewish boy on his thirteenth birthday. For that, he needed to understand enough Hebrew to read a Torah verse before the community gathered in the synagogue. But at thirteen, Joe still hadn't managed to memorize the alphabet.

'He's so clever he can't possibly be interested in those clichés about the creation of the world—as if such a trash heap could ever have been created—or in that cheap morality your rabbis peddle,' his mother complained. She was a political progressive, close to the communists, and naturally anticlerical.

'Maybe,' scoffed the Baron, 'but, by dint of being too clever, he's well on his way to becoming an illiterate fool.'

Because Joe managed, however, to heed his instructors in Zohar's presence, they decided to invite Zohar to the house twice a week, to coincide with Bensimon's lessons. And this time, the mayonnaise seemed to thicken—Joe's progress was spectacular, stimulated by Zohar's presence and his endless questions. 'For an apricot?' one of them would ask. 'You say the blessing on the fruit of the tree, of course,' the other immediately replied. 'But for apricot paste?'—which they both adored—'Hmmm. Do you also say the blessing on the fruit of the tree or the one for cooked food?'

The two boys competed to remember details of religious rules, prohibitions about foods, rituals; they could recite the daily prayers in their entirety. Joe, who a few months earlier could not decipher a single letter, surpassed Zohar at reading Hebrew. But Zohar, who listened every day to the prayers chanted by his father, was better at memorizing. They learnt as they played—their play was learning, their learning, play. They looked like two lion cubs being initiated into the hunt as they nibbled each other's ears.

Two years later, the Baron, proud of his son's progress, decided to celebrate the bar mitzvah on Joe's fifteenth birthday. He was late, to be sure, but. with the skills he'd acquired, he would not embarrass his father who wanted to invite his community's elite to the ceremony. Rabbi Bensimon suggested that his co-disciple, the young Zohar Zohar, be initiated on the same day, even though he would not be quite thirteen. They planned to hold the ceremony in Cairo's grand synagogue, Sha'ar-Hashamayim, 'The Gates of Heaven', on Adly Street, in the elegant Ismailia district.

But the ceremony nearly came to a very bad end. Joe, the older boy, was called up first. Without hesitation, he read the verse he'd been assigned, carefully following the silver finger that the rabbi made dance on the parchment to guide his eyes, word by word. But when it was his turn, Zohar embellished his reading with personal commentary: 'Seize the Egyptians' goods before you leave Egypt. Do not hesitate! Gold bracelets, rings, necklaces—necklaces above all!' No one caught the allusion except Poupy, who stifled a guffaw. 'If you know a rich Egyptian woman, steal her ring, tear off her earrings. Heap up jewels stolen from the Egyptians, hide them in your cabinets, under your beds, in nooks and crannies in your walls, in preparation for your departure. One day soon, another Moses will tally your gifts when the house of God is built.'

Alarm among the assembled. Yes, the verse told of the construction of the Tabernacle, the Ark of the Covenant, with the help of offerings, the gold and silver gifts the Jews had taken from the Egyptians before the Exodus. But no one saw any connection between the present day and the mythic tale of a flight from Egypt in the time of the pharaohs.

Yet those Jews of Egypt might well have been thinking about departure—for in the distance you could hear the jackboots pounding Europe's pavements. During those days of oriental ease, no one dreamt they might have to leave their native land, the land of their ancestors and the ancestors of their ancestors, from time immemorial—Egypt!

Motty, the bar-mitzvah boy's father, shook his head, mortified. 'What do you expect?' Poupy whispered into his ear, 'He isn't circumcised, it's not normal! His bar mitzvah most certainly can't unfold normally: "As your circumcision is, so your bar mitzvah will be." Isn't that what we say?'

'It's not the scandal that saddens me, O my brother,' Motty murmured, 'but the words he's uttered. I know it's not Zohar speaking—forces are speaking through him.'

Everyone acted as if they didn't understand, attributing the child's outbursts to his mental deficiency or lack of education. That's how, on the fifth day, 30 Adar 5698 according to the Hebrew calendar, or Thursday, 3 March 1938 according to the Christian calendar, Giuseppe di Reggio, known as 'Joe', and Zohar Zohar, known as 'the Smoke' (al-Dokhan in Arabic), joined the community of believers. 'Amen and amen!' was the cry heard on the Zohar family side, or again, 'He is strong and he is blessed,' while the di Reggio family shook their heads scornfully at the loud remonstrations of their needy brothers.

The following day, Friday, 4 March 1938, in the Arabian Desert, near the little port of Dammam, the geologists and engineers of Standard Oil were jumping for joy, yelling like madmen. They tossed their hats into the air and grew hoarse as they thanked God, America and luck. After five years of effort, the drill had reached a depth of one thousand, four hundred and forty one metres, and black oil finally gushed forth in waves. From then on, oil would fill the pockets of the Saudis, and King Abdul Aziz ibn Abdul Rahman ibn Saud would have no further worries about how to feed his thirty-two wives and eighty-nine children. A page in world history had just been turned; a new page was beginning, one that would see the Jews driven out of all the Muslim countries, beginning with Egypt.

Through what channels had Zohar intuited this?

The following Saturday night, at the close of Shabbat, Baron Ephraim di Reggio held a reception to celebrate his son's bar mitzvah. All the elite were in attendance, drawn more by the pomp of the Zamalek palace than by young Joe's religious awakening. Here was the imposing Joseph Aslan de Cattaoui Pasha, King Fouad's old Minister of Finance and president of the Jewish community, his white hair spilling out from his tarbouche and his clear opal eyes gazing from afar on his people's fate. Also the prince of finance, Salvatore Cicurel Bey, one of the owners and managers of Cicurel Department Stores in Cairo, who made heads turn when he sat at the wheel of his electric-blue, sixteen-cylinder, late-model Cadillac convertible, just like the president of the United States. And the banker, Daniel Curiel, financier to sultans and princes, neighbour of the di Reggio's, whose villa, surrounded by an immense park planted with palms, adjoined the Gezira Sporting Club. Huge, with a big bare head, his eyes hidden behind dark glasses, he came forward, hesitating, blind, on the arm of his wife Zephira, his guide, his beloved. And Raymond di Piciotto, another baron; Isaac Levi, an industrial magnate; the two cousins, the celebrated Mosseri bankers. Baron di Reggio could be proud, everyone who was anyone was there: the Menasces (also barons), patrons of the community who had arrived, brimming with snobbery, at the wheel of the latest Citroen, a Traction; the Suares, so identified with the Cairo tram that people didn't say, 'I'm taking the tram,' but 'I'm taking the suares'; the Ades, of the Ades department stores; the Rols, the Toledanos, the Hararis . . . All those who'd once carried their bundles in Haret al-Yahud, some in antiquity, others five hundred years or barely a generation ago and who were now making their way in Egyptian society. For it must be said that the Jews of Egypt, those in wool suits as much as the idlers in galabias, all came from the same cesspool, those few narrow streets crammed with synagogues and saints' tombs, known as the hara, the alley.

For good measure, the Baron had also invited Zohar's entire family. They'd dressed as for a holy day at the synagogue, travelling as a tribe with their noses in the air, through the alleys to the tram station, then besieging the door of the villa and insulting the Nubian guards.

'Didn't I tell you that your boss is my cousin?' boasted Poupy as he tugged the sentinel's moustache. 'O my son, O my soul, never scorn the stranger. How do you know he's not an angel?'

On a platform, an orchestra—with a profusion of violins, a piano and some brass—was playing nightclub music nonstop. The baron and his wife were greeting their guests with princely grace, addressing special thanks to each. A superb speech by the president of the community, who, for this occasion, had pinned on all the medals he'd earned in service to the state. His chest sparkling under a rain of light, he expressed his pride at the success of these ancient Jews enriching eternal Egypt. A grand buffet, where shadows circulated through the groves to discover, here some alcohol, there some little sought-after petit fours. Sweetness of a night in March on the banks of the Nile, when women could for a change display their foxes and their otters, and men their smoking-jackets. Beneath a tamarisk entwined with jasmine, Motty was seated in an armchair, his wife Esther beside him. He hoped to speak to the rabbi, Vita Bensimon, who'd secured the young men's education. He had a favour to ask.

'May your night be like honey, O my master!'

'May our Father keep you, O son of goodness!' the rabbi replied, 'and send you a dove to take a crap on your eyes, as He did for our ancestor Tobias, when He wanted to restore his sight.'

'From your lips to God's ears, O my master. But do you think if I regained my sight I would see at night as I do now? I perceive your soul, child of joy, it is light, like your blood. How pleasant is your company!'

'Thank you, Mordechai Zohar. Your words are sweets that gladden the heart, like the wealth of our people I see displayed here tonight.'

'As for the wealth of these people who've invited us, my heart trembles, like yours. It's not good to show off like this. As the Prophet Mohammed advised, we should stop eating while we're still hungry. Wise advice our wealthy would do well to heed. Do you know that I knew your father?'

'You're luckier than I. He departed, may God enfold him in his womb, when I was only five. How could you have known him, since you're not very old?'

'Well, I was only eight days old when I saw him. At that age, my eyes weren't yet withered. He's the one who cut me.'

At the thought that his father had circumcised Motty, Bensimon burst out laughing: 'You must have a lovely clean bird, then, smooth and round. Among all the circumcisers in Cairo, my father was known as an artist.'

They began to discuss Zohar's behaviour during the bar mitzvah, his shocking remarks in front of the rich and powerful. They were in agreement—it wasn't done! You didn't voice such prophecies in public. Who was he, after all, this urchin? Motty confessed his anxiety to the rabbi, who nodded. To Bensimon, Zohar was certainly an intelligent boy but one who used his gifts only when he chose. Motty then told the rabbi that Zohar had not been circumcised because he'd been too sickly at birth and they had feared for his life. This information plunged the rabbi into deep perplexity. The father repeated his question: was it the lack of circumcision that made Zohar so strange, as the men in his family were constantly telling him? Bensimon was a wise man, steeped in religious lore since his most tender youth. But though he searched his memory in vain, he could not find a comparable case that might have guided his deliberation—neither among the children he'd been responsible for nor in the books he'd studied. He didn't know how to answer, except to advise the father to have his son circumcised before his first sexual relations. He added that it was more than time, for he'd noticed fuzz on Zohar's upper lip. But Motty was against it. Someone who hasn't been circumcised in infancy can only be circumcised at his own request. They could not impose such an ordeal on a child if he did not long for it with all his soul, to go beyond himself in some way. If not, it would be a punishment, and entrance into the covenant should never be a punishment.

Bensimon scratched his goatee. Motty's words seemed sensible. But in that case, what to do?

'Would you do me a favour, O my master? You see I am deprived of my eyesight. As you might imagine, I cannot write.'

'Certainly, O child of light, my hand is yours, my pen will obey your voice the way rain obeys the voice of God.'

'The ninth psalm—could you write out the ninth psalm on parchment and give it to Esther, my wife, my eyes?'

The psalm reputed to protect a person from demons—Motty was convinced that such a parchment, enclosed in a leather pouch, would be an effective talisman for his son if he wore it around his neck.

The evening had progressed. Zohar and Joe were the only children allowed in the garden with the adults. Was this not the day of their arrival at religious maturity? That's when Baron di Reggio stepped onto the platform and, taking the microphone, announced to his guests that it was time for the surprise, the one they'd all been waiting for—an oriental orchestra, indeed, straight from a village in the Delta, not far from the land owned by his neighbour; he pointed to Lord Daniel Curiel. The orchestra would accompany a singer. He could already see women swooning, men closing their eyes in anticipation. He'd chosen—guess who? The extraordinary musician everyone was talking about in the papers . . . a murmur swept the crowd gathered around the platform.

'Yes! You've guessed it. You can't even imagine—the one they call Kacimo Madrid, the prince of the oud. I've chosen—Mohammed Abdel Wahab!'

An ovation rose from the assembly, like the roar from a lion's breast. The popularity of Abdel Wahab, who'd revolutionized Egyptian music, was huge. His voice, said to be 'of velvet'; his gift for the oud, the oriental lute; his true knowledge of music; and, especially, the texts of the poet Ahmed Chawki, which he set to music—all this had made him, for some ten years, a veritable idol. Women dreamt of his face with its ethereal beauty; men copied his clothes—his striped ties, his three-piece suits, his tarbouche worn to the side, his handkerchiefs folded like roses. His lover's laments, broadcast by radio into the most distant villages, were sung by all Egyptians.

He was so well known that when, after a long violin introduction, he emerged from the shadows to begin his most recent song, the wealthy wives could not keep from softly singing, 'Run, run, run . . . Take me, carry me . . . Let's go, hurry . . . my darling awaits.' Another long violin interlude, then the entrance of the percussionists, the taraboka players, villagers in galabias who tapped out the hoof beats of the carriage's horses. 'Take me with you . . . carry me. I want so much to be like you, compelled by fate. Run, run, run . . . ' He repeated the same verse over and over, accompanied by the percussion, on a bed of violins, led step-by-step with his lute solo.

Suddenly, a beat of the bendir, and a young girl emerged from the shadows. Very young, her nymph-like figure seemed like a pistil in a corolla of veils; her rhythmic step echoed the slow pace of the carriage. She undulated, twining around the love-stricken notes. It was a surprise. Everyone knew that Abdel Wahab enjoyed duets. He'd just included one in the film, *The Tears of Love*, as romantic as an American musical comedy—a popular triumph! But such a young girl, so gracious, at once enticing and forbidden—was he in love? Yes, that would explain the presence of this very young beauty. Really? Was it even possible—he, the solitary, melancholy singer? The women cried out. And his tender voice continued, 'The sun has come out. It has fallen asleep and awakened. The sun has come out. And I, I can find no one to carry me . . . Run, run, run . . . Take me to her . . . ' And the young girl fluttered from one end of the platform to the other. She drew near him, slowly, like a shadow, like a double. 'They've torn out my heart, they've torn it out . . . They've told me it lived with another. And my heart has remained with her . . . ' Here she was, drawing near again, clinging to his clothes, literally winding herself around his body with inflamed passion.

It was at that moment that she sang. Her voice was delicate, high, precise: 'O God, O God, why? Why have you taken him from me? Why have you punished me so?' She accompanied the final words with a kind of deep groan, rising from within. Then they sang the refrain together, his low notes matching her high ones, like legs twining around legs. 'Run, run, run. Take me, carry me . . . '

Their song did not last more than ten minutes, but it brought the whole crowd, as if hypnotized, around the stage. Abdel Wahab bowed, took the young girl by the hand, introduced her to the audience: 'Ladies and gentlemen, for the first time onstage, so young, yet already a queen, a prodigy of song and dance, I present to you Ben't Jinane—'

Zohar, who'd slipped into the first row, tugged Joe's sleeve. 'It's Masreya! Masreya! She's come. I called her in my dreams and she's come to me.'

'Are you mad, Zohar? It's true, she's beautiful, yes, she's beautiful. But from that to believing she's come to see you—'

Abdel Wahab sang three more duets. The young girl accompanied him; she danced and sang, adding now her body to the spaces between his words, now her voice to his long, elaborated notes. Then she was snatched by three villagers dressed in black, and they all disappeared into the di Reggio house.

Zohar, who was watching her every move, set off on tiptoe in pursuit, hugging the walls, hiding behind a column in a hall corner. Joe, caught up in the game, followed him like his breath. One of the women, along with the girl, entered an attic room, one of those assigned to the servants. The two youths crouched in the corridor, silent, their hearts beating. From time to time, Zohar went to the door, pressed his ear to it, and, hearing voices, quickly returned.

Towards midnight, Abdel Wahab climbed the stairs heavily, alone, and knocked at the room's door.

'If he's coming to make love to her, I'll kill him!' whispered Zohar.

'Kill him right now, then!' teased Joe, 'How will you manage it, you swaggerer?'

In the hall's darkness, Joe saw the knife blade shining in Zohar's hand. 'Most definitely, you're mad!'

'It's Mohammed!' Abdel Wahab shouted. 'Open up!'

One of the villagers came out and pushed the singer back, gesticulating. He struggled against her, trying to break free.

'Let me in!'

'Not on your life! I'll die before I let you in, you son of a dog! And stop shouting, night bird, you'll wake the little one.'

They argued for a moment on the doorstep. At each of his efforts to enter, the old woman, clearly the guardian of the young girl's honour, shoved him away with both hands.

'Let me in, you plucked crow.'

'If I'm a plucked crow,' the old woman spat out, 'you're nothing but a clinging louse. Do you know what I do with lice? I pick them out one by one and throw them into the fire. You'll see how your soul will burn in hell. Go and sleep off your wine in your own room, or, trust me, I'll wake the whole floor.'

Weary of battle, Abdel Wahab retreated sadly, step by step. Silence returned to the hall. The two youths waited another half hour without saying a word. Then Joe said, 'The old woman must have fallen asleep. If you're a man, go to the girl. If you make no noise, you can easily slip into her bed.

Zohar's heart was beating wildly.

'Don't be afraid,' Joe said. 'I'll keep watch. Go! I'm waiting.'

*

She opened her eyes. She smelt of jasmine. He covered her mouth with his hand: 'It's me, Zohar! Do you recognize me?'

151

He kissed her on her mouth and recognized her taste of fruit.

'Gohar? Is it really you?'

He stroked her legs, fine and long as a doe's. 'You dance so well!'

She took his hand, brought it to her lips. 'That night in the village so long ago. Do you remember? We were children—I left my heart in your hands.' She let out a little laugh.

'Quiet. You'll wake up the old cow.'

They both cocked their ears. The old woman was snoring noisily, a long whistle rising and a deep breath descending in hiccups. They hid under the light cotton coverlet. Her breasts had grown, two firm pears that beckoned his hands. He placed his lips on them. She moaned, closing her eyes. 'Shush!' She slid her hands between his thighs and touched him, keen as a cobra. Zohar felt possessed by a power that pushed him towards her, she who was already so close. He hugged her to him, nearly suffocating her. 'You make me tremble.' He kissed her mouth again. Then he kissed her breasts, her neck. 'I'm trembling as well.' When he was inside her, with his whole sex, his whole body, she was inside him; when she welcomed him, he was already there.

'You will never leave me.'

He did not answer. Filled and emptied; lost and found. He'd just known pleasure.

'Right? You'll never leave me?'

He placed his face against her neck, brought his mouth to her ear, and whispered, 'Never!' He was already beginning to fall asleep.

'Go, now!'

He wanted to protest, his body languorous, as if sealed to hers.

'Other nights will envelop us. Go!'

Naked as a worm, he gathered up his clothes. 'You are the mother of all my loves.' And he left without a sound.

On the night of Saturday, 5 March, to Sunday, 6 March 1938, the bodies were united—the bodies of those two who were but one soul for all eternity. O Zohar, you whose name echoes like a mystery, you who are never where you are expected, you who seek people where they are not—O Masreya, daughter of the land and of power, you whose destiny is open—why did you look backward? Why add the senses to your passion? Wasn't it enough to be united like Siamese twins, you who had only one soul between you? He was new, like a blade of grass, tall and proud, erect; she was already open, but barely, only half-open. Those moments in the night would be inscribed for each in an eternity that would be counted out every day of their lives.

In the hall, Zohar rediscovered Joe and their boyish complicity. The very day of his bar mitzvah, God had granted him access to the tree of knowledge. But he could not share it with his friend.

They returned to the garden where two or three groups of guests were delaying the moment of departure.

The youths resumed their endless discussion.

'So, tell me again,' Joe asked, 'another difference between the rabbinates and the Karaites?'

'The Karaites reject the Talmud.'

'We already said that. And?'

'Also the Kabbalah?'

'Of course! But what else?'

'Oh, yes! The phylacteries! Instead of wearing them on their left arm and on their forehead, like us, they hang them on the wall and look at them.'

'Ridiculous. Okay! But a more important difference, a difference that relates to your adventure tonight. So?'

'I don't know,' Zohar admitted.

Joe burst out laughing. 'The Karaites forbid relations between men and women on the night of Shabbat.'

'And so?'

'What do you mean, "And so"? Don't you know that for us, the rabbinates, it's mandated? Idiot.'

'They don't know what they're missing,' Zohar chortled.

'But where were you all this time?' his mother Esther asked.

'We were debating in Joe's room.'

'You were debating—O, my little one. As if at your age you had something to debate.'

Zohar's family returned to their ghetto on foot, their eyes lit up by the wealth of the wealthy. Zohar skipped before them, happy as no one had ever seen him before. Only Motty was worried, oppressed by a dark foreboding.

Al-Galaa Street

1938. From that night forward, Zohar's behaviour metamorphosed. The adults kept saying that now that he'd been bar mitzvahed, he was an adult. He took them at their word. Every morning, like many men in the hara, he'd go to Cafe Gedaliah. He'd spend an hour there, sell a few cigarettes, trade news and take the city's temperature before venturing out to scavenge.

One morning, a foreigner showed up. Dressed in a well-cut European suit, his head uncovered. His eyes were piercing, and he sported a magnificent, glossy moustache. His arrival plunged the establishment into silence. He called out to the flock: 'Does anyone here want to earn fifty piastres?'

Fifty piastres? And how! Everyone was willing. Gedaliah asked him, 'How many do you need—of these lucky beggars, I mean—how many?'

The men hung on the foreigner's words; he spoke French with a strong Italian accent.

'How many?' he replied. 'Why, as many as possible. As many as you can find!'

The work would take a day. One day of work for fifty piastres—what a windfall! But, the Italian added, this work required some preparation. They would have to present themselves to the Italian Consulate on that very day—he called it *Consolato d'Italia*. He gave them the address, Al-Galaa Street, and promised to explain what they would have to do when they arrived. And he asked Gedaliah, the cafe owner, to prepare the list of candidates, to gather them and to send them to the Italians, *pronto*.

Hearing this, Zohar shot off like an arrow, met Doudou on his way to the cafe, dragged Poupy from bed, convinced Elie to entrust the grocery to Esther, and off they went, three comrades led by that strange adolescent to the notorious consulate.

'Maybe they're seeking a consul?' Poupy joked.

'It's true, with your Garibaldi moustache . . . '

'And your fake monocle . . . '

'But why do you call it fake? Do I say you're wearing fake shoes on your feet?'

No one had the heart to point out that he'd put on his much-loved old combat boots without socks.

They were the first to arrive. Soon, some hundred men, those pariahs from Haret al-Yahud—an undisciplined and raucous troop assembled by Gedaliah—presented themselves to an Italian military officer in a spotless uniform.

'*Bene*! We'll proceed immediately to the administrative formal-ities, since you're all volunteers.'

'Volunteers?' Poupy asked. 'How and why, volunteers?'

'Volunteers for what?' someone else called out.

'Silence!' roared the sergeant. 'Don't think you're here to bargain the way you would in the souk! I don't want to hear a single word from the ranks.'

It was quite difficult to organize them. The Italian wanted to line them up in size order, but each insisted on being near his cousin, his neighbour, his friend. The debate grew heated. Two soldiers arrived to lend a hand to the non-commissioned officer. A shot in the air. Frightened, the Jews scattered to the four corners of the court-yard. They had to start all over again.

The Italians dropped the idea of a military formation and moved on to identification. Elie was refusing to let himself be photographed. The only snapshot in which he figured dated from the day of his marriage, when he was wearing a suit. He refused to appear like this in a photo, in a galabia and without a jacket. Doudou finally con-vinced him with the promise that, in an identity picture, only his face would be visible.

After the photo session, they had to recite their names. Elie, the eldest, spoke for the whole family. For Poupy, enlightened by the old man, the officer wrote 'Jacobo'; for Doudou, 'Davide'; for Elie, 'Lieto'; for 'Zohar', they searched a while before settling on 'Spirito'. Elie invented birth dates that more or less corresponded to their ages.

They had to wait in the courtyard for the identification of all the group members to be completed. Then the sub-officer solemnly assembled them, insisting on silence as he brandished his cane. 'You've requested Italian nationality—'

'But we didn't ask for a thing!' Doudou shouted.

'Silence in the ranks! If you didn't ask for anything,' the sergeant replied, 'then you won't get this.' And, from a cardboard box, he drew several booklets, which he waved in front of their astonished eyes. '*Il passaporto*, the passport.'

Elie dug his elbow into Doudou's side. 'Shut up now! We'll take the passport and then we'll see.'

'You're right,' the other one answered. 'Maybe we could sell it.'

The sergeant started over: 'I begin again after this untimely interruption. I see that some of you have never heard of discipline. I will assume the task of teaching you the first rudiments. I begin, then: Acceding to your request, in his infinite benevolence, His Majesty Vittorio Emanuele III, King of Italy, has consented to grant you Italian nationality. From now on, you have a passport that will allow you to travel anywhere you wish, anywhere in the world. And now, repeat after me: *Viva Italia*!'

As a chorus they shouted, '*Viva Italia*!' And Poupy added in Arabic: 'May God burn the faith of a jenny-ass' butt, and of Italia.'

They all burst out laughing, because the two words rhymed in Arabic.

'Silence in the ranks!' roared the sergeant.

'The jenny-ass,' Doudou whispered in Arabic into Poupy's ear, 'it's him!'

The other guffawed: 'So lick his butt!'

And they laughed even more.

Then they were taught to raise their right arm, fully extended, to salute. And they were given shirts, all black.

'Next week, the chief of staff of our army, Marshal Pietro Badoglio, will be on an official visit to Cairo. What do we say?'

In the ragged ranks, there was a profound silence. The non-commissioned officer shouted, 'What do we say? We don't say, we shout.'

They didn't know how to answer.

'We shout: *Viva Italia*!'

And they repeated, '*Viva Italia*.' Zohar's family spoke again of the jenny-ass. And they laughed some more.

'Next Thursday, at fourteen hours, I want you all at the Consulate, dressed in your black shirts, your feet together, to welcome the monsignor, Marshal Badoglio, your right arm held high as I just taught you, and shouting—shouting—'

'Shouting?'

'Shouting *Viva Italia*! you idiots! Shouting what?'

And they repeated again, '*Viva Italia*,' this time without hesitation. The sergeant judged his little troop ready. He promised them fifty piastres after they'd saluted the Marshal, and dismissed them.

On the return trip, Doudou, proud of his photo embossed with a raised stamp, deciphered the additional inscriptions on his passport. He guessed the meaning of the Italian words but he couldn't understand one category. Under 'city of origin' was written 'Livorno'. He studied Poupy's passport. He also came from Livorno; Elie as well, and Zohar, whom Poupy had declared to be his son. Here was a mystery!

'Why are we all from Livorno?' Poupy wondered out loud.

'And not Rome?' Doudou added. 'Rome's better, after all.'

'Or even Naples! I once knew a jeweller from Naples. He had some class. I would have preferred Naples. Do you think we can ask them to change the city of origin?'

The following Thursday, the day of the fifty piastres, they were all there, the little Jews from the hara, dressed in their black shirts, some thrust over a galabia, some stuffed into pyjama pants, some, like Doudou, in real cloth trousers—though they had lost the memory of an iron. Little Marshal Badoglio, his head covered in his magnificent officer's kepi, decorated with gilt and a crowned eagle, gave them his hangdog look.

'Is this the militia you've raised in Cairo?' he asked the consul.

'*Viva Italia*!' roared the chorus of new Italians in black shirts, their arms out. '*Viva Italia*! And *Viva Italia*! And may God toss you into the fires of Gehenna,' they added in Arabic under their breaths.

'It's good, it's good,' mumbled the marshal.

And the consul puffed out his chest. A few months earlier, he'd telegraphed Rome, proudly announcing that several hundred Italians in Egypt had enrolled in the fascist militia and were burning to fight for their country. Naturally, he requested funds to outfit them. Rome disbursed the money, which the consul promptly squandered at the casino. Now, on the occasion of his visit to Cairo, the chief of staff wanted to review the troops. Hence the rushed recruitment at Cafe Gedaliah.

The next day, the sergeant appeared in person at the entrance to Haret al-Yahud, accompanied by a soldier holding a case of deployment orders on official paper. Outfitted with their rucksacks, the subjects of His Majesty Vittorio Emanuele III needed to present themselves at the railway station the following week to relieve their brothers-in-arms stationed in Ethiopia.

'Jacobo Zohar? Do you know Jacobo Zohar?' Poupy asked Doudou.

'Toz! No! Never heard of him. If Jacobo Zohar exists, let his mother come introduce him to me. And if this dog in a suit thinks we'll go fight in Ethiopia, may his mother burn with so many flames that the light shines all the way to Livorno.'

'Livorno up the arse of Badoglio. And may Badoglio burn as well and may Mussolini put out the flames with petrol, if we're going to fight in Ethiopia.'

And the family stirred up a veritable insurrection among the holders of those precious passports. The furious Zohars led the newly minted Italians, already conscientious objectors, to Cafe Gedaliah.

'*Viva Italia*, Gedaliah, you son of a dog! Do you want to send us to our deaths in Ethiopia? May Allah strike you with blindness and the plague!'

From these events that cost the unfortunate Gedaliah the sacking of his cafe, the Zohar family was left with four passports,which would bring them, in the fullness of time, both good fortune and bad.

Khamis al-Ads Cul-de-Sac

1941. Three years had passed. Dark black hair, meticulously combed and parted on the side in the British fashion; large, slightly bulging black eyes, always startled—at sixteen, Zohar had become a handsome young man of refined elegance. He wore pleated trousers that rose high above his navel, in a style set by Hollywood films; along with light, open-collared shirts, always immaculate. He never went anywhere without his two-toned shoes, clicking their metal taps on the hara's cobblestones. And even though no one knew where he spent his days and nights, every so often he returned to sleep in Uncle Elie's grocery, on the little bed his parents had placed beside theirs.

He continued to make and sell his cigarettes; day by day, his business flourished more and more, especially after he expanded his offerings to include less licit items along with tobacco. One night, a work night when he was roaming the city in search of customers, he had what would prove to be a fateful encounter.

Not far from Haret al-Yahud, in the Karaite neighbourhood of Khoronfesh, a tiny cul-de-sac, Khamis al-Ads, threaded its way through the small, run-down buildings. There, in the house owned by the Karaite Samuel, lived the Cohen family, not Karaite but just as poor as the other tenants—Muslim, Copt, Karaite or rabbinate. Over the course of some fifty years, the father, Gaby Cohen, who worked for the watchmaker Moussa Farag, had ruined his eyes repairing the neighbourhood's watches. He died right at the start of the war, the day Germany invaded Poland, 1 September 1939, in the small hours of the morning. No doubt about it, he was dead too young, barely sixty years old, leaving a wife in tears, plus five grown children from a first marriage and three from a second. The oldest of the three was named Abraham or Albert—but this hardly mattered, since everyone called him Nino.

At the death of his father when he was seventeen, Nino was already in his second year of medical studies at Fouad I University on Kasr al-'Aini Street. An intellectual, most definitely, who cared more about reading than about his studies. He read equally well in three languages—Arabic of course, but also French and English. A tall young man, strikingly handsome, the aptly named Gamal lodged in the same building. This law student, four years Nino's senior, had for a long time served as a mentor, recommending books and encouraging him to view life in political terms. A passionate militant nationalist, he'd led Nino to discover the biographies of Kamal Ataturk and Bismarck, the works of Karl Marx and Paul Lafargue, but also the poems of Ahmed Chawki and the novels of Tawfik al-Hakim. Gamal, who'd joined the Officers' School, had grown scarce of late, but reappeared whenever he was on leave, and the two continued their unending discussion of Egypt's future.

Gamal was convinced that Egypt, mother of the world, would spawn a new era—when Arabs, the wretched of the earth, would finally regain their place among the nations. Nino, who shared his ideals, asked him what role the Jews would play. Gamal replied that in Egypt there were no Jews, only Egyptians and foreigners. And he explained further—the people's poverty stemmed from the foreigners' brazen exploitation of resources: the British primarily, but also the French, the Turks and all the other imperialist vultures preying on the country. The new Egypt would be Egyptian.

His powerful voice carried; he spoke well, he spoke truly, he spoke for the people. Emanating from Gamal was such conviction, such authority, that Nino didn't dare confess that he, although Egyptian since time immemorial, had no nationality—neither Egyptian nor foreign: he was stateless.

Ever since the father's death, the Cohen family's income had been progressively reduced to a pittance, so much so that Nino took a job working as a compounder for Assiouty, the pharmacist on Nazmi Street. During the day, he worked there making lotions and creams; at night, he studied. To stay awake, he'd developed the habit of smoking hashish. Unlike his fellows who frequented the smoking dens on Champollion or Ma'ruf Streets, he smoked alone, at home, cigarettes he rolled mechanically, without looking up from his anatomy assignments. One night, when he'd gone out in search of the drug, he came across Zohar patrolling Suares Square, not far from the Italian Consulate, near the Bentzion building. Nino, his little eyes hidden behind thick glasses and his neck sticking out above a shirt with too big a collar, was so gaunt he seemed afflicted by a serious disease. He was painful to look at.

'What's wrong, my brother?' Zohar began. 'Your head seeks the vapours of the night, but your feet don't know where to take you. I know what you need, the paste that opens the paths of the spirit, the blue dust that makes your eyes sparkle, or would you rather the jelly that makes you lustier than a lion?'

Struck by the young man's patter, Nino smiled. And so it was another face Zohar saw, a face of intelligence and joy. It was impossible to resist Nino's smile.

'And what would be best for me, Doctor Smoke?'

'First of all, some green, very fresh, straight from the fields of the Delta, and your week will be green. Then, you'll sprinkle your Craven A with some blue and you'll float on an ocean of truth. When you close your eyes, a nude woman with long hair will sit on your lap and her arse will dance between your thighs. That's what you need, my brother.'

They walked the length of the new bridge that was now called Qasr al-Nil, chatting. Finding an intelligent and clever boy who hadn't been to school, Nino undertook to convince Zohar to earn his baccalaureate. Zohar was happy to meet a young man who liked to talk, to debate, to prove, to argue. Nino spoke of Egypt, Zohar of the Jews; the first thrust himself into history; the second sang of origins. Nino explained to Zohar the reasons for his poverty: ninety-five per cent of the land belonged to a handful of wealthy families, who leased it to the fellahs, peasants who couldn't even make enough to pay the rent. 'Look! I'm not poor!' Zohar replied, drawing wads of bills from his pockets. 'You are poor!' Nino replied. 'You're poor and you don't know it. You're poor because you're all alone.' And Zohar burst out laughing, explaining that he was not alone, quite the opposite! He was a scout, the explorer assigned by the great Zohar family to discover the new Egyptian society. And he took hold of it exactly where people couldn't resist, where they'd become slaves to their only pleasure. 'What a strange idea,' Nino interjected. 'Pleasure is the path to alienation.' Zohar didn't understand the word. Nino explained: To be alienated is to lose your strength, your essence, for a third party's profit. The fellahs are alienated because all their strength serves only to enrich the wealthy landowners. The workers are alienated because their backbreaking labour serves only to enrich the factory owner. Had he ever seen a rich fellah? Or a rich worker? No! No one had ever seen any. They were alienated. The fruit of their labour was confiscated. Did he understand that? And the Egyptian people were alienated, since the profits of the nation's work went elsewhere, to foreigners, the British, the French.

'But I have only one master!' Zohar replied.

Nino interrupted him. 'You think you're your own master? You think the profits of your labour belong to you? Is that what you think?'

'No,' cut in Zohar, 'No. I have only one master and I don't know him.'

Nino was speechless before the strange reply of his nighttime companion. He bought some green from him, hugged him , and said only 'I love you, my brother!' And they walked side by side, hand in hand, as far as Shepheard's Hotel which was open all night. They parted there, promising to find each other again soon.

Zohar frequently met Nino at night, sometimes for business, sometimes solely for the pleasure of talk. That year, 1941, war broke out in the Middle East. In accordance with the treaty signed in 1936 by young King Farouk, Egypt had been constrained to welcome British forces. Cairo was crawling with soldiers, Englishmen of course, but also Australians, New Zealanders, Indians, Poles, Frenchmen from unoccupied France. In the wealthy neighbourhoods, there were now more foreigners than Egyptians. All these men, especially needy since they were separated from their families and confronted with the anxieties of combat, had to be fed, dressed, housed, entertained. Bars sprang up like mushrooms; nightclubs and brothels fell clanging onto the city. Commerce underwent an extraordinary expansion, as pounds sterling and shillings joined piastres and dollars. What's more, everything was for sale—at a premium, and in foreign currency! From old bicycle tyres to costume jewellery, from battered pots to ancient cars. Prices climbed faster than a monkey chased by a panther. The official market collapsed, the black market exploded.

Zohar's traffic thrived now that he'd given up cigarettes as too cumbersome. He procured all sorts of drugs for military men, from hashish whose price had skyrocketed, to rarer powders he found thanks to Nino's connections with pharmacists. Having grown rich from one day to the next, Zohar laboured alone, spending his nights scurrying through nightclubs and hotel bars, here to obtain the merchandise, there to sell it. Numerous British officers relied on his services; he had entry into the capital's exclusive clubs: White's, St James, the Automobile Club.

Under Gamal's auspices, Nino was meeting Egyptian military men more and more hostile to the British presence. He'd been admitted to gatherings where they were plotting against the British and against the King, where they were planning different kinds of revolution—communist, socialist, Islamic. Imbued with their ideas, Nino was beginning to long for the victory of the Axis forces: the Italians who were occupying Ethiopia, part of Somalia, and above all nearby Libya; and the Germans, whose armies were beginning to disembark in Cyrenaica, the east coast of Libya. He sometimes said strange things that startled Zohar, things like, 'If we Egyptians were to sign a secret accord with the Germans, once the British were routed, Egypt would finally be independent.'

Zohar was deeply opposed to these ideas, first of all because the departure of the British would mark the end of his business. Then there were all those stories circulating about the visceral, bestial, delirious hatred of the Germans. Did he want to find himself in a concentration camp because he was Jewish? Nino would reply, 'There are no Jews, only exploiters and exploited.' And the debate went on— the same, always. Zohar liked this debate, which reminded him of Rav Bensimon's arcane reasoning about forbidden foods.

It was during that same year of 1941, in March, a few days after the announcement of General Rommel and his Afrika Korps' victory in Libya, that Zohar introduced Joe di Reggio, his longtime friend, to Nino Cohen, whom he'd nicknamed 'the Professor'. 'You'll see,' he told him, 'his blood is light, like orgeat syrup, and he's as learned as a rabbi. A professor.'

During the intervening three years, Joe had chosen a totally different path. The year before his baccalaureate, he'd suddenly grown enamoured of sports, tennis and polo, which he practised on the grounds of the Gezira Sporting Club—but above all basketball, for which he'd joined the Maccabees, a Zionist club that sought to impart its ideals to Jewish youth. There, he was part of a top-ranked team, but he also learnt songs of Jewish resistance against British occupation and began to dream of the struggle to create a new Jewish state. This sudden orientation profoundly displeased his parents— his father who despised the socialist ideas of the Jewish colonists in Palestine, and his mother, allied (at least in her mind) with the communists, and who could not understand a liberation struggle for Jews alone. She, several times a millionaire in pounds sterling, longed for a revolution sprung from the masses that would establish justice and equality for all, not just for one group. The baroness' political sallies provoked a reaction in the salons; a scent of scandal spread all around her.

So it was that one night, all three of them found themselves at Shepheard's—Joe the Zionist, Nino the communist and Zohar, who was simply Zohar, Zohar Zohar. He was talking to them. His nighttime excursions had often led him into posh neighbourhoods, to make deliveries to his customers, on the islands of Rhoda or Gezira, in Zamalek or Garden City, in sumptuous villas where most of the high-ranking British lived. One afternoon, he'd found himself in front of the villa of Colonel Clifford Chapman, a Scot who, out of necessity, had given up whiskey for cocaine—less cumbersome and more effective. Zohar was carrying in his sack a small flask with two hundred and fifty grammes of powder, the best, the purest, reserved for pharmacies and hospitals. He'd rung the doorbell. No response. He was growing impatient at the gate, anxious about an eventual military patrol. He knew they didn't fool around when it came to drug trafficking. A woman finally appeared at a window. She announced in English that the Colonel was away. He didn't understand what she was saying. His English wasn't very good and the woman was speaking from too far off. 'What? What?' repeated Zohar. She came to the gate, a cigarette dangling from her lips.

'Good evening, young man! From my window, I was trying to tell you that my husband, Colonel Chapman, has left for a manoeuvre. He's usually not away for more than two weeks. But you never know. It's war! Were you supposed to deliver a package?'

Ann must have been thirty-five years old. Her army uniform was well cut and she'd loosened the tie on her wide-open collar. Her unbound hair flowed in blond waves to her shoulders. Zohar stood speechless, overcome by this unfamiliar beauty. He'd never seen such white skin, reddened by the sun, sprinkled with so many freckles; nor such clear eyes, the colour of the Mediterranean—and that small turned-up nose, bringing with it the edges of the lips into an eternal smile.

'*Madame*,' he stammered.

'You speak English, I suppose.'

'A little,' Zohar replied. 'Mostly French, and Arabic, of course.'

'Well then, we'll speak in English. Would you like a cup of tea?' And she invited him in.

'You don't say!' The other two were in raptures. 'The wife of the Colonel let you enter her Garden City villa while her husband was away? How beautiful was she?' Zohar relished the effect he was having. Before replying, he explained the situation in which the British officers' wives found themselves. Far from their homes, their families, their children (which they'd often entrusted to grandparents), they worked in army auxiliary services—post, telephone, hospital. For the first time in their lives, they were independent, properly earning their own income and daily awaiting their husbands' disappearance into combat. According to Zohar, they were hot, hot like coals! 'Sometimes war loosens the ties that bind solely due to social conventions,' Zohar learnedly pronounced. 'And so, you understand.' He was silent, allowing them to hear, more loudly by his silence, what their bellies were eager to discover.

'What are we to understand, you son of an ass?' asked Joe at the pinnacle of excitement. 'Are you going to leave us with our tongues hanging out like dogs?'

Zohar went on. She'd brought him into the salon, invited him to sit on a sofa. Under the pretext of tea, she'd returned with two stemmed glasses on a tray. On the little table, two carafes. 'Port or brandy? So, you're a delivery boy, a student most likely.'

By the second glass, he'd kissed her on the lips; by the third, she'd led him by the hand to the bedroom. They'd made love in full daylight, their bodies striated by rays filtering through the blinds, unable to distinguish between their panting, their heartbeats and the muffled pounding of the endlessly whirling ceiling fan.

'And after?' Nino asked.

'And after, like before!' Zohar replied.

'Oh, my friend! Which means . . . ?'

'Which means, I already told you, after like before, like after two hundred times. After, we began again!'

What was he saying, 'two hundred times'? Even if he claimed he'd done it twice, they wouldn't believe him, thought Joe. Nino was

hesitant to form an opinion, now perceiving Zohar's story as adolescent boasting, now as a real adventure he wanted with all his heart
to believe. For 'the Professor', soon to be a doctor of medicine, and
already learnt in Egyptian politics, had never gone near a girl. As for
Joe, he'd sketched the drafts of his budding sexuality in the company
of servants in the di Reggio palace (in good times and bad, there were
between ten and fifteen); but he'd never yet had a true relationship
with a girl.

They were smoking nonstop, lighting one cigarette after another,
using the butt of one to light the next.

'You wear your name well, Smoke,' Nino complained. 'You're
spreading a fog. Listen, your words are like the *khamsin* when it stirs
up the desert sand. With locusts, moreover! First answer this question: Why are you telling us this story?'

'Wait, you unbeliever! You who don't believe in God, you can't
help but doubt your friends. Listen!'

The first time, in their haste to be together, transported by desire,
they hadn't taken the time to undress. But the second time was
calmer, slower. No, well, how to explain—curious, they'd explored
each other, traveling across their bodies. Naked, she had full hips and
generous breasts, riddled with freckles. And she smelt of milk. It
was the first time he'd gotten close to a woman, a true woman—and
what a woman! He'd only kept his *higab*, his amulet, around his
neck, his protection, the little leather pouch his mother had given him
the day after his bar mitzvah, making him swear never to be separated from it.

'What is it?' Ann had asked him.

'It's to repel demons!' he'd replied, aware of provoking her.

'And it works?'

He'd confided in her a little, telling her about the kudiya's magic
in Bab al-Zuwayla where his mother had often taken him during his
childhood.

'The kudiya?' Ann asked again. 'What's that?'

'She's a sorceress,' answered Zohar as seriously as possible. 'The mistress of the demons.'

'I'll give you twenty pounds if you bring me something from that witch.'

'Something?'

'Yes! Something that would help me get rid of someone.'

The idea had intrigued him. He'd never gone alone to the house of the zars, only with his mother. Each time, he would leave with blessings and little talismans to put in his wallet, flasks filled with water into which several suras of the Qur'an had been dissolved, with which he was supposed to wash. The kudiya would draw him to her side, place her two hands on his head, and, after having repeated, 'You are our child, son of the zars. This house is yours, my prince,' she would clap her hands in that familiar rhythm of the camels while she sang, 'O Nofal, O Nofal, O Nofal . . . The prince has come, he will return . . . Aaah . . . ' And when he left, the women would lean towards him as he walked, murmuring, 'May our father escort him!' They would sprinkle fresh water over his footprints. He knew that, like his mother, he was bound to this place. He'd seen miracles no one would believe: women swallowing snakes, men burning their chests with a torch without later bearing the least sign on their skin, astounding creatures—servals, caracals, owls—emerging from walls and vanishing into the night. When he was a child, his mother warned him never to say anything to strangers about this place. These days, he kept it to himself, knowing he'd be taken for a madman or a fool.

One evening, then, he went, without his mother's knowledge, to Bab al-Zuwayla, wondering how he would formulate his request to the kudiya. But he didn't have to say a word. As soon as she saw him, she swept him into her arms, covered him with kisses, picked up a handful of earth which she imbued with his sweat by passing it under his armpits. She spread this earth on a wicker tray she used for divination, casting shells onto it, many, maybe thirty. She studied the shapes they made, some on their backs, some on their bellies, ran her fingers over them, giving herself over to mysterious calculations, beginning again. Suddenly, a wide smile lit up her face. 'O Nofal, O Nofal, O Nofal . . . The prince is in love, he wants a gift for his beloved with the marble skin.' Despite being used to this, he jumped. 'How do you know her skin is white?' She simply smiled and sang again as she clapped her hands. Then she vanished into her room, asking him to wait. An hour later she returned with a little doll, crudely fashioned from newspaper. 'Look!' she said to Zohar, 'All she has to do is throw this into the Nile from a bridge while uttering three times the name of the person she wants to see disappear.' He didn't dare touch the doll. 'And the one who should leave will disappear into the night. Take it! Take it, you fool!' She burst out laughing. 'Are you afraid of a paper figurine? She'll also need to say this sentence in our language: "In the name of Solomon, our king, who commands all the creatures of the Creation, those of the day and those of the night." Do you understand?'

He didn't know whether Ann had followed the instructions but, the following week, Colonel Clifford lost his life during the Afrika Korps' furious attack that enabled Rommel to take the village of Al-Agheila, at the far end of Cyrenaica.

It had been years that Ann could no longer tolerate her husband, but she hadn't wished for his death, just a lasting separation. Still, when she discovered what her inheritance amounted to, her sorrow disappeared as if by magic. She sported a black crepe band on the lapel of her uniform and was careful to redden her eyes with the help of an onion before appearing in public. But she grew intensely attached to Zohar, whom she welcomed in the middle of the night and whom she was reluctant to let leave.

Zohar hadn't jumped for joy when he heard about the colonel's death. It wasn't a good situation; here he was in possession of two hundred and fifty grammes of powder for which he urgently needed to find a new buyer. He consoled himself with the thought of enjoying a pied-à-terre in the most beautiful neighbourhood in Cairo; and the love of the beautiful Englishwoman, intensified by her mourning, made him discover sensations he hadn't dared to imagine.

She initiated him into lust's complex games—the torment of piercing caresses, the words that inflamed bodies, the surrenders that conquered souls. Who better to initiate you into love than a mother? Within a few weeks, Ann had become his guide to lust. He occasionally thought of Masreya, who remained in his memory as the mother of all his loves, but lust, that was something else!—a force like the growl of a wild beast that rose from the belly.

One night, Ann asked him, 'Are you bored with me?'

'Never!' he answered her immediately. 'Your body is a city, a great capital. I can never tire of exploring it.'

'You aren't lying to me? Would you say such things just to please me? Yes, you would! Young as you are, already an Oriental.'

He didn't know what to say. He who spent his nights with his head filled with his father's songs, had finally found a place where he could simply smile. But he didn't know how to explain this to Ann. He simply shrugged.

'We can't just meet at night and part before the first rays of light, like ghosts,' she continued. 'We can't just be at the beck and call of our senses, like beasts.'

'Yes?'

'We also need to meet people, friends, human beings.'

She insisted. She was probably thinking about restaurants, bars, dinners out. That's when Zohar had an idea.

'I'm going to ask you a question, but first you have to swear you won't get angry.'

'I can't get angry with you, angel of love. Can anyone control the wind? Speak! Ask me your question.'

'Do you know other military wives, like you, who don't know what to do with their nights? We could meet them here with my friends.'

*

The other two were dumbfounded. Nino sucked on his cigarette as if reattaching himself to his mother's breast. 'What?' he stammered. 'Do you mean—?' Zohar finally announced that they were invited, the two of them, Nino and Joe, that very day, to Ann's villa, where two British army wives would be eagerly waiting to meet them. 'Eager? How do you know? If you'd warned me,' Joe complained, 'I would have dressed properly.' Nino burst out laughing. With his fine cotton suit the colour of raw silk, his Scottish bow tie, his light hair whose forelock he continually pushed up, Joe looked like an American student.

'But you're handsome, Joe, you Zionist son of a dog!'

The other tried to procrastinate: 'Why do we have to go tonight? Couldn't we wait until tomorrow, or maybe next week?

Zohar started to laugh. 'Come! Let me buy you a glass of arak.'

By the second glass, they no longer had the slightest hesitation. After the third, they climbed into Joe's gleaming MG two-seater. The motor began to backfire; Joe pressed the accelerator furiously, happy to attract the attention of people out strolling. Definitely, these British had mastered the art of exhaust noise. The car took off briskly, making the rear wheels squeal. The other two took the seats while Zohar perched in the back, his butt on the luggage rack, his hands gripping the windshield. He yelled, 'Take it easy, Joe, I'm racing!'

Garden City was not too far. Nino closed his eyes, thrilled by the wind hitting his face. 'O, the peace of God, O the peace!' Joe taught them the lyrics to 'David, David, King of Israel', which he sang with the Maccabees. They began to sing at the top of their lungs, repeating it again. In their nabab's car, their hearts wide open, they were kings! Joe made the tires squeal and they exploded with laughter. That's how they crossed Qasr-al-Nil bridge. A light breeze was rising from the river, which here was called the sea, and the feluc-cas traced diagonals of light on the water. They passed a military police jeep and the officer saluted them. Probably an MG aficionado.

The night had partnered with these three young men and a thin cloud was crossing the full face of the moon. 'Look! She's smoking a cigarette,' joked Nino. 'Probably purchased from Zohar.' Communion, despite their differences. Those who believed in the people, and the one who ignored its existence: the nationalist, the Zionist, and the one who was nothing; all three stateless (or Italian), suddenly united by the same call to life's immediacy.

Filtered light, intoxicating incense. On the record player, Duke Ellington orchestrating the rendezvous of souls. Ann had arranged everything, distributing glasses and pastries here and there. Looking vampish in a black cocktail dress that fell just above her knees, with her golden hair and treacherous eyes, she was holding a long cigarette holder between her fingertips. Slightly anxious, she invited them in.

Sidelong glances. Kathleen was probably the oldest. Strict army suit, with, as the only whimsy, a rose in her severely cut hair. But her blouse gaped from the pressure of her exuberant breasts. As for Mary, she looked like a dutiful secretary—short hair, pulled back; a little blouse with a closed collar; tortoiseshell glasses; burning cheeks.

The three boys sprawled on the same sofa. They immediately began to drink. Ann made the introductions. They entertained themselves searching for a common tongue. Joe and Nino spoke fairly good English, but couldn't restrain the volleys of jokes in Arabic. Zohar, silent, savoured a new pleasure. Ann came close, offered to dance. 'Later!' he promised. Then Joe led Mary in an artistic be-bop. 'He dances, huh? Look how he dances!' Nino drew closer to Kathleen and began to talk politics. The war, the British, the Egyptians. Ann, whose spirit was brightening with the alcohol fumes, scolded them. 'There's plenty of time to talk about the war. You can do it all day on every street corner. Tonight, it's a party!'

Three British women set adrift by war's anarchy; three young Egyptians dazzled by the world's lights. The husbands no longer existed; obligations dissipated like a bad dream; differences of age, class, language, religion, or politics evaporated, diluted in drink. They danced a little. They laughed a lot, and about everything. They gave themselves one night of irresponsibility, one night of freedom, out of time. In the guestroom, Nino lost himself in Kathleen's breasts, falling asleep for a while before the love she'd finally accepted. On the living room rug, Joe strove to meet Mary's insatiable demands.

Zohar had withdrawn into the bedroom with Ann. The alcohol had made her lyrical. 'I'll take you to my house on the banks of the Thames, near Richmond Park. You'll be both my king and my valet. Haven't you told me your name means "jewel"? You are my gift! You'll be my gem brought back from Egypt.' He wanted only to join her body, to bathe in her depths as if in warm dark water, an ungraspable particle of this night of harmony. She never stopped talking, endlessly weaving the future. 'When the war ends,' she kept repeating. But he knew—this war would never end! It would last for ever. Until now, men were unaware that the earth had owners. They'd wanted to seize its entrails. They'd disinterred mummies, made its black blood gush. The earth would never pardon them. This war would end only with the death of the last humans.

'What are you saying?' Ann asked.

'Nothing!' Zohar replied, 'I was talking about my family.'

When they fell asleep, an insomniac rooster was already calling people to prayer.

It was after five a.m. when Zohar suddenly emerged from his dream. He rose to dress. 'Come back! Why do you have to leave before daylight!' Ann simpered without opening her eyes. He roused the others, leading them away from the villa.

In the car, Joe was the first to speak. 'But who is it that said Englishwomen love love? It's untrue! It's love that loves them. It drives them mad.'

They took up their song again, 'David, David, King of Israel'.

'This David,' Joe added, 'must also love Englishwomen.'

'They say he loved all women.'

'Never in my life,' Nino learnedly asserted, 'never in my life would I have imagined loving a bourgeois through a night.'

'Bourgeois and imperialist!' sneered Joe.

'Zionist son of a dog!'

And they burst out laughing and clapped their hands.

Clinging to the luggage rack, Zohar had just made a decision. If this night hadn't been a party, what would it have been? Why, a business meeting! And if these three young Jews of Egypt hadn't met these three Englishwomen solely for entertainment, what would have been their purpose? To form a partnership, by God!

Doctor Tawfik Street

The next week, Zohar launched his business. He'd been thinking about it for a long time. One of the British army's main problems in Egypt was the lack of alcohol. The British couldn't import the quantities needed for the well-being and courage of their troops, and local production was just about nonexistent. A market was thus open for a creative entrepreneur, especially since there was more and more talk of prohibition. The Muslim Brotherhood of Hassan al-Bana, stridently calling for bans on prostitution and the sale of alcohol, was gaining popular sympathy. King Farouk had promised to have a law passed, and already forbade alcohol at his receptions. Things were so bad that prostitutes were in hiding, and alcohol had disappeared from most markets—grocers and large food stores, including the Greeks'. You could still find bottles of arak in the souks of the old city, but they were selling at ridiculous prices. Nino had told Zohar how some Poles, soldiers in the British army, had threatened poor Dr Assiouty, the owner of his pharmacy, until he turned over his stock of ninety per cent alcohol. And when, trembling with fear, he'd handed over his twenty-five-litre drum, they'd paid him and even insisted on a receipt, afraid of later being accused of theft.

Although Zohar could count on Joe and Nino, his two partners in pleasure, for organization, and on the Englishwomen for distribution, he still needed to work out the problem of production. He knew there were numerous sugarcane plantations in Upper Egypt. Surely it would be easy to procure large quantities of cane there, but the war made transport nearly impossible. There were also some plantations in the Delta, less numerous, yes, but just as productive. That's where he would get his raw material. As for the technical details, fortune smiled on him by sending Jack, an Englishman from Jamaica, a homosexual on the prowl who'd tried to seduce him one evening in a club on the Avenue of the Pyramids. On his native island, Jack had operated a rum distillery for years. He'd left everything behind, drawn by Egypt's glitter, but got lost in the old city's brothels. About alcohol production—he knew his business, and soon understood that Zohar was serious. He told him, 'It all depends on how much you want. Hundreds of litres? In that case, you could set up your factory in a garage. Thousands? You'd need an isolated barn because, before extracting the alcohol, the distillery will stink up the neighbourhood. And if you want to produce hundreds of thousands, you could try everything, you'd never get by unnoticed.'

Zohar knew exactly what he wanted: quality rather than quantity. He asked Jack if he knew how to extract an alcohol which could be sold as gin—looking like it and just as strong. 'Nothing simpler,' Jack declared, 'once the machinery is set up, it will take about three months between obtaining the cane and delivering the first bottles.'

Joe di Reggio took care of incorporating the business, registering it with the Commerce Department, and managing the books. They would call their enterprise the 'Blue Water Company' because they'd decided to sell their product in navy blue bottles. They presented it to the government as a sugar-producing operation. They established their office on Doctor Tawfik Street, in the Abasseya district. Attached to the building was a huge garage which they transformed into a small production unit. Nino, the most skilled at reading and interpreting texts, was put in charge of relations with the authorities, distributing bribes to obtain permits or avoid punishment. During this preparatory period, Zohar continued his nighttime commerce so he could amass the necessary funds for the initial investments. They hired Jack the Jamaican to set up 'the factory', and dozens of little hands milled about the workshop, adjusting metal drums to build a perfectly acceptable distillation column or to shape huge copper pots destined to heat the intermediate liquors.

The Allies were retreating on all fronts. After the falls of Belgium, Holland and France, Europe was on its knees. In the Balkans, all the countries were either occupied or controlled by the Axis powers. In the Middle East, the Iraqi government had been overthrown by Al-Kilani, an ardently pro-Nazi nationalist. Haj Amin al-Husseini, the Grand Mufti of Jerusalem, vanished from Palestine to suddenly reappear in Berlin, bellowing at the top of his lungs through German radio microphones, exhorting the Arabs to revolt against the British occupiers. Egypt, which had resisted an initial Italian invasion through Libya, was now enduring Rommel's assaults; the British were losing battle after battle. Chased out of Libya, they'd retreated to Egypt, and a wind of panic was blowing through the streets of Cairo, each day a little stronger. Rommel had crossed the western frontier—he was reaching the gates of Alexandria—he was bombing Port Said. The situation was growing critical. The British could not let the Egyptian lock be broken—the access to the Suez Canal that would open the route to Middle Eastern oil and the riches of the Indies. The military police were patrolling nonstop, day and night, and their forays into bars and hotels often ended in arrests and blows. New troops flowed in as reinforcements: cavalcades of trucks crammed with soldiers, heavy assault tanks crushing the overheated macadam along the two roads that led from Cairo to the sea. In the souks, people claimed that nearly a million foreigners, largely military men, were now in Egypt.

The poor Egyptian masses tried as best they could to profit from the manna, but suffered from the scarcity of food and the exorbitant prices it commanded on the black market. The middle class—employees and civil servants—were scandalized by the behaviour of the soldiers, who went around drunk in the streets, bottle in hand, clasping Arab women, not always prostitutes, around the waist.

Nino became more actively involved in the nationalist meetings to which Gamal led him. He returned from each one more convinced of the need to struggle against the British occupiers. His debates with Joe grew heated.

'You're not after all going to support the Nazis' entry into Egypt!' Joe yelled.

'The Germans never colonized Egypt. They're not interested in occupation. To them, this country is only a gateway. They'll liberate us from the British and go elsewhere, to Iraq or Saudi Arabia.'

'You're so naive, my poor Nino! You're letting your head be stuffed by these mock revolutionaries. If Rommel enters Egypt, it will be with the Gestapo, his secret police. Do you need me to tell you what will happen to you next?'

The insult finally came. The more political it was, the more it risked turning into a fistfight.

'You're nothing but a rich kid, a filthy capitalist! What can we expect from you?'

'I may be a rich kid, but I'm not a traitor. I don't abandon my people. If you want to fight the British, go to Palestine and join the secret Jewish army fighting for our independence.'

'Our? You said "our". So who do you include in this "our"? Huh? Me, I don't take sides. My "our" is the people. And here the people is the Egyptian people.'

Joe took off his jacket, undid his bow tie, rolled up his sleeves. He was getting ready to slam his fist into Nino's nose. Zohar arrived just then and grabbed him by his arms, dragging him back.

'Let me go!' Joe yelled, 'Let me at him so I can crush him like a fly on the wall, this *mamzer*, this bastard.'

Zohar always managed to calm them, to reunite them over a glass of arak. They recalled their first night with the three English-women, and the eternal friendship they'd vowed at dawn; he reminded them of the nights that had followed, those feasts of poetry, sensuality and joy, to which they'd brought Oriental musicians and Egyptian dancers; their jaunts in the middle of the night in the crazy MG to the sea, ending at the casino. And he reasoned with them. Their company was about to launch. The Blue Water would make people forget the whiskey labels that could hardly be found any more, Johnny the walker and the two black-and-white fox terriers. They were going to be rich, very rich. There would be time

enough later to see whether they still wanted to be Zionists or revolutionaries. All their theories were nothing but child's play, cut off
from the real world.

'But he's the one, this four-eyes, this garbage-lover, who wants
to be king of the poor. As for being king, you'd be better off choosing
your subjects somewhere other than a cesspool.'

'And you,' Nino rejoined, 'Zionist, son of a dog. You think
they're so great, those Palestinian Jews of yours, who sleep in tents
on the sand, like Bedouins?'

'You're not going to start again!'

And they started again, of course. They sized each other up,
competing like two young cocks. But they always reconciled, because
they had Zohar, their friend and guide, Zohar of whom they knew
nothing, about whom they understood nothing and who sometimes
frightened them.

One day after the siesta, he summoned his two partners just as
they were leaving their homes, freshly showered, shirts immaculate
and shoes polished. As they'd done so many times, all three climbed
into the MG and Zohar led them to Bab al-Zuwayla. From his brief-
case, he drew out a hammer and a nail, a big one, about fifteen cen-
timetres long. He approached the wall that framed the big door,
climbed onto a wooden crate and started to drive in the nail. He hit
it three times, saying 'Zohar' with the first blow, 'son of Mordechai
Zohar' with the second and 'child of Esther Zohar, Paradise is
beneath your feet' with the third. Then he handed the hammer to Joe.
'Your turn now!' Joe hesitated a moment, then asked, 'But what are
you attaching to the wall?' Then he did the same: 'Giuseppe di
Reggio, son of Ephraim di Reggio, child of Elisabeth di Reggio.'
He hesitated. 'Repeat!' ordered Zohar. He repeated, 'Paradise at his
feet.' When it was his turn, Nino resisted: 'You won't make me do
ridiculous things. I don't believe in all this nonsense.' Zohar put
the hammer in his hands and mocked him. 'What? What do you need
to believe in? All you have to do is plant a nail.' So, Nino struck the

nail with rage: 'Abraham Cohen, son of Gabriel Cohen, child of Rachel . . . ' He couldn't finish and dissolved in tears. The thought of his mother always uncorked intense emotion in him. 'It's good!' said Zohar, 'It's good! Now turn and face the wall.' He placed a hand on each of his companions' heads and murmured, 'If you see bees emerging, you'll thank Solomon, king of all the creatures of creation. If they're frogs, you'll ask which of the three is a traitor. If a snake appears, move away and thank God you're still alive. And if it's a goat, then say, "Muslims, Jews or Christians, we're all children of Abraham."' He stepped back. Nino and Joe were immobile, staring at their shoes. Then they lifted their heads and looked at the nail. Three bees were circling its flat head, sparkling in the setting sun.

*

Zohar had an instinctive sense of the obligation humans owed the spirits. Before opening his shop, he had his mother come to it in the middle of the night. Khadouja, the witch, joined them, bringing one of those nondescript stray dogs that infested the souks. The poor creature, his paws pinioned, did not stop whimpering. Khadouja dropped him on the doorstep, then drew from her dress coloured powders she set alight as she uttered incomprehensible sounds, 'Baws' and 'Akhs', a sort of barking that echoed disturbingly through the night. She pulled up her dress, displaying her dark thighs, and spat out curses as she rubbed her buttocks on the ground. Then she took a long, sharp knife and slit the dog's throat, its final moan lost in the distance like a butterfly's flight. With her knife, she collected some of the blood that spurted from the carotid artery and applied it to Zohar's forehead. Then, with a practiced hand, she separated the head from the body which she buried on the threshold. She then gave Zohar the still-bleeding head: 'This head—because this shop will propel you to the head and never to the tail—this head,' she told him, 'will permit you to sleep here, in the shop, the very place where you'll receive your customers. Tomorrow, you'll come before sunrise, you'll take the head and throw it in the Nile, over your shoulder, without looking to see where it lands. Do you understand?' Zohar made a face. 'You'll do it, my son,' Khadouja insisted, 'to clear the way.'

On 21 September 1941, the day the first case of Blue Water was delivered, Zohar wasn't yet seventeen, Joe barely nineteen and Nino twenty. They were probably the youngest business owners in all of Egypt. At first, they sold a case of six one-litre bottles for twenty pounds sterling, close to double a worker's monthly wages. The first customers, high-ranking, arrived through the efforts of the three Englishwomen. Soon, lines of six-windowed Hillmans, Morris Eights, two-toned Humbers or voluptuous Sunbeams were parking in front of the factory door. You could see young soldiers piling the cases into their commanders' cars.

The success was so great that by December they'd already exhausted their stock, which made the prices climb higher. And when officials from the Ministry of Commerce came to examine their books, they left with their trunks filled with cases of Blue Water.

Nino, the most serious of the three, ran the office. He'd traded his post at Assiouty's pharmacy for this much more lucrative position as commercial director of the Blue Water Company. Joe, who looked like what he was, a young man from a good family, was responsible for bringing in new customers. He found them among those who frequented his father's palace.

At the start of 1942, you could see another kind of automobile arriving in Abasseya: Americans—Chevrolets and Ford convertibles, sumptuous Packards, Cicurel's Cadillac and even, sometimes, the palace Rolls-Royce. Zohar was a permanent presence—at once the soul of the place and its devil. He ran endlessly from one worker to another. He pressured Jack the Jamaican to increase production. He encouraged porters, warehousemen, cane cutters and attendants at the distillery, distributing bonuses each time they improved their output. He served as both personnel director and social director. And all those workers, peasants driven from their land or emigrants from Upper Egypt, sometimes from the Sudan, were surprised that such a young man could head such an important business. 'He's a demon!' one of them exclaimed. And another replied: 'A son of Adam would not know how to succeed at this without the help of the folk.' The folk—those folk were not folk, not exactly—sometimes they were called 'Muslims' in a propitiatory formula intended to chase away the terrifying prospect that they might be Jewish, or, worse, pagan. Those they called the 'folk' were the spirits, the afrits.

Rommel's diabolical Afrika Korps, agile and over-trained, seemed unbeatable. They surged in where they weren't expected, inflicted losses, retreated, attacked elsewhere. The British were constantly on the defensive, and, despite the arrival of reinforcements and quantities of materiel, couldn't manage to seize the initiative. The French and English newspapers warned residents what a catastrophe German victory, followed by a new occupation of Egypt, would be: the violence, the pillage, the exploitation of resources. Some Europeans and well-off Jews imagined exile in Upper Egypt, in the Sudan or in Jerusalem. As for the Arab newspapers, they didn't hide their sympathy for Rommel, rejoicing in anticipation of the lesson the arrogant British would receive, the ones who kept repeating how they were educating an immature populace. Benghazi fell in January, Bir Hakeim in June. The more the tension mounted, the more the Company sold its bottles of Blue Water.

Zohar moved into a little three-room flat on the building's top floor. He tried to persuade his father to give up his alcohol business, for which it was becoming more and more difficult to obtain supplies. 'Join us at the factory. I'll hire you as the accountant.' Motty obstinately refused. How could he dream of leaving the alleys, where he knew each family, where his feet knew the shape of each stone? How to leave the Haim-Capucci Synagogue, where he could put a name to each voice? He answered his beloved son: 'Why have you never learnt what to do with your time? My eyes that don't see teach me what is permanent in the world. That's what you must cling to, my son. There where life is eternal.' And he sang for him that verse from the Song of Songs that Zohar had heard so many times: 'There are threescore queens, and fourscore concubines, and virgins without number. My dove, my undefiled, is but one.' Perhaps for the first time in his life, a tear rolled down Zohar's cheek.

Suleiman Pasha Street

Since the opening of the Blue Water Company's shop in September 1941, Nino Cohen had moved into a small flat on Suleiman Pasha Street, a few steps from The American, the elegant patisserie where Joe sometimes waited to drive him to work. Aside from his lodging that brought him closer to the factory, he hadn't changed any of his habits. He went around on foot or by tram, always in Third Class. He always wore the same dark grey trousers, shiny at the knees, which he pulled up mechanically whenever he tripped on the cuffs— and the same open-collared white shirt, which made you think he owned a dozen identical ones. With his ascetic body, fresh-shaven face and a myopic's thick glasses on his nose, he looked like a seminarian. Once his workday was over, he disappeared, refusing the games of backgammon over a beer on a cafe terrace. No one ever saw him after dinner in the clubs—the Empire or the St James— where the others played poker while rehashing Middle Eastern history from the time of the pharaohs. No one saw him either in the big hotels where they'd acquired the habit of dancing until first light. He claimed he had to go home to study, that he couldn't allow himself to fail his year of medicine. And his two friends, vaguely guilty about not cultivating their own grey matter, didn't insist. But, without admitting it, they were uneasy.

For, little by little, Nino's behaviour was starting to change. He no longer spoke anything but Arabic, refusing to share in the Franco-Anglo-Arab sabir sprinkled with Italian that was their usual tongue. Instead, he used obscure expressions and declined his nouns, as in classical texts. 'If you speak Arabic, you speak Arabic, not the composite language of slaves.' Laughingly, Joe pointed out, 'Sometimes, we don't understand a word of what you're saying—it's like listening to the radio.' He made fun of him when he shut himself up for a long time in the bathroom: 'My mother says all you need to do is take a spoonful of tamarind syrup in the morning before breakfast,' implying that he suffered from constipation, and always added, 'It might brighten your mood—and spare ours!' Joe didn't let a day go by without asking what Nino was doing with his money, why he was always dressed like a beggar—you'd think he was throwing it away in brothels or at the races.

When the comments and gibes grew too insistent, Nino launched into long political harangues. He, for one, wasn't a reactionary. He didn't want to be like the khawagates, those 'gentlemen' of banks and big hotels; he wanted to join the Egyptian people who would inevitably liberate themselves from the oppressors' yoke, first that of the British, then the wealthy, the pashas, the landowners . . . Slyly, Joe would add, 'You've forgotten the Jews.' And Nino would let himself be caught. 'The Jews, yes! The Cicurels, the Mosseris, the Suares, the Picciottos, the Hararis, the Curiels.' Joe pressed his point. 'It seems that the young Curiel, the son of the banker, is not a millionaire but a billionaire. Actually, he's a communist, like you. Communism is an occupation of the rich. What's more, my mother's one too.' The tension between them mounted again. And Nino let loose, bitingly: 'My poor friend! You don't understand a thing. I'm not a communist.'

When Joe told Zohar about the dispute, he asked, 'But if he's not a communist, what's his problem?'

'I know him well,' Zohar replied, 'he's secretive. You should let him be.'

'Could I just let him say that Jews are exploiters? He should be taken on a visit to the hara, the alley. He'd see poor Jews, our relatives, lying on the pavement, their excrement caking their clothes, not having eaten for days, so hungry they no longer have the strength to get up.'

Zohar's eyes were lost in the void at this description of the hara. He saw once more the grocery of his childhood; Uncle Elie, his

great-uncle, truly a man of gentle wisdom; his mother, the strange
Esther, to whom he did not know how to express his affection; and
Motty, his father, who guided him from afar with the words of the
psalms he'd implanted in his soul.

'Let him talk,' he told Joe, dreaming. 'When he loves a girl so
much he trembles to feel the Nile breeze caressing his face, trust
me, he won't miss a single game of backgammon.'

'Unless it's a boy.'

'A boy? What do you mean?'

'I mean: unless he falls in love with a boy.'

Nino, shepherded by Gamal, went to all the nationalist military
group's weekly Thursday night meetings. But he found the activists
too ineffectual, spoilt by the army and its mad passion for hierarchy.
They stood as stiff as toy soldiers. It was always a matter of this
sergeant here, that lieutenant there. What was the point of invoking
their rank, if they were all equally poor and devoid of the least
actual power? What was one to think about a country surrounded
by war, invaded by hundreds of thousands of foreign soldiers, whose
own army had to remain paralysed, its weapons at its feet? As for
weapons, they had none, certainly not new ones, and even fewer
munitions. So, rather than playing at being soldiers from another era,
all these mostly lower-middle-class youths—who'd acquired their
positions through merit—would have done better to turn directly to
political action. That's what Nino thought in his heart of hearts.

At one meeting, he saw a man who didn't look like the others.
He wasn't a military man. Dressed conservatively in Western fashion,
with a dark suit and a white shirt, he had a smooth face and fiery
eyes, his bare head showing off his growing baldness. He never
smiled, never joked and his speech was sharp as a knife. 'We should
abandon these big useless meetings that end up in cafe gossip. The
hour for action has tolled!' the man said. The remark was chilling.
Gamal tried to save the situation by reminding them that the orator,
Abd al-Raouf al-Gassem, whom he was happy to welcome here at

the military officers' club, belonged to a nationalist religious group. 'Our goals are related,' he pointed out, 'but our methods sometimes differ.'

Abd al-Raouf drew up his tall body. 'The army is disarmed. If it thinks that pride is a weapon, it's wrong. Pride leads only to vainglory and failure. Brothers, get to work. Go into each house, speak to each fellah, remind him of his duty to our prophet—the power of unity, of community—recount the greatness of the Arab nation.'

Nino was deeply moved by Abd al-Raouf's words. The Arab nation—he was part of it. He said to himself, 'Arab of Jewish faith.' No! he corrected himself internally. 'Arab of Jewish origin.' That day, Nino did not dare approach Abd al-Raouf, content to devour him with his eyes.

At the end of the next meeting, he asked if he could walk home with him. The man looked him up and down before replying, 'Are you a Muslim, my brother?'

'Muslim?' answered Nino. 'What is a Muslim? The word means someone who has "submitted", does it not? I submit to the will of the people. And so, if you like, I'm a Muslim.'

'That's good! But do you at least say your prayers?'

And he explained that submitting to the rules of the community made life flow easily. Do you think before breathing? No! It's an action necessary to life, which you accomplish without thinking about it. That's how prayer should be performed, without thought, without effort, like breathing, at every moment of the day.

Nino found him at once intelligent and powerful. But prayer, really!

'I'll consider your advice,' Nino promised. 'But it's action I need, not prayers.'

'You're mistaken, my brother. Prayer is action, its effect on the world a distant consequence.'

'Prayer is action? I thought it was contemplation.'

'It is a whole,' explained Abd al-Raouf. 'God is our goal.'

'Don't we say God is our Creator?'

'No, my brother. The mistake is to think He is at our origin. God is not our past, but our future. And to reach that future, the Prophet is our guide. He is the one who shows us the way. If you think all you do is read words in the Qur'an, then you're not a living being but a statue of salt. The Qur'an is a way, the path that takes over your legs, your arms, your soul, and carries you. Your destination is God!'

Nino was possessed by Abd al-Raouf's ideas. They blazed in his mind like truths. He had not admitted it to himself, but the Marxist violence, the invocation of the revolts of the proletariat, the nearly mathematical reasoning of the communist brochures, echoed like distant images from cold countries. What he was hearing now, from the mouth of this man, healthy, clean and pure like the trunk of a palm tree, was true—as true as the sun that rose each morning, as true as the Nile that was a sea carved out of the desert. Abd al-Raouf was speaking of Egypt's revolution, not Russia's or America's. Here was the revelation!

'Can anyone follow this path you're describing?'

'Do you think I'd show you a road that's forbidden? It would be like flaunting a feast before a starving man and forbidding him access.'

'How—?'

Nino didn't finish his sentence, suddenly aware of the triteness of the question he was about to ask. He could guess the answer. The other would tell him all he had to do was convert to Islam. He shook his head no, reproaching himself inwardly for his naivety.

'Jihad!' Abd al-Raouf said then. 'Jihad is our path towards God.'

'Jihad?' The scholarly Nino was startled, for to him the word meant only 'internal spiritual struggle'.

'Our prophet is a warlord. He guides us by example. The community will awaken through war. Jihad is the necessity for war, and death is our most faithful ally.'

'What are you saying?'

'You need to understand, my brother, if you want to join us. Our love of death is the presence of God. This is the teaching of the Prophet.' And he repeated, 'You must love death!'

Nino remained perplexed. Death is an eventuality for any combatant. You try to avoid it, to protect yourself. You may certainly wish for your enemy's death; you may do everything you can to kill him. But what did it mean, 'to love death'?

'Are you saying we mustn't fear killing our enemy, that we need to prepare ourselves for armed struggle? Is that it?'

There were many passersby. The two men had to continuously clear a path without losing the thread of their conversation. Suddenly, Abd al-Raouf stood still. 'Look!' he said to Nino, pointing to an Arab woman strolling on the arm of a British officer. 'This woman fears poverty and death. That's why she's lost her soul. She prostitutes herself with foreigners, she dirties her body and the house of her Father. All because she fears death.'

The couple was walking a few steps ahead of them. The woman was dressed in a modern suit, rose-coloured, the skirt above her knees, her buttocks swaying in rhythm with her high heels. The military man, a British officer, clearly tipsy, was staggering as he tried to hold onto his cap with one hand.

'Look and reflect, my brother. Look where the fear of your death can lead. This is what I'm trying to tell you: we are the inverse of this woman. Not only do we not fear death but it is our own death that we desire above all. To die during jihad is our dearest wish.'

'Our death,' murmured Nino, wide-eyed. 'Our death—'

'Next Friday,' Abd al-Raouf suggested, 'come for prayer. Our Guide himself will preach the sermon. You'll probably understand these truths more clearly when you hear them from his lips.'

At the door to the mosque, before parting, Nino was startled when the man vigorously grasped his shoulders and kissed him on both cheeks. 'I'll introduce you to him.'

The mixture of cheap eau de cologne and sweat shook Nino, a strange sensation he'd never experienced, a new feeling of shared virility.

The following Friday, Nino went to one o'clock prayer at the Great Mosque. Despite the throng, he was impressed by the order and discipline. No shoving, no gossiping. Hundreds of men—perhaps even a thousand—gathered in the same place, to murmur the same words, at the same time, to make the same gestures, to prostrate themselves, to raise their open palms to the heavens, like a gigantic ballet. What a contrast with the disorder of a synagogue! He didn't know the prayers, only the first, the Fatihah, which he tried to stammer. But he was seized by an impulse that arose, paradoxically, from an impression of nothingness. Who was he amid this throng? An atom, a blade of grass in a prairie? Here's what it was to join the people. And a breath from the depths filled his lungs.

'I'll teach you the prayers and show you the suras of the Qur'an that correspond to them.'

He jumped, then recognized that acrid mixture of sweat and eau de cologne. Abd al-Raouf had slipped behind him and was signalling, by pressing his arms, when to make prostrations.

'I came to see and to hear, as you suggested,' Nino answered in one breath.

When the prayer was over, the men sat down, waiting in perfect order for their imam to mount the podium. The man, dressed in a grey suit, his beard trimmed, his tarbouche on his head, was seated in the first row. Nothing distinguished him from the group of elders beside him. He rose slowly, climbed the few steps, and moved to the center of the platform. He was greeted by total silence, impressive—not a sound, not a movement, not even a clearing of the throat.

'My brothers, I feel you all here,' began the Guide. 'I hear your soul murmuring in mine, your heart beating in mine. And I feel that I am nothing, nothing but all of you together.'

Nino was suddenly dizzy. He leant on Abd al-Raouf's arm, who held him firmly and admonished, 'Sit up straight, my brother!'

It's that the words of the Guide had joined Nino's thought, mingling with his desire, granted that very moment, of melting into the Egyptian people. He made an effort to sit up, but his unease persisted.

'And your voice is expressed through mine, my brothers,' the Guide continued. 'When you speak in your heart, I cry with my mouth and I articulate the faith we all have, my brothers, that God is the greatest!'

A murmur arose like a huge wave rolling from the depths of the assembly, 'God is the greatest!'

'And so it is that they wish to reduce us to silence—not by attacking Islam with words, in those interminable debates conducted by the false sages of Al-Azhar, no! Not through the stupefying Islam of the Sufis, who only know how to make old women dance and plunge the people into archaism. No! They want to prevent Islam from affirming its solidarity with our brothers in need, they want to stifle Islam's strict morality, which protects the virtue of our women and girls. One of our brothers who had come to join us, a hero of past wars, of irreproachable character, General Aziz Ali al-Masri, has been imprisoned. He will be judged by a court martial—to put it plainly, he faces the death penalty. Will we let our great brother, our elder, our example, be taken so shamefully? It's as if we were to allow a leg of ours to be amputated. No, my brothers! We will act because God is the greatest—and our path towards him is jihad!'

That same murmur, immense, exploded again from the assembly: 'God is the greatest.'

The Guide's sermon lasted two hours. The crowd of the faithful went out, burning at white heat. Each dreamt only of revolution, of marching against the royal palace, attacking the British military in the streets. Resistance! Nino, ashen, staggered, leaning on Abd al-Raouf's arm as he accompanied him home. Along the way, they continued to talk.

'I warned you. Our Guide's words are powerful. You're not the first to be overcome in hearing him.'

'Yes, I felt faint. I have to admit I haven't eaten anything for two days.'

'To accept these words, so that they are a balm for your soul, and not a bolt of lightning that lays you low, you must become Muslim, my brother.'

Abd al-Raouf stopped on the way at the home of Omar, a young imam who was a member of their group, and invited him to join them. When they reached Nino's, the two Muslims were surprised to find nothing but books in his flat.

'You're like our Prophet!' declared Abd al-Raouf. 'You too have meditated for a long time, very long. And like him, one day you fell, you understood and you submitted. Today is the day on which you saw the light!'

Nino recited the shahada, the profession of faith, that beautiful Arabic sentence, composed of alliteration and music, 'There is no god but God, and Mohammed is his messenger.' It was as if he were not himself—he felt that he was at once reaching the goal and experiencing the anguish of being completely, absolutely, in the world.

From that day forward, Nino was riven in two. One part was his old self, which he rediscovered every morning at the factory, in the others' eyes, in their jokes and references, and in his family, which he now endured with a vague sense of disgust. And the other was this new personality, walled-off, a little stiff—but strong—which he nurtured through his attendance at the nationalist military meetings and his occasional presence at the mosque. Because Abd al-Raouf didn't want him to be a Muslim like all the rest. He wanted to use his unusual profile—Jewish, intellectual, soon to be a doctor—to infiltrate the military and the circles of power. He came to him several times a week at the flat on Suleiman Pasha Street and spoke to him of revolution, of God and of strategy.

One day, he entrusted him with a delicate mission: an attempt to save the prince.

Sidi Gaber Street (Alexandria)

By the end of 1941, tension between the British and the Egyptians was at breaking point. To ease it, the Egyptian Government had granted Allied bases the status of foreign territories. As a result, they were subject not to Egyptian but to British law, and all aggression against them was punished by court martial. Yet a rumour grew that made the Egyptians harder and harder to control: Rommel would be the victor, and the British were planning their retreat. People were even saying that at Kasr al-Dobara, in the Chief of Staff's offices, the main activity was the destruction of the archives. Some added that they were instituting a scorched-earth policy. But the earth they were planning to burn before they left was the Egyptians', not theirs. In this atmosphere, the king, as always, tried to calm the powerful while safeguarding the future. Farouk wanted at all costs to maintain Egypt's strange neutrality, refusing to declare war on the Axis Powers.

Monday, 15 December 1941. Was the wind beginning to turn? For the first time, the British, with the help of their Commonwealth allies and Polish troops, had forced the Afrika Korps to retreat. Retrenched in Gazala, Rommel had abandoned the siege of Tobruk.

Nino arrived around eleven in the morning and rang at the gate—he'd been warned that the prince never rose before ten. The evening before, he'd taken the night train, had slept in snatches on the wooden benches in Third Class, crammed between noisy peasants and a huge woman swathed in layers of black cloth. The peasants had talked all night, gobbled kilos of bread stuffed with favas dripping oil, spat onto the floor the sugarcane stalks they chewed nonstop. They'd argued, made up, argued again. Luckily, they got off at

Tanta. He could have used the time to sleep, but thoughts were ricocheting through his head.

Once on the platform, his anxiety ratcheted up. British soldiers were everywhere, haughtily inspecting each passenger. He left the Alexandria-Misr station at seven, limping, his back aching. Outside, he quaked at the sight of armoured tanks, batteries of machine guns, dozens of troops with rifles on their shoulders. He moved forward slowly, hesitating, seeking the right direction. A young soldier, not even twenty, blocked his path. He was tall and thin, with glasses on his nose. Nino thought this soldier might have been him, if he'd been born over there. Where? An Englishman, Scots perhaps. He was red-headed. Nino explained in English that he was a student, soon to be a doctor, who'd come for a residency at the Alexandria hospital. The other didn't question him further and let him continue onward.

He strolled along the corniche, awaiting the time appointed for his visit. Thanks to the morning breeze, the more he walked, the more he felt cleansed of the night's filth. 'Aren't you ashamed?' he reproached himself. 'Why such disgust? What do you have to reproach them with? These are the Egyptian people, the people you long to serve.' And he immediately made a distinction: 'To serve the Egyptian people, yes. But first to educate it, to draw it from its abjection, its easy subservience, its filth—yes—from its filth, most of all!'

He was walking towards Sidi Bishr, the celebrated beach, the elite's summer playground. But it was far. Soon, he had to turn back, to veer off towards the Sporting Club, near the prince's dwelling.

If you had the good fortune to be invited into his palace in Alexandria—which wasn't hard, since he liked to surround himself with commoners—you ended up being brought into his office, his sanctuary. Rare-wood furniture, huge Persian carpets. On the wall, a collection of sabres, scimitars and Bedouin daggers, surrounded by wild animal trophies, mounted antelopes, leopards with huge teeth, buffaloes with tired smiles. Regal, he sat in his armchair as on a throne before inviting you to come in. At his feet, an enormous stuffed lion, more than two metres long, with a sad, stiff mane and lost eyes. He was stroking the lion's head as if it were a dog. Chin forward, a strangely naive smile, short hair plastered with brilliantine, His Lordship, the nabil Mohammed Abdel Halim, prince of royal blood, was holding a glass of whiskey in his hand.

'Would you like some tea, my young friend? Or some soda? A whiskey, perhaps? What's your name?'

He had a strange Arabic accent; it was obviously not his native tongue. In any case, it couldn't be English or French.

'I am honoured to find myself in your presence, O Prince! My name is Nino, Your Highness, and I have an urgent message for you.'

'Nino, did you say? Nino what?'

The young man cast his eyes about. On a small desk against the wall, a photo of the prince, twenty-five years earlier, in a leather aviator's cap topped by goggles; his eyes clear, piercing. Nino pointed to the photo. 'Were you in the war as an aviator?'

Flattered, the man sank back into his chair, placed a hand on a hip, crossed his legs. He liked being looked at. 'In the Luftstreitkräfte, the German Air Force, yes! I fought in the East, on the Russian Front, before joining the Ottoman Air Force. I must have been your age at the time.' He burst out laughing, the coarse laugh of a crude soldier. 'And do you know who was one of my comrades in my squadron? A close friend, I must say—Hermann! You don't know him?' Another burst of laughter. 'Hermann Göring, the German hero, now Minister in the Third Reich. You're not going to tell me you haven't heard of him.'

It was true, then! What Joe repeated almost every day wasn't just rumour. The prince was allied with the Germans, and by much more than opportunistic sympathy.

Nino rose to look at the photos more closely. 'May I?'

The prince's face lit up with a big smile. 'Of course! Look! You'll see the strength granted by an intense youth—always the promise of a successful life.'

Nino's attention was drawn by another photo. The prince, standing, dressed entirely in white, in a sweater with a rolled collar, sports trousers, tennis shoes on his feet. He was holding the collar of an enormous mastiff, as white as his clothes. 'Your dog?' Nino asked.

The prince's face darkened. 'He was my dog! I buried him last year. We were two comrades, joined for life, until death. His name was Panzer. It's a German word. Do you know what it means?'

'Dog, son of a dog!' Nino thought. 'Why the devil did Abd al-Raouf send me to this clown? Why should he be saved? Let him rot in a British prison or in the one we'll build when we take over, what difference does it make?' But Nino was disciplined. So he answered: 'No, I don't know. What does it mean?'

'Panzer, let's see. Panzer means "tank".' And the prince burst out laughing again. 'I could have called him Reich. But that would have been too much, don't you think?'

Everyone knew that Hitler had conquered the Poles, the Czechs, the Austrians, then the Belgians and the French in a lighting war, thanks to his panzers. In Egypt, people spoke daily about Rommel defying the British while playing like a virtuoso on his battalions of panzers. Rommel, whose presence hung over Egypt like the shadow of a huge black bird. So, to call his dog Panzer—he might just as well have raised a flag with a swastika on his palace gable.

The prince was an extrovert, his interests clearly displayed on his walls. He was a hunter, a killer of big game whose death dates were engraved in gold letters on each trophy's wooden frame. He was also athletic: as president of the Olympic Club, he'd posed in his fencing outfit, in a swimsuit, at the wheel of a racing bike. But the most beautiful photograph, enlarged, colourized, showed him at the wheel of a black Mercedes SSK, a diabolically fast vehicle, with a huge striped hood, traversed by six enormous chrome tubes—a racing car that could reach speeds of two hundred and thirty kilometres per hour, already, in 1930. Smiling in his leather helmet, one hand on the wheel, the other in a Roman salute.

'My my!' Nino cried. 'Such a car must be worth millions.'

'It was a gift. My German friends know my passion for cars. Do you know I was educated in Germany? I still have so many friends there.'

So that was it, that strange accent. He had German at the tip of his tongue, so to speak. As for his infatuation with cars, Nino had heard of it. Since 1936, several times a year, the prince organized rallies in the Western desert, penetrating deep into Libya. What was he thinking? It was a sure bet he'd contributed to the drawing of maps that must now be quite useful on Rommel's field tables.

The prince was not unknown to Nino, who'd once gone with his comrades to his villa in Cairo, along the Nile corniche. There, in his basement, the prince gathered groups of nationalist union members, whom his henchmen trained in guerilla warfare. Nino had watched their training. They were being initiated into street combat, the use of blackjacks, rifles, all kinds of arms. The trainers explained to the astonished recruits how to overturn a tram; how to set fire to a store, synagogue or church; how to instigate a riot.

To prepare the people for struggle was a good idea, Nino had thought at the time. He knew they would never expel the British without resorting to force. He didn't doubt the enterprise's merit, but he questioned the prince's sincerity, seeing him there on his wooden throne, dressed to the nines, his hair slicked back, barking orders to an army of servants. Ever since that first encounter, during which Nino had been content to sit silently in a corner, the prince had seemed to him an egocentric bully whose passion for himself clouded his perception of the world. But Abd al-Raouf had explained to Nino that in politics you had to work with the forces that were present. And the prince was one such force, in one hand holding the truckers' union, and in the other a fluid alliance with the German forces.

'So, do you have an urgent message for me?'

'O my nabil, we've learnt that the British are convinced that some powerful people, close to the court, are transmitting highly important military intelligence to Rommel. They are seeking the transmitters. They will probably search your house in Cairo.'

'So why didn't you call me on the telephone, you ass?' the prince retorted.

'Gamal told me that telephone communication was not safe. He charged me with bringing you the message orally. That's why, dropping everything, I came to warn you.'

All of a sudden, vehicles could be heard braking in front of the palace. The sound of boots. Furious knocks at the door. Nino looked at the prince and couldn't refrain from blurting out, 'Cohen!'

'What?'

'You asked me my name: My name is Cohen. Nino Cohen!'

Later, languishing in his cell, Nino wondered at length what would have led him to utter the name that marked him as a Jew. Most likely provocation, he concluded; also, a way to test the prince, to confirm the rumours of antisemitism that swirled around him.

Pistol in hand, the British officer stormed into the room, followed by a dozen soldiers brandishing rifles. He addressed the prince. 'Are you Mohammed Abdel Halim?'

'Excuse me, sir! Not Mohammed Abdel Halim, like a servant, but the Nabil Mohamed Abdel Halim, if you please! Prince of royal blood. Yes, sir!'

'You are under arrest. You will follow us without protest!'

The prince later learnt that this arrest was not connected to the intelligence agency's ongoing inquiry into the activities of those close to the palace. The motive was at once simpler and more direct. The preceding week, he'd attended a reception where a throng of British officers milled about. He'd appeared in his German military uniform. He'd even shouted, 'It's like new! I just had it cleaned. I want to be impeccable, as if on parade, to welcome General Rommel when he comes to take possession of the Abdine Palace in Cairo.'

The prince and Nino both left the palace on Gaber Street in handcuffs, surrounded by a platoon of British troops. God only knows why Nino was imprisoned in Cairo, on Queen Nazli Street, in the foreigners' prison. He was not a foreigner, yet not Egyptian either—merely stateless.

Osman Bey Street

Masreya had become a beauty. She'd inherited her father's stature, proud nature and aristocratic bearing, along with her mother's dark skin and clear eyes which, on her, tended towards green. But unlike her mother, she feared neither the deceitful words of those close to her nor the notoriety associated with dancers in Egypt. At sixteen, she was already a kind of star, under her stage name, Ben't Jinane, meaning 'daughter of Jinane'—which was true—or 'girl of madness', 'maddening beauty', also true. She danced in cabarets, nightclubs and music halls. Appearing with huge orchestras composed of several dozen musicians, she'd created a hybrid show, halfway between Oriental dance and American revue. Known for her loose morals, she never hesitated to dine with an admirer, as long as he was a pasha, a minister, or, at the very least, a banker—but always a millionaire.

Fate had smiled on her since her first artist's steps at the age of thirteen; so much so that with the income from her ticket sales, she'd been able to purchase a villa in one of Cairo's wealthiest neighbour-hoods, on Osman Bey Street on the Island of Rhoda, a stone's throw from the Nile. She lived there with her mother and two guardians, Ouahiba and Baheya, peasants she'd brought with her from the village of Kafr al-Amar in the Delta. Her first film, in which she co-starred with Farid al-Amesh, the celebrated singer and actor, was a triumph. Since then, her picture was plastered on magazine covers and blown up on cinema facades. 'Where are you fleeing, mistress of men's madness?' asked Farid, whose favours she refused. 'Barely blooming, you've garnered what the greatest don't acquire at their peak. Don't you think an experienced man like me could help you avoid life's pitfalls?'

She was having none of it. She knew how to take care of herself, little Masreya. She entrusted her assets to a Coptic banker, old Boutros Nabil; the management of the house to her mother, Jinane, whom she'd moved into an flat in the villa; and her career to a poet, the timid Kacim, who always had original staging ideas that made her shine. But the key to her success lay elsewhere, in her fierce defence of her independence. She liked to say, 'Woman is a panther, powerful in the wild. Captured, she grows mad or dies.' From her mother's history, she'd concluded that misery comes to women who let themselves be imprisoned by one man. And so, she decided to have many. To all, however, she forbade access to her home, meeting them elsewhere, sometimes at their houses, most often in luxury hotels along the corniche—the Semiramis for the British, the Intercontinental for the rest.

Kacim, her poet-producer, madly in love with her, was the only man admitted into her home, in the intimacy of her room opening onto a large terrace overlooking the Nile. He had her rehearse her dance numbers, inventing new choreographies and composing songs she never sang.

'My mother sings much better than I do!' she said by way of excuse.

'But your mother no longer sings, Masreya! No one will compare you to her. You could equal or surpass her, without a doubt.'

'Oh, you're not going to start again, Kacim! I don't want to sing alone on stage. I can accompany Farid or even Abdel Wahab. I've already done it. But to fill the whole stage with my voice—I don't want to, I can't!'

Kacim left again with the love poems he copied into a thick note-book from which he never parted. Every now and then, he opened it, measuring the precision and harmony of his verses: 'My beloved never looks at me, I who watch her every move.'

Early every Friday morning, cloaked in a peasant's long black gown, her head wrapped in a scarf, Masreya, accompanied by Kacim, began her circuit among her rich neighbours—senators, lawyers, businessmen. She was seeking alms. She liked these moments when she plunged back into the humility of her condition. Her celebrated face, her aura, her luminous smile, opened all doors and she requested alms to feed the poor of the old city, the people who swarmed in the filthy alleys around the Grand Mosque; she requested money to build a hospital or a social-aid centre; she requested so that Egypt might finally belong to the Egyptians. And the rich gave—they gave dozens of pounds. She returned home, her basket piled high with banknotes she counted meticulously, recording on a sheet of paper each amount beside each donor's name. Then she folded her packet of money in newspaper and went to the mosque for the mid-day prayer. Along the way, she stopped at the home of the man she called 'the Guide'. A young man appeared, cracking open the door, suspicious, 'The Guide is praying,' he always said. Lowering her eyes, she slipped the package through the gap. And he responded with a blessing, 'May our Father keep you, my sister!'

Then she took Kacim's arm and off they went, the two of them, their steps lighter, towards the mosque. And Kacim wrote in his notebook: 'She loves the one she knows not and knows not the one who loves her. My beloved never looks at me.'

Sometimes Kacim dared to comment: 'It's dangerous to associate with these people, you know. Especially now. Not a day goes by that one or another of them isn't thrown into prison.' She would trace out a joyous little dance step and exclaim, 'But what am I doing wrong? Is it wrong to collect money for the poor?'

On this day, Friday, 19 December 1941, when she returned from the mosque, still flanked by Kacim, she noticed a little two-seater parked in front of her villa. She'd never seen it before: green, black fins, top down, gorgeous tan leather seats. At the sound of steps on the gravel, the two porters, who lived in a small cabin in the garden, opened the double gate and bowed. Ouahiba was waiting for her on the doorstep, a jug of water in hand, and Baheya was holding a basin for her ablutions. She climbed the stairs quickly, curious.

'Two young men have come, O beloved! Of course I warned them that you receive no one on Friday, but they insisted.'

'You haven't let them in, have you, O guardian of my life?'

'Of course not! But they said they would return.' She approached Masreya and whispered: 'One of the two, the one with hair as black as a raven's wings, said to me: "Tell her that her brother has come to say hello." I know you don't have a brother. I told him I didn't believe him. He burst out laughing. "I'm even her twin!" he said. "Don't forget, you peasant." '

Masreya stood pensively on the doorstep. Then dismissed Kacim, who tried to resist: 'You might need me if these two strangers return.'

No. She wanted to be alone, to rest, to take care of her mother. Dejected, Kacim left with his head hanging, a line of poetry dancing through his head: 'One minute of her absence is a tomb to me. My love watches me leave and does not weep.'

From the doorstep, she could hear music. She found her mother sitting at the piano. Jinane, who could not read music, composed songs at the piano, songs that filled her soul. When she was carried away by her inner impulse, her fingers whirled wildly in a demonic dance and the world shrank to the space of her melodies. She discovered them as she created them, as if a spirit, an inspired musician, possessed her hands. Abandoned to this power, she was striking the keys so vigorously, tapping her feet and emitting little cries, that she didn't hear her daughter enter the room.

'O mother, look what a state you're in!' exclaimed Masreya.

Jinane paused, raised her eyes and smiled guiltily. She'd thrown herself at the piano as soon as she'd risen from bed; she hadn't combed, hadn't eaten, hadn't even splashed a little water on her face. Music had taken hold of her in the depths of the night, had hurled her towards the instrument.

'Wait! I think I've captured the tune in all its details. I'm afraid I'll forget it. Oh, if only I knew how to write music.'

She began again to strike the keys with a sense of urgency. Masreya raised her eyebrows and looked at Ouahiba who lifted her arms to show her helplessness. And Jinane played, and Masreya listened, gradually captured by this strange music that recalled the music of the Delta Sufis. Suddenly, they heard a voice coming from the entrance, clear as a clarinet's note, precisely meeting the melody: 'O Nofal, O Nofal, O Nofaaaa . . . '

The two women turned as one. Zohar had entered without knocking, followed by his friend Joe, who, to give himself some importance, was rhythmically twirling his little keychain around his finger. Jinane stopped playing.

'Weren't you playing the music for my words, O Mother?' asked Zohar, bowing respectfully. 'I must say, you interpret it passionately.'

Jinane barely looked at him, then began again, even more forcefully; Zohar accompanied her with words that rose perfectly from his memory: 'You who resemble the spirits of the night. You with the grace of a gazelle. O Nofal, O Nofal, O Nofal . . . ' And he clapped his hands in triplets, the rhythm of a camel caravan. Masreya's two guardians also began to clap. Masreya's feet were carried along by the song of the earth's spirits, and Joe's key danced rhythmically around his finger.

Jinane finally stopped playing. Pivoting on her seat, she addressed Zohar: 'Who are you?' she asked; then, smiling: 'The spirits' boy or a spirit disguised as a boy?'

'A boy, O Mother! My father's name is Gohar. I'm also called Gohar. Gohar ibn Gohar, that's my name,' answered Zohar, who'd acquired the habit of translating his name into Arabic.

'Gohar!' Masreya cried out.

'You know him then?' exclaimed Ouahiba.

'Do I know him? No, I don't know him. It's just that we're made from the same smoke. How can you restrain two smokes and keep them from joining? Go, bring some tea, some cakes and jellies.'

She was right, the beautiful Masreya with the almond-coloured eyes. Can smoke be confined? It slips through the strongest walls, seeps under doors, spreads into the tiniest chink, flying to find its familiars—air, ether, wind, scent.

Jinane, the mother, blinked, troubled. Gohar. Her memories flooded in. She recalled the hardest moments in her life: Masreya's father, maddened by her pregnancy; and then that child, her daughter Masreya, this gift from God, who'd restored her taste for life—from the first movement she'd noticed in her belly, and then again when the child let out its first cry, this child who filled each day of her life with joy. She saw herself again in Haret al-Yahud, in that tiny grocers' shop, with that Jewish family terrified of the death she alone could ward off. She touched her breasts. They were no longer as firm or as full, but the sensations were still imprinted on her nipples, the two nurslings sucking life. Yes. They were twins, not from the same womb, not of the same blood, but with the same life. And tears rolled down her cheeks.

'My children!' she stammered. 'My children, O my soul, O my life.'

The two threw themselves at her feet, Zohar and Masreya, each taking one of her hands and bringing it to their lips.

'O my mother!' And, beginning Mohamed Abdel Wahab's celebrated song, '*Sett al-Habayeb*,' Masreya sang, 'Mother-love, O my beloved!'

'O my mother!' Zohar sang in turn, 'May Allah keep you for us, Mother-love, O my beloved!'

And then, together, 'You whose pain is love, whose care is love, whose life is love, may Allah keep you for us, Mother-love, O my beloved.'

Joe gazed at the scene, understanding nothing. He'd often wondered about the source of his dear friend's peculiarities. And now here he was in an Arab house, at the feet of on Arab woman he called 'mother'. 'But you're Jewish!' Joe protested. 'How can your mother be Arab? How can you have a Muslim sister?' No one answered him.

The governesses returned, carrying trays. They sat on the terrace, drinking tea, tasting jellies with silver spoons they then dipped into crystal glasses filled with pure water. They recalled a little of their past, but so little. How could they? It was lost in a sort of protective mist. For Jinane, what remained was the suffering in her belly; Zohar and Masreya knew only snatches of it, which they jealously preserved in their secret dreams. Intense rediscoveries all the same, sensations difficult to describe, emotions fleeting and intense. They stayed together until nightfall, speaking of the world as it had been and as it was becoming. Naturally, they spoke of the war knocking at Egypt's doors. Alexandria and several cities in the Delta had been bombarded by the Axis forces. They thanked God for having spared the little village of Kafr al-Amar, the water buffalos and chickens of Jinane's family. Joyful, she returned to the piano, played Abdel Wahab's song, and the children, milk brother and sister, sang again, and Joe ended up joining his voice to theirs. When it was time to leave, the question finally arose. That's what Egyptian etiquette requires—you never reveal your visit's purpose until the moment of departure.

'You've known of my existence and probably my address for a long time. Everyone in Cairo knows me,' Masreya observed. 'What brought you to me today?'

'You can help me, my sister, my love!'

She smiled. 'Shut up, you idiot from the alley! Do you want them to forbid my seeing you again?'

'Who can forbid you anything? My belly calls you,' Zohar went on, 'my soul is yours.' And, remembering the words of his father's Song, he translated them for her: 'Behold, thou art fair, my love; behold, thou art fair.'

'Shut up, Gohar ibn Gohar, little Jew from the hara, or we'll end up cutting out your tongue.' She took him by the hand, led him into the hallway. 'Tell me more of your holy words.'

Zohar continued to translate: 'Thou hast ravished my heart, my sister, my spouse; thou hast ravished my heart with one of thine eyes.'

'Shush, O my mad brother whose madness I love, my mad brother who makes me mad! Shush! I quake in your presence, as if you were wind. How can I help you?'

'Do you remember how I awakened you?'

'Braggart! Snot was dripping from your nose. You knew nothing of love, I led your eyes, I led your hands, I showed you the way. Have you forgotten, you ingrate?'

'Beneath your mother's breast, that's where I awakened you, barely emerged from the belly. It's you who has forgotten.'

'Louse-ridden idiot! No one can remember such ancient days. Come, tell me quickly how I can help you. I can't stay alone like this with you in front of the governesses.'

'I must see you—tonight!'

She hesitated. She'd established a rule never to leave her house on Fridays. And then, who was this devil, really, who'd entered her life from its first moments and who set himself up each time like an owner? She needed some time to collect herself, to think quietly.

'Tonight—I can't!'

'Kiss me with one kiss, one kiss of your lips on mine.'

'Idiot!'

She placed her lips on his and a strange humming filled her ears, obliterating the world's sounds. Only the heartbeat echoing in her temples, on her neck, on her belly, in her sex. He pushed her against the wall, stroking her legs.

'How beautiful you are, O my beloved, O my gazelle.'

She pushed him away.

'Stop! No. Not here.'

'Tonight?' Zohar insisted.

'No! I told you. Tomorrow!'

'Time presses.'

O Masreya, you who know you are blessed, why did you not respect the prohibition, the only one imposed on you, not that of blood, but of milk? O Zohar, child of the spirits, why are you always questioning rules and laws? Smokes! What do you care about the sensations of your bodies? Your bodies are just an illusion. You are both smokes . . . So, avoid humans, float up into the sky, merge with the ceaseless movement of clouds—because it will cost you, don't you know, it will cost you to disturb the worlds' order . . .

They found each other again the next day at sunset. Joe had borrowed his father's black limousine, a Packard, which looked like a minister's car or maybe even the king's, with a glass partition between the driver and the passengers. He wore a black suit with a black bow tie. When she came through the gate, he rushed to open the door, removing his cap and bowing down to the ground.

'Princess of shadows, goddess of nights, consent to set your feet in my master's modest automobile.'

She burst out laughing. She hadn't yet settled onto the velvet cushions before he sped off and she fell onto Zohar's lap.

'Hey!' Zohar cried, tapping the glass.

'Where are you taking me?'

He slid open the partition and told Joe, 'Driver, to the pyramids!'

They spun along the corniche. Masreya lowered the window and stuck out her head, letting her scarf float in the night wind. She sang to passersby: 'With you, with you, the world is so beautiful with you.'

Recognizing divine Farid's song, Zohar joined in, 'Whether you reject me, whether you accept me, whatever the place, I will be with you—'

'With you,' Masreya continued, 'with you, how beautiful the world is with you.'

On the long straight stretch of the sumptuous Avenue of the Pyramids, the wind flowed into the windows and they laughed. At the Pyramids Cafe, they spoke at length. They told each other about their mutual departure from the alleys of old Cairo to attain the villas on the banks of the Nile and the plush buildings of the grand avenues. Crocodile eggs laid on the same day and buried in the riverbank's mud, hatched by chance during sunlit days, drawn towards each other by instinct and finding each other for love, they told each other everything. Like crocodiles, they were of the Nile, forever. They kissed publicly, drawing the whistles of passersby. 'Aren't you ashamed—in front of children?' They laughed some more and began again. They evoked grandiose futures: she would dethrone Tahia Carioca, eroticism embodied in a dancer, and Umm Kulthum, the voice of God; he would reign over an empire of power and money, eclipsing Cicurel and the baron Menasce. Joe, playing his part, kept refilling their glasses with champagne. They were young; they were beautiful. Nothing held them back, explorers of a newfound world they created as they moved, smiled, talked. Hand in hand, they ran through the night, shouting out their joy. And Joe watched them leave.

They climbed the Great Pyramid in the middle of the night, leaping like goats from stone to stone. When they'd climbed so high no one could see them, she sat between his legs. She was still panting when he took her lips. They tasted of orange blossoms. She wrapped her arms around him; he wrapped his arms around her; they were like two magnets, unable to part. What was this irresistible force that drove them to merge, much more than desire? Even love would be too weak. This was a power, a cataclysm. She wanted to slow his passion while his body dreamed only of being lost in her. She said, 'Do you realize we're on a tomb? The pyramids are tombs. Below us lies a king's corpse.' He burst out laughing. 'The pharaohs knew that there was no other woman but your sister.' And he closed his eyes: Egypt; she, Masreya, his double and his other half; the pharaohs; the moon that was three-quarters full; a warmth that filled his breast. He translated his father's words for her, the words of the Song of Songs, 'There are threescore queens, and fourscore concubines, and virgins without number. My dove, my undefiled is but one.' That night, at the moment when their pleasure reached its peak, when he moaned, when she cried, a kite rested on the stone above their heads, spreading its wings as if to protect them, and the air breathed a scent of myrrh.

O Zohar, you whose mouth holds ancient words; O Masreya, you whose fate is that of a nation, why turn in on yourselves, growing drunk with your love? What do you have that's so special? Don't you know that each man has a woman double hidden in the ether, each woman a man double spinning backwards beneath her feet? It's best that they never meet.

Sated with love, they descended slowly, stone by stone, holding hands and thanking Cheops. The car door was wide open. At the wheel, Joe was waiting impatiently, smoking a cigarette. During the return journey, the moment came when she asked how she could help him. Zohar explained that a very dear friend, a brother, his double so to speak, had been arrested for subversive activities. If he didn't act quickly, he would be tried by the British, perhaps in a court martial. He'd disappear into a jail for ten years, maybe longer. Masreya stiffened.

'Subversive activities? What do you mean?'

'Nationalist, communist, I don't know exactly.'

'Good! What do you want from me?'

'That you persuade the king to intervene.'

'The king?'

'Yes. The king. You alone might reach him.'

He'd just touched the heart of one of her most secret dreams. The whole world knew about Farouk's taste for very young women, especially artists, dancers, singers. Masreya, who'd known many suitors with whom she sometimes consented, albeit parsimoniously, to share the pleasures of the night, saw that Zohar's proposal could be her path to the top. She had a somewhat confused idea of where exactly she wanted to go, except that it was to the summit. And in Egypt, the summit had a name and a face: it was the king, and his name was Farouk I. When she closed her eyes, it was the king's face—as he appeared in official photographs, proud, with a broad brow, a perfect nose—that transported her. Often, she'd imagined him in the room where she danced, calling her to his table after the show,

sending her dozens of roses every day, offering her jewels, automobiles, villas. And here was her brother, her milk-twin, this devilish
Gohar ibn Gohar, holding out the mirror of her dream.

'What's your friend's name?'

'Nino. Nino Cohen.'

'And the king? How will I get to him?'

'I'll take care of that!'

'What will you do to have me meet the king?'

'I'll take care of it, I'm telling you. But when the time comes,
don't let me down!'

*

Sunday, 21 December. Joe had wangled an invitation to a reception
given by Princess Shivakiar, King Fouad's first wife—King Farouk's
stepmother—on the occasion of the year-end holidays. This time, he
borrowed both his father's Packard and his driver. In a distinguished
smoking jacket, with a notched collar and a bow tie, his sun-lightened
brown hair combed back, his freckles sprinkled around his nose,
his topaz eyes, his athletic build—he went towards the bar, drawing
the looks of the elegant. He stumbled upon Zacco Calloghiris, a
journalist he'd met at receptions in the Reggio Palace. He began a
conversation, hoping Zacco could tell him the guests' names. The
royal family's Rolls began the ballet; then came those of princes,
princesses, and other nobility. And the Greek journalist, proud of his
acquaintances, named them all.

'The prince Mohamed Ali Hassan—he's the son of prince
Hassan Pasha who is the son of Khedive Ismael. Do you know?'

Joe nodded, looking impressed.

'And there, look! The prince Omar Toussoun. He's the grandson
of the old vice-king, Mohamed Ali Pasha.'

Joe didn't know what to say. Unlike his mother, he'd never been interested in the royal family's complex genealogies. What could he do other than compare the quality of the cars? He ventured, 'His car seems older than the previous one.'

He uttered this sentence more or less randomly; most of the Rolls were black, with white-walled tyres, enormous headlights in front and radiator grilles shaped like Greek temples. Then came the ministers, preceded by the cabinet head, the aristocratic Ahmed Hassanein Pasha.

'Amazing!' Zacco was in ecstasy, 'simultaneously *sir* for the British and *pasha* to the Turks.'

Joe was growing bored. He left the bar and approached a woman, also a journalist, a little brunette with frizzy hair, like a sheep's fleece. She was covering the event for *L'Egyptienne*.

'You don't know it? Mrs Naguib's journal. A cultural review focused on women.'

Joe had never heard of it, but quickly realized that this time he had a good informant. She knew each of the women approaching the entrance.

'There, the Princess Toussoun, in that magnificent black velvet dress embroidered with beads. Impressive, don't you think? Oh— Princess Irene from Greece! I wouldn't have thought the latest styles had arrived yet from Paris. Look there, in navy blue tulle, sparkling with black sequins. It's signed Balenciaga! Yes, indeed! Truly *haute*. The latest thing—what style!'

Joe liked her, the little journalist.

'Did you notice how the bodice is narrowed at the waist? The "wasp waist". It's all the rage in Paris!'

'And you? What's your name?'

But she was much too busy recording the princesses' outfits in her notebook.

Suddenly, all eyes were turned towards the gates. A new Rolls-Royce had just entered, preceded by two motorcyclists, military men in dress uniform. This car was enormous, its top entirely down, with two windshields, a phaeton. It rolled on the gravel right up to the steps. A small woman, about forty, with a pretty face, emerged with deliberate slowness.

'Lady Killearn—grace incarnate. Did you see that luminous mauve dress?'

Joe, on the other hand, recognized her husband, a giant nearly six feet tall, huge, with a baritone voice ordering his guards to follow him. 'It's Lampson!' Joe said, 'the British Ambassador, no?'

But she loved titles. She corrected him. 'Yes, Lord Killearn. Sir Miles Lampson, if you please.'

Joe insisted. He wanted to know the journalist's name. 'And you? At least tell me your name.'

But she'd already been drawn by another personality. 'A beauty, that woman. There, in a rose tulle dress embroidered with sequins. You don't know her? Hélène Mosseri, the latest wife of Elie Mosseri!'

It was her then! Joe breathed a sigh of relief. He hadn't been sure she would come. He stared at her. Huge green eyes, rose-coloured lips and reddish hair that fell in carefully curled waves à la Hedy Lamarr—majestic!

'Would you introduce me?' asked Joe.

The journalist turned to him abruptly. 'I thought you wanted to know my name.'

Joe stammered an excuse. It had nothing to do with that. Madame Mosseri was for a business matter. But she, the journalist, he found her so attractive. She wasn't listening to him any more, happy, after all, to have an excuse to speak to the woman everyone called 'The Beautiful Hélène'.

'Come!'

This was the mission Zohar had entrusted to him, the reason he'd asked him to go to Princess Shiviakar's reception—to approach the beautiful widow. He had to introduce himself to her, gain her trust, convince her. Raised in a seraglio, Joe knew how to conduct himself in society. He adjusted his bow tie, buttoned the vest of his smoking jacket and followed the journalist clearing a path between the social elite and political personalities.

'Mrs Hélène Mosseri, do you remember me?' she asked with a forced smile. 'The interview you granted me for *L'Egyptienne*. You remember, of course. You spoke about your childhood in Alexandria, about your meeting with Mosseri Bey. I'm Reina Sawiris, freelance reporter. We drank coffee at Groppi's and talked all afternoon.'

'Of course I remember! You have an elegant pen, young lady.'

Then she turned to continue her worldly progress, Joe touched her arm. 'Madame Mosseri! Could you spare me a moment?'

She turned quickly, sending him a severe look. 'We haven't been introduced, young man!'

'Di Reggio, madam, Giuseppe di Reggio.'

'Reggio—the di Reggios of Zamalek?'

'Ephraim di Reggio is my father.'

'Well, then . . . '

She agreed to follow him to one side. He spoke to her at length. He gestured extravagantly with his hands, interrupted himself, burst out laughing, spoke some more. Reina watched them from a distance. 'So,' she murmured. 'The son of di Reggio! But where then is his baroness mother hiding?' She drew closer to him with the intention of asking that question, and overheard the last words of their conversation, 'We're asking only that you introduce her to the king, nothing more,' Joe pressed. 'You know how to create the perfect moment.'

Reina found Joe again. Together, they crisscrossed the reception. She never stopped talking. Towards ten-thirty, when the guests were leaving in clusters, he offered to accompany her. The nights were cool during those last days of December. She accepted his jacket, which he draped over her shoulders. Wedged against each other in the back of the Packard, they took the road to Heliopolis.

Villa Mosseri

Hélène Mosseri had some trouble arranging a meeting with the king during that year's end. He'd left for Luxor, to spend the winter holidays with his family, at least a hundred people—the relatives of the Queen Mother, the impetuous Queen Nazli who'd been expecting to rule Egypt through the intervention of her son, the too-young King Farouk; along with the relatives of Queen Farida, the king's wife, who, despite her youth, had decided to play the role assigned by her marriage. Things were no longer working out between these two bright, beautiful queens, each with a taste for power. Ministers, royal cousins, chamberlains and influential figures were split between the two camps.

The conflict had begun with the train's first jolt and grown envenomed at the Winter Palace Hotel where an entire wing had been reserved for the royal entourage. By the end of the first week, the battle had intensified, with acid comments on one side, deliberate meal delays and invented illnesses to avoid touristic visits on the other. Little by little, an unbearable uneasiness took hold. Torn between his mother's recriminations—she felt she was not being treated in accordance with her rank—and his wife's constant jealousy, Farouk took refuge with the two archaeologists: Howard Carter, notorious profaner of burial sites who'd opened Tutankhamen's tomb; and canon Etienne Drioton, French archaeologist-priest, looter of sacred objects for his government, appointed head of the Antiquities Department and the Cairo museums.

Unlike the war between the queens, the war between the intellectuals entertained the king. Carter put on the air of an ancient philosopher, claiming to know the site of Alexander the Great's tomb; the canon, on the other hand, his Basque beret pulled down over his ears, red with excitement and hoping to monopolize Farouk's attention, promised to reveal the secrets of pharaonic medicine. Still, the two researchers' caprices soon bored the king. Under constant surveillance by one queen or another, he could barely glance at an attractive young woman, and he certainly could not slip away for a game of cards at the casino.

The phone call drew him from the lethargy into which he'd begun to sink.

'Your Majesty, it's Hélène. I'm calling you from Cairo, Hélène Mosseri!'

He looked around to make sure no one could overhear their conversation. 'Hélène,' he whispered. 'The beautiful Hélène! You can't imagine how delighted I am to hear your voice.'

Farouk used the pretext of his sovereign duties, a mandatory visit to his subjects lost in the Southern oases, to escape. After a long detour through Upper Egypt, he reached Cairo on Christmas Day.

Saturday, 25 December 1941, 10 p.m., Ismail Pasha Street. Amid the leafy trees of a private park, the three floors of Villa Mosseri were all lit up. Hélène had fallen asleep on her sofa, limply holding the last issue of the *Revue du Caire*. Farouk, in city clothes, his head uncovered, sunglasses on his nose despite the darkness, was gliding silently behind the wheel of his red Mercedes. She'd mentioned a surprise. He'd insisted on knowing. 'Your Christmas gift, sire.' A weapon? A revolver or a hunting rifle—an American, a Remington perhaps? Unless it was about a girl, oh yes, that was it! A girl—but in that case, where would he meet her? Certainly not in the villa. What then had his friend Hélène concocted?

They hadn't known each other long, but a subtle bond had been sealed on the first day. It was during a reception, a year ago, in his chamberlain Hassanein Pasha's salons. He'd been unable to take his eyes off a magnificent old ivory-handled cross dagger resting on a cabinet in a chased silver sheath. 'Which one?' Hélène had asked him. He answered automatically: 'The one on the right, naturally. It's silver.' She'd disappeared for a few minutes. When she returned, he barely noticed a light touch on his arm. Mechanically, he placed his hand in his pocket and found the dagger there. She'd stolen it for him. They looked at each other. He smiled. She simply winked. Most certainly, this woman understood his secret desires. Her husband, Elie Mosseri, perhaps the richest man in Egypt, had married her as his third wife. He'd prematurely lost his first two, both chosen from the small circle of patrician Jews. But the third, Hélène, the well named, was Greek, young, beautiful and penniless. During dinner, Farouk whispered, 'Beware your husband. He's already made two wives disappear.' She burst into laughter and swallowed her drink. 'Don't fret about me, sire! A real woman is like the earth. She outlives those who trample her.'

Farouk had never had a real friend. An only son, the sole male heir charged with preserving the continuity of a dynasty that went back to Muhammad Ali, he'd been physically pampered but spiritually abandoned, entrusted to elderly British governesses, sadistic and stubborn. The only creatures with whom he'd formed a bond were an Italian electrician, Antonio Pulli, who replaced light bulbs and repaired the record player, and a little cat, which he carried through the corridors of the immense Koubbeh Palace. He'd turned to objects—weapons, daggers, sabres and rifles—and his extraordinary collection grew larger each day, along with the cars he amassed by the dozens in his garages. Unable to penetrate the secret of life, he fell back on mechanisms whose functioning was, undeniably, more straightforward. Emotional isolation had deadened his feelings, as if, little by little, his soul had been muffled in cotton-wool padding. So, his life force expressed itself in outbursts—of fear, mostly, with which he flirted while committing his larcenies; Farouk had become a kleptomaniac. Few within his circle knew—the faithful Antonio Pulli, certainly, who followed the king everywhere and reimbursed the cost of stolen objects whenever he could. How could Hélène have discovered the king's foible? Clearly, she had a gift, this woman who'd offered him her complicity at their very first meeting.

The guard didn't recognize him. The king slipped a generous tip into his hand so he would open the gates, and he advanced in slow motion, the engine quiet, down the driveway to the manor. He was careful not to bang the door; he climbed the staircase on tiptoe. Farouk liked to be in disguise. Sometimes, on Fridays, he'd go on foot to a mosque to pray incognito among the people. When he was recognized and they wanted to honour him in accordance with his rank, he would declare, 'No! Before God, we're all equal! There are no kings or masters'—words that earned him the admiration and love of the masses. Could they suspect, these humble believers, that their king was toying with the fear of being discovered and unmasked, seeking that little jolt of adrenaline that gave him, for a few moments, a surge of life?

He reached the landing without a sound, pushed the door and was disappointed to find Hélène asleep. He couldn't come behind her and take her by the waist with a sudden gesture to startle her. He pulled up a chair and sat down beside her.

Of course they'd had an affair. He'd even been in love with her for two weeks, three at most. Hélène's husband had still been alive. They'd made love right here, in this room, while the old man was dying on the other side of the door. She would take a long time getting ready, like a harem courtesan, anointing herself with fabulous scents, selecting seductive silk or satin lingerie. They'd sit on the sofa, side by side, following a set ritual. Everything had to seem above board, as if it were a matter of well-bred people sipping tea. She always made the first move, gently taking hold of his sex, slowly caressing it, flattering his virility. Each time, he was surprised by his erection, as if he were sure the previous one had been his last. She praised his vigour, using words meant to be poetic. 'Look how your bird's rising. It's reaching for the sky.' And he smiled, half-frightened, happy to be violating stultifying protocol for a flash of desire. During these afternoon encounters, he never wondered if she loved him. How could anyone cherish feelings for the king without an ulterior motive?

More than a year had passed. They had not had sex for a very long time. But she'd shown a complicity, beyond the senses, beyond words, the direct perception of his needs. And today, once again, she'd sensed from afar the boredom he was feeling in that Luxor hotel, far from the capital's clamour; once again, she'd come to his rescue. The beautiful Hélène, the good Hélène!

She opened her eyes and leapt to her feet.

'Your Majesty! Forgive me. I fell asleep. I didn't hear you come in.'

She took his hand and leant over to kiss it. He pulled it back abruptly, bursting with laughter.

'Come, Hélène! It's my fault. I was late. What's worse, for a rendezvous with my mistress of pleasures. What a misstep!'

He was big. He'd grown fatter, even more imposing, with his fighter's shoulders. She recalled his marriage four years earlier, in the Koubbeh Palace, on the eve of his eighteenth birthday. He'd been a magnificent young man, tall and slender, athletic, with fair eyes, sensual lips and a delicate, aristocratic moustache. But he already had that absent look, and, when he spoke, you had the sense that he was reading a text suspended behind his interlocutor's back.

They chatted awhile. As always, Farouk hid his discomfort—his primal fear in the presence of life—behind a condescending attitude People said he liked listening to others. The truth was, he'd fashioned for himself a reserved, distant attitude, somewhat mocking, which he thought befitted a king. She spoke of Egyptians' anxieties, the war that was infiltrating everywhere, like the desert sand during the *khamsin*. She came to what must be troubling him: the British troops that had invaded Cairo's streets; their trucks, more numerous than cars; the insistent reports of their demands, most notably the removal of the prime minister, the likable Sirry Pasha—all the unsettling news to be found in the many newspapers that had cropped up in every language. Farouk, always smiling, did not reply.

'Forgive me!' she suddenly cried, rushing towards the door.

She was about to call Mustapha, her majordomo, to ask him to bring them some appetizers, but the king motioned to her from afar, a finger on his lips. 'Shush! Come, Hélène, come back and sit down. Everyone thinks I'm in Upper Egypt, in Asyut.'

'You're hiding?' She laughed out loud.

'I like to,' he answered, mysteriously.

'Wait for me a moment.'

And she went to fetch her carafe of Blue Water from the second salon. She returned and said in a strong voice, 'Forgive me, sire, I need a drink.'

'You know I don't drink alcohol. Well, after all, only from someone else's glass.'

When she sat back down on the sofa, she found a package encircled with gold ribbon.

'Oh! Your Majesty always surprises me. What is it?'

'Your Christmas gift, my dear Hélène.'

'May I open it?'

'Unless you want to give it to one of your friends after I've left.'

She untied the ribbon, opened the case and couldn't help exclaiming, 'From where did you filch it?'

'From whom rather. You should be asking me from whom I filched it. From the canon.'

'The archaeologist? Great gods!'

She carefully drew out a magnificent, finely chased gold necklace in the shape of a horned viper. It was among the objects the Antiquities Department director had presented to the king at Luxor, an exceptional piece, miraculously preserved, discovered in a royal tomb of the Fifth Dynasty. The viper was perfectly recognizable, with the protuberances on its head, its open mouth, sharp fangs and forked tongue.

'I couldn't help thinking of you when he gave me the necklace. Already, four thousand years ago, our ancestors knew all about woman, a viper.'

She flung herself around his neck, kissed him on the lips. Haughtily, he gently pushed her away. She put the necklace on, admired it in a mirror, tried to hook it, couldn't. 'But I'm thinking— I can never wear it in public.'

'No! Only with your lovers, as long as they know nothing about ancient Egypt. But you'll be able to sell it when you're ruined. A fortune!'

She swallowed half a glass of that new gin you could find in the city, that 'Blue Water', far superior to the vile bottles imported from England. He took the glass from her hands and downed it in one gulp. She asked him to wait a few minutes while she dressed.

'No!' he commanded, authoritarian. 'Dress here, in front of me!'

And when she appeared before him, naked, without shame, her skin milky, her hips full, holding her breasts in her hands, tracing out some oriental dance movements, Farouk sought his sex through his trouser pocket. He was making sure. No erection; not even vaguely! He knew her too well. He feared neither her refusal nor her erotic frenzy. She didn't frighten him, no longer surprised him. He'd never be able to have sex with her again. He poured himself a fresh glass of Blue Water and, bringing it to his lips, asked her, 'Where are you taking me?'

'It's a surprise.'

*

A cigarette dangling from the corner of her mouth, she was driving the fine Mercedes very slowly. Sunk in his seat, black glasses, wide-brimmed American hat, scarf wound up to his nose, Farouk was thrilled. He spoke to her about the car, his favourite—its leather the colour of camel skin, the rare-wood panelling the same colour as the seats. It had been given to him new by Hitler himself, as a marriage gift, in January 1938.

'Do you know what they're saying in town? That Adolf Hitler is Egyptian, and Muslim, of course. His real name isn't Hitler, but Haidar, Mohammed Haidar. One of my ministers firmly believes that. He even offered to take me to visit his birthplace, at Tanta, in the Delta. People are also saying that when he wins the war, the fertile lands will be distributed to the poor, and that I, thanks to him, will be able to grind my heel on George's head. Doesn't that make you laugh? George VI, King of Great Britain.'

She parked in a little passageway off Suleiman Pasha Street. She was bringing him to a place he knew well, where he had his routines. Would he prefer to enter alone? She'd join him shortly. And so Farouk presented himself at the door of the Turf Club, elegant watering-hole for night owls, frequented by British officers and wealthy Egyptians. He didn't notice the sign posted near the door, announcing a famous dancer. The porters pretended not to recognize him, but, as soon as he turned his back, they cried, 'The king! The king!' The maître d' rushed over to greet him. He hadn't known he was in Cairo, otherwise, his table would have been ready. Would he like to join a poker table? Several were available, with men whose company he'd certainly enjoy. The British—perhaps not right now, no; the bankers, then? Or perhaps the film producers? Farouk asked for a quiet place, near the stage.

A few minutes later, Hélène came in. From afar, he gave her a little friendly nod. With the whole room watching, they played at meeting unexpectedly. She ordered some gin, and added, 'With plenty of ice!' She was a woman, after all, and so, clear and diluted, the alcohol could pass for mineral water. He asked for a large glass of orange juice.

The rounds began at the table—one minister, another, an Egyptian army colonel, another from the British army. They bowed before him, wanting simply to greet him, to affirm their sympathy. Farouk, always genial, always distant, never missed the chance for a quip. He gently scolded his minister: 'That a king should spend his evenings in a nightclub, we can understand. But a minister is supposed to work, isn't he?' He asked an Englishman, 'Do you miss your king? You can use me as an ersatz. You wouldn't be the first.'

The lights were lowered. A spotlight formed a circle on stage. First a long solo on the qanun, the Oriental zither, a voluptuous progression of notes that rose in swirls, taken up again by a band of invisible violins. The flute came next, to tease the violins, to interrupt their phrases, to mimic and contort them. Each time, the percussions reconciled them. A rumbling of drums. A man in a smoking jacket approached the microphone. His face was hidden. The audience thought he was about to speak, to introduce the evening, perhaps to sing.

She emerged from the dark, like a demon, swathed in flame-coloured veils that fluttered gracefully in rhythm with her movements. She leapt like fire, punctuating the silence with her steps. She took the microphone. The man turned to the audience, his arms limp. She twined around him and extended the microphone to him, but, when he tried to grasp it, she shot off like an arrow. The music was accompanying her now, tracing each of her steps. The spotlight rested on the jilted man's face, weak with love. He retrieved the microphone and sang: 'O God! If You let the day come when she tells me yes, I'll give up the rest of my days, the rest of my nights, and all my dreams.'

The public sighed with satisfaction. The great Farid al-Amesh himself, the singer with the honeyed voice had come for them. It was Christmas! She approached him, touching him, making him tingle, but, before he could catch her, she flew off, swathed in her veils. And when he sang, 'On my terrace, the jasmine envies her perfume,' she took the veil that covered her head and caressed his face with it. 'And the roses envy the sweetness of her cheeks.' A cascade of long wild hair. A second spotlight lit up the dancer's face; you could see her big green eyes shining like a cat's caught in a headlight in the middle of the night.

Farouk trembled. He pressed Hélène's arm. 'Is that her? Yes! That's her, right?' That open face, balanced—both angel and devil, the face of a child baring herself as a whore. It was for him, for the king, the type he liked best!

The dancer took the microphone again, then lay on the floor, from which she suddenly rose on tiptoe, taller than the singer. 'I am a serpent woman, a shameless serpent that brings harm to those who threaten it and good to those who let it be. I am the serpent woman.' Her sweet voice lined the room, offering it to men's fantasies. 'She's the mystery of my nights and her song intoxicates me more than wine. God, I beg you, let her tell me yes.' The rhythm became more oriental. Seized with frenzy, she shimmied her hips, her breasts, repeating, 'I am the serpent majesty! Bow down! You are only a man.' He continued to sing the agony of his hope, his aching desire. And, fluttering her veils, she came to meet his dreams. At the climax of their passion, the final, transparent veil revealed a nymph's body, the breasts barely covered, a star sparkling between her thighs. The singer, fulfilled at last, intoned, 'Life is beautiful to those who understand it. Life is beautiful. If you take what you are given, life is beautiful. Life is beautiful to those who understand it. Life is beautiful.' The dancer, unveiled, turned to the audience, repeating the refrain. The audience took it up in turn, applauding.

It was a triumph. The room was on its feet, singing, repeating the verse. The men drew near, hoping to climb onstage. Farid al-Amesh raised his two arms, enjoining silence. Into the microphone, he simply said, 'This evening, for you—*seulement pour vous*—the marvellous—*la merveilleuse*—Ben't Jinane!' Unending applause. She took the microphone. '*Ce soir*—tonight—the sweet Farid al-Amesh—*le doux*.' They sang four more songs, each one unleashing fervour, but, at the end they were called back and the audience clamoured for the first, Kacim's intoxicating song, 'Life is beautiful,' celebrating the pleasure taken with courtesans. They sang it again, and the audience wanted more.

The lights in the room were turned back on. Farid al-Amesh had slipped away. Farouk ostentatiously raised his arm. Masreya came to sit at his table. She looked deep into his eyes.

'Do you recognize me?' asked the king, who didn't know what to say, who thought only of touching her, seizing her.

'Your Majesty is everywhere. In the newspapers, in the cinema, on stamps, on the smallest coin, even the little millième. How not to recognize you? How can I know if you are real or only a dream?'

'The bitch!' thought Hélène, 'she's guessed that she needed to surprise him.'

'You're very young, my dear,' she told her. 'But already a great professional.'

Farouk interrupted Hélène. 'You must need something. Tell me! What do you lack? What do you need? One word from you, I beg you.'

And he sang, 'O God! Let the day come when she'll tell me yes.'

'You have an amazing memory, sire!'

He invited her for Tuesday, late in the afternoon. Slyly, she asked if she should bring her musicians. 'I don't need music,' the king replied. 'My soul sings just to see you, and my heart beats time.' He added that this would be a private meeting, just the two of them. She bowed her head in assent. Farouk felt an erection swelling his trousers. 'You'll leave your address with Hélène. A car will pick you up at home.' She asked where the rendezvous would be, but he did not reply. Later in the evening, when Masreya disappeared into her dressing room, Farouk instructed Hélène to rent a room at the Savoy for the following Tuesday. He'd promised to attend a Rotary Club meeting in the ground-floor halls. He could easily disappear after half an hour to join the dancer.

'The bellhops, the pages, the housekeepers—anyone could recognize you.'

'*Baksheesh*, my dear Hélène! Distribute it generously, I'm counting on you. When it comes to love, danger heightens pleasure, don't you agree?'

Abdine

During their first meeting, on the third floor of the Savoy, she had made his desire mount to its apogee. She'd twined around him as she sang, allowing him to brush her; she'd breathed words of love into his ears, had thrown herself at his feet, stroking his legs. 'Come,' he begged, 'Come sit on my lap, my little girl.' And she came, Masreya, the demoness, to alight for an instant. Set ablaze by her scent, entranced by her skin's softness, the king drifted in sensations of infinity. But she left just as quickly. He enjoyed this game he'd glimpsed during her song with Farid al-Amesh. 'Life is beautiful!' she murmured, 'Life is beautiful to those who understand it.' Yes, Farouk thought, but what was she doing fleeing from him like a feral cat? 'Yes!' Masreya whispered, 'Yes, Your Majesty! But you must not see me.' And she'd covered his eyes with a scarf. He'd felt his way around the room, drunk with excitement, seeking her on arm-chairs, behind the door, under the bed on all fours. She'd vanished. He removed the blindfold, searched every corner. Evaporated. He went out into the hallway, his shirt open, his tie undone. He never found her.

The next day, she received a dozen bouquets of a dozen roses each, accompanied by a sentence in his beautiful Arabic handwriting, 'The roses envy the sweetness of your cheeks.' Through Hélène's intercession, he'd arranged a second rendezvous, at the Mena House beside the Pyramids. She'd said yes, but hadn't come. He was obsessed with her; her scent haunted him; he saw her face every-where, on the women he encountered at hotel bars where he smoked his cigar or in clubs where he fingered the wildcards. He finally reached her by phone. 'Why have you fled? Ask and you'll have whatever you desire, no matter the price.' She requested a meeting at the palace. At the palace? That was difficult indeed. The place was overrun with spies who reported to the Wafd, to the British, to the Italians as well—watching for his least slip. She argued. Since he claimed to be a believer, a Muslim . . . According to the faith, a man must marry a woman, even a prostitute, before having sexual relations with her; he may divorce her upon awakening the next day. But he wanted only to devour her, like one of those pastel pink and green *loukoums* he doted on.

Yes. Whatever she wanted, yes, he'd replied. He was ready for anything. But she had to realize he was king, he couldn't disgrace his legitimate wife, the mother of his children.

In that case, she'd accept a secret marriage, performed in a room in the palace. After that, she would belong to him. Dazed with desire, he promised. In the presence of a witness, she insisted; the faith requires it. He hesitated. A third person? For a moment he felt she'd gone too far, testing his limits. But he was ready for anything just to see her again. 'And who will it be?' he asked her. 'Who will be the witness?' A moment of silence. Then she exclaimed, 'My brother!' New silence on the end of the line.

He thought of the ties that bound him to his own sister, Fawzia—the sister he missed so much since she'd left to join her emperor husband, Mohammed Reza Pahlavi, the young Shah of Iran. He'd been opposed to the marriage. 'Too far away,' he'd argued. 'But no,' he'd been told, 'There are airplanes now.' 'But these young people don't even speak the same language,' he'd tried again, 'how will they communicate?' 'In French, of course, they'll speak to each other quite well.' And then, 'The Iranians are Shiites, they don't follow the same customs!' 'No problem. There's no legal obstacle to the marriage of a Shiite and a Sunni.' Another objection came and went through his mind, but he kept it to himself. The young Reza was sickly, afflicted by tics, a sort of invalid. Fawzia, so pure, so beautiful, would never be able to endure him. The marriage indeed took place; their mother, Queen Nazli, arranged it all. And Farouk, King of Egypt, had to resign himself to being the witness. A few days later, his sister's departure for Tehran devastated him. For two years now, he'd been obsessed by one thought: to bring her back and secure her divorce. He was sure she was miserable among those half-savages in the mountains. He felt it. Yes! A brother and sister can share a subtle bond, beyond the everyday. This he understood.

He yielded to Masreya's demand. She would come to the palace with her brother, it was agreed. He would receive them in a royal audience, in his cabinet, as he did all sorts of guests. Then he would have them visit rooms off limits to the public. He would marry her in a hidden room. He boasted that there were at least a dozen in the palace, and, aside from the servants, he alone knew of their existence.

She made him wait some more. She delayed the date, claiming she first had to go to the Delta, to see her family. The secret ceremony took place only after the first of the year. Beautiful and proud, Masreya stood like a rooster; Zohar remained in the background, elegant and discreet. In front of the brother, Farouk had resumed his aloofness. Zohar reminded him that they had met a very long time ago. The king apologized. He'd forgotten; he saw so many people. Zohar told him—he was the one who'd returned Queen Nazli's lost necklace. Farouk raised an eyebrow and took a moment to study the young man—an odd figure. Naturally graceful. A foreign look. Indefinable origin, he thought. Not Arab, in any case. Greek, perhaps—or Jewish? He was intrigued by those Jewish bankers with whom he played cards and discussed finance. He admired those entrepreneurs who'd managed not to be bound by the king-dom's borders. For a few months now, new Jews had been arriving, such as they'd never seen before in Egypt, European Jews who resembled Germans or Englishmen. They were not like the ones he knew, the Levantines—less supple, less joyous, less cunning as well. He didn't dare ask how a Jew could be the brother of an Arab, a peasant from the Delta at that. Some family drama, no doubt; perhaps a second marriage?

The two men smiled at each other, exchanging pleasantries, then some plays on words. After all, they were Egyptians. A bond developed between the friendless twenty-four-year-old king, and the very young man, enterprising and clever, who strangely seemed to be both child and old man. Farouk, deadpan, asked if it didn't trouble him to offer up his sister like this to the Pharaoh. 'Your Presence!' Zohar exclaimed. 'The Pharaoh's pleasure is the smile of all Egypt.' The king gestured with his hand, as if to banish a thought. He would have so liked to believe those words.

In that little old-fashioned room known as 'the harem room', Farouk uttered the prayer that joined him to Masreya, sealing the secret union between a child of the people, called 'the Egyptian woman' and the King of Egypt whose spirit had been conquered by her, both day and night.

*

In the streets, more and more soldiers could be seen. The month of January 1942 was, in Egypt, a month of utter anxiety. New troops had left England to reinforce the Eighth Army. People were saying two hundred thousand men, maybe more, had come to add to the already-overflowing barracks in Cairo, Ismailia, Port Said, Alexandria. And they weren't the only foreigners. Fleeing countries occupied by the Third Reich, refugees numbered in the thousands— Northern Europeans, and, for a few weeks now, Greeks, terrorized and haggard. Food was growing scarce. The British army monopolized supplies, and people could find nothing to buy in the souks. The poor were hungry and blamed the black market. Everything was lacking: wheat, corn, favas, and especially the potatoes without which an Englishman did not feel as if he'd eaten. Riots broke out. Stores were attacked, groceries looted. The half-hearted measures taken by the government had no effect, since many of the ministers, themselves large landowners, were stockpiling grains to raise prices. The common people in the cities were close to famine. And the rich grew richer still.

The Axis armies had resumed their offensive; Rommel was claiming victory after victory. Anti-British demonstrations broke out in Cairo and Alexandria, to cries of 'O Rommel, come quickly, my prince! Hurry!' or 'Long live Rommel, our liberator!' People thought Berlin would rush reinforcements and that the invasion of Egypt was inevitable.

The British intelligence service was convinced the Egyptians were transmitting their regiments' positions, maps of their movements and even their battle plans to the enemy. Taking advantage of Farouk's absence during the year-end holidays, Sir Miles Lampson, the British ambassador, a giant with the voice of an ogre, summoned the debonair prime minister, Hussein Sirry Pasha, to the Kasr al-Dobara headquarters. 'Bring me without delay the radio hidden in the Abdine Palace.' He had good reason to believe there was no better place than the royal palace for broadcasting to the Germans. The Egyptian, reeling, his mouth half-open, was silent. 'Unless you do so,' menaced the Englishman, 'I'll come with a battalion of tanks and search it room by room until I lay my hands on it.'

How could an ambassador speak in such terms to the prime minister of the country where he was posted? Red with suppressed rage, Sirry replied that this was a violation of Egyptian sovereignty. 'Oh indeed,' roared the other, who had little respect for Egyptian politicians. 'Sovereignty implies a sovereign! Where then has yours gone?' The prime minister didn't know what to say. What's more, he didn't even try. In recent days, many people were wondering where the king had disappeared to. Profiting from Sirry Pasha's stupefaction, the ambassador added, 'And that's not all! You will respond at once to my government's frequently repeated demands'—that Egypt at once break all diplomatic ties with the Vichy government, whose spies were swarming through Cairo's streets, and that it recognize General De Gaulle's French government in exile. Sirry, realizing that he was cornered, that the British could topple the government and depose the king, brought them, the next day, the radio hidden under the rafters. Then he dispatched a note to Jean Pozzi, French ambassador, at 29 Giza Avenue, informing him that the Egyptian government was severing diplomatic relations with the Vichy government.

Now persona non grata, the ambassador was advised to leave the country without delay.

*

During the last days of January, Masreya yielded to Farouk on the great sofa in the throne room, beneath a portrait of him in a white uniform decorated with medals. Under pretext of a secret agent's arrival, he'd emptied the palace wing of all personnel. His entourage was convinced he was in negotiations with Rommel. They awaited the arrival of a German officer, perhaps disguised as a Bedouin. In Egypt, the most amazing stories are born from a trifle that spreads at the speed of words. Someone had seen him come in, a tall blond man with green eyes, his head wrapped in a *keffiyeh*—he could be taken for Colonel Lawrence. He had the bearing of a prince, and the king seemed pleased to welcome him. Someone else had seen him leave, as a woman dressed like a movie star, with huge black glasses that hid half her face. This new Mata Hari had slithered down the steps at a run, diving into the back of a white Cadillac.

Only the two Albanian body guards could have told the truth. But one was mute and the other would have given his life rather than reveal the least of the king's secrets. As we say in Egypt at the beginning of children's stories: 'This was, or this was not.' No one could testify that it was; therefore, it was not. For no one could have seen Masreya entering the palace; she was already there. She'd slept in a secret flat of Farouk's, to which he alone had the key. She'd spent the day with her two duennas, preparing, putting on makeup, perfuming herself for the Pharaoh.

At nightfall, when the king had gone to find her—after having made sure no one was loitering in the halls—he found her cloaked in seven veils that blazed with the colours of fire. He'd approached her, uncovered her face, and Masreya's beautiful eyes had gripped him. 'O my sister!' He was overwhelmed with emotion. But, regaining

control, he'd added, 'The palace is shining, O sweet one! Your presence lights up my dwelling. You were born for the pleasure of kings.'
They sported for several hours before, exhausted, Farouk stretched
out naked on the sofa. It was then that she slipped in, 'I have a favour
to ask of you, Your Majesty!' His eyes closed, he murmured, 'I'm
listening' And she spoke to him of the unjustly imprisoned Nino,
intimate friend of her brother Gohar with whom, he must recall,
he'd enjoyed chatting. His mind befogged, he promised, of course.
Tomorrow at dawn, he'd arrange to have the man released. Then,
suddenly authoritarian, he commanded: 'Now show me what you
know how to do.' It was 29 January 1942. In Bengazi, the British
garrison had just surrendered. Masreya as well!

Farouk took quite a long time before keeping his promise to
release Nino Cohen from the foreigners' prison. Political events
had accelerated. He'd spent part of the night with Masreya, 'the
Egyptian woman'. He'd even fallen asleep for a few minutes, right
after lovemaking. When he awoke, he said, 'I have slept in the Nile's
bed. And I've understood what pleasure the crocodiles take there.'
The following morning, discovering that his prime minister had
surrendered to the British without informing him, he was seized by
a cold rage. He stripped Hussein Sirry of his powers and decided to
entrust the new government to Ali Maher, a man opposed to the
Wafd and notoriously pro-German.

Everyone knew he was competent, but, in the current atmosphere, the irritable British, especially the ambassador, took this nom-
ination as a provocation: 'Oh, the Kid'—that's what he called Farouk
in English, *the Kid*—'wants to try to outsmart me. I'll teach him
what it is to be an officer of the crown.' He emerged like a whirlwind
from his office, rounded up a few officers, leapt into his Rolls and
reached the palace at the head of a battalion of tanks. His troops
surrounded the buildings; followed by the officers, he passed through
the doors at top speed, revolver in hand. Threatening them with
his weapon, he swept aside the chamberlains who tried to stop him
and brusquely threw open the door to the king's chamber.

Farouk, who was studying a map spread out on a table, raised his head in surprise. 'And so, Sir Miles,' he said coolly, 'you must be very anxious to go walking around like this, revolver in hand. Put your weapon aside, you're safe here.'

'Ali Maher, never!' the ambassador shouted. 'Do you understand?' He demanded that the new government be entrusted to Mustafa al-Nahhas Pasha, head of the Wafd, whom he knew favoured the Allies. If not, he barked, he could easily dig up another puppet to play the role of king.

Farouk stiffened at the insult but restrained himself. He realized that the other man was trying to trip him up, seeking an incident. He wouldn't let himself be manipulated. If he clung to his plan to name Ali Maher, the British army would depose him. Lampson would call on Khedive Abbas II, in exile in Geneva, and place him on the throne. Abbas would declare martial law, and that would be the end of the dreams of a great Egypt cherished by Farouk who saw himself as king of Egypt and the Sudan one day.

'So it's Nahhas you want?' he ended up saying, his lips trembling with rage. 'Don't put yourself in such a state, Sir Miles. You want Nahhas, you'll have Nahhas!'

When the British left the palace, Farouk, livid, emerged from his chamber without a word. His chamberlain and majordomos tried to intervene, asking him where he wished to go, but he pushed them aside. He raced down the great staircase, dressed in his city clothes, his head bare, his hair in disarray. He reached the door of his personal garage. Each driver and mechanic rushed to the side of the car for which he was responsible and came to attention, smoothing his uniform. The king hesitated a moment, glancing rapidly over the ten or so cars lined up, impeccable, gleaming. He wanted the least recognizable one. He settled on a Jeep he used to go antelope-hunting in the Southern oases. He leapt to the wheel and took off right under the noses of the guards, who, speechless, watched him leave.

Farouk always drove fast, but that day he was a madman. At the Suleiman Pasha intersection—named for his ancestor, his mother

Queen Nazli's great-grandfather, whose true name was Joseph Anthelme Sève, a Frenchman in Napoleon's army who'd converted to Islam—he clipped the rear fin of a British officer's car. The policemen whistled until they were breathless, and several military police jeeps set off in pursuit. He lost them at the Qasr-al-Nil Bridge. He crossed the bridge at top speed, his hand on his horn, veering to avoid pedestrians, donkeys and trucks. 'Hey!' shouted an old man he brushed, 'Speed is the sign of the devil!' When he reached Rhoda Island, without slowing down he turned on two wheels, oscillating for a moment before falling back to take off again more gracefully. The tyres screeched at every turn; the motor, pushed to its limits, roared, and a smell of burning filled the cab.

On Osman Bey Street, he leapt from the car, which butted against the pavement, and banged on the door. He was out of breath, sweating, his heart pounding. Ouahiba half-opened: 'The young lady is out.'

He pushed her brusquely. 'If you close your door to your king,' Farouk told her, 'what will happen to you when you present yourself in Paradise, you dimwit?'

She dropped the clay pitcher she was holding and it shattered on the floor. 'The king!' she stammered, 'The king!'

Masreya, stretched out on her bed, dressed only in a galabia, was reading the lyrics of a new song by Kacim. 'Sire!' she cried. 'What's happened to you?'

The voice of his mistress calmed Farouk. He sat on the edge of the bed, silent, his eyes blank. She took his head in her hands, placed a kiss on his brow. She raised her eyes to the heavens. 'O God! You who have offered a king to Egypt, give him the strength to face the violent and the deceitful.'

He looked at her, surprised by the aptness of her words. He undressed and stretched out on the bed beside her.

'What's wrong, my love?' Masreya asked. 'What's wrong, my soul? What's wrong, my eye? What's wrong, my king? Is it love that's troubling you so?'

And Farouk let himself be taken. More than anything, he liked to watch the rebirth of his sex, feeling the same fear that overcame him when he'd been surprised during his very first erection by his British governess, no doubt the first British spy he'd had to submit to, between his fifth and thirteenth years.

'In your hands,' Farouk murmured, 'I'm like the desert sand arranged by the wind. According to its whim, it raises mountains or hollows out valleys.'

When he left Masreya's villa, the sun was about to set, fiery orange crowning the minaret. A crowd awaited him, surrounded by a ring of British soldiers. The captain in charge of the garage had chosen a Cadillac, one of the king's favourites, with a carmine red carriage and white roof. He opened the door and bowed down to the earth. Furious, Farouk climbed in, ignoring the crowd that was hailing him.

Edmond Rostand Square

In the Cafe Rostand, across from the Luxembourg Gardens.

Women are often strangers to their own desires. It can even be that, sometimes, their sex is on fire and their head doesn't know it.

Last night, I had erotic dreams. It was definitely me in the dream; I recognized my voice, with its musical tones and *r*'s as soft and supple as camel hair. A memory came back to me—a night of madness on the banks of the Nile, aboard a *dahabeya*, a floating house, rolled in satin sheets, rocked by the lapping shore.

Heaps of memories, organized by two criteria—dates and places. Although the events of 1942 are decisive, on reflection, their image remains blurred. In 1942, I'd begun a love affair with Masreya, my milk-sister, not just little moments of sudden passion like before but a true love, so much so that we were seriously thinking about marriage. Well, I was the one who wanted it. I know it's forbidden for men to marry their sisters—for ordinary men, I mean, not for divine kings, like the pharaohs. I've read the story of the pharaoh who married the daughter he had with his sister. Could there be a purer marriage—purer and more intense?

And the necessary otherness? Otherness is reborn from its own ashes. And new gods and new idols arise from the hearts of those thought to have been reduced to the faceless throng.

I am quite old. Sometimes I wonder if death has forgotten me. Today, I no longer fear it, it has become my ally—if it comes, I thank it; if it spares me, I thank God.

Nino Cohen had climbed the ladder within the Brotherhood to become one of its leaders. It's hardly believable.

I hail a taxi. Irony of fate, the driver is Egyptian. He drives very calmly; you can barely hear the motor purring. He casts furtive glances into the rear-view mirror. He ends up speaking to me. He grew up in Cairo. Do I by any chance know Cairo? Not even forty years old, tall, with wide shoulders; a thin moustache gives his face a certain distinction. I answer, 'Cairo, city of all the secrets.' Another exchange of glances. Cairo, he specifies, *Al Qahira* in Arabic—'The Victorious'. You might wonder who this city was able to conquer; he thinks Cairo has triumphed over order. We cross the Pont Saint Michel. A broad hand gesture, indicating the Palace of Justice: 'Take Paris, for example, an orderly city. It looks like a museum, a huge museum. You can't say that Paris is victorious, not at all. Paris has lost, order has triumphed. What's left are buildings, very tidy, with clear style, but life has vanished.' And Cairo, then? How to put it? He uses a metaphor. It's as if you were watching a tree trunk gliding down the water's current when suddenly an enormous mouth opens with a terrible roar, like a lion's. And you realize it's not a tree trunk but a crocodile. Cairo is like that. From high up, you think it's dead matter—stones and sand. But up close, it's wild life.

He apologizes for his poor French. I venture to ask: Did he know King Farouk? Am I an idiot? He's much too young for that. Has he heard of him? Of course. What are they saying about him these days in Cairo? 'Oh, Farouk!' the driver replies, 'When old people talk about Farouk's day, it's as if it were a paradise from which they were expelled.'

Farouk and his cars, for example: His father, King Fouad, had given him an automobile, a real one, an Austin Seven, in 1931. He was eleven. It was already red. Later, he had all his cars—and God knows he had a lot—painted this same metallic carmine red. What's more, he decreed that no one in Egypt could own a red car. So, in his day, when you saw a car that colour passing by, you knew it was the king, King Farouk, unlike anyone else.

'It may well be true, everything that people say,' he concluded. 'Farouk was so wealthy. We Egyptians enjoyed the king's wealth. It was as if we shared it a little. But Mubarak's wealth! Every piastre of that wealth impoverished every Egyptian. Go figure . . . '

The Nile Quay—Dahabeya

Zohar was growing more uneasy, day by day. Students he met in the cafe—those who'd experienced it—had told him about the violence suffered by detainees in Egyptian jails. Nearly naked, confined by the score in tiny unlit cells; fed once a day a meagre dish of favas they had to eat with their hands; subject to the vindictiveness of Nubian jailers who flogged them to force them to sing hymns of praise for King Farouk—not to mention the sexual humiliations. What they most longed for was a breath of fresh air. The evening breeze cost one pound for a few minutes during which the guards agreed to leave the door ajar.

A month after his friend's imprisonment, a student brought Zohar a note scribbled in pencil on a scrap of newsprint. Nino asked only for some clean linen. He couldn't stand his own stink. Poor Nino! Always so fastidious, now faced with uncivilized promiscuity in the darkness of an ancient dungeon. He must have grown nearly mad—the proof was that he concluded with these few Arabic words: 'May Allah preserve you, my brother.' There was nothing strange about an Egyptian Jew calling God 'Allah'—the three religions shared the same word. If you broke it down into al-lah, it meant simply 'the god', hence 'God', giving the speaker freedom to assign the identity of his choice. Egypt had long ago understood that ambiguity was the mother of freedom. But Nino had added, 'My soul is serene. If God has willed it, I will die a martyr for the triumph of our faith.' That last sentence tolled like an alarm bell. 'Our faith?' What faith was he talking about? Zohar's flesh crawled.

Of course, Joe had been warning him for weeks. 'Zohar,' he kept saying, 'you should go see Nino, talk with him one on one. You're his friend! Do you know he's converted to Islam?' Zohar would shrug. 'So? If he's converted to Islam, he can later convert to something else. It's like a bank note, let's say a pound sterling—you can convert it to dollars; then, you can convert the dollars to francs or rubles. It's still money, isn't it? You go up, you go down, you're still Jewish, no matter what.' But Joe insisted. 'No, Zohar! You don't understand. It isn't an intellectual conversion. It comes from his gut.' Zohar couldn't believe it. When you're Jewish, you remain Jewish. Otherwise, how to explain that there were still Jews, after centuries of efforts to make them disappear? He wanted to believe that the strange sentence in Nino's note was a cry of despair—a warning perhaps, a kind of plea.

When he went back that Friday to celebrate Shabbat in the hara, his mother asked him what was wrong. His father felt his cheeks, was startled to feel them tense, placed his hand on his head, and blessed him: 'My son, may your spirit find peace.'

Zohar sat still on a chair. His father focused before saying. 'Listen, some people think they'll triumph through speed, others through strength. But you who were cradled by the words of the Lord, you know it's through recalling His name that serenity comes to our hearts. For it's the Name that soothes the spirit.'

Instead of relaxing, Zohar grit his teeth.

Motty immediately reacted. 'So it's not business that's troubling your soul—'

'No, my father! But it doesn't matter—'

Motty was turning around to bless the wine, but Esther tugged his sleeve. 'Insist! Don't leave him, Motty,' she begged. 'His arms are solid, his brain is powerful, but his soul is as light as the wind.'

Motty lifted his head and hands towards heaven, and a verse of the Song rose to his lips. His deep voice, more solemn than usual, a little hoarse at this late hour, filled the small candle-lit room. 'Him whom my soul loveth: I held him, and would not let him go, until I had brought him into his mother's house, and into the chamber of her that conceived him.' Esther placed her hand on her husband's and looked at him with a smile. She loved him as on the first day. She loved him despite adversity; she loved him despite the winds; she loved him for the joy she felt each morning when she woke up beside him; she loved him more than life.

Hearing his father's voice raised, Zohar was finally soothed. He looked at his parents and smiled. What would they ever need, these two? Adam and Eve in the Garden, that's who they were. Assuredly, it takes a blind man for a woman to relinquish all her fears.

'It's my friend Nino, O my father, he's the one I'm worried about. If I don't manage to get him out of jail, he'll die, I know it!'

Esther and Motty knew about Nino's imprisonment. Everyone knew about it. News circulated more rapidly than air in Haret al-Yahud. Motty set down the cup of wine he was about to consecrate and asked Esther to lead him to the armoire. He felt with his hand behind his shirts and pulled out a bilingual book, Hebrew and Arabic. He counted seven pages, placed his finger on a line and held it out to Esther. 'Here!' he commanded. 'Read the first words so that I can remember the beginning of the psalm.'

Surprised, Esther looked at the book, turning it over to make out the cover. She wondered why her husband hid esoteric texts he couldn't read in the linen closet. She began in Hebrew, 'Give me justice, O my God! Defend my cause against a nation of infidels.'

Under his breath, Motty commented: 'And against the place's philosophy, native, as old as the stones, as placid as the Sphinx.'

Then he continued out loud: 'Men's justice is always unjust. It is not just for men to judge men. When the Messiah comes, the judges will be judged.'

And he sang, 'Give me justice, O my God. I will go to the altar, I will take my harp, my joy and my gladness will rise towards you. O God! O my God! Give me justice, O my God!'

Motty's voice traced spirals up the walls; the candles' flames flickered in time with his melody. Esther took up the refrain with him, and her voice, high-pitched, a bit piercing, strong, the voice of the people, joined in concord with her husband's. 'O God! O my God! Give me justice, O my God!' Then Zohar began to sing as well. And the joy of Shabbat rose over the little grocery in the Alley of the Jews.

Drawn by the music, old Massouda was the first to enter, followed by Uncle Elie. 'What's going on? A secret celebration? The house belongs to our fathers, and we're excluded from festivities?'

Esther hurried. 'Come in, my mother! We'll sing together. So many voices are invoking Him tonight that we need to pray with all our might so that He can hear ours among the rest.'

Uncle Elie immediately recognized the psalm for the liberation of prisoners and asked Motty, 'Has some misfortune occurred?'

Motty was singing, 'Deliver me from men's injustice, O my God, my protector, my salvation!' And they sang together, Uncle Elie and his wife the *robissa*, Massouda, and Motty and Esther.

Zohar, his heart suddenly swelling with an emotion he couldn't name, was thinking about the world's complexity: business, where you could lose everything in a day; his risky circuit through the courts of the powerful; and what to make of the gods, those of the Copts, the Muslims, the Orthodox, the Armenians, the Jews—all different, all jealous, as tempestuous as women in love. Oh! The world is so hard, and no one knows where the true guides are hidden. This evening, he missed his childhood, when he was simply an element of the world—a bird or a tree leaf.

Esther's aunts, first Maleka, then Tofa'ha and even Adina, joined the improvised choir with their husbands. The little grocery was proclaiming its faith with a sort of fury, knowing God's deafness through experience. Motty's tenor voice suddenly rose like a kite seeking the sun: 'O my God, O my rock!' The others repeated. And Motty continued: 'O my God, O my rock! Grant me justice, O God! Defend my cause against the entire nation. Deliver me! Deliver me!'

After the songs, they sat around the table. Motty broke bread and commented one last time, 'They say this psalm softens judges' hearts and fills them with terror.'

Zohar looked at his father, thunderstruck. 'Really? Do you think our prayer will get Nino released from prison?'

Motty replied mysteriously: 'There are all kinds of prisons, my son: those surrounded by walls where you know what separates you from the world, and those so wide you don't perceive their boundaries. The desert is also a prison—would you know how to find your way out? The wandering of someone who no longer knows how to ask questions is worse than the desert. Your friend is lost. He'll escape men's prison, that's certain, but I don't know what will bring him back among his own.'

When Zohar left Haret al-Yahud, the sky was studded with myriads of stars. Less than a year before, he'd been spending his nights prowling the city in search of lovers of herbs and powders. Is that what his father called 'wandering'? At that time, he'd felt freer and more at peace than today.

Taking long steps, he swung his arms like a lord along Suleiman Pasha, surprised at the number of lighted signs despite the black-out. Fearing German bombardment, the civil defence had ordered that lights be hidden behind blue curtains. But the king himself, rebelling against the British, made his palace shine with a thousand fires. It should be said that, until now, Cairo had been spared by the enemy air force. Cairo, where the night's heat was enough to trigger drunkenness.

Zohar did not hear the Buick that suddenly drove up and parked by the pavement, right beside him. The hum of the electric top made him jump and turn his head. On the rear seat, a woman veiled entirely in black gestured towards him and pointed to the front seat. The driver, a liveried Sudanese, opened the door. Zohar hesitated.

'You don't recognize my eyes?' Masreya asked from behind her mask. 'Our grandparents envisioned whole romances solely based on an exchange of glances.'

He climbed onto the seat in one bound. As the car pulled away, he said only, 'You startled me.'

He straddled the seat back and flung himself into the rear.

'My prince!' she said, as she twined around him. 'Beauty of the world that allows me to breathe your soul's perfume.'

Then in an authoritarian voice he did not recognize, she addressed the driver: 'Mad Abdu, to the dahabeya!'

Born in the South, the land of Christians and charms, he was called Mad Abdu because he was so handsome, driving women to madness. He turned around, letting his smile blaze, and answered, 'Your orders are a caress, O my mistress!'

'The dahabeya?' Zohar was startled. 'What dahabeya?'

They were rolling along with the top down. The British out on the town turned to look at them, stunned by the sight. They saw passing by a gleaming sand-coloured Roadmaster, its chrome decorated with crescent moons, and a very young man, dressed like a dandy, ardently kissing a veiled woman. They must have told themselves that the soldiers' briefing had been quite exaggerated when they informed them about the Egyptians' primitive modesty. As soon as night fell, Egypt became Los Angeles; the quays of the Nile, Hollywood.

Mad Abdu swerved wildly at Qasr-el-Nil and began to drive along the river. He knew his mistress's tastes. He accelerated, and the eight cylinders roared out their wandering song. Masreya was calling into the wind: 'Faster! Let's go! Death pursues us, and love lies before us, far away.'

Zohar repeated his question, 'What dahabeya?'

'Mine,' she finally admitted.

He didn't need anything more to understand. 'A gift?' he asked.

He tried not to show it, but the thought pierced him like a poison and made his insides churn. The car rolled for a long time, bouncing over potholes. They were still kissing: his mouth was hers, they had only one tongue, and they were speaking about the world. 'The war hasn't yet reached the hara,' Zohar was joking; 'I just left. I like seeing them that way, insulated from evil, speaking to God and still fearing pharaoh.' They laughed about the people there, the people they encountered, the people who were not them. They touched each other through their clothes, sniffing each other like cats in heat. 'And the nightclubs,' Masreya replied, 'are filled with soldiers who don't want to go to war. Cairo has become a pleasure palace.' It was true. They were still for a moment, holding each other's hands, their eyes vacant. Did they see themselves as twins in the same womb?

'And the Buick? Also a gift?' he couldn't help asking.

She burst out laughing. 'Maybe. I was only given the keys. You have to admit that these leather seats . . . I certainly hope to keep it! But what's wrong with you, Gohar ibn Gohar? Could you be jealous?'

The road angled sharply. Mad Abdu tried three times before making the turn. They ended up in a sort of clearing. The bank had been built up. At the entrance, two palms rose like the columns of a temple. The car stopped beside the pontoon. The dahabeya, rocked by the indolent lapping along the shore, creaked rhythmically. A porthole diffused a reddish glow. Appearing out of nowhere, Ouahiba opened the car door. Masreya winked. 'Let's go, come!'

'Where are you taking me?'

'I've created a cradle on the Nile for you.'

In their haste to make love, they neglected the water at the entrance. They neither drank nor made ablutions. They didn't bother to look at the place, lit by a few lamps. In the half-light, he was her night; she was his day. 'Handsome as the moon,' they say in Arabic. The moon is masculine in Arabic. She was strong as the sun, which, in Egypt, is a god. They made love on the doorstep. They made love standing up, unable to separate, not even to take a step towards the bed. They made love without letting go of each other, Siamese twins from birth, caught in a spell. They made love without moving, afraid to part.

On the pontoon, Ouahiba, the older of the two sisters, hearing them moan, was overcome with anxiety. She murmured to Baheya: 'Maybe it's haram—but it's so powerful—it's not their fault.'

And the younger one replied, 'O my sister, I'm afraid! I can already feel the earth trembling.'

O Zohar! You whose soul is light and whose blood is as sweet as honey, why are you not satisfied to love with your heart? Don't you know that love's danger lies in the humours that well up from the body to generate the creatures of the night? O Masreya, nervous fish with eyes of light, hear me! A brother's friendship is the foundation of the world. What is it then that drives you to join your flesh? You could have set yourself up in a union of the powerful. Brother and sister, perfect twins—you could have been king and queen, that could have been your destiny, if you hadn't been seized by your passion for viscous fluids. O Zohar, O Masreya, magical children, too beautiful for the world, your ancient memory of the womb's waters has veiled the sun.

Stretched out naked on the bed, his hair sticky with love, pretending to study the ceiling, Zohar, regaining consciousness, had rediscovered the bitter question that tormented his soul. 'A gift from the king?' he asked again.

'Who else?' she sighed.

'I'll kill him!'

Was he mad? She reminded him of the role he had assigned her, to seduce Farouk to obtain Nino's freedom. She'd worked at it; he'd better believe it. His friend would be out of prison by the end of the month. And the work hadn't been easy. Yes, the king was free to do anything he pleased, but he still needed to somewhat justify the orders he gave. Was Zohar aware that Nino had taken on responsibilities at the heart of the Brotherhood? That the *moukhabarat*, the Intelligence Services, viewed him as a fanatic, an especially dangerous figure liable to trigger an uprising, place bombs or lead students in an attack on a British barrack? On his police record, she'd read: 'Inflamed ideologue, even more intractable because intelligent and educated.' Those too intelligent to be restrained were regularly strangled with a rope in their cells by the police, then thrown into the water near Aswan to feed the Nile perches.

Zohar lowered his head, not knowing what to say. Then he raised his enormous eyes, a little haggard. 'Did you really have to go that far? Now he loves you madly, to the point of offering you a floating house on the Nile and an American convertible.'

She shrugged and sighed. 'Toz on the American car, and toz on its convertible top! Toz on this mockery of a king who day by day returns closer to infancy.'

He smiled. She joined him on the sheets still damp from the flood of their passion. They interlaced, rolling, united, interwoven, braided like serpents. They were perfect, naked as on the first day, she with skin so brown at the base of her back that the folds looked blue; he fair and almost entirely hairless, like an *eromenos*. Their breathing synchronized, at that moment their hearts beat as one, precisely.

'Will you marry me?' asked Zohar.

She flinched. 'What?'

'I mean—when you're done with him. I've heard he doesn't keep any woman for very long.'

'You're mad!'

'Why?'

'Will you renounce your faith?'

'Your god, mine—we'll marry them as well. And we'll add the others: the lords, those little gods so powerful they're honoured in the neighbourhoods, in Bab al-Zuwayla—and all the gods of the earth too, if you like.'

'The lords are not gods, you infidel, they're nothing but old wives' tales!'

He burst out laughing. 'The lords draw power from your doubts.'

'Shut up, Gohar ibn Gohar. Don't blaspheme.'

'We are Egypt. You are the earth, I am the river. I am the city, you are the sun. I am the past, you are the future.'

'Listen to me, you son of nothing.'

She was about to speak when Ouahiba knocked loudly on the cabin door.

'Mistress! O mistress.'

'What's wrong?' she cried angrily through the door.

'Cars are approaching, O mistress! Many cars—the king, the king!'

Masreya leapt up, crammed into a closet the clothes scattered on the floor, on the chair, on the bed. If they found him there, Zohar risked joining his friend Nino in a dungeon.

He'd already put on his trousers. His shirt open, he threw her a questioning look. Without a word, she pointed to a trap door in the floor. He raised it. A few steps descended into the hold. He climbed all the way down, banged against a case, burrowed through the bowels of the ship all the way to the other end, then crouched under a half-open porthole. He heard Masreya going out onto the bridge. A man asked to speak to the young lady named Ben't Jinane. 'I am she, your highness!' The man explained to her that the king was in Montazah Palace in Alexandria and wished her to join him without delay. She could take her own car; the two cars here along with the four motorcycles would escort her the whole way. Could she at least have some time to get dressed? Of course. They would wait for her here, on the quay, as long as it didn't take more than a few minutes. The king was in a hurry.

Zohar waited for Masreya to come back into the cabin before he raised the trap door. He stuck his head out. 'Will you marry me?' he asked again.

Montazah

She abandoned him there, in the floating house, the dahabeya, that golden folly, and Zohar remained stretched out on the satin sheets, staring at the ceiling and smoking cigarettes. It was impossible to tell whether he was thinking or whether the thoughts were effortlessly escaping from his brain like steam from a pot of boiling water. He'd heard the Buick's motor start and the bark of military orders instructing Mad Abdu about his place in the convoy. The motors vroomed, proud, sober, strong, and those of the motorcycles, sputtering, framed them like drumrolls. 'Go! Go! The king awaits.' And rat-a-tat-tat, he saw himself opening the cabin, tommy-gun in hand, splattering those uniformed clowns. Rat-a-tat-tat. He would have liked to spit lightning from his lips, to call down thunderbolts from the sky; to howl the dreadful curses that filled his tongue, and have the elements come to his rescue. Wasn't he the lords' child? But he remained stretched out, his eyes closed; he saw them bustling outside, growing impatient as they waited for Masreya who kept adding one thing onto another—the bird cage, the hat box, the white gloves for receptions, the gold fox collar. He closed his eyes as he inhaled like a madman; he restrained himself as unknown words raced through his head, words he'd never uttered, in a forbidden tongue, Bab al-Zuwayla's. He reflected for a moment. Arabic? No. More likely a language from the South—Sudanese, or Ethiopian. When the kudiya would utter those strange words that now were returning to him in gusts and clanging through his head, the flames rose and crackled, the sky darkened, the earth growled. So, yes. He'd go out, he'd stand before them naked and howl those words; the earth would spew its burning lava and their cars would catch fire and they would be engulfed in darkness, right up to the last one. Masreya would be left at the centre of a pacified world, without soldiers, without king, without Egypt, naked like him—she, his sister, his spouse. The two of them would be all alone in the world again, and they would set to work naming the animals.

He rose suddenly and struck the cabin door with all his might, gouging a ragged hole in the varnished wood. Concerned, Masreya reappeared; she thrust her face through the opening. 'What's wrong?' she asked with a lift of her eyebrows. He shrugged, resigned, and mouthed the one burning question that was tormenting him: 'Will you marry me?'

She blew him a kiss and disappeared. He heard doors slamming, motors revving and the captain crying, 'Let's go! Let's go!' He turned over on his stomach, buried his head in the pillows and sank instantly into a dreamless sleep.

*

Escorted by the motorcycles, the Buick rolled along, swaying majestically at an irresponsible speed—maybe a hundred kilometres an hour, maybe more. All along the road, horns blaring, they passed military trucks by the dozens—tractor trailers transporting armoured tanks to the western desert to face Rommel's onslaught. When they reached the outskirts of Alexandria, the first rays of sunlight cast the palm trees' huge shadows onto the roadway. Without slowing, Mad Abdu swerved, making his tires screech on the corniche road. In the back, Masreya, her eyes half-closed, let her face be caressed by the morning breeze. Suddenly, at a bend, she caught sight of a castle, straight out of a children's book. Excited, the driver turned around: 'Montazah, mistress! It's the Montazah Palace.'

She opened flabbergasted eyes. Rising from gardens that stretched as far as the eye could see, it was enormous, the facade studded with elegant arches, the walls adorned with coloured arabesques, the corners in fine stone lace. She trembled. So much grandeur to conceal how many vanished sleeping beauties?

'The palace of the mad, yes!'

That's what they called the insane asylum in Egypt, 'the palace of the mad' or sometimes, on account of its stones' colour, 'the yellow palace'. This one was white, outlined in pink and red—the king's colour—flamboyant. As the convoy slowed to enter the gardens, a cannon blast made Masreya jump.

'What's happening?' she cried. 'Abdu! What is it?'

'It's for you, mistress.'

'For me? What are you saying? Are you insinuating I look like a German soldier?'

'May misfortune be driven away, mistress. On the contrary, it's to honour you. The king welcomes his special guests with a cannon blast.'

The two military vehicles crammed with soldiers had disappeared into the lanes. The motorcycles had separated, two by two, and stood at the gates; their drivers, hats in one hand were making a military salute with the other; the Buick was slowly advancing. Suddenly, out of nowhere, a fanfare—trumpets, bassoons, horns and a bass drum—launched into the refrain of Masreya and divine Farid's celebrated duet: 'Life is beautiful to those who want to understand it. Life is beautiful. If you take what you are given, life is beautiful!'

Tears came to her eyes. All this for her, a child of the people, still suffused with the smell of water buffalos, still mired in the Delta's mud. If only her brother, her true king, that devil Gohar ibn Gohar, could be here to share her joy. Where was he now? May God curse his faith!

The majordomo opened the door and invited her to descend while an army of liveried servants rushed to the car's trunk and removed her baggage. Lifting her head, she saw the king coming down the steps to meet her. He was not alone. On his right, a young woman with a fair face and a Vivien Leigh hairdo, dressed in a sophisticated suit—the skirt's stripes were the inverse of the jacket's—looking as if she were straight out of an American film. On his left, an elegant man in a dark suit, his glistening hair divided by a straight part. Taller by a head, Farouk, in a three-piece suit, his eternal sunglasses on his nose, was holding his arms out and smiling.

Masreya turned back to Abdu who, with his eyes, signalled her to advance. She sprang forward like a young girl, climbed the few steps in one bound and flung herself into the king's arms. He hugged her to him—huge, hot, inhuman; sultan, insulting; ogre, prince, vampire; dispenser of kindness, maniac; commander of the faithful—he hugged her so hard she thought she would suffocate. What did he mean by all this? He turned to the elegant young woman beside him: 'My dear, I present to you the celebrated Ben't Jinane, the most promising of our artists. She's so young. I've somewhat adopted her.'

And he hugged Masreya to his chest again, adding, 'She's like my daughter—or rather, my sister,' he corrected himself with a knowing smile.

'I never had a father, you understand?' Masreya said, 'My mother was a singer.'

'I present to you Nazli Hanem, my cousin from Alexandria,' the king interrupted. 'And her husband, Omar Bey. They're spending some of their holidays at the palace. Go quickly and freshen up— we're leaving for the sea.'

Mad Abdu accompanied her to her room, asking questions all the way. 'Don't stray too far,' the driver advised. 'He's past the time for jealousy. He could dismiss you. Don't get too close, the ground is burning. Stay at just the right distance for desire.'

'Oh, Abdu my madness, if we were living at the time of the Mamelukes, I'd appoint you chamberlain of the harem.'

'We've changed eras, mistress. As in the past, women have intelligence. Today, they've also acquired the means. They're the ones who stand behind the curtain while, one after another, men fall at their feet.'

For two weeks, she was queen in her palace. Following Abdu's advice, she neither governed nor commanded, neither demanded nor pleaded. Shining and joyous; calm, solemn, and serene; at the hour when the moon hid, she reigned as mistress of desire.

The first day, they fished for tuna along the shore, zigzagging between the British destroyers. Farouk stood on the gleaming wooden bridge and drove the motorboat as fast as the dolphins. His hair in the wind, he mocked the British officers who threatened him with their tommy-guns. After dinner and the poker game that kept them up past midnight, he gave himself over to Masreya's airy fingers in his apartments. The next day, they hunted in the marshes and shot quail and duck under the nose of the commandos of the Long-Range Desert Group—until a colonel came expressly to ask that the king leave the militarized zone. Farouk replied in perfect English: 'You're blundering through my land, my young friend. You should instead ask your men to play a little farther during my hunt. They're frightening the birds.' This king who defied the British, who provoked them at the heart of their military operations, was only awaiting the moment when he could surrender to his queen of the night.

During the day, she kept herself apart, letting herself grow black in the sun, in her pristine bathing suit, humbly answering the guests' questions. In the evening, she sometimes danced for them, and these philistines, these innocents with deep pockets, understood her gift: the capacity to open your heart that falls to souls spawned by the earth's forces. Masreya, mysterious and limpid, sensuous and severe, light as her dance steps, whose name drew its depth from the palms of the Delta: 'the Egyptian woman'. She was the incarnation of Egypt, entrusted for a few days—you could say for a few instants—to a pharaoh on his way to mummification.

And Masreya's reserve, that silence about her own desires, which Mad Abdu had advised, inspired the king to confide in her. He opened his heart, perhaps for the first time, to this child born old, carrying in addition to her own the age of her Gohar ibn Gohar, her twin, her true love. Farouk spoke to her again of his sister, the divine Fawzia, whom he called Wizy, that sister whose beauty had crossed the ocean. They were praising her as far as America—the cover of

Life magazine, art shots taken by the greatest photographers, including Cecil Beaton. But then her husband, that damned Shah of Iran, he'd observed him when he came to Cairo to present his marriage offer. A madman! This demon-possessed man had set up this woman of perfect beauty, his sister, the sublime Wizy, in his chambers, then left from the very first night to gratify his lust with a man, his valet. Yes. A faggot, that's what this so-called emperor was, who let himself be taken on all fours by his servants—a follower of Lot. And Farouk swore to Masreya that he had only one thought in his head from morning until night—to repatriate poor Wizy. Masreya consoled him, and in his moments of distraction, he called her 'my sister'.

A few days later, the king decided to organize, with the help of the nabil Mohamed Abdel Halim, the relative he'd succeeded in releasing from the British jails, an automobile rally through the Western desert. In the middle of the wartime desert, while the tanks of the Eighth Army were shattering beneath the shells of Rommel's dreadful 88 mm anti-tank guns, the king planned an excursion, followed by a cortege of millionaires on holiday, to visit the common people of the oases. It's true the war was raging in Libya, but British encampments teemed along the border, especially around the oases of Siwa and Baharia.

At night, when he returned to Masreya, the king exulted: 'If they permit me to ramble through the desert, they make a mockery of their war. If they prevent me, they'll be taking a stand against the common people of Egypt.' And he burst into a satanic laugh, this child king to whom, from the beginning of his adolescence, nothing had been forbidden, except—he remembered—masturbation. Masreya tried to dissuade him. 'No, O my king, no! They'll think you want to spy on them, to transmit their positions to the Germans. Remember what happened in February.' But he laughed even more and puffed up his chest in front of his beauty, and in his thick voice cried, 'I am Farouk, King of Egypt and the Sudan! Do you know what my name means? Farouk—the one who separates. Yes! Who separates truth from lies, good from evil. What I'm saying is true. What I'm doing is good, for my people, for my country.' O, madness of the powerful, who don't know how to retreat, even when pursued by death! Masreya calmed his excitement as she caressed him. The scene was always the same, a sort of ancient ritual to the gods. He offered himself naked on his back, sperm whale beached on silken sheets, and she set about trying to resuscitate his sex, with her hands, her feet, her lips, binding and unbinding, imprisoning and releasing him. She always succeeded; he called her his magician.

A man had entered the palace in the middle of the night. He'd passed through the gates on a bicycle and was immediately apprehended by the royal guard; but when he showed a note written by the king's majordomo, they went to alert Farouk. The king received him in his office. Who was this unknown man, slender as a heron in his rumpled uniform, with a large hooked nose and skin the colour of burnt earth like the people of the South? Rumours spread. How could an ordinary low-ranking military man, a lieutenant in the ground forces, specialist in telecommunications, have obtained a private rendezvous with the king? At two in the morning, moreover. Those who'd seen him walking through the halls said he seemed desperate, constantly looking behind him. Was he being pursued by the British? The two of them talked for a long time, without a witness.

The next day, Farouk announced to the British commander that he was abandoning his plan for a rally but still intended to go to the Siwa oasis. He wanted to let Masreya discover this wonderful place, this garden at the heart of the desert, to dive into the fountains where Alexander had once bathed. The British, happy to avert another crisis, authorized the expedition, on condition that it contain only one automobile. The king, suddenly reasonable, assured them they would be just two, his guest and himself. Happy from then on, he joked endlessly about nothing, guzzled dozens of orange sodas and nibbled countless pistachios he drew from his pockets by the handful. His cousin, who knew him well, confided to Masreya: 'He has his ways—especially when he's done something wrong. Perhaps he stole a crystal ashtray from the casino. I remember the day he killed the guard's dog with one shot. We weren't even ten years old. He was acting the same way.'

The night before the departure for the desert, more excited than usual, Farouk rushed Masreya who was taking her time in the bathroom. From the bed, where he was stretched out naked, he called out, 'Do you think perhaps I pay you to linger in front of mirrors?' She didn't answer. He called her name. Silence. He was up in an instant. In the time it took to put on a dressing gown, the door slammed; she'd left. He wandered through the corridor, shouting like a madman. The sleepy guards rushed to him, but his arms swept them away with a bull's strength: 'Where is she, that whore? Where is the Egyptian woman hiding?' He raced down the grand staircase, his robe flapping behind him like a pelican's wings, followed by the armed guards. She'd disappeared. He woke up the two hundred servants, the soldiers, the maids, from the basement to the attic, and ordered them to search for her. They lit up everything. They scoured the nooks and crannies of the palace; brandishing torches, they ploughed through the garden; they called, they pleaded, they menaced. Cars sought her along the road; others bumped along the sand towards the beach. Masreya had melted into the night. At four in the morning, dripping with sweat, Farouk gathered his staff and showered them with insults: 'Idiots, dimwits, incompetents. To think that I maintain you, all of you, as many as you are! When one feeds animals, one gets services in exchange: milk, meat. From you, I get nothing. Nothing! You're parasites!' And he sadly trudged back up the great stairs, downcast. Only the little groom dared raise his head. And he's the one who saw her, Masreya with the beautiful face, leaning on the bannister, watching the king climb up. He cried out as he pointed to her, 'There she is! She's here, the devil!'

Her? Here? It was not possible. How could she have escaped the systematic search of the palace? The women started in: 'May it be according to your will, O lords!' No, she hadn't hidden; she'd simply gone through the walls. It's easy for creatures of the night. 'Have you seen how she dances?' insinuated one woman with a knowing look. 'No child of Adam can wind around herself that way, like a snake.' 'In the name of God,' added another, 'with my own eyes I saw her catch fire like a match. She was burning and she was unharmed—the more she burnt, the more beautiful she became, the black one.' The women, terrified at having rubbed elbows with a witch, cried, 'May misfortune be upon us!'

The king, hypnotized by the sight of his beauty at the top of his stairs, rushed like a dog finding its master. 'Look,' murmured a woman, 'look how he crawls.' And another one breathed, 'She uses a black pomade, a sort of unguent with which she paints her sex. She prepares it on the balcony under the full moon. I've seen it!'

Farouk was already on the landing, a little breathless. 'O gift, O sweetness! Were you frightened by my loud voice? Come, I'll give you the most beautiful jewels to make you forgive me.'

He didn't ask her a single question, this pharaoh with a heart of sex. He only wanted her to seize him, as she alone knew how; he would close his eyes, she would take him, and he would be reborn. And to placate her, he confided in her—he knew she liked to hear him talk business.

'Do you know who I entertained last night? That man who slipped into the palace, do you know who he was?'

'No. How would I know?'

'Just think, there are hundreds like him, who've had enough of the British. They first wrote me letters when they learnt about the violation of Egyptian sovereignty by Ambassador Lampson, last February. They were ashamed of our army's cowardice in not reacting to the insult. They assured me they were ready to take up arms to defend their king's honour and their country's independence. The man who came to the palace the other night is named Anwar. He's part of a group of officers working to a create a link between the Egyptian and German armies.'

'He has relationships with the Germans?' asked Masreya, surprised the king would compromise himself with rebels.

'Yes! They have a transmitter that has enabled them to reach German intelligence. Very soon, in the coming weeks, Rommel will attack. I think he'll take Alexandria and push on to Ismailia and Port Said to control the Canal. That's when the Egyptian army should arise from its torpor.'

'Is it wise, O my king, to take sides with one of the armies in the war? Haven't you been careful instead to maintain Egypt's neutrality? What if Rommel doesn't attack? If he loses the battle?'

'That's why we must help him! You see, politics is complicated. What you say, and even its opposite, you don't have to do. And what you do, you especially should not say—not even its opposite. Do you understand? I will bring Anwar with us into the desert. I'll have him pass as my driver. He will know how to locate the British positions and transmit the information to the Germans—he's a specialist.'

So that was it, Masreya realized, that was his plan: to have the liaison officer of the rebel military men pass as his driver. That's what was making him happy and excited at the same time. His cousin was right, the child king had again done something foolish, only this time it concerned the entire nation. Masreya was frightened, but not for herself. Could you be worried about a natural element, a mountain or a river? For that's how she lived, as part of the world, eternal. She was afraid for her brother, her twin, her Gohar ibn Gohar. If the Germans were to occupy Egypt, they would hunt the Jews, they would kill them or deport them far away to camps lost in the depths of the frozen steppes. And she would lose her double, her shadow, her breath, her soul, her love.

'You won't do this, O my king!' she said, forcing herself to remain calm. 'It's too dangerous! You won't bring Anwar.'

He stretched out naked on his bed and asked in his gentlest voice: 'Come, take me! Do what you know how to do.'

They didn't sleep long, barely two hours. The sun was already burning when they settled into the rear of the red Cadillac. Wearing a new uniform, Anwar was at the wheel. Farouk was in a good mood.

He placed his hand on his new driver's shoulder: 'May your morning be filled with goodness, O Anwar, the happy one.'

The man turned. He had a certain elegance—dark skin, a handsome face, large surprised eyes and a delicate moustache that gave him a slightly British look.

'O my king! May your morning light up the world, you whose brightness equals that of the lord sun.'

He cast a furtive glance at Masreya and lowered his eyes. Anwar was polite, respectful of religious precepts. He steered westward.

Leaving Alexandria, first they followed the shoreline and made an initial stop at Damanhour, not far from Masreya's village. Farouk was happy to show up like an unknown man among the Delta's peasants—to sit, to sip a soda, to chat like a simple bourgeois in a cafe in this small town in a distant province. The naifs' fear, when they suddenly discovered they were in the king's presence. And then his mischievous joy. They left the place, with hundreds pressing against the car, crying, 'Long live Farouk!' Farouk I, this king who was not afraid to venture out beneath wartime bombs to get news of his people. He laughed. 'Do you see how merely my presence makes them happy?'

As Masreya remained silent, he insisted, 'So, what do you say?'

She answered then. 'Your presence is sweet to them, O my king. It is your absence that makes them grieve.'

At these words, Anwar turned around. His eyes were more expressive than his mouth. Who was this young woman with razor-sharp speech?

Along the road were legions of soldiers bent beneath the weight of their weapons; cohorts of trucks, engines like lions roaring in clouds of sand; assault tanks, mechanical elephants with trunks of fire; and cannons by the hundreds, countless phalluses erect like dragons of death. Farouk knew each gun model, each truck design, the origin of each armoured vehicle, and Anwar took photographs with his miniature Minox.

They stopped in fishing villages transformed into fortresses; at Al-Alamein, well-named 'two worlds', the exact spot where the Occident meets the Orient; at Sidi Abd al-Rahman, the home of a centuries-old saint, his eye darting at them from the depths of his tomb. Anwar feverishly noted the placement of airfields and fuel reserves.

At yet another fortress bristling with bayonets, Marsa Matruh, where they were roughly greeted by a nervous colonel, they left the coast to plunge into the dunes—beautiful women's breasts, infinite, caressed night and day by a whistling colossus. Anwar found his way using a solar compass invented by the celebrated Major Bagnold. They could hardly get lost, though, for they were being shadowed by a twin-engine plane from the Egyptian Air Force; it flew over them every three hours, parachuting water, rations, cold sodas. The next day, at midday, they reached Siwa, whose presence had been announced for a while by flights of birds. They were not more than twenty kilometres or so from the Libyan border. Infernal heat, immensity, solitude as far as the eye could see, from which emerged fragments of dromedary skeletons and rusted trucks, a chaos of rocks and hovels of beaten earth, all of that same dusty yellow. And the royal red car, the Cadillac itself, had taken that colour, already almost a statue of sand. Masreya shivered.

'Is this still human land?'

'There!' Anwar shouted.

A narrow path between the rocks—first they heard something like a waterfall; then saw suddenly, rising from the earth, a palm tree, and then another—palms, a veritable forest of palms; and at the centre, a basin, a sort of pool, built in the time before time. The water bubbling up continuously. The solemnity of the moment when they saw being emerge from nonbeing, life at the heart of the desert. In his own way, Farouk was a believer—egocentric, superstitious, disorderly—but a believer all the same. He approached the water, performed his ablutions, prostrated himself and began to pray. Anwar prostrated himself beside him and prayed too. They moved forward, and, when they emerged from the forest, saw an ocean—yes, an ocean!—at the heart of the desert, a huge lake, with a rocky island in the centre and palm trees on the banks and very ancient ruins. Men had lived here in the time before time, men who grew rich from caravan bivouacs, men for whom each stone corresponded to a star. There were men in the past here of whom we know nothing; then the men from Ramses' time, men who already welcomed soldiers, from both the Levant and the Occident—these same desert men who today lodged soldiers of the Eighth Army, perhaps those of the Afrika Korps tomorrow. Happy people of the oasis, sometimes thieves, sometimes gift-givers, always enriching themselves with objects, songs, new words.

These shepherds, hunters, farmers, brigands, merchants and poets—poets above all—were singing. For their king, whom they'd never seen save in his likeness on banknotes, they brought out big gazelle-skin drums and one-stringed violins and launched into an improvisation contest. The visitors did not perfectly understand their language, Arabic certainly, but with foreign words from other times and places. But they understood that these men were singing about their good fortune in welcoming the King of Egypt, pharaoh lord of the chariots; reciting in verse the beauty of the woman who accompanied him, princess of desire; and the grace of his driver, whose pipe gave off a lingering scent of gum. And they foretold, not for the king, nor for the woman, but for the driver, a destiny worthy of the ancient gods. He, the nobody, would reestablish the pantheon, the place of the hundred gods, then disappear in one day, in a burst of fire. Anwar grew dark; he believed in soothsayers' predictions.

They drank fermented camel's milk, and, when the music filled the space until it mingled with its own echo, Masreya danced for them. She rose, the woman with the body of a goddess, red veils over her dark skin, with her full moon eyes and wild hips. 'Oh, this is most certainly Egypt's king!' cried the men, overwhelmed by so much beauty, 'And this woman is a princess!' And they repeated, 'This is certainly Egypt's king!'

O king of the two Egypts, see how the desert, where food is always a gift, fosters the birth of beauty, while the palace of abundance breeds ugliness.

Farouk had the most endurance—drinking, eating, a tireless reveller, laughing, speaking of nothing, joking as if at court surrounded by his generals and ministers of masquerade, his coquettes and fine gentlemen, his khawagates in suits, canes and hats.

When they had made friends, those from the infinite city and those from the desert, the men led Anwar to the battalion of Australian tanks camouflaged at the centre of the palm forest. And he kept on photographing until he'd run out of cartridges for his Minox.

The desert men had prepared tea for the king—a great ceremony, with white tablecloths and napkins, porcelain cups, silver spoons and pots—to one side, in the shade of a sand dune. They'd set this moment aside for him and her alone; they'd sifted and smoothed the sand, placed the table at the precise centre of the desert ocean. Farouk was standing, waiting for Masreya, a red veil on her shoulders, to take her place on the felt cushions.

From the height of his two metres, immense, enveloped from head to toe in folds of fabric, a man poured the tea, blacker than coffee, sweeter than honey—for the king first, then for his favourite. Afterwards, he'd withdrawn into the distance, behind a dune. Here, in the desert, creatures appear and disappear in an instant.

In this improvised salon, they spoke.

'I wanted to show you Egypt at its borders. You've seen it. I wanted to see you dance with sun and sand as backdrop. I've made the gazelles jealous.'

And Masreya, with the elegance of the wind, in a low voice, uttered these words, 'You will be a great king if you forget yourself. You will be forgotten if you think yourself great—'

A sound interrupted her. In the distance, the vultures were the first to hear it. They'd lifted their heads, stirred their wings in a disorderly motion and taken off, first one, then two, then the others.

They'd all flown back into the sky when the haze began to roar and the earth to vibrate. It appeared in the distance, outlined, an enormous sky whale swaying above the surface of the dunes.

'Armstrong Albermarle!' cried Farouk.

Masreya was surprised, so he explained, 'The plane's an AW 41 Albermarle. We can relax. It'll return us to Cairo with no trouble.'

The sound grew terrible, a stormy thunder that lasted minutes at a time. A wind from the horizon made their faces burn—their cheeks, their ears, their eyes. Then you could hear the metal pleading, the wheel's rubber submitting to the stones, objects clattering. The twin-engine touched down in a yellow fog and rolled for a long time, reaching the far end of the sand runway where it made a half turn, then returned, sputtering, to the foot of the wretched earthen buildings.

The propellers were fanning the wind impatiently. The journey would end here. The metal trembled; the men, fledglings famished for love, circled the smoking cabin, mother bird with outspread wings. They would be embarking for Cairo. Two military men, descended from the plane, would drive the car back to the Abdine Palace. The Alexandria holiday at the fairy palace of Montazah, the expedition into the desert, would end the moment the king stepped into the plane—she knew it.

'O king, O lord!'

He turned back to her in one movement: 'Your word is a caress to me, princess! Order, it is my pleasure.'

'O my lord, it's now been several months since I spoke to you about my brother's friend detained in the foreigners' prison. Will you let me think for one moment that the King of Egypt and Sudan cannot command the dark jailers on Nazli Street?' And she turned around to hide a tear.

'By my head!' swore the king. 'Do you hear me? By my eyes, by my soul! Tomorrow! The sun will not set before your brother's unfortunate friend will return home to eat at his family table.'

She turned then, her eyes red, kneeled before him and kissed his hand. The desert men shot their rifles into the air. Their wives dug into their throats to draw out the festive ululations, the shrillest. It seemed as if, in the distance, the jackals were responding. Perhaps it was simply their joy's echo reverberating in the vastness.

*

Upon its return from the Siwa oasis, the plane landed at a military runway in Helwan, a posh Cairo neighbourhood. The ambassador, Sir Miles Lampson, was standing at the foot of the walkway, hiding the sight of the Egyptian prime minister, Mustapha al-Nahhas, flanked by his ministers. A battalion of British special forces had surrounded the plane, preventing anyone from approaching. Farouk emerged first, in white sports trousers and tennis polo shirt, smiling, his hand raised to greet the people. When his eyes grew accustomed to the sunlight, he saw the forest of pot-shaped British helmets, bristling with bayonets. Frightened, he took a step back, thinking that this time Sir Miles, his avowed enemy, was coming for his head. Feverish, his hand damp, he squeezed Masreya's arm. She was standing behind him. The ambassador greeted him with a satisfied smile that augured nothing good.

'Happy to know you are back, Your Majesty!'

'What is this?' Farouk exclaimed furiously. 'A kidnapping?'

'Not at all,' the ambassador reassured him, 'you can return to your palace as you wish, if you allow us to search you.'

Choking, the king looked around. Not one Egyptian soldier, not even the Albanian guards—they hadn't accompanied him on his journey nor come to welcome him. Even his ministers, those incompetents chosen by the British, were holding back. He was alone.

'Not here,' grumbled the king, resigned.

'Would you rather return to the plane so we can proceed with the search?' asked Lampson.

He hesitated, thought of the scandal, told himself to maintain his dignity. He angrily turned out his pockets; they held nothing but a handful of pistachios that spilt onto the ground in a futile spray. Then he moved forward, cleaving the battalion with a rapid step, his head high.

But the British searched the plane systematically. They found the Minox and its cartridges hidden at the bottom of a travel bag, and documents, too, that revealed contacts with agents of the Abwehr, the German intelligence service, along with a list of officers' names and tracts calling for struggle against the occupier. Anwar was imprisoned, tried and condemned to a long sentence. Masreya, conducted to the Kasr al-Dobara headquarters and questioned at length, was not released for two full days. The interrogating officer treated her like a harlot, alternating off-colour jokes about the king's sexuality with threats of imprisonment. Distraught, the beautiful Egyptian woman ended up sharing her thoughts with this Englishman—who remained insensible to her charms. 'Why are you so upset? You have nothing to fear. You won't be chased out of Egypt by men, but by the gods!' She was not freed until she'd agreed to furnish information to British intelligence.

As for the king, his humiliation had been stinging; after rage came bitterness. Sorrowful, he made himself scarce, avoiding ceremonies attended by the British, having grown stingy with his usual repartees and bursts of laughter. He was seen more and more at the mosque. And when he appeared in public, he made sure it was with his family, accompanied by his wife, Queen Farida, and his little girls.

The events at Helwan airport remained secret; everyone had a stake in silence. But the fire was smouldering beneath the embers. The British thought they had Farouk, who feared that his amorous escapades would be exposed in broad daylight; meanwhile, Farouk was silently contemplating vengeance.

Queen Nazli Street

10 November 1942. On this day of freshness and light, Nino left prison, an ancient hermit in a filthy galabia, a ragged wool cap and a bundle of laundry on his shoulder. He'd spent close to a year in this medieval dungeon where he left behind a tamed rat, his comrade in misfortune. He could recite the whole Qur'an by heart and sported on his chest a fakir's shaggy beard, on his forehead the black prayer bump Egyptians jokingly call a *zebiba*, a raisin.

Dragging his bare feet over the pavement's sand, he moved forward blinking, overwhelmed by the street's bustle. Joe was waiting for him at the wheel of his backfiring MG.

'Hey! O Nino! Where are you going like that? Are you lost in the seventh realm of the kabbalah? Come, climb in!'

Nino stopped and squinted his myopic eyes towards Joe, who repeated with a laugh, 'Come, climb in! It's me, Joe, your friend, your companion, your partner.'

No sooner settled on the seat than Nino was asking, 'Isn't it time for the call to prayer, my brother? Take me first to the mosque.'

The summer of '42 was the summer of Al-Alamein. For months, Egyptians had untiringly repeated the name of this little port. Al-Alamein was splashed on newspaper front pages, crackled on radio broadcasts, accompanied newsreel images of tanks charging into trenches. Some sang it with hope, chanting: 'Go, Rommel! Go, Rommel! Show them your strength, let your nature shine forth.' From the depths of his dungeon, Nino had been among those. For others, the words were laden with anxiety about the end of the world. In a few weeks, they thought, Al-Alamein would fall; the Germans would take Alexandria, Cairo a few days later. Morale was so low, predictions so dire, that during the month of July the

British burnt their archives and dispatched their wives to Palestine or Iraq; the Jews studied maps in search of a destination. Jerusalem? For how long? America? But with its quota policy, America had almost completely shut its doors. Further away, then, Australia? The devil only knew. To whom would they apply for a visa, having become the earth's vermin, stateless?

Al-Alamein, the name that means 'two worlds'. Those facing each other in a global apocalypse? Or those facing Egypt, which needed to choose between a European future or an Arab revolt against the West?

Summer of anxiety. The heat had been scorching, the asphalt melted under automobile tires. But, benumbed by the wait, no one dared think of their villas in Alexandria, or even less of Ras al-Bar, so close to Port Said and the Canal, primary objective of the Axis forces.

Not once had Farouk summoned Masreya, nor come to visit her on Rhoda Island or in the dahabeya, nor taken her on a wild adventure to the edges of the land. It was as if he'd forgotten her. Perhaps her memory, mingled with the humiliation Ambassador Lampson had made him suffer at Helwan airport—damned British!—had grown distasteful to him? He was like that, this impulsive and changeable child king who paraded his instincts like medals and confused his desires with the country's needs, who believed that when he ate Egypt grew fat and when he had felt pleasure the earth itself was fertilized.

Strange summer. Kites immobile at the zenith; time appearing to stand still, holding its breath; people looking constantly behind them, jumping at the slightest sound, even the most familiar, but which now shattered the soul like an explosion.

Every night, Masreya welcomed Zohar in her floating house. Every night, after love, Zohar asked her to marry him. And every night, she was on the verge of accepting. Before she fell asleep, she would murmur, 'Let me think about it. I'll answer you tomorrow.'

But, by morning, the words of love had dissipated. As the proverb has it: 'Night's sweet words are like butter—they melt at the sun's first rays.' In the light, Zohar lost substance, his image faded, as if he'd been only a dream. She never thought about him during the day, not until evening when he materialized beside her without a sound. 'I heard nothing. Where the devil did you come from? Do you go through walls like a djinn?' During that entire summer, Masreya, the Egyptian woman, was neither married nor divorced, suspended, like her country, her head vacant and her heart torn.

As he drove, Joe was telling Nino: 'You missed Churchill's visit. He landed in Cairo, a colonial cap on his fat head, a khaki shirt, in shorts and socks. You should have seen him, a lion in disguise. It was so funny.' Nino was staring at the street, as if entranced. British soldiers by the dozens, clearly tipsy, cigarettes dangling from their mouths. He clenched his teeth, his fists. 'Why do you compare him to a lion? Huh? He's a dog! An imperialist dog, the source of all our trouble.'

Joe smiled. He had no desire to argue. Today, he was ready to forgive his friend everything. Moved, he studied Nino's emaciated face, his thin arms, his fingers with their blackened nails, and his eyes—his eyes, above all!—hollowed by despair; two dark little pearls at the bottom of morose chasms. 'Have you lost your glasses?' he asked. Nino took an infinite time to reply. 'A guard crushed them beneath his heel on the first day. But what does it matter? Do you think there's anything in this world worth looking at?'

On 31 August, the news burst, terrifying but also comforting, like the first clap of thunder after a stifling day. Rommel was launching his attack, the biggest, the ultimate—packs of panzers, mounting the assault on Al-Alamein. Newspaper headlines screamed like sirens. People asked each other in the street: 'Any news from the front?' Like snakes stalking their prey, rumours slithered through the city: Rommel had pierced the British defence; he would charge Alexandria; the first German sidecars had been seen in the suburbs—people extolled the beauty of the blond combatants, tanned by the sun, with their rapacious grins and tommy-guns. Some had circled the town, had lost their way near Tanta, heading towards Ismailia. They were offering chocolates and candy to village children . . .

These rumours spread, and anxiety mounted—the anxiety of not knowing, and the anxiety of knowing all too well the fate reserved for some. Tension, anxiety, hope.

'In the factory, we never let up,' Joe was saying. 'We sold Blue Water by the case, the customers were so afraid of running out.' Nino turned around roughly. 'Blue Water? What blue water?' He seemed to have forgotten the name of the alcohol that had made their fortune. 'You remember—Blue Water, the rum of the three Jews, the sweat of Haret al-Yahud.' Nino scowled and spat out a curse in which you could hear the names of unclean animals, dogs and pigs, associated with the word 'Jew'. And Joe, who'd resolved to act as if he were with the old Nino, pretended to rejoice. 'We have nothing to complain about. The more the blondes make war against the red-heads, the more gold pieces pour into our coffers.' And, always a tease, he added, 'You've earned a great deal of money, my friend! Lucky devil! You spent nothing in prison.' He placed his hand on his thigh. 'Dear Nino, never a smile, always your brain going a mile a minute.'

'My name is no longer Nino!' the other said, pushing Joe's hand away.

The reply was chilling, but Joe continued to joke. 'Oh, okay. So, what's your name now? Abraham? That's your real name, isn't it?'

'Abu l'Harb! From now on, you will call me Abu l'Harb.'

Abu l'Harb: 'Father of War.' What had he gotten himself into, this maniac? Joe shivered. He'd heard that detainees sometimes went mad in prison. He knew that in the Brotherhood they gave pseudonyms to those who vowed to fight to the death, sacrificing their lives. Once again, he avoided conflict by design—by habit as well. After all, Egyptians are Levantines, who know that conflict feeds on too much detail. So, as if he'd heard nothing, he continued.

'What was I telling you just now? Oh yes. A week ago, radios announced the rout of the German forces, but the Egyptians didn't want to believe it—so much so that the British had hundreds of prisoners march through the streets of Cairo. And the Egyptians approached them, touched them, questioned them. Afterwards, rumours spread through the city that the prisoners weren't German, that it was a ruse, that the British had dressed their own soldiers in German uniforms to hide their defeat.'

'The British are liars,' Nino muttered.

But on this 10 November, victory was complete. Montgomery had defeated Rommel's Afrika Korps and the redheads were gloating. Flags festooned buildings, soldiers invaded cafe terraces. Everywhere you went, you ran into passenger cars honking for joy. Indoors, hands were busy, greeting, serving sweets, flashing the 'V' for victory. Restaurants overflowed again. Rhythmic, shameless music spilt from windows; men's glasses swirled lewdly while women's arses swayed like the doors of hell.

Nino kept his eyes lowered, constantly moving his fingers, strangely mechanical. All along the way, Joe—friend, faithful rival, brother and adversary—tried to call Nino's soul back to life, to their former carefree life of sunshine, affection and smiles.

'Do you remember Kathleen? Of course you do. The Englishwoman with breasts as big as watermelons! I don't know how many nights you spent with her.'

'The Prophet too knew indecency and a profane life before he was called. Thank God, prayers have cleansed my memory.'

While Nino threaded his prophet's steps through the alleys adjoining the Great Mosque, Joe impatiently tapped out a Charleston tune on his Bakelite steering wheel. A cluster of urchins surrounded the car, climbed onto the running board: 'Is this a race car, O sir? Does it go faster than the tram?' Joe joked with them, 'It's not a race car, you idiots, it's an airplane. Look, if I accelerate, it'll fly up into the sky.' He revved the motor and pointed skyward; they looked at his finger and burst out laughing.

Nino returned from the mosque accompanied by a tall, heavy man with a trimmed beard, in a grey suit and a white shirt. They stopped some distance away, continuing their conversation as they looked in Joe's direction. The man pointed to the car and shook his head disapprovingly, then gave Nino a shoebox-sized package wrapped in newspaper. Nino listened, his head lowered, appearing absorbed; the other multiplied his anxious looks. Finally, they embraced and shook hands for a long time.

'Are you feeling better?' Joe asked when Nino sat in the car.

He didn't answer, unwrapping the package and hiding its contents. Then he drew out a string of wooden prayer beads and began to tell them one by one. Joe watched in fascination as Nino's fingers separated, grouped, counted and recounted the little balls; he heard him murmur words in Arabic, among which he recognized *bismillah*, 'in the name of God', and other phrases in which God's name returned repeatedly.

'What are you asking me?' Nino finally replied. 'If praying does any good? Listen, once a prayer is over, I think only about the next. Nothing else! Do you understand?'

'Do I understand? Yes—no—I don't understand. I don't know,' Joe ended up saying, determined to avoid a confrontation.

But when he saw Nino take a revolver out of the package and thrust it into his galabia's pocket, he could no longer restrain himself. Grabbing him by the sleeve, he asked, 'What's this, Nino? Have you gone mad? You're not thinking of doing something foolish, I hope?'

And the other, still telling his beads, his eyes closed, chanted louder and louder. And so, Joe could no longer keep from exclaiming, 'Do you think it pleases God to see you armed like a bandit? One hand on your beads, the other on a revolver. Is that it? Is that what it is to believe in God?'

Nino turned back to him, red eyes bulging. 'God is everywhere. What can you understand, son of a devil, you who were born with a silver spoon in your mouth and who never touched anything except objects made with Shaytan's gold?'

He was no longer shouting. His voice came from his gut, deep, hoarse, ringed by an echo. But he was terrifying in his determination. Suddenly he thrust the barrel into Joe's side.

'He is here!' he added menacingly, 'Here, in this weapon. God is this weapon when it rids the world of those who prevent us from following the laws He has ordained, when it cleanses the world of those who sully it. God is in the bullet that pierces the skin to eradicate in one instant the breath of life you don't deserve. God exists through your death, through the death of each unbeliever!'

And he cocked the gun. At that instant, Joe thought he would pull the trigger. He braked violently and parked the car in a cloud of dust, then turned to his friend: 'Nino,' he shouted, 'Put it away!'

The other still had his madman's eyes.

'Put it away! Hide it in the bottom of your pocket. Forget! Forget all this! It's like a bad dream. It's over. I'm not your enemy. I'm Joe, Joe di Reggio, don't you remember? A Jew like you. We like jokes and frothy anisette. We like sun and pretty girls, the ones with narrow waists and breasts like cannonballs. And for us, there's nothing better than a dive into the pool at the Sporting or Shell Clubs. Joe! Don't you remember the laps we used to swim at the pool? You always beat me, you bastard, easily. You could do ten in a row without stopping.'

Despite Nino's stubborn silence, he continued.

'Have you thought about your family? Your mother? Every day, she's told me, every day, she has your image before her eyes, from dawn to dusk. At night, she dreams of you, always of you. Come! Have you forgotten her *bele'hats*? No one can cook meatballs with cumin like her. And your sisters? They're waiting for you. Ever since they heard you were imprisoned, they've remained behind closed doors, trembling at the slightest sound of footsteps on the stairs. But trust me, they've lacked for nothing. Ever since your absence, may God help us, not one week has gone by that I didn't reassure them, sustain them. Put away the gun, you look like a madman.'

Nino ended by uncocking the gun. His hand was trembling. His teeth clenched, his voice quavering, he finally said, 'Don't speak to me of God! Never!' And he opened the door, as if to escape.

'But where are you going?'

Nino turned and looked Joe in the eyes without replying.

'Come! Close the door. We're going to find Zohar. He's waiting for us in a very special place. It's a surprise, you'll see!'

Nino remained immobile, a stone statue, a monument of rage. Joe leant across his legs to slam the door; then he took off, tyres screeching. He began to talk, garrulously—to forget what had just happened; to chase away this silence in which he saw a world suddenly emptied; to dissipate his fear; to preserve the illusion of ongoing, everlasting friendship. He spoke about the money they'd earned, the connections they now had at the highest levels, in the ministries, in the British army, among prominent Egyptians. He told him how, from one day to the next, they'd tripled the selling price of their bottles, so insatiable was the demand. He explained how they'd made so much money it was impossible to spend even a tenth of it. He described the plans to develop and export their product, tomorrow in the Sudan and the Congo; then in Europe perhaps.

He was untiring. Nino was sunk into the seat, his eyes half-shut, telling his beads. But Joe no longer looked at him. He was speaking to another Nino, in front of him, over there, who looked like the old one, with whom you could discuss medicine, pretty girls and philosophy; this Nino who would return, he was sure of it, after being purged of his suffering. And, swept along by his rhetoric, because at that age you can't hold back a thought for too long, he said, 'I don't understand, you see. The nabil was freed less than a month after your arrest. They had much more to reproach him with than you. Why did they keep you? Why for so long? Despite all our efforts. What happened?'

It was as if Nino had been waiting for this question. Emerging from his torpor, he explained: 'It was written! God wanted it that way. He needed to be alone with me, the way a newlywed joins his wife on the first night, without witness. He withdrew me from the world, He whom I love passionately, and there was no one in that place where I found myself, no one but Him, no one but me.'

He closed his eyes again, absorbed by prayer. Joe was speechless. 'He whom I love passionately.' For a moment, he hadn't understood. It occurred to him that his friend had fallen in love with a man. He even thought of the man he'd seen at the door of the mosque. Then he realized: No! The One he loves passionately is God.

Still, the sentence had a strange ring. Could you be in love with God? It's a figure of speech, not something you really experience. Moreover, should you say God or gods? Is there one god or many? The god of the Muslims is not the god of the Jews, most definitely! Which of the two had arranged this strange sequence of events on this Tuesday, 10 November? He must not be peaceful, that god.

That morning, though, Cairo was bathing in an atmosphere of beauty. The mildness of the air, an unreal glow shining from the heavens, a delight in nature. Why doesn't the harmony of the world soothe human souls? Nino might have calmed down, melted into his friend's arms, and wept, above all wept. Joe would have been unable to resist. Men so often replace grief with anger. Nino had stiffened, restraining his rage between clenched teeth. But it was through what came next that fate's bitter cruelty was revealed.

O God! O gods! Whoever you are: God of the Jews or the Muslims; of the Copts, the Greeks, or the Armenians; gods of the Egyptians perhaps, so gracious in their delicate hieroglyphs. O gods! Is it that you never have pity for humans?

Nino might have tarried at the mosque, chatted longer with his friend from the Brotherhood, stopped at a cafe to drink a very strong, very sweet coffee the way he liked it, cooled his hands through the touch of a glass of iced water. He might have hailed a street vendor of *ta'meyas*—those deep-fried patties of fava flour with the taste of childhood, which he'd missed so much in prison—or a vendor of licorice or orgeat or tamarind juice. Joe would have joined him. He longed to reintroduce him to worldly pleasures. Instead, like puppets whose strings were being pulled from another world, they'd spun at a devil's pace in their devil of a car. For the devil is speed.

Zohar was not expecting them so soon. As on all the preceding nights, he'd slept beside Masreya, and, at dawn, as soon as the first birds noisily greeted the sun, he'd asked that same burning question: 'Will you marry me?' She hadn't answered. He'd glimpsed her bare feet moving through the floating house. He'd followed her, like her shadow; he'd gone before her, like her breath; clung to her, like her skin. 'You,' she said, touching Zohar's chest with her finger. Then, pointing to herself, 'Me.' He replied to the tune of a song by timid Kacim, 'You and me.' And Masreya accompanied the birds with her song. 'You are born from me, I am born from you, O my soul, O my life. You are born from me like a tree from the earth, I am born from you like a branch from a trunk.' Sitting on the bed, he regarded her back; she was combing her hair in front of her mirror. 'You and me,' the Egyptian woman sang, 'You came out of me; I emerged from you.' He continued, moved, 'O my soul, O my life!' She turned around, a smile lighting up her face.

'You're mad, Gohar ibn Gohar, mad! Our love is childhood.'

'Our love is my life.'

'Your life is childhood! Do you know what Sett Jinane told me?'

'Your mother?'

'Yes, my mother. Do you know any other Jinane? When we were children, barely two weeks old, a rabbi made a *'herz* for us.'

'A 'herz? An amulet?'

'Yes. Magic writing, on a sort of parchment. In Hebrew, diabolical writing, like you, in a sorcerers' language, yours, with the names of demons and spirits inscribed all around it, in circles—the names of your saints. Whenever anyone tried to read it, the letters began to dance. It's true. Jinane was frightened. She kept it for a long time, rolled up in the bottom of a flask, wondering if she should keep it or destroy it.'

'Where is it?'

'When she learnt you'd turned me away from the path of God . . .'

'That *you* turned me away.'

'That *we* turned away from the path of God . . . she thought the amulet was the cause. She decided to destroy it. She searched for it in her cabinets, she searched for it in her garden, she searched everywhere.'

'The amulet had fled?'

'What do you mean, "fled"?'

He explained to her that an amulet was not a thing but a being. Because it had been inscribed with powerful names, breaths of life, it was alive, like an animal. And when you try to kill an animal, it reacts, it screams, it takes flight.

She again repeated that he was mad. In her view, Jinane had simply lost the amulet. One day, she would find it, and that day Zohar would disappear. One morning, she would look at the door of her house but he would no longer be there, even the walls would have forgotten his outline. She would search her memory and his name would have been erased; she would slip into her bed and her feet would meet nothing but the freshness of clean sheets.

He raised his head, stunned. Did she really think their love was nothing more than a rabbi's sorcery? She was standing before him, her hands on her hips, naked. Her long wavy hair barely hid her breasts, which were, he thought, the exact size of his hands. She was beautiful, so tall, so brown, her hips proffered like a promise.

'You are beautiful, O my soul!'

He drew near. She flowed into his arms. A scent of musk and fire emanated from her, driving him mad with desire. He buried his face in the hollow of her neck, became even more drunk.

'Your name resounds within me,' she murmured. 'It pervades my spirit. My head is filled with it.'

They were standing, naked, their legs entwined, lips against lips, belly against belly, he hugging her, she hugging him, and still they longed for each other. Even when they were joined in the act of love, she with her legs wrapped around his waist, he encircling her with his arms, thus linked, sealed, they were still too far from each other. For they longed to dissolve, to be united, lost—to be merged, to be merged, more than anything.

'The amulet,' murmured Zohar, 'I can feel it! It's not you, it's not me, but it's what surrounds us and keeps us bound like this, for ever. Do you understand me?'

Each time, it was the same. He thought it was too much, too strong, too perfect; it wouldn't go on. Each time, he thought it was the last. Which is why he repeated, as if it were a spell, 'bound for ever'. She closed her eyes. The force that drew them towards each other frightened her. She didn't know how to resist, but she sensed the imminence of danger. She let herself slip into the abyss, dark and warm, where the echo of his name reverberated. She didn't hear herself cry; he didn't hear himself moan. They no longer heard anything but a sort of musical note in the distance, like a diapason that would never stop vibrating. The cabin door suddenly opened. But they did not hear it.

Joe was the first to enter. He tried to hold Nino back, but he was already in the room. The two lovers rolling on the satin bed formed for them the image of one creature, a fish twitching in a net. The two men, lost just a moment ago in political passion, were dumbstruck. The fish leapt, gasped, wriggled. And the intruders were both gripped, one overcome with rage, the other with laughter—Joe accompanied the lovers' spasms with laughter, Nino ground between his teeth the insults he longed to hurl upon them.

Their pleasure exploded.

But it wasn't as usual, when they abandoned themselves, sated with love, one against the other, warm animals, so close to the eternal fields, their bodies still quivering, subject to unknown wills;

as when they closed their eyes on fleeting dream images in which she was the earth and he the rain, where he slipped on the clay and she let the rain bathe her. No! They leapt out of bed, Zohar suddenly aware of Nino's gaze. No! Masreya rose up on her buttocks, pulling the sheet towards her, covering her chest and letting out a shrill scream. And he stood, young Zohar, his soul on display, blooming—this warrior of heaven, suddenly deprived of armour.

'May you be cursed, Gohar, son of a dog!'

It was the first time Nino called him by his Arabic name—the name that appeared in the paper when he returned Queen Nazli's necklace, the name Masreya used in jest, in derision. In Nino's mouth, it rang like a slap.

'May you be cursed, Gohar,' Nino repeated, 'may your faith be cursed, may your race be cursed.'

'But forgive me!' Zohar ventured weakly, 'Forgive me! I didn't hear you coming.'

'And she, this harlot, may she be cursed as well! Let her burn in Gehenna. When she is stoned in front of the Great Mosque, I'll come and with my own hands tear out her eyes.'

A thought occurred to Zohar, which at first he found absurd. Nino was a Cohen, one of those authorized to bless—and to curse as well, most certainly. Did he know that, Abraham Cohen, who until now everyone called Nino? Did he remember?

'Be careful what you say, O Nino! Don't forget you're a Cohen,' he reminded him. 'Your words can animate the world.'

At these words Nino flew into a veritable rage. 'A Cohen? Pffff!' And he spat on the floor. 'God destroyed the earth for the very reason you've shown me. There is no God but Allah. Allah is great. He unsealed my eyes. And I thank him. Remember, he unleashed the flood, torrents of water to cleanse the world. And you've just shown me the filth He decided to clean, the corruption from which He wanted to wash us. Do you know what was happening then, during the time of our Father Noah? Humans were coupling with animals. Yes! Men with sows and women with monkeys. And what have I just seen? A woman, a Muslim, wallowing in the mire with a monkey, a Jew. And so, this woman, this Muslim, is not a woman but a sow!'

His red eyes bulging, he was howling loud enough to split one's eardrums. The, still howling, he drew the revolver from his galabia pocket. 'Aren't you ashamed, Gohar, son of a dog? Not only is she Muslim, she's your sister! Your milk-sister, in other words, more than your sister! You're truly like those dogs and those monkeys that couple with their own excrement.'

O God! O gods! God of the Jews or the Muslims; of the Copts, the Greeks or the Armenians; gods of the Egyptians, so gracious in their delicate hieroglyphs, O gods! Is it that you never have pity on humans? Why have you driven Nino mad at the sight of the purest love, the love of the belly, of milk? He fired; the bullet skimmed Zohar's hair before lodging in the wood of the door. O God, O gods! Why destroy in one instant the friendship that binds? Why replace it with the hate that dissolves, fragments, and destroys?

Joe struck him, and Nino fell.

On this 10 November 1942, Rommel had been conquered. From the sun outlined in kohl, light was descending, perfectly blue, like a pyramid. Life was abuzz. Hundreds of chilly northern birds splashed and fluttered in the marshes. For the first time, the Nazi army was in retreat. And Zohar loved Masreya. O God, O gods!

After Al-Alamein

It was at Al-Alamein that the war's direction was reversed. Before this battle, the Germans were surging across the world; after, the world would progressively surge across Germany. Once again, History was being written in Egypt, at Al-Alamein, the well named, where one sky collided with another during that autumn of light.

Since that day of sunlight, day of victory, nothing was as it had been. Rommel, ill, left Egypt with no hope of returning, conquered by the desert, dysentery, his Führer's narcissism and British obstinacy. The Egyptians would have to rely on their own strength to get rid of the British. They were not saddened, hardly surprised. *Ma'lesh*! 'So what?' they said, using an expression much more common in the Egyptian tongue than the celebrated *maktoub*, 'It is written.' 'So what?'—which meant that the match was about to begin again, as in a game of draughts or backgammon. In Egypt, everything happens at the cafe. 'So what.' They simply had to adjust their thought to the march of destiny. They toppled towards religion. The Brothers grew more numerous, more powerful, better organized, deploying an original political formula—communism plus God. The true communists, who worshipped a moustachioed divinity from the Caucasus, were reduced to a handful of intellectuals, pursued by the police and chased by the Brothers whenever they ventured near the workers. Military men—moderately religious—formed cells, clubs and groups, and dreamt of striking the British and seizing power. As for the king, commander of the faithful, Bluebeard dreaming he was Machiavelli, he never stopped defying authority—strange king, he who should have embodied it.

Ever since that day of light, day of madness, nothing was as it had been among the three Blue Water comrades. Joe's punch had left

Nino dazed on the floor. Zohar had rushed to pick up the revolver, which he immediately hid under the sheets, in a safe place, under Masreya's buttocks. As soon as he came to, Nino disappeared. Joe left to look for him in the streets. He criss-crossed the neighbourhood in his car, prowled around the Great Mosque, pushed as far as the Salah-al-Din intersection, near the old mosque of Muhammad Ali. No trace. He returned, distraught, depressed, anticipating disaster. He wandered about till it was quite late, then suddenly had a hunch. Why hadn't he thought of it sooner?

It was ten by the time he went to the Khamis al-Ads cul de sac where the Cohens lived. He climbed the rickety steps four at a time. At the landing, he heard shouts inside, along with tears and ululations, as if at a funeral vigil. Gripped with anxiety, he knocked at the door. Loula, the elder of Nino's two sisters, opened immediately and, weeping, threw herself into his arms. 'Oh, it's you, Joe! May heaven be blessed! May God preserve you, Joe, may God preserve you. A terrible tragedy has befallen us.' He saw the mother on the floor, sitting right there on the tiles, her clothes torn, screaming, her hair on end, mad with grief, laughing and crying at the same time. Joe didn't dare ask. Nino had been in an accident, he'd been taken to the hospital, perhaps. Instead, he consoled Loula, held her arm; he brought the mother a glass of water, gave her his handkerchief. But she began to slap herself: first one hand, then the other; then both at once: 'There! That's what I deserve. I've lost my son, my first-born, my eyes, my soul. I've lost him through my own fault.' The psychological pain was too intense; she eased it by inflicting physical pain. Then, seized by anger, her eyes rolled back; her face scarlet, she began to curse God and her dead husband: 'O God, our Father! Do you take a child from its mother? You're called a just god. But it's not true. An unjust god, a piece of filth. That's what you are! Where is it written that it's justice to take a son from his mother like a piece of bread from the mouth of the poor? And my husband, that Gaby, that son of a dog, who abandoned me and three children without a piastre.' Then she rolled on the ground and wailed like a dying animal—a deep, piercing cry.

As soon as he left the floating house, Nino had gone to his mother's, rushed in like a madman, demanding money. She hadn't seen him for almost a year. She'd jumped, cried out, tried to soothe him: 'My son! Come in! Sit, have a glass of water. Come, sit beside me. Let me see you, I barely recognize you. You look exhausted.' O mothers! Mediterranean mothers, you talk too much, do you know that? Much too much! Sometimes your words form a curtain, like a torrential summer rain, a fog, an infernal din of meanings.

And Nino was strange, dressed like those beggars who pull at your sleeve at the mosque door. He stamped his feet and demanded she turn over everything she owned. She'd wiped her hands on her apron and approached him. She wanted to take him in her arms. That's when he shoved her away so violently the poor woman's head hit the arm of the chair. When he saw her stretched on the floor, her face bloody, her legs bare, he howled: 'Get away from me! Don't come near me! Don't touch me, you dog!'

The two sisters, their hands over their mouths, were standing petrified in the doorway. At last the mother stammered, 'Your mother—may you be covered in filth!—I'm your mother!' And, pointing to her stomach, she added, 'How can you act like this. Here, look! I carried you for nine months in this belly.'

At those words, he grabbed a chair and smashed it against the table. 'Allah is the greatest!' Nino shouted. 'You are not my mother! My mother is the Brotherhood.'

The sisters let out the same cry: 'May God protect us from evil.'

'Brotherhood?' his mother asked, sitting up on one elbow. 'What cursed brotherhood are you talking about?'

Then, understanding what her son had just said, she slowly rose up, on her knees, and, fixing her gaze on him, she hissed, 'What are you saying, Nino? Have you renounced your god? Did you throw out the god of your ancestors like a pair of worn-out shoes?' She spat in his face. 'May you be covered in filth!' And she raised her hands to the heavens: 'Your father, may God cradle him in his womb, if he hears me, that bastard who never knew how to make you obey. His final weakness was to die.'

'My father is alive! He shows me the way with a hand of steel. My father is our Supreme Guide, Lord Hassan.'

She replied with a long cry, her voice changed. She was no longer speaking to the living but calling on the dead, her husband, as if he were in the next room or perhaps at the end of the street: 'Gaby! Gaby, may your faith be cursed, O son of a dog, do you hear what your son is saying? Yes, you hear, I know you do. And, as always, you don't react, you do nothing. Gaby! Come back! I beg you. Gaby, come back!' And she collapsed, face down, in tears.

Nino slipped into his mother's room, ransacked the armoire, threw her linens on the floor, pocketed the few banknotes he knew were hidden under the pile of old bedsheets, then reappeared in the living room. His mother was on the floor, groaning; his two sisters were silently weeping, hugging each other. The grief, the disorder, the chaos triggered his rage. With a kick, he sent another chair flying.

'Allah is the greatest!'

'Allah?' his mother repeated. 'Oh. May God be with you. For you will be cursed, my son. Night and day, you will be cursed. Eyes open, eyes closed, you will be cursed. Rising up and going down, you will be cursed. Going out, you will be cursed. Cursed when you return.'

O mothers! Mediterranean mothers, your power is infinite. Your womb is goodness, you give life in closing your eyes, don't take it away by opening your mouth. You must know that your child's soul writhes under your heel.

'Allah is the greatest!' repeated Nino. 'My name is Abu l'Harb.'

And his mother said to him, 'May your name be erased from the Book!'

And he went out, slamming the door so violently that the walls of the little flat shook. Afterwards, his mother was taken by a true fit of madness. She tore her clothes as if her son were dead, slapped her face, scratched her cheeks. And when one of the sisters, hoping to console her, said, 'Don't cry, Mother! Nino will return, I'm sure of it,' she said, 'Never say that name again in front of me. Nino is no more. Nino is dead!'

*

Nino disappeared for long months. No one heard anything about him—neither his friends, nor his family, nor his colleagues, the medical students on Kasr al-Aini Street—except for one who was close to the Brothers, the young Chaker al-Kenati. In the university's courtyard, he told anyone who would listen that the end of the world was near, since even the Jews were converting to Islam. One of them, he said, was teaching in a madrasa in Ismailia—a doctor with a tongue of fire. His name was Abu l'Harb.

Zohar didn't seem worried about Nino's evolution. 'He's with the Muslims,' he said to Joe. 'Leave him alone. You're with the Zionists and I'm with the king. We should thank God all our eggs aren't in one basket.' The other, his mouth open, was rendered speechless by such cynicism. And Zohar was busy, racing from one end of the factory to the other, calling the palace to obtain a transport permit, entertaining a department-store manager or a bank owner, rushing to the workshop to supervise the bottling of the latest stock.

It must be said that after the victory at Al-Alamein, commerce had flourished as never before. In a few months, the Blue Water Company's sales revenue had quintupled. Orders were pouring in— from the grand hotels where it was impossible to find a room if you hadn't reserved months in advance; from bars, nightclubs and 'European' restaurants sprouting up like mushrooms all over the city; also from hashish dens on Champollion Street which included Blue Water in their vaporous cocktails. Joe wondered from where Zohar drew such energy.

The evening of 10 November, night of freshness, night of misfortune, while Joe was consoling Nino's family, Zohar went alone to

Rhoda, Osman Bey Street, to Masreya's villa. He knew she was on her dahabeya; he wanted to take this opportunity to speak with Jinane, her mother. When he rang, Ouahiba, frightened, mechanically uttered the French sentence she'd had so much trouble learning: 'Mademoiselle est sortie! The young lady is out!' Zohar gently pushed her aside, shut the door, hugged her so close as to drive her mad, and murmured: 'Listen, my daughter! If you want to make a grain of wheat grow, you need to cultivate a hectaire. Do you know that?' He pinched her cheek. She knew this proverb that meant: 'If you want to marry a maiden, you must seduce her whole family.' Ouahiba's fear multiplied. So this madman really wanted to marry his milk-sister? Didn't he know, this man possessed by Shaytan, that it's an insult to the earth, to the belly of mothers, to the order of the world? She cried, 'May misfortune be upon me! Why must he thus defy God?'

At the top of the stairs, Zohar found Oum Jinane seated on a rug in front of a sack full of photographs. She was looking at them, one by one, singing, 'Give me a kiss, O king's son, give me a kiss! You've found me, a young girl by the river. You've taken my grace and my beauty. Reward me! Give me a kiss, O king's son, give me a kiss.' Her voice rose through the trebles with a wing-like movement, and she held the note effortlessly, the way an eagle, lifted on warm air, rests motionless in the sky. Once again, Zohar thought it was the voice not of a woman but an angel. He approached her silently, placed a kiss on her head and stayed there a moment. He was not sure she was aware of his presence, she seemed so absorbed. She was holding the yellowed photograph, taken out a thousand times, put away a thousand times, curling, worn from her eyes' caresses, and continuing her song, 'See the child I've given you, son of the king. Beauty among beauties! Reward me! Give me a kiss, O king's son, give me a kiss.'

To provoke her, to draw her from her torpor as well, he grabbed the photo. 'I'll give you all the kisses of my mouth if you give me your daughter.' She quickly lifted her head. 'No.' she cried. 'Give me back that one. I have another you'll like better. Come, you turbulent child, who understands the speech of the spirits better than that of Adam's children.' At these words, Zohar stopped teasing her. He sat beside her, also on the floor, and together they went through the contents of the sack.

She showed him a view of the village of Kafr al-Amar, where she was born. She pointed out the water buffalo. 'She's my mother!' she said. 'She's the one who fed me. The one who listened to my first songs. Worship the water buffalo—for us Egyptians, she's a goddess. Worship her, child of the lords!' And Zohar kissed the photograph. Then she showed him a hut in the same village. A peasant stood in front of it, leaning on a staff. The top of the hut barely reached the peasant's navel. 'That's where they confined me, on all fours, when I came back to the village carrying in my womb the creature Gergess Hakim, Port Said's poet, had sown. I was chained to a tree stump, alone for months. That's where I first heard them, the voices that sang the earth's music, that's where I learnt how to sing with them. Worship this hideaway that welcomed the earth's speech, child of the lords.' And Zohar kissed the photograph.

She showed him others. She showed him Abdel Wahab Mazloum Pasha, Masreya's father. On a big sheet of newspaper folded in four, you could see the deputy, a tall man, in a striped European suit, with a large polka-dot tie, a silk handkerchief folded as a rosette, emerging from Parliament, surrounded by a mob of journalists. 'It's from the day they announced his death, poor man! His photo was in all the papers. May God cradle him in his womb.' Jinane shed a tear, without ostentation, a simple little tear that followed the curve of her cheeks all the way to her lips. 'Give me a kiss, O king's son,' she moaned again, then told him, 'He's your sister's father, child of the lords. Honor his memory!' And Zohar kissed the deputy's photograph.

She was already holding another one, small, very dark. 'Look! Here are the children of happiness, may God forever accompany them. May He guide them in moments of darkness, may he offer them joy of heart in full daylight.' And she hunched over her tiny photograph. It was two infants, two nurslings, one with thick dark hair, blooming and happy; the other bald, with drawn features, his limbs like sticks. 'The little one there, that's you!' Jinane said. 'And the chubby one with hair already, and beautiful cheeks—May God keep her!—that's your sister, Masreya.' He saw and was overcome with vertigo. 'Swear, in the name of the lords, that you won't breathe her air, that you won't walk in her footsteps, that you won't feed on her flesh. Swear, you whom I saved from death! Swear in the name of your fathers, the lords!'

Zohar was entranced, and brought the tiny photograph up to his face. His eyes grew clouded, and Jinane's words reached him as if from afar, incomprehensible. 'You're not going to be sick, are you?' worried his milk-mother. His legs were twitching, his hands clutching at the air, as if he were trying to catch invisible branches. And you could hear the rattle in his throat, in his belly, that of a trapped animal, suffocated. 'No,' he was stammering. 'Swear!' Jinane insisted, 'swear, child of the lords!'

With an abrupt movement of his hips, he rose. Jinane shouted, 'May it be according to your law, O lords!' Standing, swaying, he placed his two hands on the head of the woman who was more mother than his mother. And, hesitating, he said 'You lied, O my mother, when you claimed you'd lost it. I know it's here, hidden in this house. If you give me the amulet, the membrane that surrounded the two of us when we came into the world, then I'll utter the oath. I will swear in the name of the lords that I will not marry Masreya.'

The two of them were at the top of the staircase; she stretched on the floor, he standing over her. Ouahiba and Baheya had returned, alerted by the cries.

'O my mother! He's a devil, a devil!' cried Baheya, the younger one.

The other one chuckled, 'Yes, my sister, but a devil in love. What do you expect? It even happened to our prophet. He rightly said there's no cure for this state.'

That's when Jinane commanded Ouahiba, 'Go then and fetch the bottle of oil, you blabbermouth, the one I forbade you to use.'

'Under the sink?' Ouahiba asked.

'Yes, of course! Do what I say without any further talk. That one and no other!'

When she returned with it, Jinane took it from her and, showing Zohar the scroll inside the bottle, said, 'See this oil—the olives were pressed in Kafr el Amar, in my village. I hid the amulet here, in the bottle. The words written on it almost eighteen years ago have left the parchment and imbued each drop.'

She held the bottle out to him. 'Take it and keep it my child! What I'm giving you now will be an armour. Before going into battle—whether you are fighting for your people or your family, whether for honour or wealth, cover your body with the oil from the flask and no evil can touch you. And now, swear!'

And Zohar swore. He swore by Nofal and all his family, by Bahri, by Manzoh, by Safsaf. He swore he would not marry his sister Masreya, that he would never speak to her again, never go near her again, no longer desire her. He swore that he would separate himself from her the way an infant who enters the world is separated from the placenta that has accompanied him during his long journey through the damp and glowing darkness.

And he tumbled down the stairs firmly holding the flask of oil in his hands. He knew, Zohar did—he knew he would never be able to keep his oath.

Qassasin

Although war was devastating the world, the year 1943 promised to be the apogee for the ancient land. Money was flowing in. The stock market was at an all-time high, cotton was reaping prodigious profits. The rich were growing richer as never before. And the poor, always more numerous, always more impoverished, were content to live in peace, confined in the fertile valley. Farouk, who symbolized resistance to the occupation, was adored. The Egyptian people had fallen in love with its king. When he appeared at the mosque or on the balcony of the Abdine Palace, a young white beauty with blue eyes, a huge crowd acclaimed him with cries of 'Long live Farouk, King of Egypt and the Sudan!'—that Sudan whose crown he never stopped demanding from the British protectors.

In February 1943, Farouk celebrated his twenty-third birthday with a sumptuous reception. Yet, although he fooled people with his outwardly regal demeanour, his inner world was in ferment. From his earliest youth, he'd had only one partner, Death, which he tried to confront head on. He met it first in the form of luck in card games, among kings, queens and jacks. He wanted to penetrate its secret, to set up infallible martingales. He thought that to vanquish Death, you needed to annihilate chance. Poor king, poor madman! Nothing worked. You always end up losing at the casino, just as you always end up dying. And so Farouk cheated, relying on the fact that his gambling partners could never accuse the king. Daredevil, master of mockery; he spoke of himself as the fifth horseman: the fifth king in a game of cards.

His kleptomania was also becoming all-consuming; in the royal entourage and at British headquarters, he was known as 'the thief of Cairo'. Skilled at pilfering valuables, he laid his hand on silverware, gold watches, diamond earrings, precious weapons—all of which went to enrich his collections, filling whole rooms in his palace. At the precise moment when he stuffed a coveted item into his pocket, he watched his own fear of being caught, his heart beating to hear someone cry, 'The king is a thief!' For the king was naked, awaiting the child who would unmask him. And it was indeed a child who nearly did so.

Farouk had been indulging in another risky game: the conquest of very young women. Singers, dancers, debutante actresses, whom he accosted as at a brothel in the capital's swellest clubs. He would take them for a night, a week or a month, showering them with gifts, aroused by their acquiescence, becoming the honeypot in which their dreams of being queen entrapped them. Then, from one day to the next, he would abandon them. Cairo was abuzz with tales of the thousand and one nights of Farouk: with Annie Bernier, a young French singer passing through Cairo; with Irene Guinle, the beautiful Jew from Alexandria; with Asmahane and her jade-green eyes; Samia Gamal of the wild navel that scorched the drums. Had they all succumbed? The rich get richer!

This time, he'd set his sights on a well-bred young girl, the gracious Viviane, heir to the Cassuto & Company department stores, barely fifteen, with whom he'd shared a dance at a palace ball. She was fresh, she was beautiful; above all, she seemed to him pure, pampered by her parents, prominent and well-connected Jews. That's what heightened his excitement, what allowed him to defy, once again, the black angel that floated above his head. He made advances, sent her bouquets of flowers, passionate letters. He invited her to his palace, promising gold and diamonds, clothes, luxury cars, a dream life. But he received no response. He had no idea that his letters were being opened by the head of the household, Samy Cassuto, who had entrée into the British headquarters at Kasr al-Dobara.

When the king plotted to have the girl abducted by four thugs who would await her in front of the Lycée Français in a car from the royal garage, the cup was full. The father intervened with the British

ambassador; a decision was made to waylay the king, to let him
approach his prey and to catch him with his hand in the bag. Sir
Lampson was exultant. This time, he had him, the 'Kid'. In broad
daylight, he'd expose this little carnival king's moral blackness to the
Egyptian people. And this time, he'd sign his abdication, the madman!

It was in this atmosphere of impending crisis that Zohar had
himself dropped at the palace by Ann, his British friend. Before
going, he'd bathed and anointed himself with the amulet's oil. He
bowed to the king.

'I recognize you!' said Farouk, who forgot nothing. 'Aren't you
the brother of the beautiful dancer Masreya, with a body as supple
as a snake? What's your name?'

'Gohar, Your Majesty. Gohar ibn Gohar!'

'Yes. I'm happy to see you again, Lord Gohar. You must have
an important reason to petition the king. What do you want?'

Under his breath, Zohar murmured a prayer to Sett Safsaf,
guardian of the Sahel, then took the plunge: 'I've come to save your
crown, sire!'

He explained to Farouk the trap Lampson was in the process of
setting. He gave him the names of the henchmen, the Albanians in
the royal guard. They'd been identified; they were now being followed by British agents. He explained that the British had all the
handwritten letters he'd sent to young Vivian; they were ready to
publish their contents to the press. Farouk seemed indifferent. Was
he that oblivious? Zohar knew how to find the words that would
burn his soul. He let him know that his enemies were not only at
British headquarters but here as well, within the royal palace, and
that they were spying on him both day and night.

'Who then?' grumbled the king, furrowing his brows.

'Near the queen, sire!'

'The Queen Mother?'

He'd been suspecting his mother, Queen Nazli for a while. She
was a woman of power and a shameless lover, her chamberlain's

paramour. She'd imposed the status of Queen Mother and could not understand why her son kept her out of political decisions. She never stopped scheming, that one.

'The bitch!' Farouk roared. 'Doesn't she know that if I lost the crown she'd be swept away in a few hours? No more beautiful clothing, sumptuous jewels, armies of courtiers.'

'It's not only the Queen Mother, sire!'

'What? What does that mean, "not only"? What are you saying?' He grabbed Zohar by his lapel. 'Will you explain yourself, child of the street?'

Zohar gently freed himself, and bowed to the earth. 'I didn't want to disturb Your Highness. If my words are disagreeable to my sovereign, all I need do is crawl away.'

'Oh no!' shouted Farouk. 'You'll tell me what you know, everything you know. Furthermore, now that I think of it—why are you coming here to warn me about the dangers that surround me? What do you want from me?'

Zohar smiled, thinking of Sett Safsaf, guardian of the sands, with her saffron veils and ankle bracelets, she who dances to the rhythm of the dromedary. He knew that she'd granted him his wish.

'Why does one address gods and kings, Your Majesty, if not to obtain good fortune?'

'Well!' said the king, 'We'll see what your information is worth. I'm listening.'

'I don't need to teach the king that, whoever the woman, jealousy can be found at the bottom of her heart. We all know that the queen, your wife, is expecting another child. Her health is fragile, her soul trembles at the thought that, for the third time, it might be a girl, that you might take umbrage, repudiate her, perhaps. And so the queen—perhaps you already know this—listens with a willing ear to tales about her king's virility.'

Farouk started. Rising from his armchair, he began to pace back and forth.

'Farida! How can this be? I chose her from among a thousand! I went to find her in her family when she was just a child. I gave her a queen's life.'

'It's no use mourning, Your Majesty. A king cannot accuse a subject of betrayal without confessing his own weakness. On the contrary, he must act to prevent treason. By force, perhaps. Even better, by cunning. And always to present his smile that lights up the kingdom like a sun.'

Zohar explained his plan and the king's heart was eased. Farouk had often brushed against his destruction, his ruin. He must be being watched over by a divinity, who, at the last minute, had come to pull him from the jaws of Death. This time, he thought, luck, which had accompanied him since childhood, which had allowed him to escape unharmed from each trap, to triumph over his companion, his only rival—the one he did not know how to name but whose presence he sensed behind him at each step, the lugubrious, the intense, the cursed, who knew how to make his heart beat—this time, luck wore the face of this handsome brown young man.

'What did you say you were called, O boy?'

'Gohar, sire!'

'You are not unskilful. And your words let air into enclosed places. What do you want in exchange?'

'And for my information, sire!'

The king burst out laughing, with that enormous laugh he some-times had, which discomfited his entourage, a laugh that rose from his belly with instinctive, rhythmic twitches.

'You're a little too sure of yourself, my young friend. But I wish to reward your advice. Tell me what you desire.'

And Zohar told the king about the business he'd founded a year and a half ago, the bottles of Blue Water that consoled the unhappy, gave courage to the timid and cured the melancholy. Indeed, affairs were prospering, money was coming in, may God be thanked, but in this time of expansion, with all those foreigners roaming around the city, their pockets stuffed with sterling, he had the opportunity to earn much more. On Suleiman Pasha Street, a few doors down from Groppi's patisserie, there was an old garage, property of the crown, that had been abandoned. He wasn't asking for much, modest artisan that he was, only the use of this place. He would create a club—'The Rendezvous of the Pashas'—which would become the watering hole for night owls. Of course, bottles of Blue Water would be for sale there; people would drink, certainly, in the afternoon starting at four o'clock; but mostly they would come at night, to hear singers, to play cards, to talk politics in an atmosphere of luxury and voluptuousness. The king could rest assured he'd be paid without delay whatever rent he asked.

'Alcohol,' said Farouk, who suddenly remembered he was Muslim. 'Alcohol, all the same!'

'Blue Water, Your Majesty!'

'Alcohol,' repeated Farouk, when, suddenly, a thought crossed his mind. 'But you haven't said anything about your sister.'

Zohar leant his face to one side. 'My sister, Your Majesty?' He hesitated. 'What can I say? She's walled up in sorrow. Someone who has once spoken with angels no longer enjoys dialogue with her peers. She lives cloistered in her house on Rhoda, and I fear—'

He was silent a moment. 'I even fear for her life, sire.'

Masreya was still performing in the capital's clubs. Her radiant face was plastered on Cairo's walls, touting the virtues of a French brand of soap. Her romantic adventures with ministers and businessmen were regularly featured in news stories. Zohar and Farouk both knew she was most certainly not shrouded in melancholy. But that's how Levantine speech moves—generous, sensitive to the desires of the interlocutor, anticipating him, paving the way for him to move forward. Farouk seized the opportunity.

'Poor thing! With this war and these cursed British, one almost forgets one's friends. I will invite her for a night out.'

'She'll return to life, Your Majesty!'

*

That's how Farouk came to recall the pleasures that Masreya knew how to lavish, the very day he had to renounce those he was anticipating with the Jewish child, heir to the Cassuto department stores. He approached Masreya anew and, so that she would pardon him for his long absence, presented her with a gold ankle bracelet lifted from the Museum's collections—a jewel that had once belonged to the celebrated Queen Hatshepsut some three thousand years ago.

A year had passed since the victory at Al-Alamein. The Allies had landed in Sicily and Calabria. Mussolini had fallen and the gracious Marshal Badoglio, the visitor to Cairo who'd naturalized, we recall, a battalion of louse-ridden Jews from the ghetto, had taken his place at the head of a nation in tatters. In October, Italy declared war on Germany; the Jews of the hara could once more be proud of their passports obtained at the consulate on Al-Galaa Street, that anarchic day in 1938.

It was the morning of 6 November 1943. The sky was grey; from his balcony, the king was watching the city come to life. The evening before, he'd had a stormy conversation with the British chief of staff. The Afrika Korps had been reduced to nothing. The few survivors, pursued along the Libyan coast, had just surrendered. What was he waiting for to declare war on Germany in turn? The position of neutrality he'd adopted at the outset of the war, to preserve his independence despite the British presence, was becoming ridiculous. Once again, Farouk didn't know what to do. He decided on a trip to the seashore, there where the Allied army was stationed, near Ismailia. He donned a yachting outfit—loose linen trousers, white woollen turtleneck, captain's cap—and ran rapidly to his garage. His chamberlain, Hassanein Pasha, tried to hold him back with some pressing business. Farouk pushed him away firmly, 'Tomorrow, Hassanein, tomorrow!'

In front of the twenty or so cars lined up, each with a liveried driver and mechanic at its door, he hesitated a moment, his finger on his lips. He looked like a sultan, at the door of his harem, choosing his consort for the night. The Rolls? Too official. The Packard? Too stiff. The Lincoln? Too American. His eyes lit on the Mercedes, the infamous 540K that Adolf Hitler had given him for his wedding It was a little dated—he'd gotten married in 1938—a big convertible, low enough to graze the tarmac, two white leather seats, a chrome radiator grille at the end of a long hood striped with hundreds of gills, the curve of the front fins echoed in the sunburst of its tail—a folly! Its chrome gleamed. He wanted to run his hand over it. And to take off, defying the British, at the wheel of the Führer's Mercedes, along the Canal, the very one they were protecting as the gateway to their empire.

He pointed to the Mercedes. The mechanic rushed to polish it one last time with a cloth. The driver slipped behind the wheel and started the engine, eight cylinders in a row, a precision mechanism, a rough and deep sound, promising power. Farouk took the wheel and sped away in a cloud of dust. He needed no more than ten minutes to reach the banks of the Nile. Masreya was waiting for him in her dahabeya. She emerged swathed in white veils, her head wrapped in a silk scarf. 'All my horses for my princess!' Farouk told her. She leapt into the passenger seat and they raced along the desert road at the speed of wind, towards the coast.

Farouk was driving fast, very fast, at his car's maximum power. Other drivers, seeing the headlights of the royal roadster in their rear-view mirrors, moved aside, some even choosing to stop in the ditch to yield the right of way. Deftly, he avoided obstacles: a turn of the steering wheel to the left, another to the right. He also spoke—cursing the carts and their donkeys, upon which he bore down at more than a hundred and twenty kilometres per hour; cursing the ignorant peasants who crossed the big road without even looking, most likely to avoid bad luck; cursing the British assassins who barred the way with their enormous tanks. He was talkative, happy to escape his obligations once more. As men often are, he was proud of his coach and the marvellous engine of this Mercedes. Did she know that the factory had made only twenty, all destined for heads of state or movie stars? Just think, this engine could propel an assault tank or even make a plane fly—this engine, for them alone, at their service.

'You're mad, O my king! You've retained the madness of child-hood.'

'I was born to be king,' Farouk replied. 'It is my misfortune. I've continued so until today. It is my luck!'

Masreya, her soul vibrating like a lute string, sensed that he was troubled. Had she understood that you invoke luck only when you run the risk of destruction?

'What is happening, O my king? You're worried, I know!'

'Politics, my child, politics!'

She understood that he felt he was in danger. Eternal gambler, he'd chosen to leave the city so as not to draw the bad card, not to lose the game. They crossed the two hundred kilometres separating them from the sea in a few hours, without a single stop. He was in a rush to reach the shore, to breathe the open air, to be dazzled by the spray. They made their first stop at the entrance to Alexandria, on Agami Beach; the sea, limpid emerald, opened their souls. After lunch, he promised to give her the grand tour, the promenade of kings, from Alexandria to Port Said along the corniche, the beach road and then the desert road.

At the restaurant, no one recognized him. His playboy clothes, his sunglasses, his cap. He was miffed. It was only when he was paying that the waiter remarked, 'You remind me of someone.'

'The king, perhaps,' he ventured.

'Oh no, not him! The king is not so fat.'

The sentence stung like a slap. He remained speechless for a long time. It wasn't until later, when they were passing Stanley Beach, deserted during this winter month, that he finally said, 'What a peas-ant, that restaurant waiter. Hasn't he seen my face on banknotes? He's probably only interested in the amounts.'

'Calm yourself, O my king,' Masreya soothed him. She saw that he was afraid of disappearing, of exiting the stage without a trace.

Poor kings, poor fools! You should never leave your palaces! Shut yourselves up in your panelling, drape yourself in velvet, count your gold and spare the world. You trail death behind you. Poor kings, poor fools, respect your nature, govern in secret!

The king was speaking, confiding his concerns. Ever since the reversal of the war's course, the British had grown more and more authoritarian, imposing their decisions, including on internal affairs. Strong in their garrisons, with their cannons and their planes, they were acting like lords of the land. They paid the Egyptians no more mind than ants and mosquitoes. Some day, Farouk's courage would be acknowledged—he who, despite his youth, had been able to stand up to them, alone, without an army, relying solely on his intelligence and charm. He wondered if that day would ever come. Masreya, the Egyptian woman, moved by such loneliness, spoke to him gently: 'By my head, O my king, by my eyes, by my soul, I who go everywhere, I swear that I hear only words of love about you. Patience, my king, patience. Your greatness will be recognized!' And Farouk's heart was somewhat eased.

Ever since the Ezbet Mansheya crossroad, two motorcycles had been shadowing them. Farouk had spotted them. It was useless to accelerate, unbridling his hundred and eighty horses, hunched over the wheel as he tried to master their rearing; the cycles didn't relent. He could even hear the distant growling of their motors. 'I can't make out their faces,' he told himself, 'but I'm sure it's still those dogs at my heels.'

Night had just fallen when they reached Ras al-Bar. Hoping to scatter them, he decided to abandon the coastline for the narrow roads that snaked through the fields. But the motorcycles, powerful and agile, drew closer at every turn. Farouk was nervous, and a dull fear began to pervade Masreya. She knew that the British dreamt of making the king disappear and she knew their agents' efficient methods. She'd heard talk of how, at the beginning of the war, they'd disposed of Ghazi, King of Iraq, he who'd shown off his independence by invading Kuwait without forewarning his British guardians. He'd died in a car accident, poor fellow. It was an assassination, and everyone knew it.

She began casting backward glances.

'They're still there!' she warned him.

'What do you expect? Dogs!' the king muttered. 'The more you run, the more they chase.'

When they crossed the little village of Damietta, not seeing them any more, she hoped for a moment that they'd stopped. But as soon as they left the village, the two little lights returned, glued to the rearview mirror. She could now make out the drivers. They were encased in leather, with caps and thick goggles, but their delicate moustaches were not those of Egyptians.

That's when Farouk gave her an absurd command, which she would never have dreamt of. Not here, not now, not in this night, with this gut-wrenching fear and these curves that kept appearing in the headlights' beams. 'Come! Show me what you know how to do!' he said, pointing to the little swelling between his thighs. Surprised, she didn't know what to say. 'Come!' insisted the king. 'What are you waiting for?' A sudden turn of the wheel threw her against him. She closed her eyes, whispered a prayer and began to unbutton his trousers. She was amazed. Usually, Farouk's desire was slow to unfurl; he needed the wisdom of Masreya's hands, the tenderness of her lips and the goad of her words to animate it. But this time, though he was busy controlling his car, the king immediately bloomed in full splendour. Without a doubt, fear is a powerful aphrodisiac! 'Take it,' the king commanded, 'Take it in your mouth!' They were nearing Qassasin. She no longer thought of anything, letting nature control her movements. Neither Masreya nor Farouk, whose eyes were half-closed, noticed the motorcycles' disappearance. Two minutes later, at the entrance to the village, she lying crookedly, her head under the wheel, he with his body sundered, the top battling the road and the bottom abandoned to the science of caresses, Farouk did not see the enormous GMC truck appear, emerging from an adjacent road with all its lights out. A cry escaped him. The reflex of pressing the brake with all his might. Too late, much too late! The brief screech of tyres at the instant of his pleasure's explosion; then the sound, dreadful in the night, a sound of collision and fragmentation, of metal and glass. Followed by another sound, cataclysmic, like the eruption of a volcano, that of the truck buckling under the impact. The Mercedes was heavy and solid; it dragged the truck some twenty metres. And one final sound, metallic, a bar of metal rattling, rolling down the road. Then there was silence, a strange silence, broken by a rhythmic beat, the tick-tock of an unseen clock or the drip of petrol from the tank.

Farouk tried to open his door. Jammed. The other one, the passenger door, had vanished. Masreya rose with difficulty, looking him in the eyes. She seemed to be in pain. Blood was trickling down from her eyebrow.

'I'm wounded,' the king cried.

She did not reply. She slipped slowly from the car. She kept close to the ground, on all fours. Already British military men were coming from the truck and approaching the car.

'*Are you okay, sir?*'

Wasn't it enough that God had witnessed their depravity? Was it also necessary for the British to stare at them? Masreya began to run. Clearing out of there. Escaping. Escaping humiliation, the cowardice of the king, who would think only of saving his skin. She wanted to see herself in a mirror, as soon as possible, to find her image again, intact. She ran straight ahead through the fields without looking back, sinking into the night.

Poor kings, poor fools! You should never leave your palaces!

1952

The Rendezvous of the Pashas

On the evening of Saturday, 6 November 1943, at the wheel of the Mercedes 540K given to him by Hitler for his wedding, King Farouk, his soul tormented and his sex on fire, rammed into a British army truck at the entrance to the village of Qassasin. The soldiers had difficulty extricating him from the car. His clothing torn, half-naked, he could not walk or even stand upright. Urgently rushed to a British military hospital, collapsed, haggard, he kept repeating incoherent words: 'She got me, that devil! I felt her, behind my back, pushing me towards the truck.' The collision was unusually violent, the car having struck the obstacle at nearly eighty kilometres per hour. 'I'm dead, I'm dead,' the king kept repeating. And he asked, 'Who are you? Angels? Demons?'

The king owed his life only to the sturdiness of his heavy Mercedes, with its chassis fashioned from the finest steel. To tell the truth, he wondered whether he was alive and kept asking: 'Am I in hell? Tell me, please!'

At the hospital, he received emergency care and sedatives. As of the next day, official communiqués were reassuring, mentioning only a small pelvic fracture and a few contusions. While it was true that, despite several fractures, his wounds were relatively benign, his dis-orientation lasted for weeks: he was being pursued, a black presence was hovering over him—in his room, in the hospital corridors, outside, in the courtyard. He refused to eat, fearing he might be poisoned; to go out, claiming someone was waiting for him behind the door; to speak, certain his words were being recorded. He answered the doctors tersely, eying them suspiciously.

In Cairo, rumors ran rampant. Suddenly, with the king out of the picture, it was whispered that the British had tried to assassinate him and were keeping him prisoner—some said he'd been locked in a villa on Cyprus; others, that he was in India. Nothing was further from the truth. The doctors would have preferred to release him as quickly as possible—this demanding invalid, resisting treatment, growing more aggressive by the day.

After five weeks, the king's condition finally improved. Farouk no longer spoke of Death, that creature he'd been defying since childhood and which had overtaken him on the outskirts of a little village in the Delta. He relaxed a little, though still without establishing personal relationships as was his wont. He left the British hospital on 14 December, after having decorated with the Order of Ishmael the doctors and eight nuns who'd nursed him. The people of Cairo came to greet him at the city gates, festooning him with flowers and exclaiming, 'Long live the king! Long live Farouk!' No one noticed his changed face, frozen, the sunken lids and fixed eyes behind his sunglasses; the stiffer gait; and the profound lassitude that weighed down his shoulders. The people truly loved Farouk, and they professed it to him once more. But was this the same Farouk returning as conqueror to his city? The little king, handsome as a god, hadn't he been kidnapped by Death during the accident on 6 November, replaced by a baleful shadow?

*

The last two years of the war were years of grace for the Blue Water Company. Farouk kept his word and agreed to rent the building on Suleiman Pasha Street to Zohar. What's more, he secretly took a thirty per cent share in the business. The success of the Rendezvous of the Pashas exceeded their wildest dreams. The setting was refined, with plush sofas, modern music, luxurious hangings, rugs, scents and that Blue Water, always purer, always stronger: 'Purer than water,' the ad said, 'stronger than life, Blue Water, the water of life!'

For artistic programming, Zohar relied on a French producer, Augustin Levert, a resister, escaped from a camp. He presented the biggest stars—Tino Rossi, Maurice Chevalier, Charles Trenet and the celebrated Jeanne Bourgeois who called herself Mistinguett. It was a blessing to hear them sing there, on that little stage, beneath huge copper fans, a Blue Water cocktail coloured with Curacao in your hand—at home, so to speak.

Everyone who was anyone in Egyptian high society met there, liberated from stringent propriety by the makeshift character of the times. British officers patronized the venue, hoping to find beautiful Egyptian women; khawagates, European and rich Egyptian gentlemen, came to meet ministers and deputies; all of them sought a glimpse of the king. Farouk was such a regular that his table was set every night. You had to stand in line on the pavement for hours to join the 'Pashas', and inside you couldn't find an empty spot; not one column without a night owl in evening clothes leaning nonchalantly against it. After dinner, the establishment became a club where only members were admitted. Then there were tables for poker and gin rummy, discreet smoking dens, and, on stage, oriental music and belly dancers. Farouk dragged his languor there, his gaze occasionally brightened by the shimmies of a belly, the curve of a hip, the point of a breast. The war was nearly over, and, with the gradual departure of the troops, Egypt was sinking into an economic crisis. Yet the Rendezvous of the Pashas glowed to the skies, a sulfurous star, the pinnacle of the Egyptian dream, halfway between the gentility of London and the mad sensuality of an oriental Hollywood.

At twenty years old, the owner, Zohar Zohar, had grown rich, very rich. But he had no idea where his money went. He was simply happy to know he had enough to buy a villa or a new car. He did nothing about it, though, absorbed in running the factory, still in Abasseya, and in the management of the Rendezvous on Suleiman Pasha Street. His money was in his business; he never touched it. Zohar was the Blue Water; the Blue Water was Zohar. He'd lost his two associates, the other two young men named on the Art Deco label that adorned the bottles. He sometimes heard word of Nino— his brilliant sermons at Ismailia, his passionate denunciations of the

British occupation, his calls for armed struggle, sacred combat to open the doors of Paradise. But he could not bring himself to take it seriously. In his view, Nino was hiding, sheltered at the heart of the Brotherhood, the last place you'd look for a little Jew.

Later, he began to get really worried, when, in December 1947, Nino transformed into a war imam—wasn't that the name he'd chosen, Abu l'Harb, 'father of war'? 'My brothers, I appeal to your conscience. Remember your oath. The Qur'an is our law—you've sworn it. Death is our most faithful ally—to die during jihad our dearest hope. The time has come!' And he called for a crusade.

A few weeks earlier, on 29 November, the UN General Assembly had adopted the plan for the partition of Palestine. The State of Israel would be created in May. So, by Almighty God, Nino exhorted the faithful to defend Arab territory, to uphold the honour of Islam. And his beautiful solemn voice, always calm, drawing on ancient texts, citing the Supreme Guide, delivered dreadful messages of hate. 'Kill the Jews! Kill the dogs! Go and defend your brothers in Palestine, and kill them down to the last one. And if you cannot go, kill them right here, in Ismailia, in Tanta, in Alexandria, in Cairo, throughout Egypt.' It must be said that, for a while now, he'd been going around with the Grand Mufti of Jerusalem, Hadj Amine al-Husseini, welcomed by Farouk after the French Ministry of Foreign Affairs had opportunely let him 'escape' from his guarded residence in France. 'Kill the Jews wherever you find them,' the Mufti had declared, 'that pleases God, History and our faith.'

When, during the last days of 1947, Zohar heard these declarations by Nino and the Grand Mufti, he was chilled. Not that he felt menaced, for he thought he was safe in the shadow of the powerful, but he envisioned a pogrom like those of the past, the masses rendered mad by their god's jealousy, surging through the alleys as they howled, 'Slaughter the Jews!' How would they defend themselves, the poor people in the hara? What could an old man like Uncle Elie do? And his father, blind Motty? And the women, his great aunts—Maleka, Tofa'ha and above all Adina, who couldn't hold her tongue? She would certainly incite the rioters. God knows what could happen.

With a brush of his hand, he chased these thoughts away. But the preachers' calls for murder had burnt a scar into his soul that would never fade.

Zohar did not realize that Egypt was changing. Yet he frequently came across the king, whom he could freely observe on the pillows at the Rendezvous of the Pashas. In Egypt, from the time of the pharaohs until the end of History, the king, whether called Pharaoh, Prime Minister or President, was the land. Farouk was slowly drifting, like a foundering ship, unmoored, abandoned to the tumult of his impulses. He'd capitulated, not to the British, who were losing ground daily, but to his eternal rival. Death, which he'd insolently defied since childhood, had caught up with him one November night in 1943; he'd felt it, he'd even seen it, that black shadow hovering over him, and he'd heard it. On that night, Death had come and howled in an infernal din (which is its language): 'The king is naked!' Naked he was, his fly open, his clothes torn, before the mocking British troops. What a disgrace!

Ever since that day, his manias had overrun his life, driving out the handsome little love king. Always a thief, he became one like never before—so much so that when he went to dinner in Cairo's fine homes, silverware and valuable objects were hidden. He became bulimic, swelling like a sad balloon. When Zohar asked him, 'Your Majesty seems upset. Is something here not to his taste?' he replied, 'How can I be happy? Look at me—a bald king, obese, nearly blind, and, as you're well aware, entirely mad.' His pursuit of young women, which might once have passed as a foible, became obsessive. He always needed more, testing his virility, once more, always, to know if he'd won the game against Death. But the hunt—hunters beware!—is like the gaze, always reflexive. Whoever sees is seen. Sooner or later, the hunter will be hunted.

Her name was Liliane Victor Cohen. Members of the king's inner circle claimed that his taste for Jewish women was due solely to his father's fiat. Fouad had one day uttered this enigmatic sentence: 'A Jewish woman cannot help but be exceptional.' Farouk was trying to prove it true. Dark-haired, with milky skin and heart-shaped lips, both fresh and sensuous, pure and voluptuous, she was no more than seventeen. Born into a poor Alexandrian family, she'd decided to become a movie star. She was dancing in a small cabaret on the corniche when she saw the king in the room. She came and gyrated around him, climbed onto his table, brushed his clothing in time with the music. His head looking up between her outspread legs, hypnotized by the proffered flesh, he seized her on the spot. He thought he'd captured her; it was she who'd harpooned him.

The next day, he asked her what she wanted. 'To be in a film, sire!' In 1947, she had her first role in *The Red Mask*. The public fell under her spell. The Arab cinema had its Marilyn. In a few months, she became Camelia, the Egyptian vamp, as innocent as Shadia, as erotic as Hind Rostom. It was publicly known that the very young actress was the king's mistress. Each time he tried to leave her, she threatened suicide. And when he wanted to hold onto her, to spy on her, she escaped abroad with a director or rich patron. He feared scandal, had jealous fits, sent armies of spies at her heels. He agreed to get a divorce, promising to marry her. Like any adulterous husband, he'd tightened a noose around his own neck. Zohar, who sometimes witnessed their scenes, should have understood. If Farouk had let himself be captured, it was that Egypt was adrift. It would topple, fall into the arms of other powers: Farouk was Egypt.

Joe di Reggio, Zohar's companion since childhood, who'd followed him, fascinated by his volatile soul, always in motion, ungraspable—'You're like a spirit,' he told him, 'you appear out of nowhere; no one never knows where you come from. Sometimes it's for the good, sometimes, I'm not so sure'—Joe di Reggio was staying away, for a woman's love often tarnishes the sheen of an old friendship.

After that terrible scene in the Khamis al-Ads cul-de-sac on 10 November 1942, Joe had been shaken. Until that moment, his world had been one family, where he moved with ease, knew the places,

loved the people, expressed his gifts in the fluidity of a serene universe. But on that day, the world had been turned upside down.
Before that mother torn by grief, before that son rendered mad by
a god, Joe's spirit had been drained, like water in a sink. No more
faith, no more truth, no more landmarks—just this brute suffering,
this agonized cry of Nino's mother cursing God. That moment and
that place became an altar, from which meaning would one day arise.
Every week, Joe returned to the street, often on Friday night, to celebrate the Sabbath with the little family in mourning. No doubt he
came to console Nino's mother, and to help her make ends meet,
bringing what he called 'her son's pay', the salary for work he had
not been doing for ages. Nino's mother, missing a son, pampered
Joe as if he were her child. And he, son and heir of the celebrated
banker di Reggio, did not dare admit to himself that he was finding
here, in this squalid room in this tumble-down building in this foul-
smelling cul-de-sac, more pleasure than in his palace.

Someone else metamorphosed over the course of weeks, in time
with his Sabbath visits: the blond Loula, the elder of Nino's sisters,
not yet seventeen. First she began wearing her hair in a pony tail,
pulled high, like American starlets. Then her waist narrowed, cinched
by elegant white- or red-leather belts; then her skirts grew shorter,
billowing over lace-edged slips. When, fresh and joyful, her face
painted like a doll, her cheeks sprinkled with freckles, she drew her
chair right next to his at table, a scent of woman and jasmine per-
vaded Joe's spirit. Saturdays, he took her to the Metro Cinema to
watch American films. Sometimes, he put his arm around her shoulder and she leant against him. Then they spent hours at Groppi's
patisserie, speaking of the future before impressive ice-creams. In
those years, Egypt was a balcony from which you could contemplate
people and places in panorama. She would have so loved Paris,
France. When the war ended . . . 'If it ever ends,' Joe interjected.
'May God keep us!' Loula cried, 'It must end.' Joe looked doubtful.
At that moment, she didn't understand.

He took her to his sports club, the Maccabees. They spent time with the young Zionists, sang in Hebrew all night long, accompanying themselves on guitar around a campfire. One night, after the songs, the dances, the long discussions about the need for a Jewish State, they looked deep into each other's eyes. Their decision was made. They would go there, to Palestine, the two of them, to establish a family.

That night, Joe did not bring Loula back to her cul-de-sac. He rented a room at Shepheard's; as they were crossing the threshold, he searched for a phrase, a blessing. But religion had never been his strong suit. So he simply murmured the Jewish credo—that, he knew by heart—actually, only the two first sentences: 'Hear O Israel, God is our god, God is Oneness.' In that luxurious room with its balcony wide open to the Nile, for the first time, they were but one. Oneness . . . This, then, was God. A man and a woman, their bodies entwined, their souls fused . . . Oneness.

When Zohar heard that Joe was engaged to Nino's sister, that they were frequenting Zionist groups and planning to settle in Palestine, anguish tightened his throat. Unlike Nino and Joe, Zohar did not participate in politics, but he felt it in his body. In 1945, the war over, the Brotherhood was centrestage. Its nationalism seemed more credible than the Wafd's, and, *a fortiori*, the king's. The Brothers were Egyptian, born from the people, truly opposed to the British presence, and, above all, they were Muslim, Muslim first of all. The people recognized their own anger in the Brothers' slogans; they saw themselves in the Brothers' way of being and in this religion that united them with their past. Under the Brotherhood's impetus, riots erupted in Alexandria—three synagogues were torched; Jewish hospitals, Jewish schools and Jewish shops looted. Jews had been attacked—poor merchants, old people—beaten, thrown to the ground, trampled. Dozens had been wounded; several were dead.

At the Rendezvous of the Pashas, ministers and bankers sneered. 'A revolution? Don't count on it. The Egyptian people are like that. When they itch, they scratch, then they sneeze. And then everything calms down.' Events seemed to bear this out, for a few days later, life resumed its indolent course. Everything seemed as before. But Zohar sensed that to be a Zionist in Cairo in 1945 was like thrusting your arm into a crocodile's gaping jaw. And to be a Zionist in the company of a warrior imam's sister—Abu l'Harb, 'father of war', who preached holy war—was like tickling the crocodile, inviting it to bite.

At first, Joe wanted to share with Zohar his love for Loula and the future Israel. He tried to involve him with the Maccabees. He invited him to seaside outings with his youth group. Zohar always refused, replying with strange words. 'Remember, you are not alone, we are three, Joe! The Blue Water, the eau-de-vie of the three shebabs. Don't ever forget it!' But what was he doing carrying on about three young men? The whole world was in turmoil; the British were repelling camp survivors who wanted to go to Palestine. They were sending boats filled with immigrants back to Germany—to Germany, that cursed land, gorged with the blood of their relatives! And he, Zohar, thought only about business. Could anyone be so indifferent to the suffering of his people?

They didn't fight, not quite, but grew apart. Joe sometimes went to the factory on Doctor Tawfik Street, but it was always in the afternoon, after the siesta, when he knew Zohar would be busy on Suleiman Pasha Street with his millionaires, his generals and his ministers. Joe no longer went to the Rendezvous of the Pashas.

*

'May Your Majesty's day be as limpid as a drop of fresh cream in a crystal cup.'

'This day, Gohar ibn Gohar, son of a dog, is black as pitch, and I feel like the mud at the bottom of the Nile.'

It was barely 7 p.m. on 22 October 1948. Farouk had just learnt that his fleet's flagship, the frigate that bore his name, *The Emir*

Farouk, had sunk, carrying a crew of seven hundred men to the bottom. While it was cruising along Ashdod, the Israelis had sent a dinghy loaded with explosives against its flanks. It took no more than four minutes for the ship to disappear beneath the surface. A few hours later, a telegram informed him that three thousand elite soldiers under General Taha Bey were besieged in the Fallujah Pocket. His army, which he'd sent to Palestine to expel the Jews, and his generals, who'd promised to conquer their Tel Aviv neighbourhoods in two weeks, had been defeated by those who'd been presented to him as a barefoot band equipped with ancient blunderbusses.

'Your cousins, the Jews,' added the king, 'do you know what they've done to me?'

'We don't choose our family,' Zohar tried to joke.

'Listen to my advice, Lord Gohar, a king's advice: change your family! Do it before it's too late.'

And for the first time since they'd known each other, Farouk invited him to sit beside him. Affectionately, he put his arm around his shoulder.

'Sooner or later, Egypt will belong only to the Egyptians. And the nature of Egyptians is to be Muslim.'

'And why not the religion of the pharaohs?'

Farouk burst out laughing.

'Secretly, my friend, secretly!'

When he evoked the danger of being Jewish in Egypt after the war, the king knew whereof he spoke. Under the influence of new German advisers who'd secretly entered the country, old Nazis who'd managed to flee occupied Germany, he'd had Parliament—which was entirely in his control—vote in new discriminatory laws. They weren't quite those of Nuremburg, but they were heading in that direction. During the month of June, a new law prohibited the Jews from leaving the country, for fear they would swell the ranks of the Israeli army. Another stipulated that seventy-five per cent of employees in public or private businesses must henceforth be 'true

Egyptians'—in other words, Muslims—de facto excluding Jews and Englishmen. And since the start of the 1948 war, young people were being arrested for 'Zionism', now a crime against the State. They were detained by the hundreds in the foreigners' prison or in desert camps.

In the room, customers were just being seated for dinner. Farouk pinched Zohar's cheek, as one does with children: 'O my son, I beg you! Come join us, stay with us! I don't want to see my evenings at the Rendezvous of the Pashas disappear.'

*

On the same 22 October, at the same time, in front of his house in Zamalek, Joe, freshly shaven, perfumed with an intoxicating scent he'd purchased at the Nessler perfumery—a new eau de toilette called 'Daughter of the Sudan'—was eyeing himself in the rear-view mirror of his convertible MG: Scottish cap on his wavy hair, bowtie, blue-striped white evening shirt. He ran his hand over his chest to remove some invisible dust, turned the key and pressed the ignition. He liked the rough sound of the exhaust, a little wild, promising speed. That evening, he was taking Loula dancing at the Automobile Club. Several of the Maccabees had planned to meet in that safe spot, patronized only by high society, to finalize the details of their departure. One of them had access to a powerful motorboat, able to reach Haifa. During wartime, it was not so easy to leave a port like Alexandria. So they would leave the country by way of Ras al-Bar, the seaside resort, as if it were an ordinary excursion. Landing in Israel was more dangerous. It was Joe's specific mission to make contact with officials in the Jewish Agency, who would warn the Israeli army about their arrival. They didn't want to be strafed by the coast guard just as they were reaching their goal. They were burning to join the fighters of the Hagganah, no longer able to endure their anxious inertia in this Egypt they felt more hostile by the day.

Port Said Street was jammed. He veered left, his thumb tense over the horn's little knob at the centre of the steering wheel. But in front of Zahir Baybars Mosque, a dense mob was moving forward, chanting slogans: 'Palestine for the Arabs! Slaughter the Jews!' Impossible to cross the tight ranks of these angry men, brandishing sticks. He braked and shifted into reverse. A few yards, and a truck arrived, barring his way. He braked again and attempted a half turn. But the crowd was around him. Men were approaching the car, touching it. Children were playing with the handle, opening the door. Then a large man, his eyes red with rage, came forward. 'I recognize him!' he cried. 'I saw him with the Maccabees, with the Zionists.' A rumour rose, echoing through the ranks. 'He's a Jew! A Zionist, son of a dog! Slaughter him! Slit his throat!' The fat one, in front, grabbed Joe by his beautiful striped shirt. 'You play basketball with the Zionists. You're a Zionist, aren't you?' And he shook him. Joe abruptly loosened the man's hands, slipped out of his MG and stood in front of the mob. He spoke to them in Arabic. 'I am not a foreigner. I'm an Egyptian like you.' All his limbs were shaking—with fear, yes, but also with rage. The first row stopped yelling. They stood speechless, as if they didn't know what to make of this well-bred young man who spoke their language, an Egyptian after all. But in the back, the cries were redoubling. 'Slaughter the Zionist!' And they shoved hard, seeking to reach the enemy. Poor Joe, alone before these hundreds, had in one instant become responsible for the humiliations endured for centuries; the mob had found its rallying cry against the Jews once more: 'Zionist!'

The fat man raised his stick, looked back, seeking his companions' assent, and shouted. '*Allahu akbar!*' He brought the stick down on Joe's skull. '*Allahu akbar!*' the others repeated.

On that evening of 22 October, Loula waited a long time for her prince, her love, who was planning to take her dancing at the Automobile Club, where she'd never set foot.

The Grand Rabbi of Egypt himself led the procession when, two days later on 24 October because the 23rd was a Saturday, the

Jewish community, on foot and in the greatest silence, carried Joe di Reggio's remains to the Bassatine Cemetery. Aghast, the people of Cairo watched them go by. Women ululated, cries rose here and there: 'Poor fellow! Such a handsome young man.' Who are the true Egyptian people, those who the night before howled for the Zionist's death, or these, sincerely afflicted, rendering a last tribute to his youth's beauty?

Zohar had stayed at the Rendezvous of the Pashas, lost in contemplation of the label, 'the eau-de-vie of the three shebabs'. With a hesitating hand, he spilt the last drops from his glass. He'd emptied the bottle. Joe was dead. He hadn't felt strong enough to attend the funeral. Joe was dead and he couldn't understand why. For years, together, they'd flirted with danger, with the luck of carelessness. And here, since—since when actually? Since the end of the war, most certainly . . . These demonstrations in the street, these outbreaks of violence, these hints of pogroms . . . the atmosphere was no longer the same, he could feel the noose tightening—and his throat. The movement had accelerated after the UN vote approving the plan to partition Palestine. And the debacle of the Egyptian army.

The king, once so elegant, the dandy king, who swelled each day, a mountain of fat, who made scenes in the cabarets, a dancer on each arm; the king whose elitist cynicism, with carefully wrought, refined English sentences, had given way to filthy words that made him unrecognizable, gross insults, scatological behaviour—this, Zohar knew instinctively, the Egyptians would never forgive. They loved Egypt in their king.

And the rumors persisted. Farouk's men abducted women against their will. Husbands, fathers, brothers who tried to resist were harassed, sometimes imprisoned. People spoke, too, of disappearances, of unexplained deaths. But people said so many things. In the Orient, speech is made to sing its dreams and to tremble at its nightmares, not to inform!

Suddenly, a dreadful explosion. The windows rattled. A deep rumble reached Zohar's ears. Then, outside, a low hiss, followed by a second detonation, not as loud but more intrusive than the first. A heavy silence for almost a minute. Then the mob's shouts, close by. He went out onto Suleiman Pasha Street. People were running towards the square. The last building housed the Cassuto & Company department store, which belonged to the father of that young girl on whom the king had set his sights five years earlier. After the scandal that nearly erupted, the parents had packed little Vivian off to France, to pursue her studies. They'd hoped to marry their daughter to the young Joe di Reggio. The Cassuto building was on fire, and Joe was dead. And when he saw the mob rushing through the store windows to loot everything they could put their hands on—rugs, curtains, lamps, chairs, objects, things, more things, those things the people lacked—Zohar retched and left reeling in the opposite direction.

He wandered through the city for a long time. His steps naturally led him to Bab al-Zuwayla. He moved forward, his head down, his soul absent. He took alleys he knew well; no one called him, no beggar extended his open palm, no child clung to his garments pleading for a coin. He seemed to have become transparent, invisible to passersby. When he crossed the threshold of the neighbourhood, the kudiya, mistress of the zars, the one who'd initiated his mother and permitted his conception, greeted him as always by clapping. 'O Allah! Here is the son, child of Nofal, our lord! Come! Come welcome our child!' She hugged him, his head pressed against her enormous soft breasts that smelt of laundry and incense. He cried, Zohar, he who had never cried before; he was suffocating, Zohar, with tears, with affliction, with a tight heart and a knotted throat: 'My mother! O my mother!' And she hugged him harder, the kudiya, and he entered into the earth as into a down quilt. 'Your absence was a monster that devoured my soul!' he cried. The kudiya clapped again: 'What a liar he is! He knows how to talk, this one who lives with thieves.' She intoned the measures of the song that had accompanied Esther's first dance, the night of her initiation into the lords' dance: 'O Nofal, O Nofal . . . Those who descend are happy in the depths.' Then she burst out laughing. Changing in an instant, she suddenly assumed a severe look: 'My absence? Son of a dog! Aren't you the one who's forgotten your mother, the kudiya? You who don't find the time to come to us, who are satisfied to send servants with perfume offerings for the ceremonies, don't you think they've asked for you, the lords? Every day, they ask about you: "Where is he? Has he forgotten his father's house?" ' She enumerated the spirits, the zars calling for Zohar. 'Don't you think they would have wanted to dance with you? The red master, our king with the beautiful hair of fire, and his wife, known as Jenneya. And Bahri, the one from the sea, and his sister, the one in the felucca. And Manzoh, the *bawab*, the porter. And the owners of the earth, who called you at each ceremony, those from the high kingdom and those from the springs. And mother Safsaf, who guards the desert shores. Yes! Mother Safsaf! You know how she loves you!'

And she burst out laughing again, the kudiya, the severe one.

That's what Zohar loved most at Bab al-Zuwayla. There, nothing was serious, everything could be cured: the difficulty of life and the impossibility of enduring death. 'Look at my belly, son of nothing, son of the lords!' And she lifted her dress up to her breasts. Above a strange woollen undergarment, she had a tattoo he'd never seen: 'Look at my belly,' repeated the kudiya. The tattoo represented the face of a child, his mouth open, his tongue slightly sticking out. He had slanting eyes, an endearing little mug. His nose was the kudiya's navel. And she began to undulate in a belly dance, holding the hem of her dress between her teeth. The little tattooed boy grimaced, then laughed, then cried, then laughed as she moved. And Zohar smiled and smiled. And the other women surrounded them and clapped to create a rhythm for the dance. The tattoo child made signals to Zohar, a wink of an eye, a movement of the lips, like a kiss. And Zohar smiled some more and ended up laughing. Then he threw himself into the kudiya's arms. 'Relieve me of my suffering, O my mother!' And he buried his head in the pillows of her enormous breasts.

She'd understood, the deep, wise, intuitive priestess of origins; as soon as he'd crossed the threshold of her place, she'd understood that he had lost his way, her child with the burning heart. 'Eat a little! Eat some of the sacrificial meat and some *bamia*, the gumbo as sticky as molten iron. Eat while you wait for me. I'll make a claw for you. You'll wear it around your neck, and, when a power greater than you seizes your will, you'll take the claw between your fingers and you'll say the words I've taught you.' He ate and drank and joked with the women, the owners of Cairo; he cried and they cried with him; they touched him and kissed him, they who had seen the pharaohs descend from the kingdom of Kush. The kudiya returned and gave him the claw, as big as a tiger's, made of buffalo leather and a snake's bone, and said: 'The lords don't travel. They are like trees. Children go away. They are like birds. Remember, child of night, you are not one, but two! And if ever you believe you know with whom you make one, think you are not two but three.'

And Zohar kissed the kudiya's hands and brought them to his forehead. 'Go,' she said then, 'Go your way.'

And Zohar left Bab al-Zuwayla with his head held high, inwardly repeating the sentence like a mantra: 'Think you are not two but three.

The Palace

Light of night, child of the alleys . . .

You paced old Cairo from your earliest childhood, and today you no longer recognize your city. You who once felt the happy strength of a world in each woman of the people with a throaty voice; the curve of a hip; the weight of a breast in the hollow of your hand; the perfumed flesh of a lip between yours; in each man in galabia and tarbouche; the acrid scent of the porter who carried you in his arms; the coarse hand on your cheek . . . From now on, you were suspicious of each man, each woman you encountered. You saw the leopard's terrible violence in men's faces, poison at the corners of women's lips. And to reassure yourself, you gripped the magic claw buried deep in your pocket, the magic claw you'd never yet hung around your neck.

Light of night, child of the alleys, do not fear, this world is coming to an end, dying . . .

Zohar hailed a taxi and gave the driver an address: Osman Bey Street, on Rhoda. Was she still living there? He hadn't seen Masreya in six years. Dropped off at the gate, he hesitated to ring. He wouldn't be able to endure his milk-mother Jinane's sweet-faced gaze, her angelic voice that would remind him of his oath never to see her daughter again. And the very words to which he fell asleep each night, 'my sister, my love, the appeared, the disappeared': he closed his eyes and smelt the perfumes of her body; he opened them, closed them, and then again. The little gusts of wind gathered to draw the shape of his beloved. He trembled at the thought of his hand feeling her legs. He searched for pretexts. After all, he'd just lost his friend. He was miserable. He needed to see her. He rang.

'May God spare me from ill fortune and all the shaytans!' cried Ouahiba when she saw him through the half-opened door.

He pushed her inside, not giving her time to close the door again, and pressed against her.

'Shush! You'll wake up the devils, you fool! Do you think you're alone in the world? If you only knew the multitude that surrounds you: at your feet'—he pointed to the ground, she looked down—'in the air'—he pointed upward, she raised her head—'all the afrits you don't see. They hear your cries and come running. Especially when you invoke the name of Shaytan.' He made his voice reverberate as he pronounced the devil's name.

'May God keep us!'

'And they press against you!' He pressed harder against her.

'In the name of God! May he distance the shaytans!'

She pushed him away: 'Why have you come back?'

'Speak quietly now.' He placed his hand over her mouth. 'Is Oum Jinane in the house?'

'It's been a long time since the mother left for her village, Kafr al-Amar, in the Delta. She said she'd rather take care of her buffalo cows than the asses passing through this house.'

'Shush! Speak less loudly. She no longer lives here?'

'No! Only Madame and Monsieur'

'Monsieur? What monsieur?'

And she told him, Ouahiba, the simple, the dreamer, the faithful. Masreya had known many men after having given up her brother. (May God forgive her!) And then Cherif had come—Zohar must know him, Cherif al-Afgani, the deputy. He'd even been minister for a while, under the government of Sirry Pasha or of Hassan Sabri, she wasn't sure. Lord Cherif had put the house in order. He'd placed two guards at the entrance and when one or another of those scoundrels, those nighthawks that had populated her mistress' bed, tried to return, he found himself at the police station.

'You're lucky, Gohar, son of no one. Today, with all these riots, the guards have gone into the city to help the police. That's why you were able to reach the door.'

'Is she married?' asked Zohar.

When the servant didn't answer, he insisted. 'Masreya—is she married to Mr Cherif? Speak!'

'The lord Cherif is not a night owl like you. He's a khawaga.'

At that moment, Masreya came down the stairs, dressed only in a green silk dressing gown. The years had ripened her a bit, accentuating her shape draped in velvety satin. River of reflections from her long hair curling over her shoulders, her face bathed in tender sweetness, she was moving forward slowly, step by step, as if she wanted to savour this moment of witnessing the disappearance of absence. He watched her come, his eyes fixed, smiling to himself about the air of majesty she sought to give herself. She drew closer. He moved forward. She took the last steps at a run.

'Gohar!'

And she came to press herself against him. She buried her head in the hollow of his shoulder and hugged him as hard as she could, inhaling him through each pore. Then she looked at him, studying his face to learn his fate. She repeated his name. She kissed his mouth. With her hand, she caressed his back, his belly, even his sex. From the first glance, they had become again naked nurslings, each attached to one of Oum Jinane's breasts. He was the first to speak. 'I've waited for you for years in the corner of my darkness.'

'O God!' lamented Ouahiba. And she shook her head from right to left, trying through her denials to ward off the coming disaster. 'May it be according to your will, O my God!'

But who knows God's will? She thought she was uttering an exorcism, Ouahiba, the faithful, the carnal, the curious. But, through her words, she validated the unforeseen, accepting that spirits, devils, reunite the two halves once more. Perhaps she did it knowingly, who can say? Perhaps her soul rejoiced, even while claiming the opposite, to let love pour from the heaven of one into the heaven of the other. In Egypt, opposites are often identical.

'I've also waited for you, Gohar, my brother, my beloved, my betrothed. Who's the one who left that 10 November?'

He kissed her mouth, caressed her with his hands, hugged her, took her with his strength, carried her with his words to the edges of the world.

'And who has returned today? Isn't it me?'

And he lifted her in infinite whirlwinds; they ran without moving.

'Come!' he told her. 'Let's go elsewhere, where no one knows the milk that nurtured us.'

'Where?'

'To the end of the world!'

And it was here! On the floor, on the carpet of the great hall. Couldn't they have waited, if only an instant? They let themselves gently fall to their knees, the one adoring the other, without knowing who was the believer and who the idol. They rolled into one ball of flesh and nerves, tension and sweetness. Like the first time, ten years ago, when they were thirteen, they unbridled their wild nature. They seemed a pair of rutting cats, or rather, tigers.

Ouahiba left the room at a run. But she didn't get far. Hiding in the kitchen, holding her sister Baheya's hand, her ear glued to the wall, to spy on them, to watch over them, to protect them; perhaps, to try, once more, to discover their secret, yes!

They rested a moment, intertwined, panting.

'You will return?' she asked him.

'You will be here?' he asked her.

'You must leave now! Quickly!'

'I know. But before that . . . '

'No, Gohar, no! He's coming, I can feel it. He's on his way.'

He would have wanted to tell her about his suffering. He would have wanted to recount his years without her. He would have wanted, once more, to try to convince her to leave with him, or even to stay in this country, the two of them, elsewhere, at the borders, in

Nubia, or the Sudan. But he had just realized that the force that bound them, born before language, made a mockery of words.

'Go!' Masreya repeated. 'Go, now!'

Go, light of night, child of the alleys, you whose name is planted in a book like a tree in the earth. This world is coming to an end, dying.

And when the outlines of a world grow blurred, overlapping with those of other worlds, a witness to the changing time appears. On 10 November 1948 was born in Abasseya the grandson of the grandson of the Grand Rabbi of Egypt, Rabbi Yom Tov Israel Cherezli, who knew, during the ministries of the Khedives Ismail Pasha and Tawfik Pasha and until Mustapha Fahmi Pasha, how to govern Israel in Egypt. The old people recounted how on that day, in the mosques, in the Coptic churches, in the Catholic churches, in the synagogues of Cairo, eyes rose all at once, and the faithful did not know why.

On 17 November 1948, after ten years of marriage, Farouk divorced his wife, Queen Farida. Wind, rain, even some snowflakes were seen in Alexandria—Egyptians were cold during this month of November. 'In his wisdom, God has decided that the sacred bond that united two noble spouses be undone.' Then the king uttered the ritual phrase, 'I repudiate you! I repudiate you! I repudiate you!' Dreadful words with which, according to tradition, a man separates from his wife; perfect inverse of those with which a sorcerer calls the devil, inviting him, three times, to enter his house. Already, in 1943, the beautiful Farida—endlessly provoked by her husband the king's misdemeanours, no longer able to withstand the acid torment of her own jealousy, undermined in his esteem by the successive birth of two daughters—had taken a lover, the elegant son of Princess Chiwiakar, a distant cousin of Farouk's. She became pregnant a third time, and everyone in the court wondered—from her husband? Or from her lover? In Farouk's entourage, the sulfurous Pulli and Karim Tabet, his private advisers, persuaded him it was a plot of mythic dimensions. Farida would bring a son into the world, a foreigner's child into his house, who, when the time came, would seize power and bring an end to the sacred dynasty founded by the great Mohammad Ali. It was a daughter. On 15 December 1943, the gracious Farida, the third child of King Farouk, opened her astonished eyes on the world. But the poisoned thought had been planted, and, since then, the king suspected the queen more than anyone else. The polite indifference that governed relations between the royal couple gave way to animosity, disgust and rancour.

And then, other projects germinated in the king's mind. He had to secure the throne, to give birth to a son, an heir. Clearly, Farida was incapable of doing so. What confirmed his conviction was a remark let fall in passing by Princess Nimet Allah. The same story had unfolded in the previous generation, she explained. To his father, the severe King Fouad I, three girls had been born in succession during a first marriage. Fouad had then chosen a new wife, a very young girl from the haute bourgeoisie, beautiful, educated, intelligent, Queen Nazli. Her first son was a boy, and it was he, Prince Farouk! So, if it was true that a family's fate is repeated from father to son, he needed a helping hand. When you learn the future, you should help the world give birth to it. He decided to divorce the queen. But, as for conceiving an heir, Farouk did not take that route.

Liberated from his marriage, this bond that had constrained him to a semblance of normalcy, Farouk abandoned himself, body and soul, to the forces of night. At the Inn of the Pyramids, at Risotto, at Mohammad Ali, at the Rendezvous of the Pashas which he preferred for a long time over other clubs, Farouk spent long nights of ennui. There, games of cards, gambling and laughter with courtesans brought him some fleeting excitement. He joked loudly, cheated as he played, feasted as he belched. At the end of the evening, hunters presented their catch, young beauties with a talent for love. He carried them off in powerful cars he drove himself at the speed of Shaytan. And if any other car slowed his progress, he shot the culprit's tyres with his revolver. You make way for the king! Yet his car was recognizable, especially his latest acquisition, a sumptuous Bentley Mark

VI—not the standard model, but one designed by Figoni and Falaschi—painted a Californian candy red—the only one in all of Egypt, it goes without saying; the only one in the world, perhaps. He kept the girls in isolated villas until morning for unbridled orgies. He went to bed at sunrise and rose at the siesta hour. Addicted to excess, he always needed more. At breakfast, he wolfed down whole boxes of caviar, two dozen eggs, a roast chicken. He sometimes had terrible hiccups, which lasted for hours at a time, despite the litres of cold orange soda he gulped down with spasms of his whole body.

On this evening of the last day in November, the girls at the Rendezvous of the Pashas were ordinary, too vulgar for his taste, and the courtesans were asleep, tired of entertaining the king. It must be past two in the morning. He didn't have the heart to go back to the palace. It was because a recurring nightmare had been haunting him for several weeks, and he feared finding it again, hidden in the folds of his sheets. Zohar was busy behind the bar.

'Lord Gohar, you who are like me a child of the night, come have a drink with me.'

And Zohar came to the table of the lost king, to whom everything had been given at birth except promise—a king born without a future.

'What would please Your Majesty?' asked Zohar.

'Nothing! Just a few minutes of your time, to talk.'

And he recounted his terrible nightmare, which awakened him with a start, drenched in sweat, panting. Lions, hordes of lions, were chasing him. He tried to escape them, but the animals ran faster than he. If he hid, they found him by sniffing his track. To climb up a tree, perhaps. But it was impossible; the trunk was too slender, too slippery, with nothing to hold onto. So he ended up falling to the ground, and, when he felt on his skin the fetid breath of the animal ready to devour him, he rose from sleep, panic-stricken.

'They see in me a kilo of flesh,' he explained to Zohar, 'on which they can feed for days.'

'Your Majesty is doing me a great honour in thinking I might be of some help in elucidating this dream. But I am no one, sire, just a little Jew from the alley.'

'Come, Lord Gohar, you're far too modest. And the Jews, I know, are expert at handling dreams, ever since Joseph and the Pharaoh. Just tell me: do you think as I do that these lions represent the forces that have decided to destroy me, the bloody British and those womanish Wafds, and the barkers in the mosques, and the followers of the Great Mufti of Moscow, and my mother Queen Nazli's clique? Don't be afraid to tell me, because I already know!'

Zohar trembled to be addressed like this. It was not good to contradict the king during these tumultuous years. He brought his hand to his neck, searching for the magic claw, felt it with his fingers and answered only: 'I don't know what to say about your dream, O my king. What better advice to give you than to put yourself in the hands of God? Let His Majesty pray before going to sleep, invoking the aid of the Almighty.'

'Get away!' the king sputtered, as he rose to leave. 'I'll know how to master them myself, those lions!'

And he raced in his Bentley to the Cairo Zoo, which he had opened in the middle of the night. Howling like a madman, he ordered the terrified guard: 'The lion cage! Bring me to the lion cage, you fool!' And there, he continued to shout, addressing the animals: 'Oh, so you want to take my throne! It's not enough that you're king of the beasts, you want to take away the crown of the children of Adam! You're ogling my wealth, are you? If I were reduced to dust, it would be easy for you to take it. If it were only a matter of my throne and my fortune—you also want to feed on my flesh, do you?' And with that he discharged his revolver into the two unfortunate sleeping lions.

Poor king! Who could have made him listen to reason? Princess Chiwiaker was dead; also dead was his chamberlain, the aristocratic Hassanein Pasha, the only two elders whose word Farouk somewhat respected. The royal family, the princes and princesses, the uncles and the cousins, assembled secretly in a sort of emergency council. If they let the king do as he pleased, they would all be lost in the wreck, ceding their place to God only knows what mismanagement. 'He's mad!' said Princess Fawkieh, the eldest. 'Completely mad!' added Prince Mohammad Ali Hassan. 'In the streets, all you hear are slogans against the immoral king with dissolute habits, who engages in adultery and hellish games.' The princes and princesses, the nabils and nabilas, were unanimous. They had to depose the king. But how? If they'd only been able to agree on the means.

Light of night, child of the alleys, flee! Run far! This world is coming to an end, dying.

When, on 4 December the Muslim Brothers assassinated the chief of police, and, on 28 December, Prime Minister Al-Nokrashi Pasha, claiming responsibility for the attacks and declaring they were eradicating corruption through word and blood, Zohar couldn't help thinking that this what the king had been dreaming about a few weeks earlier. If he'd been Joseph, he would have warned the pharaoh. One of the lions in the dream represented the terrible Brothers. But Farouk was now inaccessible, surrounded by a clique of corrupt figures who profited from the least word exchanged with him. Gone, that politics of an oriental prince, fashioned from cunning and unexpected initiatives, defending on the one hand the thoughts of a peasant encountered in a village, on the other a banker who'd played cards with him one night in a club—this politics that rendered him unpredictable, allowing him to navigate troubled waters. From now on, he would use power like an ordinary dictator. He decreed the dissolution of the Brotherhood, and, on 12 February 1949, had its Supreme Guide, its creator, Sheikh Hassan al-Banna, assassinated. The Brothers, dreaming of martyrs, finally had one, their own, the greatest, the most prestigious. It's a well-known fact that the dead revive the living.

If the commoner dreams about problems at work or in his family, it stands to reason that the king dreams about problems of state. Farouk's nightmare was not in error: it was indeed a pride of lions that wanted to feed on his flesh—not just one but a whole herd of starving lions. The Muslim Brothers were not the only ones, far from it! Some fifteen officers, intelligent and educated, were organizing meetings with the goal of overthrowing the regime and establishing a socialist military republic. It was during this floating period, when everything seemed possible, that Nasser, their head, established his committee, surrounding himself with talented men like Anwar al-Sadat, Abdel Hakim Amer and General Mohammad Naguib. A few weeks later, the new organization, with a network at every level of the army hierarchy, took the name, 'Free Officers Movement'. The lions were emerging from the forest and beginning to rally.

Ever since that night of November 1948 that ended tragically at the Cairo Zoo, Farouk was no longer to be seen at the Rendezvous of the Pashas. Zohar continued to manage his still-flourishing business as he tried to throw a veil over the disintegration of the world around him. He fled from anxiety by losing himself in easy conquests. He sought Egyptian women, women of the people, still imbued with the clay of the Nile banks or with the odours of the fish they sold at auction in the market. Often, he initiated them into the intoxication of the senses; sometimes, he stumbled upon sisters, initiates in the cult of the zars, young followers of the lords, from the neighbourhood near the Barbarin Gate, or the New House, or the Citadel, and, for one night or just for an hour, he closed his eyes to inhale the perfumes of his world. For him, women were Egypt's future. Despite the evidence, he wanted to preserve the illusion of a land extricating itself from poverty and, thanks to its women, entering into a happy modernity. A new advertisement had appeared on the city walls, touting Coca Cola, now being manufactured in a Cairo suburb. Masreya, his sister, his goddess, dressed like a Westerner in a low-cut designer suit, had her legs crossed on a beach chair. Her skirt, riding halfway up her thighs, hinted at the hidden place of desire. Just below, a bottle of Coke, its foam flowing freely. The message was clear: it was impossible to resist! 'Quench her thirst!' the indecent ad promised. The billboard produced its effect. Men sometimes paused for long minutes, dreaming in front of Masreya's perfect legs; women smiled at her; and Zohar spoke to her in his heart, reciting that same verse of the Song: 'Thou hast ravished my heart, my sister, my spouse; thou hast ravished my heart with one of thine eyes.'

One day, he was startled. It seemed as if the billboard had answered him. Masreya had winked; she'd murmured within his soul: 'Go, light of night, child of the alleys. You were not made to suffer.'

Power was adrift. It would return—everyone knew—to whatever force managed to chase the British from Egypt. Each group had its claim. The Brothers drew their influence from the moral question, insisting that the British presence led to corruption and depravity. The Free Officers focused on the military question and the scandal of the 1948 defeat. The Wafd, returned to the government with Nahhas Pasha, posed as the guarantor of law. That left only Farouk, the unconquerable, who now frequently wandered afar. Obsessed by his passions, from the first days of Ramadan, he left to spend the summer months in France, at Deauville, in Biarritz, in Cannes, in Monaco, where he could eat all he wanted during the weeks of the Muslim fast, looting the casinos, winning and losing sums that defied the imagination, snaring young girls by offering them a few minutes of fantasy.

*

Saturday, 26 January 1952, 1 p.m. Zohar presented himself at the gates of the Abdine Palace, at the handlebars of his Vincent Black Shadow, a new British motorcycle with extraordinary power. The two cylinders were backfiring in rhythm, trying to catch their breath after the journey. He raised his goggles onto his forehead so the two guards could identify him. He entered the courtyard, surprised to see dozens of cars, British, American mostly, and even a few Rolls. The

Vincent's acceleration, vented through two exhaust pipes, echoed storm thunder on the palace walls. He pulled up, slipping in front of the huge door that Khedive Ismail, wildly in love with Empress Eugenie, had baptized the 'Gate of Paris' in 1874. A final thrust of the accelerator to leave a few drops in the carburetor tanks before cutting the contact. He leapt off his bike, dashed to the grand entrance and quickly climbed the stairs.

'Where are you running so fast, O sir?'

He stopped short and turned. Antonio Pulli, damned soul, in his eternal smoking jacket, a faint smile on his lips, was staring at him, hands on hips.

'His Majesty—'

'I don't think His Majesty can see you, Mr Zohar.' And, with a deceitful air, he added, 'Unfortunately.'

Zohar shrugged scornfully and continued to climb. The other man hurried after him, passed him and barred his way.

'His Majesty is hosting a banquet to celebrate the birth of the prince. Important people are here, you understand. Many, many people!'

'I'm coming from Opera Square—'

Taken aback, Pulli stood still. 'You—you came from there?'

'Yes. I was able to thread through on my bike. Go, tell the king. I must speak to him. Time presses!'

For several months, the competing forces had been engaged in a terrifying bidding war. The Muslim Brothers had cast anathemas. 'The Muslim religion forbids collaboration with the British under whatever form,' Hassan al-Hudaybi, the new Supreme Guide, had declared. Whoever ventured to work with the miscreants risked death. The dockworkers at Port Said, infiltrated by communists and the fascist movement, 'Young Egypt', were refusing to release merchandise destined for the army and British businesses. Prime Minister Nahhas Pasha, weakened by widely reported accusations of corruption brought against him, had decided to strike a decisive blow by unilaterally dissolving, on 8 October 1951, the 1936 treaty allying Great Britain and Egypt. He appeared to have won the match. The people acclaimed him. On all lips was the same phrase: 'Free and independent at last, for the first time in centuries!'

After that, by all accounts, the British should have left. They decided not only to remain but also to reinforce their military presence. Rallying cries resounded everywhere. The municipality of Alexandria began to unchristen streets and squares bearing names of British officers: Kitchener, who'd offered the Sudan to Egypt, disappeared; also Allenby, who'd repulsed the Turkish attacks against the Suez Canal in 1917. Chambers of commerce decreed a boycott, asking members to cease all economic relations with Great Britain. The government raised the stakes by encouraging employees to desert; it even went so far as to propose a law that would prohibit Egyptians from working in British companies. But the Brothers placed the bar even higher, declaring armed struggle against the occupier.

On the first floor, Farouk was waiting for him. He'd gotten so fat that no one paid attention to his big size; he must weigh close to three hundred kilos, at least! Dressed in a suit with a checked vest to minimize his girth, he was standing stiffly at the top of the staircase, one hand on the banister. With his military bearing and his marble face, he was simultaneously imposing and absurd, this king who did not observe common laws, not even the law of kings. When he saw Zohar, his face brightened a bit.

'Sir Gohar! Where are you running so quickly, my friend?'

'Sire, I come to warn you. What's happened in Ismailia—'

'I know, I know!'

'The people are rumbling. This time, it's the people. Not the ministers, not the deputies, not the journalists. sire, I implore you! They are here, today, in Cairo, just a few steps from your palace. May Heaven help you! I saw them in Abasseya this morning. The police—the ones who should have reestablished order—the police themselves were streaming through the streets, shouting and breaking windows with their clubs.'

'I understand them! Didn't those damned British assassinate their colleagues, the police auxiliaries, in Ismailia yesterday?'

'I was leaving the factory, a few steps from the barracks. I followed them. They've joined the students at Al-Azhar.'

'And so?'

'You must have heard them passing right here, at Abdine, at the foot of your palace. sire! You must have heard them yelling.'

Farouk sneered. 'Was it worse than what they're saying about me in the press?'

'The people, sire! They were shouting, "Farouk, you're finished. Farouk, you're dead." '

'You see!' the king concluded, turning back to his reception. 'Nothing unusual.'

'I followed them from Opera Square,' Zohar added. 'They set fire to the casino. The panicked employees were exiting, and they beat them with clubs. Then they went to Barclay's Bank, surrounded it. They were shouting: "We'll burn the idolaters, worshippers of the pound Sterling!" And then—'

Zohar was running out of breath.

'And then, sire, it was terrible! They doused the bank lobby with cans of petrol. The employees were begging to be let out. They were fighting them and pushing them back inside. They were standing on the pavement, clapping. They were yelling, "The Shaytan Sterling burns in hell!" And they set it afire, may Your Presence forgive me. They tossed burning torches, and the flames rose to the second story. The bank employees, men and women, were howling, wriggling, still alive in the furnace.'

This time, the king stood still. He looked Zohar in the face. 'And what do you want me to do about it?' he asked, turning his palms up to heaven.

'Deploy the army, sire! Now! Right away!'

'Do you know what I'm celebrating today? Do you know why there's such a crowd in my palace? Ten days ago, the prince was born—the heir apparent!'

And King Farouk had tears in his eyes as he called to mind that birth he hoped would be his salvation. A year earlier, in that atmosphere of tumultuous anarchy, he'd taken the step of remarrying—a very young girl, seventeen years old, a poorly educated bourgeois, Narriman Sadek. Princess Nimet Allah's words were coming true, she who'd predicted the repetition of his father's fate. After three daughters from a first marriage, the first child of the second would be a son, an heir who would perpetuate the dynasty. And he was born, the royal infant, little Prince Ahmed Fouad, who would save his father and the kingdom. On this 26 January, the King of Egypt was holding a banquet, a gigantic reception attended by all the high-ranking army and police officers.

And so, since they were all present, Zohar suggested, he could convene them here and now, declare a state of emergency, impose martial law and put an end to the rampage devastating the city. He took the king by the sleeve and dragged him to the window. In the distance, they could see smoke rising, by Qasr-al-Nil and Suleiman Pasha.

'If you would permit me a direct word, Your Majesty—'

'Speak, Lord Gohar. Speak, do!'

'The throne is tottering.'

'You're too emotional, my young friend. A few madmen striking some blows, that's all! Tomorrow, the sun will rise over the Nile and it will be the same as today.'

Zohar shrugged. Then he said to Farouk, carefully pronouncing each syllable, 'I wish a long life to the young prince, sire.'

'Come, calm down! Have you at least thought of that dancer with the hips of a goddess?'

Zohar stared at him, speechless. 'What dancer?'

'The one you introduced me to at the Automobile Club a few years ago. You'd promised me.'

Farouk never forgot a thing! Nothing!

*

Zohar tumbled down the great stairs, Pulli at his heels.

'Mr Zohar! Mr Zohar! Has the king decided to act?'

He, at least, realized that the world hung in the balance.

He did not answer the chief courtier. He did not slow down; he did not even turn around. He leapt onto his bike, vigorously kick-started the motor and took off for Suleiman Pasha Square.

It was 2 p.m. People were running through the streets, some to join the rioters, others to escape. Shepheard's Hotel was aflame. They'd piled up chairs, rugs, paintings, wood furniture, telephone cables at the centre of the huge lobby, and, as at an auto-da-fé, sprinkled petrol and gunpowder over the mountain of objects. Howling, they'd set it alight. There, too, as at Barclay's Bank, they prevented the employees from leaving, pushing them into the fire with blows from their clubs.

Zohar crossed the river and parked his bike, hiding it on the other side of the Gezira Bridge; then he returned on foot. He heard the slogans: 'Total war against the British.' 'Let the British lick my arse,' and 'Send the shaytans back to hell.' He wanted to return to his club, the Rendezvous of the Pashas on Suleiman Pasha Street. But the streets were blocked by the complicit crowd that watched as small groups of arsonists went from building to building, choosing their victims from lists they consulted. And the crowd rushed through the broken windows and looted whatever was left of devastated offices and ravaged stores. Of course the British businesses—the Turf Club, Smith & Sons, the Thomas Cook Travel Agency—were on fire, as were almost all the offices and shops along Qasr al-Nil Street. Wherever it started, the fire spread from floor to floor of the building and then to neighbouring buildings. Nightclubs, bars, cafes, all those places of luxury and perdition in the eye of the Brothers, were aflame, their customers cursed, beaten and put to death if they resisted. But, once out of the building, the cafe, or the shop, people did not flee; they remained right where they were, hypnotized by the fire.

Zohar jumped. At the corner of Suleiman Pasha, he heard an explosion, rumblings, followed by shouts of joy from the mob. The fluorescent Metro-Goldwyn-Mayer marquee had just tumbled down, its hundreds of bulbs exploding in fireworks over the pavement. The Metro Cinema and the Ritz Bar, both in the same building, had just ignited like torches. That screen was giving its last show, that screen before which Cairo's inhabitants had learnt from American musical comedies or syrupy Egyptian romances how to kiss on the lips; the Ritz was serving its last cocktail. Standing some ten metres away, his face burning, Zohar was thunderstruck. A little voice echoed through his head. 'Run, little devil, run!'

Behind him, another voice, a thick heavy voice, hoarse from so much smoke, ordered, 'Find the Jews!' And he began to run, as if he'd been flogged, his body suddenly electrified. A mob had gathered in front of Cicurel Department Store, Egypt's pride, where you could find all Europe's wealth. He slowed down, hid in a crevice of the wall. He heard again: 'Come. They're Jews! Slaughter, slaughter!' Men and women were emerging from Cicurel's, and people in the crowd were hitting them, shouting, 'a Jew!' shoving them back into the furnace, thumping them with sticks. And the rioters were laughing and running and burning and destroying—strong in number, strong in their reasons, strong in the silence of the strong. And the flames were beginning to lick at the facade, and other employees emerged screaming, greeted by blows with sticks. The windows exploded from the heat's pressure, and shards fell tens of metres away in a fire of crystal. And always the mob, behind the rioters—the mob that flowed into the store to grab, before the ultimate purification, a pair of shoes, some gloves, a sheet, some shelves, a chair.

An hour earlier, at lunch time, there must have been customers at Groppi's large patisserie. Now, the storefront was black with smoke, the windows shattered. A few flames still flickered above the smoking ruins. The mob had gone elsewhere, seeking other victims, other spoils. A man was standing in front of the facade, wearing an apron that must once have been white. He was lifting his arms to heaven as he uttered imprecations: 'O our Father! Why? Why?' He was crying. A few metres away, Zohar looked up: 'The Rendezvous of the Pashas'. The sign was intact, red on a white ground, in French, in an original script that recalled Viennese signs during the mad years. He looked to the right, then to the left, to ascertain that no one was following him; then opened the door and rushed inside. He ran through the room, where a few rays of light were entering through the closed blinds. What was he doing there? He slipped behind the bar and hastily withdrew some bills still in the cash register. All the way at the back of a drawer, his hand met a hard object, the size of a notepad. His Italian passport. He needed to renew it. He'd brought it to the club thinking he would use a free hour to go to the Italian Consulate. And then he'd forgotten. He slipped it into his back pocket. He glanced above the bar, scanned the dozens of bottles of alcohol beautifully lined up. A shiver coursed through him as he thought of how the Muslim Brothers would howl if they saw this sight.

He should have wondered, Zohar, if he was on their *Kristaltag* list. They had meticulously inventoried the clubs patronized by the king. But he was like that, child of the alleys, his muscles tense and his soul nonchalant.

He decided to leave. But to exit through the double door that opened onto Suleiman Pasha Street seemed too dangerous. He crossed the club, passing through the kitchens until he came to the little door at the back of the building, opening onto the alley, kingdom of stray cats, where the trash was piled. He opened it, preparing to leave. The rioters were there. They must have spotted him. They were waiting for him, with their clubs, their knives, their cans of petrol. There were at least thirty of them. He shut the door and ran into the club. The door didn't resist them for long. He heard them hurrying in search of him. 'The Jew! The Jew!' they were howling.

In the few seconds that remained before their eruption into the great room of the Rendezvous of the Pashas, that great room that had welcomed the powerful, the artists and the beauties of Egypt, where political secrets had been whispered and romantic trysts enacted, he unhooked the claw hanging from his neck, squeezed it in his hand and sought the words deep within his soul. They were his father's, chanting the Song of Songs: 'Make haste my beloved, and be thou like to a roe or to a young hart upon the mountains of spices.' They echoed through him and made his lips tremble.

'We have you, you filthy Jew, son of a dog!'

They cast stones at the lined-up bottles and laughed as they burst, spilling alcohol; they broke glasses, cups, pints. And they surrounded him, menacing, mouthing reproaches. The remarks succeeded each other, to stimulate the spirit, to give them the courage to commit murder.

'This was Shaytan's den.'

'They drank, they smoked, they fornicated.'

'They committed adultery.'

'They looted the poor peasants.'

'And now it will burn!'

'The fire of God that washes away filth!'

'In burning Sodom.'

'In burning Gomorrah.'

'In burning Sodom and Gomorrah, God has given us the command to burn Shaytan's dens on earth.'

'*Allahu akbar*!'

And they sprayed petrol onto the red velvet chairs the king had loved, the red of the palace; the carpets with infinite designs that bore, inscribed at their centres, calligraphed in gracious arabesques, King

Farouk's name; the hangings of heavy silk; the rare-wood furniture inlaid with ivory.

When they approached him, when they'd surrounded him so tightly he felt suffocated and closed his eyes to await the lightning bolt that would cross his brain beneath the cudgel's blow, while he squeezed the claw and kept repeating sentences and sentences—the entrance door opened wide and he heard a voice—that voice—

'That's enough now!'

Silence.

And the voice again.

'Stop! I know him.'

It was Nino's voice.

'Nino!' Zohar cried.

'My name is Abu l'Harb!' Then, louder, addressing both Zohar and the rioters: 'We are not assassins! Do not fear, we will not hurt you. We only want the foreigners to return to us the country they've stolen. This debauched place, where people spent wads of bills, the wages peasants and workers never saw, this den of Shaytan, will burn in the fire of hell. But you, you may leave. You will leave the country today if possible. You will leave tomorrow or the day after if you cannot leave today. But if next week we find you still in Egypt, whether it be here or in Alexandria, in Ismailia or even in Minya, Aswan or Asyut, we'll slit your throat like a sacrificial animal.'

'Slit his throat! Slit his throat!' howled a rioter.

'Slit the Jew's throat!'

Zohar stood up with difficulty. He looked at Nino for a long time. Nino had barely gained any weight since leaving prison. His cheeks were hollow, covered with a rough beard, his jawbones twitched. His brilliant black hair was marked by a few silver hairs, his little eyes sparkled behind the thick lenses of his glasses.

'You haven't changed so much,' Zohar told him. 'You always sought purity. It looks like you've found it.'

And Zohar saw Nino's smile reappear, a smile that lit up the world.

'Yes,' he said simply. 'Go now! Go and never return.'

Zohar asked if he could have a glass of water. In Egypt, one never refuses to offer water. They brought it to him. He spilt a few drops onto the ground and said simply, 'May it be according to your law, O lords, owners of the earth!'

He drank a mouthful, set the glass on a table, and left without looking back.

Fleurus Street

That's how I went out of Egypt, my only baggage the kudiya's claw and the amulet's oil entrusted to me by Oum Jinane, my dear milk-mother, may God cradle her in his womb.

And the divine Farid was singing, 'With you . . . With you . . . The world is so beautiful with you.'

Six months later, Nasser and his Free Officers overthrew Farouk. The king departed from Alexandria aboard his yacht, the *Mahroussa*, hailed by a hundred-and-one-gun salute from the Egyptian Navy; he left to drag his spleen from the Riviera to the Cote d'Azur, from casino to nightclub, until his death in 1965.

Although I left Egypt, Egypt never left me. Sometimes I think it is only my shadow that departed while I stayed there, alone, wandering as in my youth. At night, in dreams, I trail the clatter of my two-tone shoes on the cobblestones of Haret al-Yahud, and when I lift my head, I hear singing: 'Whether you accept me, whether you reject me . . . whatever the city, whatever the land, wherever you go, I will go with you . . . The world is so beautiful with you.'

Uncle Elie died suddenly the day after my departure. He used to repeat a sentence he claimed to have drawn from sacred texts: 'There are two kinds of dead—those who were already dead before their death and those who live for eternity.' At the Bassatine Cemetery, where the jewels, my family the Zohars, are buried, he guards for eternity the generations of our dead, just as, while he lived, he protected the generations of the living.

My parents, Motty and Esther, joined me in Geneva after the events of 1956; the aunts followed two years later, all except Aunt Maleka and her husband Poupy, who waited a long time, in the alley emptied of its Jews, for the reestablishment of the world they once knew. In the hara, many used their Italian passports on which Egyptian Customs officials, at the moment of departure, placed the stamp, 'No return.' They lived like ghosts, here or there, some in France, some in Italy, Switzerland, the United States—keeping alive the hope that one day their relics would dry for centuries on the burning sands of their old land.

And I too, once a light of Cairo's nights, I wandered for years in the darkness of the Occident, always singing to myself the beauty of the world with her.

Nino rose to great power in the Brotherhood which entered into open conflict with Nasser's new regime. But some of the Brothers reproached him for his Jewish origins. Early in the 1960s, there was even a plot against him. He was accused of being an Israeli agent. Nothing could be further from the truth! Perhaps the Brothers thought that someone who once betrayed his people would end by betraying his cause. They had not understood his character. Nino was an upright man who sought to submit life's infinite variations to the mind's rigour. But after the bloody repression that befell the Brothers in 1965, he opposed the new political position that extolled generalized holy war against the entire planet. He left the movement and opened a cafe in Cairo, on Ma'ruf Street, patronized by intellectuals and writers. As far as I know, until his death, he never married. I must say, of all the people I knew in Egypt, he alone found a way to remain.

We Jews of Egypt, we were there with the Pharaohs, then with the Persians, the Babylonians, the Greeks, the Romans; and when the Arabs arrived, we were still there . . . and also with the Turks, the Ottomans . . . We are indigenous, like the ibis, like the water-buffalo calves, like the kites. Today, we are no longer there. Not one remains. How can the Egyptians live without us? And in my head, the divine Asmahane, Farid's sister, continues to sing: 'Come, O my beloved, come!'

Although I have left Egypt, she has never left my soul, she whose name means 'the Egyptian woman'. The world was so beautiful with her . . .

Masreya, my milk-sister, my love, became a great movie star under the new regime, until she fell into disgrace, victim of paranoia during the years of lead. Afterwards, she lived as a recluse in Rhoda, with her daughter, Maagouba, who, I've been told, has the same angelic voice as her grandmother. Every year, I send her a flask. I go to a custom perfumery and with the saleswoman I concoct a mixture of myrrh, oud and jasmine, into which I add a few drops of the amulet's oil.

I am very old. Every so often, I wonder if death has forgotten me. The day, necessarily soon, when it remembers me, may God grant that it also take my twin, Masreya, my intended, my forbidden, at the same moment, the same instant. It's so hard to find your loved one in the world of the dead, in that mob of a hundred and fifty thousand who arrive there each day.